WILL TANNER,
U.S. DEPUTY MARSHAL

EVIL NEVER
SLEEPS

WILL TANNER, U.S. DEPUTY MARSHAL
EVIL NEVER SLEEPS

William W. Johnstone
with J. A. Johnstone

PINNACLE BOOKS
Kensington Publishing Corp.

www.kensingtonbooks.com

PINNACLE BOOKS are published by

Kensington Publishing Corp.
119 West 40th Street
New York, NY 10018

PUBLISHER'S NOTE
Following the death of William W. Johnstone, the Johnstone family is working with a carefully selected writer to organize and complete Mr. Johnstone's outlines and many unfinished manuscripts to create additional novels in all of his series like The Last Gunfighter, Mountain Man, and Eagles, among others. This novel was inspired by Mr. Johnstone's superb storytelling.

All Kensington titles, imprints, and distributed lines are available at special quantity discounts for bulk purchases for sales promotions, premiums, fund-raising, educational, or institutional use. Special book excerpts or customized printings can also be created to fit specific needs. For details, write or phone the office of the Kensington sales manager: Kensington Publishing Corp., 119 West 40th Street, New York, NY 10018, attn: Sales Department; phone 1-800-221-2647.

PINNACLE BOOKS, the Pinnacle logo, and the WWJ steer head logo are Reg. U.S. Pat. & TM Off.

ISBN-13: 978-0-7860-4215-9
ISBN-10: 0-7860-4215-X

First printing: June 2018

10 9 8 7 6 5 4 3 2 1

Printed in the United States of America

First electronic edition: June 2018

ISBN-13: 978-0-7860-4216-6
ISBN-10: 0-7860-4216-8

CHAPTER 1

"Good morning, Will," Daniel Stone, U.S. Marshal for the Western District of Arkansas, greeted his deputy cordially when Will Tanner walked into his office over the jail. "Have you been taking a little time to rest up since you brought Ben Wheeler in from Muskokee?"

Will was immediately suspicious. As a rule, Dan Stone was businesslike and took little time for idle conversation. He had a feeling he was about to be given an assignment he didn't particularly want. "I reckon," he answered. "Doin' a few chores that needed doin'. Figured I'd have to hang around for Wheeler's trial."

"I doubt they're gonna need any testimony from you," Stone said. "There were enough witnesses that saw him shoot those two fellows." He shook his head. "No, Judge Parker won't need to tie you up for that trial."

Here it comes, Will thought.

Stone continued. "I know you just got back from a long trip, but I also know how you hate sitting around with nothing to do. So I've got the very assignment you need."

"I kinda figured you might," Will responded.

"It ain't nothing bad," Stone quickly insisted. "It's an easy job, matter of fact, just transport a prisoner down to Texas and turn him over to the Texas Rangers. That's all."

"Who's the prisoner?" Will asked.

"Billy Cotton."

"Billy Cotton?" Will questioned. "That's the young boy Alvin Greeley brought back with those other two outlaws, ain't it? Why are you turnin' him over to the Rangers? The three of 'em robbed the store in McAlester, didn't they?"

"Well, not really," Stone answered. "It turns out that Billy Cotton just happened to be drinking with the two who done the robbery when Alvin arrested 'em. Come to find out, Billy was telling the truth when he said he wasn't with 'em when they damn near killed that fellow that owned the store."

"He wasn't?" Will replied. "Then why don't they just cut him loose and let him go home?"

"Like I said, the Texas Rangers have a warrant out for him, so we agreed to turn him over. He wasn't guilty of anything in Oklahoma, but he'd been up to something in Texas, I reckon."

"Seems to me, Greeley would be the one to take him back, since he was the one who arrested him," Will said.

Stone was well aware of the friction between Will and Alvin because of a case they had worked together when Will was still fairly new to the job. "Ah hell, Will, I know what you're thinking. To tell you the truth, I think Alvin was pretty rough on the boy, so I'd appreciate it if you'd take him back to Texas. I thought you might take advantage of the trip to check on your ranch down there. I know it's been a while since you have. We can have the Rangers pick him up in Sulphur Springs. That's a short ride from that ranch of yours, ain't it? I'll wire 'em when you go and they can meet you there. Now that's a handy arrangement, mixing business with pleasure and I'll pay your usual mileage down there. Whaddaya say?"

"But no mileage for the trip back," Will stated.

"No," Stone said, "'cause you won't be transporting a prisoner on the way back."

"All right, I'll take him. First thing in the mornin'."

"Good," Stone said. "And before you start back, wire me, in case there's some business down in that part of the Nations that needs taking care of." He grinned. "You might get your mileage paid for the ride back home if there is."

Will had a few things to do to get ready to leave in the morning. Foremost on the list was to get new shoes on Buster and the bay packhorse. While that was being done, he decided to back up his supplies for the three-day ride down to Texas with enough food to feed his prisoner and himself. Cartridges for his Winchester were getting low, also, so he would take care of that, too. And coffee—he could do without all the other things, even the cartridges, but he had to have an ample supply of coffee. After leaving the supplies he bought in the small storeroom he rented at Vern Tuttle's stable, he walked over to the blacksmith to pick up his horses and return to the stable with them. "I ain't sure how early I'll be here in the mornin' to saddle up," he told Vern. "Depends on when they turn that prisoner over to me."

"Well, you know I'm always here early," Vern assured him. "If I ain't, that feller's horse is that sorrel yonder in the back stall. His saddle's in the stall with him."

When all his preparations were completed, he stopped by the jail to let Sid Randolph know he was picking up a prisoner in the morning. "I heard," Sid informed him. "They already sent me the paperwork tellin' me to turn one Billy Cotton over to Deputy Marshal Will Tanner," he proclaimed grandly. Then he chuckled over his attempt to be clever. "What time you want him, Will?"

Will paused to consider that. He normally set out before breakfast, but maybe he should let his prisoner eat his breakfast before starting. He couldn't help thinking about also fortifying himself with a good breakfast from Ruth Bennett's table before starting out again. It was an easy decision. "I'll pick him up after he's had his breakfast," he said. "See you in the mornin'."

His chores done, he decided to stop by the Morning Glory on his way back to Bennett House. It was still a little while before supper would be ready and he decided he was in the mood for a drink of whiskey before he ate. "Well, howdy, stranger," he was greeted by Gus Johnson when he walked in the door. "I heard you were back in town." Gus was down at the end of the bar, talking to Dr. Peters. Will walked over to join them.

"Howdy, Gus, Doc," Will said, nodding to each in turn. "Just thought I'd stop by to see if you're still in business. Maybe I'm just in time to get a shot of the same medicine Doc's drinkin' there."

"No matter what ails you," Doc said, "a little drink

of whiskey is the best thing I can prescribe." He tossed it back and smacked his lips, contented. Doc's fondness for alcohol was well known, but it had no effect upon his practice. Most folks around Fort Smith felt he was more proficient at his profession drunk than sober. "I haven't had occasion to patch you up lately," Doc said when Gus moved down the bar to get a glass for Will. "You're about due to get shot. It's been a while."

"I reckon," Will replied. He knew Doc was joking, but it struck a somber warning in his mind that he had paid no heed before. There was a sobering promise of tragedy awaiting all men who wore the deputy marshal's badge in Indian Territory. And the longer a man wore that badge, the more the odds went up against him. He thought of Fletcher Pride then, as he often did, and the vacuum in Ruth Bennett's life when he was killed. *It's the reason I don't walk back to the boardinghouse right now and tell her daughter, Sophie, I want to marry her,* he thought. He was suddenly startled when he realized it was the first time he had confessed it, even to himself. He glanced at Doc, aware that Doc was giving him a questioning look. "I'll try to see if I can give you more business from now on, so you can pay your likker bill," he said, and tossed his drink back.

"How 'bout some service to your other customers?" Alvin Greeley yelled from a table in the back corner of the room. "I need some more of that sorry coffee you sell." Will had noticed the other deputy when he came in, but had chosen to ignore him. Greeley was not a regular customer at the Morning Glory, so he had not expected to see him there. He was eating supper with Lucy Tyler sitting at the table with him, probably because there was no one else to pass the time with. She had just gotten up from her chair, heading toward the bar, when Greeley called after her. "What's the matter, Lucy? Ain't my company good enough for you?"

"Hush up, Alvin," she called back to him. "I need a drink and it don't look like you're gonna spring for it." She moved up beside Will. "You wanna buy me a drink?"

"Why, it'd be my pleasure," he said, and nodded to Gus to pour it.

"That man will talk a body to death," she complained. "I figured that if I didn't get up from there pretty soon I was gonna go crazy." She tossed her drink back, then placed her hand on Will's forearm. "When are you gonna marry me and take me outta this place?"

Will laughed. "Well, no time soon, I reckon. I've gotta take a prisoner down to Texas in the mornin', so it won't be for a while."

"If you're leavin' town in the mornin', it might make your ride go better if you stay with me tonight. I'd give you a special rate."

"I swear, that's mighty temptin'," he said, stroking his chin and pretending to consider her offer. "But I've still got some things to take care of before I go, so maybe some other time."

"Fiddle!" she scoffed. "You say that every time. I think you're true-lovin' some gal, maybe that little girl at the boardin' house."

"I promise you, that ain't the case," he said, and was about to say more to placate her when Alvin Greeley could hold his tongue no longer. Will was sorry to see him push his angular body up from his chair and walk toward them, slumped over to one side, favoring a shoulder smashed by a bullet wound that had never healed properly. In Will's first year, he had worked one job with Greeley and found that he just couldn't get along with him. He had decided to simply forget about it and do his best to avoid the man. But for some reason, Greeley had let the incident fester inside him until he developed a deep resentment toward the young deputy. After that first time, Will had worked mostly alone, and on several cases when he was forced to kill or be killed, Greeley had seen that as an opportunity to put the young deputy in a bad light. So he complained to Dan Stone, and everyone who would listen, that Will was too quick to shoot, and would always prefer to kill rather than capture. Greeley fancied himself the senior deputy, now that Fletcher Pride was gone, and he seemed to think he deserved respect from the junior deputies. Had Will known Greeley was in the saloon on this night, he would not have stopped in. Greeley's usual hangout was the Smith House Saloon. He had a room there, so Will hadn't expected to run into him in the Morning Glory.

"Dan Stone told me you was gonna transport Billy Cotton back down to Little Dixie," Greeley said.

"That's right," Will answered.

"Billy Cotton was my prisoner. I captured him, along with them other two buzzards. I told Dan I'd take him back down there when we're done with the trial. It oughta be my responsibility to transport him back to turn him over to the Rangers. I reckon Dan figured it'd be a nice easy little trip for you to pick up some mileage money."

"If you got a problem, Greeley, it ain't with me. It's

with Dan. I didn't ask for the job, so you're wastin' your time complainin' to me about it."

Greeley was obviously disappointed in Will's reluctance to argue with him, so he goaded him on. "That boy ain't really such a bad one. He got his back up a little a couple of times, but I straightened him out. I'm just worried that he won't make it as far as the Poteau River before he gets a bullet in the back of his head."

"Whaddaya mean by that?" Will demanded, knowing what he was referring to and not willing to let that pass.

"You know what I mean. Everybody knows you bring in more bodies than live prisoners," Greeley charged. "That ain't no secret."

Will caught himself just before calling Greeley a liar. It was a lie, and nobody but Greeley believed Will was too quick on the trigger. It wouldn't do for two deputy marshals to have it out in a saloon, however, and he was afraid if he called Greeley a liar, it would force him to fight. It was best to just walk away, so that's what he did. "Here's for the drinks," he said to Gus. "I expect I'd best get on home."

He turned and started toward the door. He had almost reached it when he heard the scream. "Will!" Without thinking, he spun around and dropped to a crouch, just in time to avoid the pistol swung like a club at his head. He came up from his crouch with a hard right hand to Greeley's gut, doubling him over with pain. Greeley sank to his knees, holding his stomach with both arms wrapped around himself. It was only a moment before the contents of his stomach came up to deposit Mammy's fine supper on the saloon floor. Will watched him for a moment to make sure he wasn't going to get up again before looking at Lucy and nodding his thanks. He left then, feeling a little sick inside himself for the disgrace Greeley had brought to them both.

"I'll be leavin' in the mornin', be gone for a week or more," Will told Ruth Bennett when he walked in the dining room for supper.

"Oh?" Ruth replied. "I hope it's not something dangerous."

"No, ma'am, I'm just gonna transport a prisoner down to Texas, but it's right close to my ranch in Sulphur Springs, so I'll most likely stay over a couple of days just to see how things are going at the J-Bar-J."

"Well," she said, smiling at him, "maybe that will be like a little vacation for you. I mean, after you turn the prisoner over. I think it might be a good occasion to give your room a real cleaning. It's about due."

In the kitchen, Sophie paused to listen to the conversation between Will and her mother. She picked up a platter of pork chops and carried it into the dining room. "So you're gonna be gone again," she said to Will as she placed the platter down before Leonard Dickens, one of the older boarders. "You just got back. Looks like Dan Stone would give you time to catch your breath before sending you back out again."

Will shrugged, not knowing exactly how best to answer. "It's the nature of the business, I reckon. Dan had something he needed to have done and I'm the only one handy right now. Like I told your mama, it's a good chance to visit the ranch. It's been a while since I've been there and Shorty kinda likes to have me check with him now and then."

More than a little interested in the conversation between the two, Ruth had to ask, "Do you ever have any plans to give up the marshaling business and go back to the ranch?"

Will hesitated a moment. "I don't know, but I've been thinkin' about it a lot more lately." He made sure he didn't glance at Sophie when he said it.

Ruth looked at once at her daughter to see the faint smile on Sophie's face. She said nothing, but she wanted to warn her. *Don't you go getting your hopes up, young lady. Getting him to settle down on a ranch would be like telling a hawk not to fly anymore.* Sometimes it was all she could do to keep from screaming at her daughter in a desperate plea to stop her from traveling the same road she had. She looked at Will. "Are you going to be here for breakfast in the morning?"

"Yes, ma'am," he said. "I reckon I'll most likely be the first one at the table. I wanna get an early start, but I don't wanna miss breakfast here." He told himself that it would take some time to transfer the prisoner into his custody, anyway, so he might as well settle for a late start.

After supper, he went out on the porch while the women cleaned up the dishes to sit and talk with Leonard Dickens and Ron Sample, who had been living at the boardinghouse long before Will came. They were the eldest of Ruth's boarders and they usually sat on the porch after supper to light up their pipes and discuss the news of the day. Will often wondered how they could have any news to discuss, since it seemed they never left the boardinghouse. "Ain't gonna be many more nights before it'll be right nippy settin' out here on the porch," Leonard commented.

"I expect so," Ron agreed. "Then it'll be back to the

parlor till spring." Directing his question at Will, he asked, "Gets pretty cold sleepin' out on the prairie, don't it?" When Will confirmed that it did, Ron went on. "You start puttin' some years on you and it'll get a damn sight harder to keep warm. You need you a good woman to keep you warm, and you ain't likely to find one as long as you're ridin' all over Injun Territory, lookin' for outlaws. Ain't that right, Leonard?"

"That's right," Leonard said. "And I expect he knows it. You can tell that by the way he looks at Sophie every time he thinks she ain't lookin' at him."

"You must be smokin' loco weed in that pipe," Will said, with a dismissive chuckle. But the comment gave him reason to be concerned. Had he been that obvious?

"Some lucky young man is bound to tie that little gal up before much longer," Ron said. "Garth Pearson thought he had her lassoed, but she's got too much spirit for him. You'd best step up there, if you're of a mind to. She ain't likely to wait much longer."

"Whaddaya tellin' me all this for?" Will responded. "That's Sophie's business."

At that moment, the front door opened and Sophie came out. "What's Sophie's business?" she asked. No one answered, so she asked again. "What's Sophie's business?" She looked directly at Will for an answer.

"Settin' up the coffeepot in the mornin'," Will came back with the only thing he could think of. "I was just sayin' I'd like to get an early start in the mornin' and I might have to get by on nothing but coffee."

Sophie was not satisfied that he had answered her honestly, especially when it was accompanied by snickers from the two older men. Fortunately for Will, the evening light had faded enough to hide the sudden blush that had come to his face. "Well, I reckon I'm gonna turn in," he said. "I've got a long ride to Texas in the mornin'." He stepped quickly to the door and went inside.

Sid Randolph met Will by the side door of the jail. Standing behind him, another guard was holding the prisoner by the manacles locking his hands behind his back. "Mornin', Will," Sid greeted him. "Looks like you're ready to ride. I've got your boy here, Mr. Billy Cotton." He handed Will a paper with the order and authorization by Judge Isaac Parker. "I see you ain't got no jail wagon, Dan Stone said you wouldn't have one. You want me to unlock his wrists?"

"Yep," Will answered. "Unlock 'em, then lock 'em again in front of him. No sense in makin' him ride all the way to Texas with his hands behind his back. Accordin' to this paper here, I'm authorized to shoot him at the first sign of trouble." The remark was meant to give the prisoner something to think about, even though the paper he held said nothing of the kind. He took a long moment to study his prisoner while the guard handcuffed him again. Billy Cotton looked even younger than Dan Stone had described. He said he was eighteen, but he looked no more than fifteen or sixteen. He stood there, patiently waiting for the cuffs to be locked, his head down, with no effort to make eye contact with Will. Will remembered that Stone had remarked that he thought Alvin Greeley might have been a little rough on the boy and it occurred to him that Stone's remark could very well be an understatement. Looking still closer, Will asked Sid, "Was he wearin' those bruises around his eyes when Greeley brought him in, or did he get 'em here?"

"He had 'em when we got him," Sid answered. "My guards don't use any force on our prisoners unless they start it." He paused to look at Billy. "And he ain't done nothin' but sit in a corner of the cell room since he got here. Ain't said more'n two or three words the whole time."

Will took a long look at his prisoner before introducing himself. "I don't know if they told you or not, but my name's Will Tanner and it's my job to take you down to Sulphur Springs in Texas. It won't be a hard ride if you've got your mind in the right place. You don't give me any trouble and I won't give you a hard time. If you try to escape, I won't hesitate to use my rifle to slow you down. Do we understand each other?"

"Yes, sir," Billy replied. "I won't cause you no trouble."

The young man's respectful, even gentle, nature aroused Will's curiosity. He didn't seem at all like the typical young hellion that aspired to operate on the wrong side of the law. "What kinda warrants are out for you in Texas?"

"Somebody saw me ridin' with some of my cousins," Billy said.

"Is that against the law in Texas?" Will asked with only a hint of sarcasm.

"No, sir, but most folks around Red River County know that the Cottons and the Treadwells are cattle rustlers. So I reckon they figured I was a rustler, too."

"Are you sayin' you're not?" Will asked.

"No, sir . . . I mean yes, sir, I'm sayin' I'm not."

"When Deputy Greeley caught up with those two men down near the Mountain Fork River, you were with 'em, right? So you were ridin' with 'em up in Choctaw country." Will was still trying to pin him down.

"No, sir," Billy replied. "I rode up to Buford Ramsey's store at Little River to see his daughter, Sarah. She works in her daddy's store and told me to come back to see her one time when I was there before. I went back to see her again and we sorta hit it off. I sure as shootin' didn't expect to run into Joe and Barney there. Those two men are my cousins, Joe Treadwell and Barney Treadwell. They tried to tell that deputy I wasn't with 'em when they robbed that store up in McAlester. They just happened to show up at that tradin' post when I was there—didn't have no idea they'd run into me. We tried to tell the deputy, but he said he knew better'n that. After we got to Fort Smith was when he found out I wasn't lyin'."

Will listened patiently and found himself believing the young man was simply the victim of some mighty bad luck. "How'd you get those bruises around your eyes?"

"I didn't set down quick enough," Billy replied. "That deputy told me to set down on the ground while he unlocked the leg chains. I didn't understand what he said, so I didn't move quick enough, I reckon. He whacked me with the barrel of his rifle a coupla times."

To Will, that sounded typical of Alvin Greeley. Victims of his arrests often showed up in court with cuts and bruises. Will found it ironic that, in view of this, Greeley seemed to constantly campaign to paint him as a lawman who preferred to put a bullet in the back of a man's head than go to the trouble of bringing him in alive. It was a reputation he did not deserve and certainly one he didn't want. "Well," he decided, "step up in that saddle and we'll get started."

They rode off toward the river, headed for Indian Territory, Will leading with Billy's reins tied to his saddle, and his packhorse following behind on a lead rope. Billy seemed to be content sitting in his saddle. Will figured it was a far sight better than the hard bench of the jail wagon he had made the trip to Fort Smith in. Will figured he was not being too careless when he discounted the possibility of any trouble from the mild young man. He figured it close to one hundred miles to that trading post on the Little River, down in the area known as Little Dixie. It was a small section of Oklahoma near the borders of Texas and Arkansas that had gotten its name because of the number of Southern sympathizers that moved there after the Civil War. He had an idea that it might be worthwhile to stop there on his way to Texas to hear what folks there said about the arrests of the two Treadwell boys and Billy.

It was a good day to ride. Dog days of summer brought some unexpected pleasant days with nights chilly enough to remind folks that winter was not that far away. Will decided to follow the Poteau River trail south, once they crossed over into Indian Territory, planning to rest the horses at a favorite spot about twenty-five miles from Fort Smith. Because of their late start, it was past noon when Will turned Buster down a path that led through the trees that lined the riverbank. After they dismounted, Will handcuffed Billy's hands around a small tree while he took care of the horses and built a fire. "You like coffee?" he asked

Billy while he was filling the small coffeepot he always carried.

"Yes, sir," Billy replied respectfully.

"Well, we'll have us a cup while the horses are restin'," Will said. When the coffee was ready, he walked over and unlocked the manacles. "It'll be a helluva lot easier to drink your coffee if your hands ain't wrapped around a tree." He was going on a gut feeling that the young man offered no threat of violence, nor an attempt to escape. Even so, he would keep a sharp eye on him in case he was wrong and had to take action in a hurry. Once Billy was settled on the bank, Will handed him his cup.

"Much obliged," Billy said.

Convinced that the young man had been honest when he said he had never stolen any cattle, Will purposely tried to engage him in idle conversation. It wasn't long before Billy was talking freely and the longer they talked, the more convinced Will became of Billy's innocence. He told Will about his desire to marry Buford Ramsey's daughter, Sarah, and work his own small farm in Little Dixie. She had already said she would marry him and that was after only his second visit. "I reckon it was one of those love-at-first-sight things," Billy said. "We were both ready to get married right away." It was just bad luck that his cousins had shown up when they did, bringing Alvin Greeley right behind them. "I just wanna get back to Sarah, so we can start our life together," Billy said.

Finally Will decided it was time to get started again. Billy got to his feet and dutifully extended his wrists for the manacles. Will hesitated, wondering if he should trust his gut feelings that Billy didn't have an evil bone in his body. "I'll tell you what I'm gonna do," he said. "I'm bound to deliver you to the Texas Rangers in Sulphur Springs. I believe you when you say you ain't guilty of any crime and I'll do my best to convince the Rangers that they ain't got no reason to hold you. That's about the best I can do for you." He didn't tell him that he was thinking over the possibility of letting him escape before they reached the Red River. The only reason he probably wouldn't was because that would brand Billy as a definite fugitive from justice.

"I surely do thank you, sir," Billy said, showing genuine excitement for the first time. "I knew you were a good man right off." He was so excited, he fairly leaped into the saddle, anxious to get started. Will had trouble keeping the grin off his own face as he led out through the trees that bordered the river.

Thinking about it later, he thought he might have heard the impact of the bullet when it struck Billy, a fraction of a second before he heard the report of the rifle that fired it. With no time to think, his natural reactions had taken over and he wheeled Buster around a stand of oak trees, seeking cover from the shooter. He yanked hard on Billy's reins to bring the horse behind the trees with him. At that moment, he didn't know that Billy was hit and he drew his rifle as he jumped out of the saddle to help him dismount. When he reached up to grab his arm, Billy collapsed sideways to land heavily on him. Since he was holding his rifle in one hand, he had only one arm to catch Billy, causing him to stagger backward before regaining his balance. Only then did he discover the bullet hole in the young man's shirt, right between his shoulder blades.

As quickly as he could manage, he laid Billy down

behind the largest of the oaks. Then he crawled toward the edge of the trees, trying to see where the attack had come from. The only place that afforded a shooter a spot to hide was a wooded ridge about seventy-five yards from the river. So he cranked a cartridge into the magazine and held his Winchester ready to fire at the first sight of a muzzle flash from the next shot. But there was no second shot. Still he waited as the seconds ticked slowly by, until the minutes began to pile up. When there were still no more shots, he had to figure the sniper was lying in wait for another target to show himself. *Waiting for me to come out in the open,* he thought. He had to see how badly Billy was hit, but he was reluctant to take his eyes off the ridge when there was a chance the bushwhacker might move to a new spot himself. After another wait of about ten minutes, with all still quiet, he decided he had to act.

CHAPTER 2

I can't sit here in the bushes all day, he thought, and started scanning the open ground between him and the ridge. Several mounds caught his eye as possible points of cover, and he thought that maybe he could advance on that ridge by running from one mound to the next. *Not a chance in hell,* he counseled himself, but he considered himself a fair runner. So before he could talk himself out of it, he sprang to his feet and took off as fast as he could run for the first mound. Only after he slid to a clumsy stop behind the small swale of sand did he speculate that he should have taken his boots off. The high heels weren't meant for running.

Surprised that their bushwhacker had not taken a shot at him, he peeked over the top of the mound. When there was no reaction from the ridge, he took a deep breath and ran to another mound, this one closer to the row of laurels at the foot of the ridge. As before, there was no shot. He dived behind the second mound and paused there until his breathing slowed down again. He found it hard to believe the sniper took that one shot, then left. Who was he? Likely some relative of an outlaw he had arrested, seeking revenge for his hanging. Will wondered if the shooter realized he had shot Billy and not him. Probably not, and thinking he had gotten the man he came after, he rode away. But Will had to make sure the sniper was gone.

With one last dash to gain the cover of the laurel, he took off, and again there was no shot. By this time, he was convinced that the assassin had run, so he kept going, climbing the ridge to the top to find no one there. A quick look around turned up a footprint that led him to the spot where the rifleman had lain. Will looked back toward the oak trees beside the river as the shooter would have seen them. It was a clear target area and in Will's opinion, open enough to have given the shooter time for a second shot—had he wanted it. *You shot the wrong man*, he thought, still finding it hard to believe the assassin didn't take the second shot.

Half a dozen yards down the back side of the ridge, Will found the spot where the shooter had left his horse. And tracks down the slope told him he had hurried down the back of the ridge in a direction that would lead him to the trail north toward Fort Smith. His thought was to go after him, but first he had to go back to help Billy, so he hurried back down the ridge toward the trees where he had left him.

Billy was lying right where he had left him, never having moved or shifted his body. Will guessed his prisoner was dead, even before he knelt beside him. There was no response to his efforts to revive him and the blank gaze of his open eyes confirmed there was no life left in the body. A little wave of sorrow swept over Will for a moment. In the short time he had been exposed to Billy Cotton, he had come to the opinion that the guileless young man was no more than an innocent bystander and was probably guilty of no crime. And now to die because he had been mistaken for him was really hard luck. "I reckon that cancels the trip to Texas," he said aloud. The decision to be made now was whether to bury Billy, or take him back to Fort Smith. And that led to the question of the shooter. He preferred not to waste any more time before going after him, not sure he wouldn't make another attempt if he found out he had shot the prisoner and not the deputy.

Another thought struck him then, one that seemed too twisted to consider, but could not be discounted right away. What if the shooter had not killed the wrong man? What if he was so sure he had shot the man he came after, that he saw no need for a second shot? Who would stand to gain by the killing? The first answer that came to mind was Alvin Greeley. It was outrageous to think a man would go to that extent, but if Will returned Billy Cotton's body to Fort Smith with a bullet in his back, Greeley would tell the world, "I told you so." It would go a long way in justifying his claims that Will killed for the convenience of not having to transport prisoners. It was still hard for Will to believe that even Greeley was not above such a murderous act. On the other hand, Greeley might have been shamed enough by the incident between them in the Morning Glory to seek revenge. And it might seem better to Greeley to see Will saddled with the reputation of a cowardly back-shooter. He thought of the satisfaction Greeley would enjoy if Dan Stone would demand Will's badge. It made more sense, the more he thought about it. Greeley might like to see him dead, but he wanted him disgraced more and that's why he didn't take that second shot.

His mind made up, he stood Billy's body up and got his shoulder under it, then he lifted it and settled it across the saddle. He took pains to tie it on firmly before it got too stiff to bend, knowing that he needed to start after the bushwhacker as soon as possible. And he felt he was getting farther and farther behind every minute. Deciding his horses were ready to travel, he stepped up into the saddle. If he could pick up the shooter's trail, he might be able to catch up with him, if not right away, then maybe when he camped for the night. At the backside of the ridge, he found tracks coming down the slope and they clearly headed toward the wagon trail he had followed from Fort Smith. Upon reaching the trail, he dismounted to study the fresh tracks that led onto it. Even though there were traces of other travelers on the road, his own tracks among them, he found that the freshest tracks led toward Fort Smith. They had to be those of the sniper, so he headed back to the city.

About halfway back to Fort Smith, he reached a point where he wanted to make sure of his chase. At a shallow bend in the Poteau, an old Indian trail forked off to the west. If the man he followed did not intend to ride on to Fort Smith and chose to ride west into Indian Territory instead, he would likely take the Indian trail to avoid having to ford the Arkansas River. He dismounted and made a careful search of the ground beside the road. The light was beginning to fade away to evening, but there was still enough to examine any tracks he found veering from the wagon road. He found none that were new enough to be the man he followed and after a few minutes, he mumbled, "The son of a bitch is headed to Fort Smith." No longer concerned with finding tracks, he stepped back up into the saddle and headed Buster straight toward Fort Smith.

He had no proof that Alvin Greeley was the sniper who put a bullet in Billy Cotton's back, but he felt that was the case without doubt. While it was debatable whether Greeley had intended to kill Billy, just the bullet hole in his back would be enough to cause speculation about the truth behind Greeley's accusations. At this point, it was his word against Greeley's and he had to make sure of his suspicions before he charged Greeley outright. The first thing he wanted to know was if anyone was sure that Greeley had been in town all day. If he was, it would be easy enough to prove. Someone would have seen him at the Smith House Saloon, the stable, or maybe Dan Stone's office. One sighting by anyone during the day would be enough to prove Will's hunch wrong. He decided his first stop upon reaching Fort Smith would be Vern Tuttle's stable, since Greeley kept his horses there—this, even before taking Billy's body to the undertaker.

"Howdy, Will," Vern Tuttle sang out when Will pulled up in front of the stable. "What are you doin' back here? I thought you was on your way to Texas." He looked past him at the body lying across the sorrel. "Who's that?"

"That's Billy Cotton," Will answered as he wasted no time stepping down. "He's the young boy I was transportin' down to Texas, but somebody shot him. Have you seen Alvin Greeley today?"

"Greeley?" Vern responded. "Yeah, matter of fact, he brought his horse in a while back, that gray he rides. Why?"

"I was just wonderin'. Is it in the corral?"

"Yep," Vern replied, and walked around the front of the stable with him to the corral. "Yonder," he said, pointing. He watched Will then, his curiosity aroused by the young deputy's interest in Greeley's horse. Will walked over to the side rail where the gray was standing, watching him approach. The horse was calm and peaceful, unlike his owner. Still studying Will's curious manner, Vern commented, "He looked pretty much wore out when Greeley brought him in, looked like he'd been rode hard. I gave him a portion of grain and watered him good." He waited for an explanation, but when it didn't come, he asked, "How come you're so interested in Alvin Greeley's horse? You ain't never had much use for him or his horse."

"Still don't," Will said, not ready to make any accusations, but convinced more than ever that Greeley had shot Billy. The cold facts only proved that Greeley had ridden somewhere that day, and returned with a tired horse. He could have gone anywhere. *How the hell am I gonna put him at that camping spot on the Poteau?* He knew he was going to face Greeley with the accusation, but for now, he figured he'd best take poor Billy Cotton to the undertaker. So he left his packhorse there and told Vern he'd be back to leave the other two horses later.

Ed Kittridge was just before closing up for the day when he saw Will pull up at the front of his building. "Five minutes later and you'da missed me," he said when Will walked in. "Who's the corpse?"

"Young fellow named Billy Cotton," Will answered.
"Gunshot?"

"Yep, right between the shoulder blades."

"You shoot him?"

"Nope. He was in my custody when he got shot, though, so I reckon that makes him my responsibility."

"Who did?"

"Can't say," Will replied. "But I've got a pretty good idea who it looks like. I'll tell Dan Stone you've got the body. I'll see if I can still catch him in his office."

"All right," Kittridge said. "Give me a hand gettin' him down off that horse. Looks like rigor mortis has already started settin' in." Rigor mortis had indeed progressed from the organs into the limbs, rendering Billy bent and stiff. They lifted the awkward corpse up off the saddle and carried him inside where they laid him on a table. "He'll be all right till mornin'," Kittridge said. "I'll straighten him out then. I'm goin' to supper now."

As he had told Kittridge he would, Will then rode over to the courthouse to see if Dan was still in his office. He very much wanted to give Dan his side of the story before Greeley started spouting his accusations. When he got to the courthouse, he hurried up the stairs over the jail to Stone's office to find the door still open. Dan came out the door, preparing to lock it, just as Will walked up. "Will," Stone exclaimed, surprised. "What are you doing back here?"

"I brought Billy Cotton's body back," Will explained, capturing Stone's interest immediately. He then went on to tell Stone the whole story of Billy's assassination. He withheld his suspicions about who the sniper was, preferring to get his boss's reaction.

"Damn!" Stone exclaimed upon hearing the story. Like Will, his first thought was that the shot that killed Billy was actually intended for Will. "I reckon it was your lucky day. Too bad about your prisoner, though. I reckon his luck ran out."

Satisfied that Stone had accepted the story, just as he had told it, Will then proceeded to investigate his theory on who the sniper might be. "What's Alvin Greeley doin' today? Did you send him anywhere today?"

"Greeley?" Stone responded. "No, I didn't send him on any job today. He's most likely hanging around town somewhere, waiting for the trial on those two he brought in. Why?"

"I was just wonderin'." He had intended to tell Stone why he thought Greeley was the sniper who shot Billy, but decided at that moment to hold back until he could find some means of proving the accusation. Seconds later, he found he was to have no choice, for Greeley suddenly appeared at the top of the stairs.

Will and Stone turned to watch Greeley lumber heavily down the hallway toward them. It was obvious that he had been drinking. "Well, I see you're already back," he fired at Will. "Another prisoner brought in with a bullet hole in his back. And this'un supposed to be innocent. By damn, I told you!" This he aimed at Dan Stone. "You shoulda sent me to take that poor boy back."

While Stone stood astonished by Greeley's ranting, Will saw it as an opportunity to let him tangle himself up in his story. "What the hell are you talkin' about, Greeley?"

"You know damn well what I'm talkin' about," Greeley sputtered. "That boy, Billy Cotton, brought in, shot in the back, like all them others you were supposed to be bringin' in for trial."

"How'd you know I brought Billy in?" Will asked. "And how'd you know he was shot in the back?"

Greeley paused a moment before answering. "Why, they was talkin' about it at Smith House," he said. "Musta stuck a gun in his back when he wasn't lookin'. Couldn'ta been nobody else that done it."

Will looked at Dan Stone. "I rode straight in to Vern Tuttle's stable, then I took the body to Ed Kittridge right when he was goin' home for supper. He said he'd work on it in the mornin' 'cause he was in a hurry to get home to supper." He looked back at Greeley. "I didn't pass a soul on the street. How the hell could anybody know about the body?" He turned back to Greeley. "So how the hell did anybody in Smith House know about it this soon?" Greeley sputtered drunkenly, obviously trying to think of a response. While Stone gaped, still astonished, Will made his accusation. "There ain't but one person who knew I brought Billy Cotton back tonight and that's the son of a bitch who shot him in the back. Kinda makes me wonder how you knew about it so soon. Where were you today, Greeley?"

"Why, you . . ." Greeley started, then checked himself. "I was right here all day, in my room at the saloon, catchin' up on my sleep. It ain't no business of your'n where I was." He looked at Stone as if asking for help, but the marshal already saw where this was leading.

"In your room all day," Will repeated. "Then how come you brought that gray of yours back to the stable this evenin' plum near wore out, accordin' to Vern Tuttle?"

Greeley couldn't answer right away. His alcohol-soaked brain was turning too slowly to think, and the look on Dan Stone's face gave him more cause for worry. He knew too late that he had tried to spring his trap too soon. He had been too anxious to shine the shadow of doubt on Will. Now he frantically tried to untangle the web he had caught himself in. "Wait a minute. I forgot about that feller that wanted to buy my horse. I told him he could take it for a ride. I reckon he musta run him half to death." He searched Stone's face, trying to determine if he believed it. When it was obvious that he did not, Greeley reverted to his aggressive nature. "I don't like the way this is goin'. What the hell have you two been cookin' up? Has he been tellin' you lies about me?"

Greeley was working himself up into a rage that was plainly boosted by the whiskey he had imbibed and Will decided it was worth a try to give him a little more rope. "Ed Kittridge said he saw right away that Billy was shot from a distance. It doesn't make much sense to think I'd shoot him at a distance, does it? I'd figure it was someone more like you that shot him, but you ain't a good enough shot to hit a man square between the shoulder blades—even at thirty yards, like that shot was."

"Ha!" Greeley grunted contemptuously. "More like seventy-five yards." A dead silence followed immediately as he realized what he had just said.

"Yeah," Will said calmly, "that's about what I made it, seventy-five yards from that ridge you were hidin' on."

Rapidly sobering, Greeley took a few steps back.

"He's tryin' to play some kinda game on me, Boss. He's a lyin' son of a bitch. I've been the best deputy to wear this badge for over eight years. You know I wouldn't do somethin' as bad as what he's sayin'."

It was a situation that Dan Stone could not imagine he would ever be in and he was almost at a loss as to how to respond. But clearly Greeley would have to answer for the outright murder of a prisoner in custody and it was all caused by his ridiculous envy of Will Tanner's reputation. "I reckon I'm going to have to ask you to hand over your badge and your weapon, Alvin."

"I'll be damned!" Greeley responded and drew the .44 before either Stone or Will could react. "Ain't nobody arrestin' me for shootin' a no-account little cattle rustler. Now, both of you unbuckle them gun belts real slow and let 'em drop on the floor."

"I'm not wearing a gun," Stone said. "You're just making it hard on yourself, so hand that gun to me. You're too damn drunk to know what you're doing."

"He's wearin' one," Greeley said, motioning toward Will. "Drop it, or I swear, I'll shoot you both down." Will didn't doubt that he meant it, he was just irritated that he didn't anticipate Greeley's reaction to be so quick. With no choice now, he slowly unbuckled his gun belt and let it fall to the floor. "Now, go back in that office," Greeley ordered and he followed close behind them, his .44 aimed at Will's back. As soon as they stepped inside, he pulled the door shut, picked up Will's gun, and ran for the stairs. At the top step, he paused, anticipating pursuit and when the door began to open, he fired three shots into it. Then he rushed down the steps to the door. Outside, he ran down beside the courthouse, cursing Will Tanner.

Inside the office, Stone and Will had dived for cover when Greeley starting shooting. Two of the bullets knocked holes in the thin center panel of the door and stuck in the plaster wall behind Stone's desk. "That son of a bitch has gone crazy!" Stone blurted.

"Where's your pistol?" Will exclaimed, and rushed to get it from the desk drawer Dan pointed to. "I reckon you're gonna want me to arrest him now," Will said as he checked the .44 to make sure it was loaded.

"Well, I reckon so," Stone drawled, still huddled in the corner behind a leather-covered stuffed chair.

"Figured that," Will said, and crawled up to the door to peep through one of the new bullet holes in the center panel. After a moment, he reported, "I can't see much through this hole, but I don't think he's still waitin' for us to open the door." He reached up and took hold of the doorknob, then eased the door open very slowly, for he was sure that Stone was right. Alvin Greeley had gone crazy, and Will was frankly surprised that he hadn't shot both him and the marshal when he had the chance. It was not so unusual that a man would ride on both sides of the law. There were quite a few examples of this over the years, but it usually involved large payrolls, or bank shipments too tempting to pass up. Greeley wasn't after money, and now he had dug himself a hole too deep to climb out of. "He's gone," Will said, when the door was open far enough to see the entire hallway. "He's on the run and I need to catch up with him before he has time to clear out. He's on foot, so I'm goin' to the stable. Maybe I'll catch him there before he gets saddled up."

"You watch yourself!" Stone exclaimed as Will went out the door. Not certain exactly how crazy Greeley was, he was a little concerned about the possibility of a return visit from him before he got home safely to Mrs. Stone. He wished now that he had asked Will to escort him home before looking for Greeley, at the same time feeling shameful for even thinking about it.

Outside the building, Will was relieved to find his two horses still standing at the rail. He climbed on Buster and headed for the stable, thinking that would be the first place Greeley would go. When he reined Buster to a stop, he jumped down and asked, "Seen Greeley?"

Vern Tuttle met him at the door, having heard the shots. "Not since you were here a little while ago. What was the shootin' about?"

"A little trouble at the courthouse," Will said, and gave him a brief explanation, being in too much a hurry to go into detail. He was puzzled because he figured Greeley would get out of town as quickly as he could. The next place to look would be the Smith House Saloon. Greeley had a room over the saloon and was no doubt still there packing his things. He paused to take a look at Buster, knowing the buckskin had not had ample rest since having just traveled about twenty-five miles. He wasn't going to be in the best shape to compete with Greeley's gray, if it came to a chase. "I might wanna borrow a horse from you if I have to," he said to Vern. He pulled his saddle off Buster and turned him out with the other horses in the corral while Vern did the same for Billy Cotton's horse. Then he drew his Winchester from the saddle sling and said, "I'm goin' to look for Alvin Greeley. If

I miss him, and he shows up here, try to stall him as much as you can, but don't go so far as to rile him. He ain't in his right mind right now." Cranking a cartridge into the chamber of his rifle, he hurried out of the stable on foot, heading for the Smith House Saloon, leaving a mystified Vern Tuttle trying to figure out what was going on.

Will had figured correctly. Greeley was in his room at the Smith House, but he was not packing up to leave. He had messed up and he knew it, but he blamed it on Will Tanner. Tanner was the cause of all the resentment and rage that had been churning inside his gut for some time now. And every day, it seemed, he heard more and more praise for Will's successful arrests from the other deputies, until he was sick in the gut. Lately, whiskey had become the only remedy for dealing with his hatred and a large dose was called for at that. So the festering sore had finally come to a head. He had not intended it to end this way, but so be it, he had said a little too much and showed his hand. "Let the son of a bitch come after me," he muttered under his breath. "He'll find out he ain't goin' up against a two-bit outlaw like Billy Cotton. After I kill Tanner, I'll shoot the next one Stone sends, or Stone himself, if he's got the guts to face me." Satisfied with his decision, he checked to make sure his gun belt was full and his .44 was loaded. Then he picked up his rifle and went downstairs to the saloon.

Lou Barton, the bartender, looked up to see Greeley walk down the stairs, carrying his rifle.

"Where you headed, Alvin?" Lou asked, thinking the deputy was on his way out.

"Right back to that corner table," Greeley replied. "And I'll need a bottle of that sour mash whiskey you sell and a glass. Put it on my bill." He turned and went straight to a small table in the rear corner of the room. He sat down in the chair behind the table with his back to the wall and laid his rifle down in the chair beside him.

Lou couldn't help casting a sideways glance at the surly deputy marshal as he pulled a bottle from under the counter and picked up a clean glass. Greeley was drinking a lot more than usual lately and always seemed to be irritated about one thing or another. But something must have lit his fuse tonight. He acted like he was preparing for war when he came storming in the saloon a few minutes before. Without saying a word to anyone at the bar, he went straight up to his room, taking two steps at a time. And now he was sitting at that back table, looking as if he was expecting an unwelcome guest.

"You expectin' company, Alvin?" Lou asked as he placed the bottle and glass on the table.

"I wouldn't be surprised," Greeley snarled, and uncorked the bottle.

Lou was rapidly getting the feeling that some trouble might be on the way to his saloon and Greeley's short answer tended to reinforce it. "I hope there ain't gonna be no trouble in here tonight," he said. "Good thing we got us a deputy marshal to keep the peace," he added. Greeley didn't bother to reply, his response was a scowl from under his heavy dark eyebrows. Lou was distracted then when a couple of his regulars got up from their table and walked out. "A little early for you fellers, ain't it Jim?" Lou called after them.

"We'll see you tomorrow," Jim replied.

"No poker game tonight?" Lou asked.

"Reckon not," Jim answered. "We'll most likely start one up tomorrow night."

Then he went out the door, leaving Lou to fret over the loss of business. He couldn't explain it, but there seemed to be a heavy tension in the atmosphere inside the saloon. Maybe it was his imagination, but he suspected that the two who just left felt it, too. He turned to take another look at the scowling lawman seated at the back table. *Maybe that's what made them decide to clear out*, he thought, seeing the menacing image that Greeley projected, hunkered over his glass of whiskey like a grizzly bear protecting a kill. He walked back behind the bar and started rinsing out shot glasses, anticipating the late crowd that usually wandered in. It was only a few minutes later when the cause of the tension in the air walked in the door.

Expecting Greeley to open fire as soon as he caught sight of him, Will stood cautiously just inside the door, his rifle aimed at the solitary figure seated at the back table. He felt sure that Greeley was waiting for him inside the saloon when he saw a couple of patrons leaving hurriedly. Even though Greeley didn't immediately open up on him with the pistol in his lap, or the rifle on the chair beside him, Will maintained a cautious attitude. "I figured you'd be comin' to call," Greeley growled, his words slurred by the additional whiskey he had consumed. "Comin' to make an arrest, are you?" He sneered and said, "Better go back and get some help, 'cause you ain't man enough to take me in by yourself."

Will realized that the reason lead wasn't already flying was because of Greeley's need to express all the bitterness he felt toward him. "Dan just sent me over to get you to come back and talk to him about this trouble. Because of your long service as a deputy marshal, he wants to see what caused you to do what you did and make it as easy on you as possible." While he talked, he made his way casually over to the bar, thinking to use it for cover in the event Greeley decided to bring the confrontation to a head. Judging by the look of open contempt on Greeley's face, he could guess that he was working on a short fuse that was liable to cause him to explode any minute. The only reason he hadn't was because there were still a few things Greeley wanted to say to him. "Whaddaya say, Alvin? Let's walk out of here together. There ain't no need for anybody to get killed."

"I wouldn't walk two steps with you," Greeley shot back. "You think you're hell on a saddle, don't you? You make a few arrests and think you're the whole law in this district. I was running outlaws to ground in Injun Territory when you were tendin' cows on that two-bit ranch of yours. And you ain't likely to ever be the deputy I am. You ain't got the makin's."

Will glanced at Lou Barton, who was seemingly paralyzed by the confrontation taking place between the two lawmen. Will motioned for him to get down behind the bar. Lou jerked his head back as if suddenly being awakened, then immediately ducked down. Looking back at Greeley, Will said, "You might be right, I might not ever be the deputy you are.

You've had your say now, so let's go on back to the courthouse. Leave the rifle where it is and put that .44 on the table. Do it with your left hand."

"Like hell I will!" Greeley spat, and pulled the trigger on the .44 in his lap. Anticipating it, Will pulled the trigger on his rifle only a split second later, never flinching when the slug from Greeley's pistol smacked into the counter inches from his leg. The slug from his rifle caught Greeley high in the chest, causing him to go over backward while trying to reach for his rifle. Before he could right himself, Will quickly moved to kick both weapons out of his reach. In pain now, Greeley lay helpless, staring up at Will, knowing he was seriously wounded. "Finish the job," he implored.

"Killin' you ain't my job," Will said, "just like killin' Billy Cotton wasn't yours. We'll get you outta here and get the doctor to take care of you."

Confident that the shooting was over, Lou released himself from the ball he had made of his body under the counter and crawled out to stare at the wounded deputy. "I swear . . ." was all he could say until Will told him to go outside and send somebody for the doctor.

"Tell Doc to bring his buckboard," Will said. "Greeley ain't in no condition to walk." He returned to Greeley's side. "Sorry it had to come to this," he told him.

"Go to hell," Greeley grunted painfully. Will responded with a shrug. "I shoulda shot you as soon as you walked in the door," Greeley went on.

"Yeah, reckon you shoulda," Will said.

In a little while, Doc Peters walked in the saloon, grumbling. "Well, you've finally gotten to where you're shooting each other. I shoulda known you were the one doing the shooting," he aimed at Will. "It seems like you don't ever send for me except when I'm about to sit down to eat my supper." He bent over the wounded man and started to examine the bullet hole. "That doesn't look too good, Greeley. I'm gonna have to get that bullet outta there before it causes more damage. You ain't gonna die, but you ain't gonna be moving around much for a while." He looked back at Will. "We need to get him to my surgery."

"All right," Will replied. "But he's under arrest, so he'll be goin' to the jail when you finish with him." Since there were no other deputies in town at this time, Will would have to stay with Greeley until Doc finished with him. Then he would take him to jail. It was not a situation that he was comfortable with. He and Greeley had never gotten along since their first exposure to each other, but now that circumstances had led to this face-off, he didn't like the feeling of having shot another lawman. "Can't you take that bullet out in the jail?" Will asked Doc, anxious to be done with his part in this thing.

"Oh, I suppose I could," Doc replied. "I could even lay him down in the street outside and dig the bullet out there." He paused to grace Will with a look of sarcasm. "Hell, no, I need to operate in my surgery where he's got half a chance of not getting infected."

It was later in the evening when Greeley was ready to be transported to the jail. He was not looking too good when Will was met at the facility under the courtroom by the night jailor. "I heard you were bringin' him in," Ron Horner said when he unlocked the door. "Helluva thing, ain't it? I mean, Alvin Greeley, don't seem right."

"No," Will said. "But that's the way it is. I reckon he just got mixed up in his brain. He's your problem now, and I'm damn glad of it. I didn't like my part in it." He stood back as two guards carried Greeley inside on a stretcher with a sheet over him. He looked as if he was barely hanging on. Will happened to notice that one of the guards was wearing a gun belt with an empty holster. It just crossed his mind as odd, before he realized what it meant. In the next instant, the gun fired from under the sheet, sending a slug inches from Will's head to imbed itself into the wall behind him. Stunned, the two guards froze, still holding the stretcher while Will rushed to defend himself, but another shot from the pistol lashed out from under the sheet before Will had time to cock and fire his rifle, silencing Greeley for good. He was aware only then that Greeley's second shot had found purchase in the shoulder of one of the guards.

So it was done, and this time for good. He told himself there was nothing he could have done to prevent it, short of leaving the service. And he had not been inclined to do that. "Best get your man over to Doc Peters while you can still catch him in his office," he told Horner. "Don't tell him I had anything to do with it." He took a moment to consider the events of that day. "I need a drink," he decided.

The events of the evening had put him too late for supper at Bennett House, so he decided to stop at the Morning Glory for that shot of whiskey he thought he needed, and maybe see if Mammy had anything left in her kitchen. Gus Johnson was standing in the open doorway when Will walked up. "Evenin', Will," Gus greeted him. "What was the shootin' about earlier?" Will told him about the trouble that ended with Alvin

Greeley's death. "Well, I'll be . . ." Gus exclaimed. "I know he went after you in here the other day, but I'da never thought he'd go that far. I swear . . ."

Will shrugged. He didn't want to talk about it anymore. "I reckon I'm too late to get anything to eat. Has Mammy thrown everything out already?"

"I don't know. I'll see." He walked to the kitchen door and called out to her. "Mammy, is it too late to get something to eat?"

"Hell, yes," Mammy's shrill voice called back. "I'm already cleanin' up my kitchen." Gus turned back toward Will and shrugged helplessly. Then the voice called out again. "Who's wantin' to eat?"

"Will Tanner," Gus answered. "He said he figured it was too late."

"Tell him to hold on a minute and I'll fix him something. It won't be fancy, but it'll be better'n nothin'."

Gus walked back to the bar, grinning. "Mammy wouldn't do that for just anybody. I think she's got a soft spot when it comes to you."

"She ain't the only one," Lucy Tyler said when she walked up to join them. "I'm startin' to wonder if Mammy ain't the one you're true-lovin' that keeps you from goin' upstairs with me," she teased.

"I reckon there ain't no use tryin' to deny it," Will said. He picked up the shot glass Gus placed before him and tossed the whiskey back.

In a few minutes, Gus's fragile little gray-haired cook came from the kitchen carrying a plate and a cup of coffee. She paused when she saw them standing at the bar. "You gonna set down to eat, or are you gonna eat standin' up?" Without waiting for an answer, she placed the plate with three biscuits on one of the tables and stood there until he walked over to sit down. Will was well aware that he was getting special service because he always made it a point to compliment her cooking, even when it wasn't good. "You almost missed out tonight," she said. "But there's usually a biscuit or two left and I sliced off some of that ham I had for supper."

"It looks like a banquet for a prince," Will said. "I reckon that's why you're the best cook in the territory." She responded with a subtle snort, the closest she ever came to a smile. "I appreciate it, Mammy. I shouldn'ta put you to the trouble." She snorted again, spun on her heel, and returned to her kitchen.

Lucy sat with him while he ate his biscuits and ham, making small talk until one of her regular customers came in. When she left, Will had one more shot of whiskey, then headed for home, knowing he would be expected to report to Dan Stone first thing in the morning. It seemed odd to him that Stone had chosen to go home instead of accompanying him in the arrest of Alvin Greeley.

"You missed supper," Sophie commented when he walked into the front parlor, surprising him, for he thought she would have already retired for the night. "Are you hungry?"

"Uh, no, ma'am," he answered. "I got something at the Mornin' Glory. I figured I was too late to catch supper here."

"The Morning Glory," she echoed, but with a hint of exasperation. "I declare, you're more like Fletcher Pride every day. Well, I saved some biscuits in the oven in case you came home half-starved."

"That was mighty nice of you. If I'd had any idea you'd done that, I surely woulda come straight home. I just didn't wanna trouble you or your mama." And then it occurred to him. "How'd you know I was comin' home tonight?" When he had left that morning, he had told them he wouldn't be back.

She hesitated before answering, knowing she had been caught in her charade. "Female instinct," she said, unable to come up with anything better. "Women know certain things before they happen." The grin slowly forming on his face told her that she was only making it worse, the more she said. "Well, I've gabbed enough with you tonight. I'm going to bed." She promptly turned and headed for the stairs. Halfway up, she looked back and said, "There are some biscuits in the oven, if you want them."

"Yes, ma'am. Thank you, ma'am." The incident would give him more to confuse his thinking about her.

CHAPTER 3

It had been a while, half a year in fact, since he had returned to the J-Bar-J ranch in Sulphur Springs. That was when the trouble with a family named Cheney had to be resolved. He thought about the job Shorty had done with the place since he had left him in charge. With Cal and Slim still there to help him, Shorty had built the cattle ranch into a respectable operation. Will wondered if he would have been as successful had he stayed there instead of letting Fletcher Pride talk him into pinning on the badge of a U.S. deputy marshal.

At times, he would feel an urge to return to work with cattle, but the thought of settling down in one place again was not one he had been able to abide. Now he caught himself thinking about returning to the ranch more and more, wondering if it would work. He admitted to himself that the start of all this speculation had come about solely because Sophie Bennett had called off her engagement to Garth Pearson. That had been some time ago now and he was still not certain if he was just wasting his time thinking about her. He had an idea, although he was not certain, that Sophie looked favorably upon him—openly liked him, in fact. But was it more than that? On his last night there, when he had encountered her in the parlor, she acted almost as if she was a worried wife, waiting for him to come home. He was sure of one thing, if he became so bold as to propose marriage to her, and she refused him, he would have to leave the boardinghouse for good. Further complicating his life was another thing he felt strongly about, his feeling that it would not be fair to her to ask her to be the wife of a deputy marshal, an opinion that her mother shared.

Shorty still looked at him as the boss, even though Shorty was half owner, courtesy of Will's generosity. Shorty insisted that they all hoped he would come back for good. It had been a good visit and he was glad now that Stone had urged him to ride down to Texas after the shooting of Alvin Greeley. The trip had been under the guise of hand-delivering the papers that confirmed Billy Cotton's death to the Texas Rangers. They could have just as easily been notified by telegraph, but Stone had evidently thought that Will would benefit from a short vacation from the business of chasing outlaws. The visit turned out to be a very short one because he found a telegram awaiting him in Sulphur Springs telling him to respond to a call for help from Jim Little Eagle, the Choctaw policeman. Will was not surprised. Stone was working short-handed, so it was useless to even think about a vacation. So he had started out that morning, planning to ride Buster about twenty-five miles before stopping to rest the buckskin and his bay packhorse at a creek that flowed into the Sulphur River. He had rested his horses at that spot more than once. It was about halfway to the Red River and the Oklahoma border.

The call to Fort Smith had come from Durant, a town in the Nations, only a day and a half's ride from Will's ranch in Texas. It would have taken about four days for another deputy to ride down there from Fort Smith, if he made good time. It would be a hell of a lot longer if that deputy traveled with a jail wagon, a cook, and a posse man. Jim Little Eagle had wired Fort Smith asking for help. Two white men, assumed outlaws from Texas, had decided to raise a little hell in that settlement, resulting in the killing of a Choctaw Indian and a white man who had been unfortunate to have gotten in the way. Since there was a white man killed and white men who did the killing, Jim Little Eagle had no authority to act without help from the marshal service, so he telegraphed for assistance. A good man, Jim Little Eagle. Will knew that he would have preferred to run the two outlaws to ground himself, but his authority was restricted to Indians, in spite of the fact that one of the dead was a Choctaw. It might be questionable to think about catching up with the two outlaws after this much time had passed. According to Dan Stone, the shootings had taken place two nights ago and it would take Will a day and a half to reach Durant. So he would be following a trail three and a half days old to begin with.

He reached the spot by the creek a little after noon, according to the sun sitting high overhead, and he unloaded his horses to let them rest and drink the good water he always found in that particular creek.

Planning to give them a good rest, he built a small fire to make a pot of coffee and have a breakfast of salt-cured ham and a biscuit he brought from the J-Bar-J. When the horses were rested, he would ride another twenty-five miles to reach the Red River and camp there for the night on the Oklahoma side of the river.

Thoughts of Billy Cotton crossed his mind again as he sat by his fire. The senseless killing of the innocent young man sickened him still. Everything Billy had claimed proved to be true when he had stopped at the trading post on the Little River. His only crime had been coming to court the store owner's daughter and being unfortunate enough to run into two of his cousins. Sarah Ramsey had been in the store when he stopped in, but she was not interested in hearing his condolences over the death of her intended. In fact, she seemed to take Billy's death rather casually, inconsequential even, and he wondered if Billy might have been mistaken about the young lady's interest in him. He wanted to tell her that he had found Billy Cotton to be an honest young man and earnest in his desire to make a home for her. He decided not to bother, for it was obvious that Billy had been far too naïve in his picture of their relationship. Will left the store on the river with feelings of sympathy for Billy Cotton. The boy's life must have been one long string of bad luck.

Luther Treadwell nodded a silent *thank you* to his sister when she filled his coffee cup before he continued talking. "I swear, Jeb, it pains me somethin' fierce to have to bring you the news about Billy. I'm feelin' mighty poorly about Joe and Barney gettin' arrested for robbin' that store in McAlester. They'll get a little prison time, but that ain't gonna hurt 'em any. But, dang it, Billy ain't never done nothin' to get arrested for, and then to get shot in the back by a damn deputy marshal, that just ain't right. Liam and Ethan got it firsthand from a feller that owns a stable in Fort Smith. The word they got from him was they found out Billy didn't break no laws and so they sent him back to Texas with a deputy marshal to make sure he got back home safe. They hadn't rode more'n half a day when the deputy shot him in the back, just to save him the trouble of a long ride, I reckon." He paused and shook his head when he saw his sister's eyes filling with tears. Both families felt the wrong done to Jeb and Estelle's youngest son. Billy was different from his other sons. He was a gentle soul who seemed to have never outgrown the innocence of childhood and his brothers and cousins had never pushed him to follow in the families' bent toward cattle rustling. "Well, I don't have to tell you that the Treadwells are ready to help you avenge Billy's death, if we have to take on every damn deputy marshal ridin' outta Fort Smith to do it," Luther continued. "The Texas Rangers ain't ever been able to catch up with the Cottons and the Treadwells, so I know damn well them marshals ain't likely to whip us, neither."

Jebediah Cotton maintained a stonelike determination on his face throughout his brother-in-law's speech. He would have his vengeance, that much he knew, and he would count on the Treadwells for help, just as he always did. Ever since he married Luther Treadwell's sister, the two families had joined together, earning their living on the wrong side of the law, their coalition growing over the years with each coming of age of their many sons. "I 'preciate it, Luther," he finally spoke.

"You know you can count on us," Luther stressed. "It's a matter of family. What happens to one of us, Cotton or Treadwell, it don't make no difference, it happens to the family. And it won't take long to settle with this coward that shot your Billy in the back." He turned to one of his sons. "Liam, what did you say that deputy's name was?"

"Will Tanner, Pa," Liam answered. "That feller at the stable in Fort Smith said Will Tanner was the deputy that was supposed to bring Billy back."

"And he was at Ramsey's Store a couple of days ago!" Liam's brother, Ethan, blurted excitedly. "Right across the border from here—told Ramsey his name was Will Tanner."

"He must think he's bulletproof," Jeb Cotton said, "showin' his face this close to Texas after what he done." He looked around for his wife. "Estelle! Write his name down on the wall by the fireplace." She dutifully obeyed, going to the fireplace and selecting a half charred stick from the fire to use as her pencil. Then she printed the name *Will Tanner* on the wall next to the fireplace. Luther got up from the table and took the burnt piece of wood she handed him. He stood staring at the two words, even though he could neither read nor write, until he felt he had seared them onto his brain. Then he threw the stick back in the fireplace, pulled out his large Bowie knife, and slashed an *X* through them. "Feel that mark on your soul, Mr. Will Tanner, 'cause you're a walkin' deadman."

"How we gonna find him, Pa?" Cecil Cotton, Jeb's eldest, asked.

"We'll start by ridin' over the river to Ramsey's Store," Jeb replied. "Liam said Tanner was there a couple days ago. We need to know where he headed from there. We'll get on his trail somewhere and we won't get off till he's dead." His words caused the air to become heavy in the dark room, the only light coming from the fire in the fireplace. The Cottons and the Treadwells were a lawless family, but up to now, their transgressions were confined to stealing cattle. The robbery of the store in McAlester by Joe and Barney Treadwell was one of the few times anyone in the family had departed from the cattle business. And their arrest served to indicate they should stick to the business they knew best. They had always sought to avoid gunplay unless absolutely necessary to insure their safety. Suddenly the carefree manner in which the boys had always regarded their rustling was replaced by the reality that they were now on a grim mission of assassination.

"What about them Rangers camped up on the ridge?" Emmett, one of the Cotton brothers asked. His question brought their collective minds back to the business that had called for the two families to meet at the Cotton ranch on the Sulphur River. For several days now, there had been a posse of Rangers camped on a long ridge about two hundred yards north of the house, watching the comings and goings around the ranch. They apparently thought no one at the ranch knew they were under surveillance. But Cecil had spotted a flash of light when the sun reflected off a field glass trained on the barn. It was a simple matter to get on his horse and ride down the riverbank until far enough to circle around the back of the ridge without being seen. Making his way up the back of the slope, he discovered the Rangers, four of them. There was no mystery as to why the Rangers were watching. Reasonably certain the Cottons and the Treadwells were responsible for the cattle rustling in Red River County, the Rangers, however, had never been able to catch them in the act. It struck the outlaws as highly humorous that the Rangers had been driven to the desperate practice of camping above the ranch in hopes of seeing them start out on a mission to steal cattle.

Expecting Luther Treadwell and his sons to come to his house to discuss plans for the immediate future, Jeb Cotton had been shaken by the news of his youngest son's death and the arrest of Luther's two sons. He had to force his mind back to answer Emmett's question. "I think it's time to leave this part of the country for a while," he said, looking at Luther as he spoke. "I reckon you'll agree that it's got so that none of us can make a move without the damn law lookin' over our shoulders. So I figure it's time to let things cool down a little."

"You thinkin' about that camp up on the Cimarron?" Luther asked, referring to a hideout they had used on numerous occasions when raiding cattle ranches in Kansas Territory. The camp was actually located just south of the Kansas border in the Indian territory of Oklahoma.

"I was," Jeb declared, "dependin' on what you thought." He hesitated a moment before continuing. "This news about Billy has got to come first, though. I can't rest peaceful till I know that son of a bitch that shot him is dead."

"I understand that, Jeb," Luther was quick to assure him, accompanied by grunts of agreement from his sons. "Tanner has to pay. That comes first. That boy was a blessin' to you and Estelle." He paused for everyone to nod their agreement, then said, "Like we were already thinkin' about, though, it's time to move out from under the eyes of the Texas Rangers. So why don't we work on both things at the same time? Like you said, we could cross over to Injun Territory to Ramsey's Store and see if we can pick up Tanner's trail outta there. He came down there for some reason, so I expect he's in the Nations somewhere. After we settle with him, we can lay low up on the Cimarron for a spell, maybe work our trade on some of those herds in Kansas."

There was much to do before the men of the two families were ready to ride. Food had to be prepared for both the men heading for the Nations and the women who stayed behind. It was not the first time the women were left to shift for themselves, although for Estelle Cotton this would be the first time that her youngest, Billy, would not remain to take care of the chores. For the Treadwells, that position was usually filled by Joe, but Joe, along with his brother Barney, was presently residing in the jail in Fort Smith. Consequently, Estelle and Mary Belle decided they could make it best if they stayed together, each one looking out for the other. They were both handy with revolver and rifle, and not shy about using either. "Hell," Mary Belle said, "I'm lookin' forward to the vacation." And it would no doubt be a vacation for both women, long accustomed to waiting hand and foot on the men of the two families.

"I expect we'll stay over winter," Luther told her, "dependin' on how our luck runs and what the cattle situation looks like up Kansas way. We'll head straight up to the Cimarron camp as soon as we've settled with that deputy. If things look better up that way, I might send the boys to get you."

"Don't be in a rush to get back," she said. "Me and Estelle will be all right." She cocked her head to the side. "Ain't that right, Estelle?"

"We sure as hell will," Estelle replied. "Just make sure you take care of that bastard that killed my baby."

All the preparations were completed by sundown the next day, so they departed that morning, six riders, on a trail that led straight north to the Red River. Behind them, two liberated women celebrated with a fresh pot of coffee, while a curious group of four Texas Rangers filed down the back slope of the ridge to follow them at a safe distance. It was to be another fruitless endeavor for the Rangers, hoping to at last be on hand when the outlaws moved to steal cattle from one of the ranches along the Red River. They followed the six outlaws until they struck the river, then watched frustrated when the outlaws went straight across and into Oklahoma Territory.

Louella Ramsey paused to look at the gang of riders approaching from the south. She propped her broom against the side of the door and stuck her head inside. "Buford! There's a bunch of riders comin' up from the river," she warned. "Six of 'em, leadin' packhorses— I ain't seen any of 'em before." She hesitated as the riders drew closer, then changed her mind. "Wait, I have seen two of 'em. They were in here the other day—on their way to Texas. Maybe they're all right."

"Maybe," her husband said as he joined her at the door. He had taken the precaution to pick up his shotgun when she first called out, just in case. They had experienced very little trouble since building the trading post on the river, but when a gang of six approached, it was difficult not to feel some apprehension. The decision to be made now was whether to openly display the shotgun and show his concern. Buford quickly decided it was not going to be of much use against six men, so he propped it against the wall inside the door and stepped out on the porch to greet his visitors.

"Afternoon," Buford called out as the men pulled their horses up in the yard and dismounted. "What can I do for you fellows?"

Luther Treadwell answered. "We'll stop here and give the horses a rest—maybe build a fire down by the river to cook a little breakfast—if that's all right with you. My boys told me you didn't sell no cookin' here. Otherwise, we mighta bought breakfast from you."

"That's right, we ain't set up to sell meals," Buford replied. "But I've got ham and sowbelly if you're needin' some to cook. Other staples, too, if you're needin'."

"We might need a few things we're runnin' low on," Jeb Cotton said. "Chewin' tobacco and coffee beans I can think of right off. You got any?" Buford replied that he sure did, and Jeb continued. "We'll be needin' some information, too." He gestured toward their sons already leading the horses to water. "You see, we're a special posse of Texas men and we were supposed to meet up with a U.S. deputy marshal at your store, name of Tanner. We ran into some trouble, so we got here a little late and I'm afraid we missed him. Have you seen him yet?"

"Will Tanner," Buford said. "Yes, sir. He was here all

right, but he never said a word about meetin' up with anybody. And that was a few days ago."

"Maybe you can tell us which way he went when he left here and maybe we'll catch up with him," Luther said.

"He left in the same direction you fellers just came from, south," Buford replied. "Said he was on his way to Texas."

"Texas?" Jeb blurted. "What the hell would he be goin' to Texas for? He ain't got no jurisdiction in Texas."

"He most likely went down there lookin' for us, since we weren't here," Luther quickly suggested, hoping Jeb wouldn't let his emotions blow their story apart. He appreciated the fact that Jeb's son was killed by the deputy, but it wouldn't be wise to let word get back to Fort Smith that a gang of outlaws was after one of their deputies.

"Oh, sure," Jeb replied, recovering at once. "That's most likely what happened."

Luther nodded. "Yeah, we can talk about it while we fix something to eat." Turning back to Buford, he said, "We could use a little sip of corn whiskey to cut some of the Texas dust outta our mouths. I know you've got a jar or two under the counter there, so add that to my chewing tobacco and coffee beans." Not bothering to deny the existence of the illegal whiskey in his store, Buford just did as he was instructed and set the jar on the counter. "Yes, sir," Luther went on. "Ol' Will Tanner, I ain't seen him in a while. Is he still ridin' that horse, I forget what he calls him?"

"The buckskin," Buford supplied. "Least, that's

what he was ridin' when he came through here. I don't know what he calls him."

"Same beard and mustache, I reckon. I ain't seen him since before he shot young Billy Cotton in the back."

Buford shrugged. "He was clean-shaven when he came in here and he said it was somebody else that done for Billy Cotton."

"'Course he did," Jeb sang out immediately. "He ain't likely to own up to it, now is he, shootin' an unarmed man in the back like that?"

Luther could see that Jeb was getting heated up again, so he settled up with Buford and said, "Pick up that jar of whiskey for me, Jeb, and we'll go have us a drink before we eat. I'll bet the boys could use one, too." He was pretty sure after Jeb's outburst that Ramsey would likely doubt his tale about Tanner meeting them, but it really didn't matter now. There was little more they could learn from the store owner.

Still bristling over talk about Will Tanner, Jeb asked again as they walked back to join their sons, "What the hell is he goin' to Texas for? He ain't got no business across the Red."

"How the hell do I know?" Luther came back. He was becoming a little impatient with Jeb's inability to control his feelings. "I know how bad you wanna settle with Tanner and I promised we'd hunt him down— and we will. But we can't go back and search all over Texas for him. His business is in Oklahoma, so he'll show up back here in Injun Territory pretty soon. We'll strike his trail somewhere. We just gotta be patient till we do. Now, while we're waitin' for him to show, we'd best see about settin' up our camp up on the Cimarron. Winter ain't that far away, so we need to make sure we've got everything we need up there."

"I reckon you're right, Luther. I ain't been able to think straight ever since I heard about Billy and that damn deputy. We'll get up there and set our camp up. We'll have all winter to look for Will Tanner. He's gonna leave a trail somewhere."

After resting the horses and having a breakfast of coffee, sowbelly, and pan biscuits, the outlaw family climbed into the saddle again and started out on a trail that would lead them to Durant after a full two-day ride.

Before noon, Will Tanner guided the big buckskin along the short street that served as the center of the town of Durant, a settlement that showed considerable growth since he had last been there. He went first to a small shack down past the stables that served as the headquarters for the Choctaw Nation Police, which at the present time meant Jim Little Eagle. Jim was seldom there, since he lived in a cabin just north of Atoka, thirty-five miles away. It was no surprise to Will to find the cabin door padlocked, so he rode back up the street to Dixon Durant's general store.

"Will Tanner!" Leon Shipley called out when he saw the rangy deputy walk in the door. "We was wonderin' if it would be you that showed up—knew one of you deputies would."

Overhearing his clerk's greeting from the storeroom, Dixon Durant walked out to meet the deputy. "Will," he acknowledged. "I expect you're looking for those two men who shot Joe Johnson."

"Dixon," Will greeted him. "That's a fact. Did you

say it was Joe Johnson that got shot? I'm sorry to hear that." Johnson was the station master at the depot. Will knew who he was, but had never exchanged more than a handful of words with him. He knew, however, that he was not the kind of man to get mixed up in a gunfight. "The word I got was that they shot an Indian, too."

"That's right," Leon replied. "Don't know his name, but he used to hang around in front of the saloon."

"Any chance you've seen Jim Little Eagle?" Will asked.

"Jim was here the next day, but he set out to track 'em and we ain't seen him since," Dixon said. "He said to tell you they headed out the road to Tishomingo."

Will nodded, then asked, "Don't reckon anybody knows their names?" As he expected, the two outlaws hadn't dropped any names. "How'd Johnson happen to get shot?"

"Wrong place at the wrong time," Dixon replied. "He just happened to walk out of his office to go home, and I guess he was just a convenient target."

"Well, I reckon I'll get along, then," Will said, knowing he wasn't going to get any more information from Dixon that might help him. From what little bit he had just learned, the two outlaws were a half-wild pair that would most likely account for more innocent victims unless they were stopped pretty quickly. Since he was not going anywhere until after his horses were rested, he decided he might as well see if anyone in the saloon had any useful information. As it stood now, he would be on a trail four days old, and he didn't know who he was chasing. He hoped that by some chance, someone might know their names.

"What can I do you for?" Pete Watkins asked when

Will stepped inside the door of the hastily built façade that fronted a large tent proclaiming itself to be a saloon. A tall, skinny man with dark-set eyes and a bushy mustache, Watkins openly looked the stranger over. "What's your poison?"

Will glanced over toward the stove beyond the end of the short bar and was pleased to see a large gray coffeepot resting on the edge of it. "It's too early in the day for me to start on anything but coffee. Can I get a cup here?" He had not eaten breakfast before he started out that morning and he was beginning to get signals from his stomach to remind him.

With a look of indifference on his face, Watkins shrugged. "Yeah, I'll sell you some coffee—nickel a cup—but I've got some real smooth rye whiskey, just come up from Texas last week. That'll start your day better than a whole pot of coffee."

"I'll just take the coffee," Will said.

Watkins shrugged again. "I can't make much of a livin' offa folks like you." He reached under the counter and brought out a cup. Placing it on the bar, he said, "Help yourself. Better take this rag, that pot's pretty hot." He continued to study Will as he went to the stove to pour his coffee. When he returned to the bar, Pete asked, "Ain't seen you in Durant before, you just passin' through?"

"You might say that," Will answered, then paused to test the coffee. It was as strong as he had expected. "I get over here from time to time. Your saloon wasn't here the last time I came through." He tried another sip of the coffee, making no effort to hide the grimace it inspired.

"That's good coffee, ain't it?" Pete asked.

"You could say that, dependin' on how you like

your coffee, I reckon. It's damn sure a nickel's worth."
Pete laughed at his remark. "Understand you had a
shootin' outside your place a few days ago," Will said,
changing the subject.

"Yeah, you hear about that?" Watkins came back,
but offered no more.

"Word I got, there was two of 'em and they were
liquored up pretty good when they left here."

"Yeah, there was two of 'em," Watkins replied, starting to get suspicious then. "You ain't by any chance a
lawman, are you?" He immediately regretted having
suggested the rye whiskey, not sure what the lawman's
stance might be.

"Matter of fact," Will answered. "I figured maybe
you could tell me a little something about those two,
since they spent most of the time they were in Durant
in your saloon." He saw Watkins immediately draw up
like a clam. He really didn't care if the man sold
whiskey or not, as long as it wasn't to Indians. He
could have informed him that he wasn't even supposed to operate a saloon for white men in Indian
Territory, a law that was seldom enforced.

"Well, there ain't much I can tell you. They was just
passin' through and stopped here for a drink. I didn't
ask 'em no questions and they didn't cause no trouble
in here. The shootin' didn't happen till after they left
here, so I don't know nothin' about it." He was reluctant to give out any information he might have had. It
wouldn't be good for his business if word got out that
he had helped a lawman. He was hoping for a lot of
business from outlaws crossing over to Indian Territory to avoid the law as well as that from honest folks.

Will was well aware of the man's reluctance to give
out any information to a lawman, so he tried to set

him at ease. "My name's Will Tanner. I'm a U.S. deputy marshal out of Fort Smith. You'll be seein' me from time to time, just like businessmen in other towns in the Nations. Those two men killed two people right outside your door. And if they're not stopped, they'll kill some more. Anything you tell me is just between you and me, so I'd appreciate it if you could tell me the names they go by. Whaddaya say?"

Watkins was still obviously uncomfortable with the situation, apparent by the way he kept looking back and forth as if checking to see if any of the few patrons in the saloon were listening in. Equally afraid to get on the wrong side of the law, he finally offered up what little bit he knew. "I swear, Deputy, they didn't give their names. I heard one of 'em call the other'n Elmo, if that'll help."

"That'll help," Will said. "What did they look like? Describe them for me."

Watkins paused to recall as much as he could. "Well, there wasn't nothin' special about either one of 'em, just average-lookin', I reckon." He paused again, then after a few moments, thought to say, "One of 'em wore his pistol with the handle forward."

"That helps, too," Will said, thinking that described a man who wanted to get to his gun fast. "Did you get a look at their horses?" Watkins shook his head and said he had had no reason to go outside, not even after the shooting and the two had galloped away.

Will was about to ask about Jim Little Eagle when Watkins volunteered it. "That Injun policeman was in here askin' about it, but there wasn't nothin' I could tell him. Figured there wasn't much he could do about it anyway, since they were white men."

Will wasn't surprised. "You ain't been in business

here very long, so you ain't found out that it pays to get to know that Choctaw policeman. His name's Jim Little Eagle and I work with him all the time." He reached in his pocket for a nickel and placed it on the bar. "What's your name, friend?"

"Pete Watkins," he replied, somewhat reluctantly.

"Good to meet you, Pete. Thanks for your help and I hope you do well in Durant." He walked outside then. He stood there for a few minutes until noticing the blacksmith, Martin Baymer, standing by his forge, watching him. When he caught his eye, Baymer motioned to him. Will untied his horses and led them across to the blacksmith.

"Martin," Will acknowledged when he walked up.

"Howdy, Will," Baymer returned. "You in town because of the shootin'?" Will nodded. "I figured. I saw it. I had to hunker down behind my forge with the bullets flyin' around. Two crazy son of a bitches, one of 'em shot ol' Lame Foot, that Injun that was always hangin' around the new saloon. It was for no reason I could tell. I saw 'em when they came outta the saloon and I reckon it just made one of 'em mad when he saw Lame Foot standin' near his horse." He turned and pointed toward the tiny railroad station. "Then Joe Johnson came walkin' outta the station and one of 'em, the one wearin' his handgun backward, whipped it out and shot Joe down. Just for the hell of it, I reckon. Anyway, he was the same one that shot Lame Foot. I don't think the other feller ever pulled his gun."

"Did you see their horses?"

"Sure," Baymer replied. "They was tied right across the street from me. One of 'em's ridin' a bay. The other'n's riding a sorrel with white stockin's on the front legs and they've got one packhorse, a sorrel."

"Did you happen to catch their names?"

"The horses or the riders?" Baymer joked, chuckling. "Nope, we never got around to introducin' ourselves with all that lead a-flyin'."

Will smiled in response. "Much obliged, Martin." He told himself that he had wasted his time in the saloon. He should have talked to the blacksmith first.

"I told all this stuff to Jim Little Eagle," Baymer went on. "Told him they high-tailed it outta here on the road to Tishomingo. He took off that way after 'em—too long after they left, I expect."

"Maybe so," Will said, "but I reckon I'll ride out that way and see if we might get lucky." He said so long to Baymer and rode about a mile down the road to Tishomingo to a point where it crossed a small stream. Leading his horses a little distance off the road, he dismounted and prepared to cook himself some breakfast. He wanted to rest his horses a little longer and he was still hungry. He was also thinking that he'd like to get rid of the taste of the vile liquid Pete Watkins called coffee. "Damn," he cursed, and spat. "He musta used gunpowder instead of coffee beans."

When he deemed his horses ready to go, he stepped up into the saddle and started out again. His hope was to find Jim Little Eagle because there was no possibility of tracking the two outlaws. There were too many tracks on the road, including those left by Jim, and he wouldn't know one set of tracks from any of the others. Maybe Jim had picked up their trail soon enough to stay on their heels. Failing that, and in the event he never caught up with Jim, his only option was to ride on to Tishomingo in hopes the two outlaws passed through there.

It was only a twenty-mile ride to Tishomingo and he planned to stop a couple of miles short of that at a small trading post on Blue River, owned by Dewey Sams. Possibly, Dewey had seen the two men he chased if they had taken that trail into town. It had been some time since he had ridden this trail into Tishomingo. Dewey and his wife, Melva, were nice folks and he was curious to see how well their store had done. Consequently, he was disappointed when he approached the store to find it seemingly abandoned. There was no sign of life anywhere around the log structure, the barn, or the corral. He sincerely hoped nothing bad had happened to Dewey and Melva. They were the kind of people that would bring civilization to this wild part of the territory.

He crossed over the creek that ran beside the store, then pulled up short when he discovered a horse tied at the corner of the porch. It had not been visible from the other side of the creek. A second glance told him the horse was a bay like the one Jim Little Eagle rode. Cautious now, he pulled his rifle from his saddle sling and dismounted, only to hear Jim call out. "Hey, you don't need that Winchester, Deputy, I'll come peacefully." He had stepped outside the front door where he had been standing when he caught sight of a rider approaching. He wore a big grin on his face.

"Jim, what the hell are you doin' here? I sure as hell didn't expect to catch up with you this quick."

"Waiting for you. How you get here so soon?"

"I was down at my place in Texas when I got the word from Dan Stone," Will said. He nodded toward the empty store. "What happened to Dewey Sams?"

"He decided to move his store into Tishomingo when some other people started moving in there. I think he was afraid he was gonna be left behind now that the town is getting bigger. Somebody will find this place before long and likely set up a homestead."

He was glad to hear that Dewey Sams and his wife had not fallen upon bad times. "Have any luck trackin' those two outlaws?" Will asked. He was prone to assume he didn't, since he was waiting in this abandoned store for him to come along.

"Yes and no," Jim answered. "I picked up the tracks of three horses that stayed right on the trail to Tishomingo. There wasn't any sign of 'em in town, so I went to talk to Tom Spotted Horse. Tom said they stopped at the general store for just a little while, then rode on, since they couldn't get any whiskey there."

"Did Tom know which way they rode when they left town?" Will asked. "I'm surprised he even told you they were in town."

Jim chuckled. He knew Will wasn't too fond of the Chickasaw policeman. "Tom ain't as bad as he lets on. He just doesn't like white folks and he doesn't try to hide it. We work together when we need to."

"But he didn't make any effort to find out what those two were up to, did he?"

"No, but to be fair, Tom didn't get any notice about them, and they didn't cause any trouble in Tishomingo, so he didn't have any reason to detain them."

In his past dealings with Tom Spotted Horse, Will had found the man to border on belligerent when it came to cooperation with the marshal service. He still had not surrendered to the white man, Will supposed. He was good in dealing with his native brethren, but with white outlaws, he didn't care what they did as long as it was not in his town. "I expect I'll check in with Tom to see if there's anything at all he might have picked up about those two. Then I'll see if I can cut their trail outta town. I reckon you'll be gettin' back to your territory now."

"Unless you need me to go along with you," Jim said.

"No need," Will said. "You've got your responsibilities in your section and there ain't but two wild drifters to worry with. So I'll take it from here. Say hello to Mary for me."

"I will," Jim said. "You be careful, Will. There might just be two, but you ain't got no jail wagon or a posse man with you." He shrugged and added, "Not that you ever have."

Will was half-decided to forget about checking with Tom Spotted Horse as he continued on to Tisho-mingo. But Dan Stone always encouraged his deputies to maintain a good relationship with the Indian police, so he figured it was the proper thing to do to at least let him know he was in town. It was getting along in the afternoon by the time he rode into the small gathering of buildings built beside Pennington Creek, so he went straight to the log cabin that served as the official office for the Chickasaw Nation. Tom evidently saw him approaching, because he stepped outside the cabin to wait for him on the stoop. "Tanner," he greeted Will simply, his face the usual stern image one reserved for an unwelcome guest.

"Howdy, Tom," Will returned, making some effort to appear friendly. "I reckon you know why I'm out your way."

"I told Jim Little Eagle everything I know about those two white men," Tom replied.

"Did he tell you they killed two men in Durant?"

Tom shrugged indifferently. "Nobody tell me nothin' before they show up in my town. They don't do nothin' in my town. They rode on. Your problem now." He watched Will intently, his face expressionless. "Long day, I go home now." He started to turn around to go back inside.

"Hold on a minute, damn it," Will said, stopping him. "It would make my job a helluva lot easier if you could give me any information I could use to track those two murderers down."

"I told you, I don't have no information," Tom said.

"Which way did they go when they left town," Will pressed, "east, west, north, south?"

Tom shrugged. "I don't see."

It was obvious that the sullen Indian would not help, even if he could. Will might have been concerned that he had somehow offended Tom in the past, but he knew it was the same with the other deputies who had occasion to work with him. He thanked him for his usual fine cooperation and turned Buster's head toward a recently built board building with a sign that read SAMS BROTHERS. He could use a few things from the general store and it would be nice to have a civil conversation after his visit with Tom Spotted Horse.

"Evenin'," the man behind the counter greeted him when he walked in the store. "Somethin' I can help you with?"

"Evenin'," Will returned. "I'll be needin' some flour and some salt, and a slab of sowbelly. I reckon that'll do it for now." The clerk hustled immediately to weigh out his purchases. He pulled out a side of bacon from a barrel and held a knife over it until Will indicated how much of it to slice.

"Ain't seen you in town before. You gonna be with us a while, or just passin' through?"

"Passin' through," Will answered. "I was expectin' to see Dewey Sams when I walked in. Is this his place?"

"Will Tanner, right?" The boisterous voice came from the doorway to the back room before the clerk could answer and Dewey Sams walked in. Will turned to face him.

"Howdy, Dewey," Will responded. "I'm surprised you remember me. Last time I saw you, you were out at your other place on the river outside of town."

"Sure I remember you—glad to see you again." He swept his arm around toward the front of the store. "We moved, lock, stock, and barrel into town." He motioned toward the man wrapping Will's bacon in a cloth. "This is my brother, Jake. I don't believe you met him when you came by our place by the river. Jake, this is Will Tanner. He's a U.S. deputy marshal." Back to Will then, he asked, "What brings you back this way, Deputy?"

"Two men who just rode through your town within the last few days," Will replied.

Dewey turned immediately toward his brother. "I knew it. Me and Jake both knew there was something about those two that made you careful not to turn your back on 'em. What did they do?"

"They killed a couple of men in Durant," Will said.

"I knew it!" Dewey repeated. "Those two came in here, lookin' to buy some whiskey. I told 'em we didn't sell whiskey, that nobody was supposed to sell whiskey in Indian Territory. Well, the big one didn't like it very much and I think he was fixin' to cause some trouble till his partner calmed him down. They walked outta the store and I was afraid they'd come back in, so I grabbed up my shotgun just in case. They rode off, though, took that trail by the post office, headed west, and I was glad to see 'em go."

Will almost chuckled, thinking that Dewey had just blurted out more information on the two outlaws than Tom Spotted Horse had supplied upon questioning. "I'm running blind on these two jaspers," Will said. "I don't even know what they look like. Anything unusual about either one of 'em?"

Dewey scratched his head while he thought about it. He looked at Jake, who shrugged in response. "Nothin' special, just average-lookin' fellers, I guess."

"One of 'em was skinny as a broom handle and he wore garters around his sleeves and he had his pistol on backward," a feminine voice declared. Will turned when Melva Sams came up behind him. She went on. "He was wearing a vest like some of those the Indians wear, with beads stitched around the pockets. I think he thought he was something special, with his mustache trimmed to a fine line and slicked down. The other one looked just the opposite, looked like he'd never had a bath in his life and there were grease stains all over the front of his shirt." She paused to register an expression of disgust. "There were a few grease spots in that shaggy beard, too. His name was Elmo. At least that's what his partner called him."

Will couldn't suppress a chuckle then. "How do, Miz Sams, 'preciate the information. I was fixin' to ask you folks some questions, but you already answered about all I can think of."

She blushed when she realized how she had rattled

on. "Well," she declared, "a body wouldn't know if it was night or day, if they had to ask one of these two. Why don't you stay for supper? I was just fixing it when I heard you out here. I'll bet you don't get many good meals when you're out riding all over creation."

"You're right about that," Will said. "But I wouldn't wanna put you out none. I'll just make my camp up the creek a ways and cook some of that sowbelly I just bought."

"Nonsense," she responded. "We've got plenty. I'm frying potatoes, I'll cut up a few more to add to them, biscuits are baking right now. I'd best see to them before I burn 'em up." She turned to go back to her stove. "You're stayin' for supper, I insist."

Left with no choice, Will enjoyed a hearty supper with the Sams family before taking his leave to ride about a quarter of a mile along the creek where he made his camp for the night. The visit was enough to take his mind off the reason for his being in this part of the Nations again, if only for the evening. There were good people moving into the Oklahoma Territory every day to offset the area's reputation as a hideout for outlaws. Sometimes that was hard to remember.

Already figuring that it would be useless to try to track the three horses, he decided to head toward the Arbuckle Mountains. It was a day's ride from Tishomingo and judging by the road the outlaws took out of town, it appeared that might be their destination. Considering the path they had taken since leaving Durant, it struck him that they knew where they were heading. Many an outlaw on the run had picked the Arbuckles to hide out. And he had to admit that he didn't have any idea where else to search. There were no towns of any size in the direction they rode, but if he was lucky, he might cross their trail somewhere. There was one trading post on the trail he would ride that was a possibility. It was conveniently located on a wide creek halfway to the mountains, just the right distance for a rider to think about resting his horse.

With the lack of settlement in that part of the territory, the Arbuckles offered almost everything an outlaw on the run could want. It was a small range with mountains no higher than three to five hundred feet above the surrounding land and covered an area of about thirty-five miles east to west, and only ten or fifteen miles north to south. Although small, the mountains provided numerous springs and streams, and a maze of caves and hollows, designed by nature to hide an outlaw's camp. The only things not provided that were essential to most outlaws were saloons and brothels.

CHAPTER 4

The sun had not reached the noon position overhead when he came upon the log buildings of Jeremy Cannon's trading post beside the Blue River. There was a fairly new outhouse between the store and the cabin behind the store, which was the only change Will could see since he had last been up this way. One thing he could count on as having never changed was Cannon's disgust for the law. He depended on a great portion of his business to come from outlaws on the run. His trading post was well known among those who operated outside the law, even though he had only built it a couple years before. Cannon moved into the territory after the death of Lem Stark, and the closing of his store. Lem was another favorite of the outlaw. Cannon built his store farther up the river than Stark had, placing it about halfway between Tishomingo and the Arbuckle Mountains and a logical place to rest the horses.

There were six horses in the corral beside the small barn, which told him Cannon was still in the business of trading horses. One in particular caught his interest, a sorrel with white stockings on its front legs. The blacksmith in Durant had described one of the outlaws' horses as a sorrel with markings like that. Will didn't expect to find the two he sought hanging around Cannon's, but it would pay to be cautious, now that he had seen the sorrel. So he cast a wary eye around him as he guided Buster up to the hitching rail beside the lone horse tied there and dismounted.

"Well, now, if this ain't a sign it's gonna be a fine day," Jeremy Cannon blurted upon seeing the deputy in his doorway, making no effort to disguise his sarcasm. "U.S. Deputy Marshal Will Tanner," he announced. The one customer, a gray-haired man with a bushy gray beard, seated at a small table against the wall, looked up immediately, alerted by the booming voice. Will had no interest in the customer, nor the fact that he was obviously drinking bootleg whiskey. "What dragged you up this way, Deputy? If you're lookin' to arrest somebody for sellin' whiskey, Zeb over there ain't no damn Injun," he challenged, his deep voice still at a loud, rumbling pitch. "And he's havin' a drink of my private stock." It had occurred to Will before that Cannon must have been named for his voice, which sounded as loud as an army cannon. The first time he had met the man, he suspected Cannon might have been talking so loudly to alert a fugitive who might be hiding in the storeroom. But he soon realized that it was Cannon's normal volume. Everything about him was oversize to excess, and he used it to his advantage.

"Good to see you again, too," Will said, matching Cannon's sarcasm with some of his own. "I'm not interested in Zeb's whiskey. I'm more interested in the two fellows who stopped in here a couple of days ago, headed toward the Arbuckles." The reaction registering on Cannon's face told him that he had guessed right.

The expected denial came immediately. "I don't recollect seein' nobody like that pass by this way in the last week or two. What are you chasin' 'em for?"

"Murder," Will replied. "They killed a couple of people in Durant."

"Is that a fact?" Cannon feigned concern. "I'm damn glad there ain't been nobody like that around here. I expect you've hitched onto a cold trail, Deputy. Now is there anythin' I can do for you in the store?"

"Nope," Will said. "I think you've told me what I wanted to know and I just stocked up on supplies in Tishomingo. So I'll say good day to you." He turned and walked out. He was outside on the porch when he heard Cannon call him a son of a bitch, no doubt thinking he was mumbling it under his breath.

He smiled and stepped up into the saddle and turned Buster's head toward the river, planning to ride out of sight of Cannon's place before stopping to rest the horses. He could be wrong, he allowed, but he felt confident he was riding the same trail that the two outlaws rode, basing his feelings solely on Jeremy Cannon's facial expressions. The sorrel he had spotted in the corral was evidently not the one he thought it might be—unless the men he chased had traded horses there. He doubted that was the case, there were a lot of horses with the same markings. The problem facing him, however, was where Elmo and whatever his partner's name was found a place to hole up in the Arbuckle Mountains. There were hundreds of caves and gulches in those mountains and he would have no choice but to search until he struck their trail. *That's what they pay me to do*, he told himself, and guided the big buckskin gelding toward a grassy apron near the river's edge.

"Damn, Slick," Elmo Black complained as he used a spoon to lift a slice of bacon out of his frying pan. "Look at this damn bacon we got from Cannon. There ain't hardly no lean in it a-tall. By the time it's done, all the fat's cooked out of it and don't leave you a wad no bigger'n a chaw of tobacco. It does leave you plenty of grease to slick your hair back, though." To emphasize his last remark, he wiped his hands on the sides of his head.

"Why don't you eat it raw and you won't lose all the grease," Slick Towsen japed. Tall and bone-thin, Slick never spared his partner the contempt he felt for his insatiable appetite. Lacking in physical dominance, Slick relied on his speed with the Colt .44 he wore in any altercation he might find himself in. It gave him an advantage and he practiced on a regular basis, at times on live targets, like the Indian and the station operator in Durant a few nights before. Although understanding why he shot the Indian standing near their horses, Elmo had questioned the reason for shooting the stationmaster when he stepped out the station door. "Reflexes," Slick had told him. "It was right after I shot the Injun. That feller popped outta the door like he was fixin' to shoot at me, and my reflexes are so fast, I cut him down before I had time to think about it."

"You ever think about what's gonna happen if you

run up against a feller faster'n you?" Elmo had asked at the time. *No matter how fast you are,* he was thinking, *there's always somebody faster.*

"That ain't never gonna happen," Slick had answered, confident that there was no man faster. "You're fussin' about that bacon," Slick continued. "What you oughta be bellyachin' about is the trade you made for that paint you're ridin'. Ol' Cannon skinned you good on that deal."

At once on defense, Elmo insisted, "Hell, what you talkin' about? That horse'll run rings around that sorrel I traded Cannon."

"If you say so," Slick replied. "I hope you're right, 'cause I'da never gave Cannon your sorrel and thirty bucks extra for a horse he most likely bought from an Injun for a jar of whiskey. That horse ain't ever been shod."

"Damn right," Elmo came back. "And I'll remind you of that next time you're puttin' shoes on that bay while I'm spending my money in the saloon." He gulped down the last of his bacon and got up on his feet. "I'm goin' to see how my new horse is gettin' along," he said, and walked toward the mouth of the narrow cave where they had set up their camp next to a waterfall. Standing with his back to him, Slick suddenly spun around, whipping out his .44 ready to shoot. "I wish to hell you'd stop doin' that," Elmo complained. "One of these days that gun's liable to go off." Slick made no reply. Smiling, he gave the .44 a twirl around his finger and holstered it.

They were an unlikely pair to be partnering. Truth be known, they didn't really care much for each other. Happenstance had sent them to ride the trail up from Texas to cross over into Indian Territory. There were four of them when they robbed the bank in Sherman, Texas, and fled west to a secluded creek three miles from town where they stopped to divide the money. Concerned about a posse, Preacher McCoy, the leader of the gang, decided they should split up and meet again at one of his favorite spots to hole up. Neither Lon Jackson nor Slick Towsen was with him and Elmo when he last camped in the Arbuckles, so he took Lon with him and headed out to the west to strike an old Indian trail up into the Oklahoma Territory. Slick and Elmo started straight north toward Durant. The holdup was a rich payday for all of them, so the plan was to meet up in the Arbuckle Mountains in a cave that Preacher and Elmo had used before, and wait until the Texas Rangers gave up on them. Then they would target some of the cow town banks in Kansas, or return to Texas. Preacher was convinced that four was the best number to work with, enough to over-power any bank guards or town sheriff, but not so many that the money had to be split too many ways. Elmo had always thanked his lucky stars that he had joined up with Preacher McCoy. Preacher always made the right decisions when it came to robbing a bank or holding up a stagecoach and this last bank had been the biggest payday they had ever enjoyed. The only decision of Preacher's that Elmo questioned was the selection of Slick to make their fourth. That thought was interrupted by a question from his partner.

"Where the hell are those two jaspers?" Slick asked. "I thought they'd be here before we got here. Maybe they decided they'd be better off if they didn't join up with us."

"They'll be here directly," Elmo said. "You ain't rode

with Preacher long as I have. When he says he's gonna do somethin', you can call it done."

"Hell, you had to turn around twice before you found the trail leadin' to this waterfall," Slick complained. "Maybe Preacher can't find this cave."

"He'll be here," Elmo assured him. "The bushes has growed up a lot since we was last here, so one trail looks like another. What are you worryin' about, anyway? You ain't got no place to go. Look at me. I'll just sit back and rest my bones in this nice little hole we got here. Fresh water runnin' right by the door, plenty of grass for the horses, and plenty of money to buy whatever we need from ol' Cannon."

"Yeah, less the thirty dollars he slickered you out of," Slick said, not willing to let him forget it.

"You're talkin' to a rich man," Elmo declared, thinking of his share of the bank money. "I won't ever miss that little thirty dollars."

Slick grunted scornfully. "Why do they call him Preacher, anyway? What's his real name?"

Elmo had to pause to think. "You know, blamed if I know what his real name is. It's been Preacher ever since I've been ridin' with him—and for good reason. We robbed a bank down near Dallas not long after I joined up and was lookin' for a place to lay low for a while. We found this little settlement called Thomasville. They had a little church, but they didn't have a preacher. The men were takin' turns givin' the sermon every Sunday. Well, don't you know, ol' Preacher showed up one Sunday and took over the lesson. Stood right up there and preached a fire and brimstone sermon that had them folks' eyeballs bulgin'." He paused to chuckle over the memory of that time. "He was the official preacher for six months, till we figured it was safe to move on. By that time, Preacher was in charge of holdin' on to the collections, so we rode outta town with a little extra money. It was not a lot, 'cause those folks didn't have much to spare, but it was enough to buy some whiskey and tobacco for a while. Yessir, it was a mighty peaceful six months. You shoulda seen ol' Preacher tellin' those poor farmers to change their sinful ways and walk the straight and narrow path to righteousness. He almost persuaded me to give up my wicked ways. I asked him one time if he had really been a preacher, but he never did give me a straight answer."

"Is that a fact?" Slick scoffed. "Well, if he don't show up here pretty soon, I reckon I'll do the preachin'."

Having noticed the tendencies before, Elmo felt he'd better warn Slick that there was no question as to who was the leader of this gang. He had seen challenges to Preacher's leadership before and it didn't bode well for the challenger.

"All right! You two outlaws come outta that cave with your hands in the air. Ain't no use to try to slip out the back, we've got you surrounded." The booming voice rang out from the trees outside the cave and echoed in the narrow canyon.

Still in their blankets, Slick and Elmo scrambled up and grabbed their weapons. "Hot damn, hot damn," Elmo repeated over and over while he scurried to the mouth of the cave to position himself behind a large boulder just inside the opening. Slick took cover behind another rock on the other side.

"Ain't gonna give you no more warnin'. Come on out, or I'm comin' in to getcha."

"Come ahead, you son of a bitch," Slick mumbled to himself, ready to fire at the first soul that appeared in the opening. In the next moment, he was astonished to hear Elmo throw his head back to release a loud guffaw. He was baffled more when Elmo got up from behind the boulder and walked through the opening.

"I give up," Elmo called out, "but I believe you're gonna have to go in to get Slick."

"We'll just let him stay in there," Preacher called back, and the three of them had a good laugh over the ruse.

"Come on out, Slick," Elmo called back over his shoulder, and went to greet Preacher and Lon where they sat on their horses across the creek, well out of the line of fire from a shot from inside the cave. "Where the hell you been?" Elmo asked. "We've been here since yesterday and I'm damn ready for some company besides Slick."

"Me and Lon just weren't that anxious to join up with you two buzzards," Preacher joked. "We was better company by ourselves."

"That was really funny," Slick commented sarcastically when he finally walked out of the cave to meet them. "You damn near got a bullet for your little joke."

"Hell," Lon said, "we could hear you two snorin' half a mile back down the trail. We coulda walked right in that cave and cut both of your throats."

"How come you're gettin' here this time of day?" Slick wanted to know. "It ain't hardly daylight yet."

"We was plannin' on gettin' here last night, but I swear, it got so dark I couldn't find the trail up here," Preacher said. "There're so dang many of these little springs, I wasn't sure which one was the right one. We gave up and camped down at the foot of this mountain and when it was light enough to see this mornin', damned if we weren't campin' right beside the start of the trail up here." He laughed at the irony of it. "But I reckon that's what makes this place a good hideout. It ain't easy to find all these caves."

"That's what I was tellin' Slick," Elmo said. "See any sign of anybody comin' after you?" he asked.

"Nope," Preacher answered. "We didn't slow down till we crossed the Red. They'da had to really hump it to get up a posse in time to come after us. How 'bout you? Run into any trouble?"

"Not really," Elmo replied, "none we didn't start ourselves. We stopped in Durant to wet our whistles and Slick decided to shoot a couple of people, but nobody followed us up this way. There wasn't nobody *to* follow us in that little town."

This caused some concern on Preacher's part. "Whaddaya mean, he shot a couple of people?" He frowned at Slick, waiting for his answer, already aware that Slick was always too anxious to shoot somebody. It was one of the reasons Preacher had suggested splitting up after the bank robbery, thinking about the dead bank teller they had left in Sherman—killed because he didn't move fast enough to please Slick. It was not the first time Preacher had doubts about his decision to let Slick join up with him.

Slick shrugged. "We came outta the saloon and there was an Injun fixin' to steal our horses, so I shot him." He shrugged again as if thinking that was explanation enough.

Preacher looked at Elmo, who shook his head slowly.

"You said there was two," Preacher said, looking back at Slick. "Who was the other'n?"

"Some feller just popped outta the railroad station," Slick said. "It was dark and he looked like he was goin' for his gun, so I had to cut him down."

"Damn it, Slick!" Preacher exclaimed. "That's the kinda thing that gets a couple of deputy marshals on your trail. Ain't no use stirrin' them up if you can help it. We're gonna have to stay outta Texas for a while because of that bank teller you shot down. Now you start out first thing by shootin' two men in Oklahoma. You think the marshals ain't gonna want to start lookin' for us?"

Slick leveled a hard stare at Preacher from under dark eyebrows. He didn't like being lectured to like a schoolboy. Maybe this was Preacher's gang, but that might change, he was thinking. "Like I said, it was unavoidable." A long pause followed and for a moment, it looked as if the disagreement might escalate into something more violent. "Hell," Slick finally said, "don't nobody know where me and Elmo went, anyway."

"That's right," Elmo said, trying to avoid trouble between the two. "Let's get the fire goin' and cook us up some breakfast."

"That's the first smart thing anybody's said this mornin'," Lon commented. "Come on, Preacher, let's take care of these horses."

"Right," Preacher agreed. He went then to unload the horses and move their packs and saddles into the cave. Although saying nothing more, he was thinking the time might not be long in coming when he found it advisable to put a bullet into Slick's head. He had made a good living on the opposite side of the law, had been at it for quite a few years, primarily because he was smart enough to strike and disappear. He would not hesitate to kill if it was unavoidable, and that had been necessary a few times, but he believed it best to avoid it if possible. It was murder that got the law riled up to hunt you down forever. Lon Jackson was primarily a gunman, but it was a business with him and he went about it in a cold, professional manner. He found no pleasure in it, but he had no qualms about using a gun if the job called for it. He posed no potential for unnecessary trouble due to a hot temper, as opposed to Slick, who actively sought a reputation as a fast gun. The more Preacher thought about it, the closer he came to giving the would-be gunfighter notice that he was finished with Preacher McCoy's gang. That would reduce their number to three, and he always felt that four was the optimal number. Having considered Slick and Lon, his mind moved on to Elmo. Elmo had been with him since his first stage-coach robbery. Elmo was just Elmo, fat and unkempt, but even-tempered and cool in the midst of a robbery. He voluntarily took on the cooking, primarily because he was always hungry. Preacher could always count on him and that was his most valuable asset. He was as faithful as an old hound dog.

It was late afternoon when Will approached the lower slopes of the mountain range. He was suddenly struck with a feeling of melancholy when memories of his first visit to these mountains came rushing back to him. This was the place where Fletcher Pride was killed, when Will was a new deputy on his first assignment. Pride and Charley Tate were both shot by Max

Tarbow and his men while Will searched for their camp on another mountain. There was nothing he could do other than to avenge them. He had done that, but he still carried a feeling of guilt and regret that he had not been there to back Fletcher up.

But that was a few years past and what was important now was to search his memory of the many caves and gulches he had explored in these mountains. Some he recalled in detail, due to the perfect conditions they offered if one was looking for a hideout. There were a couple, on opposite sides of the same mountain, he planned to search first. He had found ashes from fires and some articles of trash left behind when he was there before, evidence of a long stay by someone. That search would begin first thing in the morning. For now, he had to find a good place to make his base camp. Like the outlaws he hunted, he needed a camp not easily detected, where his horses had grass and water. So he followed a game trail he had tracked before, knowing it would lead him to a glen where the stream ran wide over a rocky bottom and there was grass on the bank before the trees. When he came to it, he was glad to see there were no recent remains of fires. He took care of his horses, then gathered wood for a fire.

Later, when sitting by his campfire, drinking coffee made with the fresh clear water from the steam, he considered his chances when confronting the two men he chased. He would have to count on the element of surprise, especially since one of them was apparently quick to pull a trigger. So he was going to have to be careful in his scouting to be sure he saw them first and not the other way around. Had he known his quarry was four, and not two, he might have wished for a posse man and a jail wagon to transport his prisoners.

Daylight brought the four outlaws out of their cave by the waterfall. As usual, Elmo was the first up and already had a fire built outside with some more of the fatty bacon from Cannon's store frying in the pan. Preacher walked down past the creek to untie the horses so they could graze on the meadow beside the pond. He lingered there a few moments to watch his horse, a coal-black horse, more accurately described as a blue roan. He was proud of that horse and never missed a chance to brag about it, and how smart it was. Just to satisfy himself, he performed a little test he often repeated. Pressing two fingers to his lips, he whistled two short bursts. The roan raised his head and immediately came to his master, who greeted him with a smiling face and a generous amount of petting.

Back by the cave, Slick and Lon made an appearance outside and were greeted by Elmo. "Good mornin', sleepyheads. Welcome to Elmo's. Help yourself to the coffee and cook your own bacon. I'm fixin' to make me some pan biscuits. If you mind your manners and ask me politely, I might share 'em with you." He squinted up at Preacher when he walked up to the fire. "What's the matter with you, Boss? You got your face squinched up like you just ate a sour pickle."

"Is that right?" Preacher replied. "I reckon I was just thinkin' about somethin' sour." In fact, he had been thinking about something that didn't sit just right with him. He was rehashing a conversation he'd had with Lon before turning in for the night and the topic was Slick Towsen and his tendency to go off half-cocked. Slick's potential to bring unnecessary trouble down upon the four of them didn't sit well with Lon, either. "We might have to do somethin' about it," Preacher had said, and left it at that for the time being, but he knew that it would not likely be a friendly parting. Lon had nodded, having the same thoughts.

After doing away with Elmo's biscuits, the four were left with very little to do. The horses were grazing peacefully by the edge of the stream, enjoying the rest and the lush grass. The conversation eventually got around to their plans after they had cooled their heels in this restful retreat. The major decision to be made was whether to return to Texas where they had spent most of their time, or move on up through Osage country and into Kansas. Lon didn't really care. He was willing to go with whatever decision Preacher made, and Elmo would follow without question. Not so, Slick. "Hell, there's four of us riskin' our necks on these jobs," he insisted. "Maybe we need to have a say in what we're gonna tackle and where we're gonna do it. I say we know Texas a helluva lot better'n we know Kansas. Texas covers a lot of territory where nobody knows us. That's the smart thing to do, go back to Texas."

"That woulda been a whole lot easier if you hadn't shot that bank teller and made us all real famous down there," Preacher said. "I expect the Texas Rangers already have our descriptions and there's most likely WANTED papers out on us by now."

"Hell, what if there is?" Slick spat in disgust. "I

swear, you three beat all I've ever seen. I'd enjoy facin' down one of them Texas Rangers."

"We've got our way of doin' things," Preacher said. "You knew that when you joined up with us."

"Yeah? Well it ain't my way, I reckon," he huffed, then got up and walked over closer to the edge of the creek, leaving them to grumble about his increasing irritability.

"I was wonderin' how long it'd be before he started practicin' with that .44," Elmo said after a few minutes. "Every time we stopped for more'n five minutes on the way up here, he'd have that gun out, cleanin' it, playin' with it, practicin' his fast draw."

Preacher and Lon looked over in Slick's direction and watched him go through his motions for a moment or two before Preacher released a weary sigh and commented. "He is fast as greased lightnin' with that gun, ain't he? But I reckon it's time we settled that problem." He nodded at Lon and Lon nodded in return. Nothing more was said about it until Slick ambled back over to the fire.

"You figure you're pretty fast with that six-gun?" Lon asked.

"I ain't never run into anybody faster," Slick replied.

"I mean when you ain't doin' your little play-like game with yourself, when it comes down to dyin' if you ain't faster than the feller you challenge?"

"Maybe you'd like to find out for yourself," Slick answered, certain that Lon would immediately back down.

"Why, I might at that," Lon said. "I think I might be a little faster when it comes to killin' a man than you are."

"Ha!" Slick snorted. "You're talkin' like a crazy man, or maybe a hound dog bayin' at the moon. Ain't but one way you're gonna find out. I'm givin' you fair warnin', this ain't no game with me. If you stand up in front of me, I'll gun you down faster'n you can blink your eye."

"Fair enough," Lon said. "Let's get to it. You call it like you want it." He drew his .44 out of his holster and checked to make sure it was fully loaded, loading one more cartridge in the one chamber he usually kept empty. Dropping it back in his holster, he walked out away from the fire and waited.

Fairly astonished that Lon had so casually called him out, Slick was halfway certain that Lon was merely japing him. Maybe Lon could use a little lesson on when to keep his mouth shut, he thought. "All right," he said. He checked his weapon and eased it back in the holster, lifted it and settled it a couple more times to make sure it would come out smoothly. He favored Lon with a satisfied smile, then turned to Preacher and said, "You heard the whole thing. He called me out, not the other way around, so there ain't no reason for complainin' after it's done, right?" Then another thought occurred to him. "This is just between Lon and me, so when I'm done with him, anything he's got, including his share of the bank money, belongs to me. Any complaints?"

"Oh, there won't be no complaints from me or Elmo," Preacher assured him, amused that Slick was dividing the spoils before the showdown was even started. "We'll play whatever hand is dealt."

"All right, then." He turned back to the piece of business he was now eager to finish before Lon had a chance to claim he was just japing. "Lon, I ain't never had much use for you, but I'll give you one more chance. You admit that you're a yellow dog and I'll let you pass."

"'Preciate the offer, Slick. You may be a mite faster than me, but I figure I'm a helluva lot smarter, so let's get this over with."

His comment caused a second of confusion, but Slick shook it off as foolishness, or a ploy to work on his mind. Speed and accuracy wins any duel, he assured himself, and strode out to position himself for the gunfight. He had ridden with Lon long enough to know the man's moves and knew there was no way Lon could draw faster than he. "Just let me know when you're ready," he said as he turned and walked off a few more paces.

"I'm ready," he heard Lon say. When he turned to face him again, Lon's gun was already out and aimed at him. The horrifying shock of his final moments was forever registered on his face as Lon's bullet tore into his gut, followed a split second later by a round in his chest. "Like I said," Lon drawled, "I'm smarter than you."

"That's for sure," Preacher agreed. "It takes a damn fool to take a chance on the other feller bein' faster'n you. Hell, if you wanna kill a man, shoot him when he ain't lookin'. Reckon we've got some more bank money to split three ways."

"Looks to me like I oughta get a bigger cut of his money since I'm the one who did the shootin'," Lon said, joking. "Like he said, this was just between him and me and he was plannin' to keep all my share.

I even went to the trouble of lettin' him play his little game before I shot him."

"Hell, no," Elmo piped up. "I'da done it, only I'da just shot him in the back without all that fuss. Besides, you oughta give us your share for lettin' you have the pleasure." The lighthearted bantering went on for several minutes with no qualms about the murder of one of their own partners before Elmo got up and walked over to check on the body. After a minute, he informed them, "He's deader'n hell, all right." He chuckled and commented, "That was one helluva surprised look on his face when he turned around." He started going through Slick's pockets.

"I expect most of his share of that bank money is in his saddlebags," Preacher said. The next half hour was spent on the dead man's inventory and the splitting up of his possessions. When they had finished, there was nothing left on the body but the clothes he wore, and that was only because Slick had been too skinny for any of the others to wear his clothes. The one exception being his beaded vest, which Lon took a fancy to. They decided to sell his horse and saddle when an opportunity presented itself, then divide that money. All three were satisfied that the day couldn't have started out better. Slick's surly disposition would hardly be missed and twenty thousand dollars split three ways was a sight better than the same amount split four ways.

The only thing left to do was to dispose of the body. Since no one cared enough to dig a grave, Lon took it upon himself to remove it from their campsite. "I'll drag him far enough away from here, so we don't have to smell him when he starts gettin' ripe." He saddled his horse, tied a rope around Slick's boots, and dragged the body through the trees to a deep ravine about seventy-five yards from the waterfall. He pushed the body over the edge of the gully and watched it fall some twenty feet to the bottom. "So long, Slick," he said. "It was a pleasure."

CHAPTER 5

Will pulled Buster up short when he heard the two shots. As near as he could tell, they seemed to have come from higher up on the other side of the mountain he was now scouting. He waited, listening, but there were no more shots. A hunter? He doubted it because both shots came from a pistol. There was a possibility that there were others camping out in these mountains, but he felt confident the shots came from the two men he pursued and could mean he wasn't going to have to scout the entire mountain range to find them. He backed Buster a few feet, then turned him back down the mountain, the slope at that point being too steep to traverse to the other side. When he descended to the base, he rode around the mountain until he came to a ravine that appeared to rise almost to the top of the mountain. He decided it to be his best path up the mountain, not too steep to keep Buster from climbing it, so he started up, keeping his eyes scanning the steep sides of the ravine ahead of him.

As he climbed higher, he heard a waterfall some-where above him; he had been here before. The

waterfall dropped from a rocky ledge some thirty feet
to form a small pond a few yards from the mouth of a
cave. It was an ideal arrangement for a camp, he
thought, as he pictured it in his mind. He continued
on and was within sight of the top of the ravine when
Buster suddenly paused and began shifting back and
forth from one foot to the other. Having been focused
on the trees above the top of the ravine, Will had
missed seeing what caused the buckskin to stop so
abruptly. "Damn!" he swore under his breath when he
saw the body lying several yards in front of his horse.
He took only a few seconds to look around him to
make sure he wasn't in the shooter's sights, then
pulled his rifle from the sling and dismounted. He realized right away that there was no one waiting in
ambush. It was apparent that the body had simply
been disposed of here, so he went forward to take a
look. At first glance, he identified the body as one of
the two men he trailed. The description Melva Sams
had given him came immediately to mind, *skinny as a
broom handle and he wore garters on his sleeves.* The only
things missing were the ornate vest and the gun belt
with the reversed pistol. Evidently, he and his partner,
Elmo, had a falling out. It was strange, he thought, for
he had been told that it was this one who was quick to
use his weapon. The two bullet holes in the man's
shirt accounted for the two he had heard, and they
were both from face-on. *Maybe this will make my job a
little easier*, he thought, *with just one man to worry about.*
He pictured in his mind the cave they had picked to
hide out in. He had been there before, but not from
this side of it. Nonetheless, he was able to remember
the setting enough to know that he was no more than
a hundred yards from the waterfall and the mouth of

the cave. He was inclined to hurry now, thinking that maybe he could catch Elmo outside, so he quickly climbed up to the edge of the ravine to see if he was in luck.

He was right in thinking he could get a clear look at the cave from the rim of the defile, but what he saw gave him pause to wonder if he had stumbled upon the wrong party. For there were three men seated around a fire, their horses hobbled near the pond at the bottom of the falls. But the description of the man lying dead at the bottom of the ravine was too close to the one given by Melva Sams. Surely it was the same man. He squinted, straining to see the three men more clearly to identify the one called Elmo, but he could see that he was going to have to get closer to be sure. Even then, he would be relying on Melva's vague description of the unkempt partner. But if it was so, it meant that the two outlaws he chased from Durant had met up with two more, and he had not come prepared for that. Two were going to be hard enough to handle and three might be too many without a posse man and a jail wagon to transport them. That wasn't his only problem. He had no idea who the other two men were. He could fairly well guess they were somehow criminally connected to the two he was after, but he didn't know for sure. He couldn't arrest them for simply being in the mountains, but he could charge the three of them for the murder of the man whose body he had just stumbled upon. He suspected there might be an alert for four outlaws crossing over into Indian Territory, running from Texas Rangers, but he was not close to a telegraph to find out. Another possibility came to mind. What if there were more of them inside the cave? *If that's the case,* he told himself,

I'm damn sure going to need help. In that event, he could only keep an eye on them and trail them if they left these mountains, so he could at least know where they were when he could get some help. But for now, he decided he was going to work his way in closer to see if he could get a better look at the three and maybe at least figure out which one was called Elmo. He figured the best way to do that was to follow the ravine the rest of the way to the top, so he backed away from the rim.

Moving quickly up the ravine, he reached the top after a short climb and crawled out onto a rocky shelf. The waterfall and the cave were below him now and he could still see the three men sitting by the fire. A thick stand of fir trees above the waterfall would provide cover enough to allow him to move down close to a position where he should be able to get a good look at them. So he made his way carefully across the rocky ledge, being careful not to dislodge any loose gravel that would give him away. Once in position, he found he could see well enough, but the noise of the waterfall made it impossible to hear their conversation. *Damn,* he thought, *I didn't think about that.* He remembered the interior of the cave from having explored it before. There was a back opening in the long cave that could be used as a quick exit in case of an emergency. It was little more than a small hole near the top of the cave, but it was big enough for a man to squeeze through and it was on his mind right now. If they were inside the cave, he could hear them talking by squeezing inside the rear opening. He needed to know who he was dealing with, so if that was the only way, he'd have to wait until dark when they went inside for the night. From where he sat now, however, he felt pretty sure one of the three he could see by the fire must surely be the man Melva Sams had described. So he was confident that he had caught up with the two he had originally followed from Durant. *Hell of a way to try to arrest three outlaws,* he thought. To add to his displeasure, he felt too strung out. He was on the mountain, perched over the cave, his buckskin was tied below the cave in the ravine, and his packhorse was tied back in his camp on the other side of the mountain. So far, he wasn't sure what he would ultimately try to do, arrest all three, or just keep tracking them until he had an idea they were going to stay put long enough for him to get some help. He couldn't help recalling the many times Dan Stone had warned him that there would come a day when he would pay for ignoring the usual policy of taking at least one posse man, a jail wagon, and a cook with him. It looked like that day had come, even though this time he had an excuse because he had been at the J-Bar-J in Texas when he got the assignment. These thoughts didn't help his frustration at the moment, so he backed away from his perch, resolved to return after dark.

Having returned to the ledge above the cave in the fading light, Will waited while the three outlaws tied their horses to a rope tied between two trees to keep them from wandering during the night. He studied the two men with Elmo in an effort to size them up. One was clearly the leader, judging by the way the other two responded to him. He was a sizeable man, broad-shouldered with a neatly trimmed black beard. The third member of the party was rangy and clean-shaven. They lingered by the fire until evidently deciding the night air was beginning to chill and it would be more comfortable inside the cave. Elmo picked up a couple of burning limbs from the fire and took them inside to restart one they had in the cave. "Gimme a few minutes to get the fire goin', then bring the coffeepot in with you," he said. "Ain't no use wastin' the rest of that coffee."

"Hell, we'll make some more," Preacher said. "We can afford it."

"Maybe ol' Slick will pay for another pot," Lon said, getting a laugh from his partners.

Above them, still unable to hear their conversation, Will watched until the other two followed Elmo inside the cave. Then he left the cover of the trees and made his way down to the rear exit of the cave, moving cautiously up to the small opening. Inside, he met a solid stone wall, but having been there before, he knew a narrow path led around it to provide access to the cave itself. He found that there was no problem with hearing, for the voices echoed clearly inside the hollow chamber.

"That's a damn fine canvas sack," Preacher said, holding it up to admire it. "It's a shame to have to burn it up."

"Too bad they printed their name on it," Lon said, and held up a similar sack. "Bank of Sherman, I could put this bag to good use in place of my cotton war bag I've been usin'."

"Can't you just turn it inside out?" Elmo asked.

"No," Preacher replied at once. "Ain't no sense in takin' any chance on somebody findin' those sacks with us. You take a look inside that bag and you can see the paint shinin' through. No, sir, we'd best burn 'em up."

That was enough for the man crouched in the cramped passageway at the rear of the cave. The three, along with the corpse at the bottom of the ravine, had robbed a bank, the bank in Sherman, Texas. There were bound to be some quick orders from the marshal's office going out to apprehend them. He backed carefully out of the passage, convinced now that he had to act, but it was going to take some thought. Three men, holed up inside a cave, was going to be a challenge.

"That's enough for me," Lon announced, and tossed his cards in. "I'm ready to turn in, anyway. Three-handed poker ain't much of a game, maybe we shouldn'ta shot ol' Slick. We coulda had four for poker." That pretty much ended the card playing for the evening. Elmo was already nodding between hands as it was. He had lost interest long before that.

Preacher released a long sigh. "I reckon I'm ready to go to my blanket, too." He followed Lon outside to answer nature's call before going to bed.

"How long ya think we oughta hole up here?" Lon asked, standing in the cool early autumn evening.

"Maybe a week," Preacher answered. "We'll ride down to Cannon's in a couple of days to see if he's heard anything, or seen any marshals up this way." When they had both emptied, they went back inside to find Elmo already asleep. Preacher pulled his boots off and rolled up in his blanket. In a few moments, he sat up. "You hear that?"

"Yeah, I did," Lon answered. "Sounds like somethin's after the horses. Might be a mountain lion prowlin' around. I've still got my boots on, I'll go see what's stirred 'em up."

"Better take your rifle in case it is a mountain lion," Preacher said. He watched Lon go out the opening, then lay back again to close his eyes. In a few moments, he drifted off. After a while, he awoke again and started to shift over to his other side, noticing then that Lon was not in his blanket. At first, he didn't think much of it, but then realized the fire had burned almost down to the point of going out. It had been a long time since Lon had gone to check on the horses. Knowing something was not right, he sat up, wondering if Lon had slipped up on a bear or something. He started to pull on his boots, just then realizing that Elmo was up.

"I heard somethin' after the horses," Elmo said. "I wasn't gonna wake you up, thought I'd go see what's botherin' 'em." It occurred to him then. "Where's Lon?"

"He went to check on the horses," Preacher said. "But that was a while back. At least I think it was a while back, I fell asleep, so I ain't sure."

Elmo chuckled. "I'll go see what's botherin' 'em."

He walked down past the pond to the trees where they had tied the horses by the stream. "Lon," he called out as he approached the horses, but there was no answer. The horses were restless, and were milling about, having somehow gotten untied from the rope. He walked into the trees only a few feet before stopping. "What tha . . ." was as far as he got when he saw Lon, his hands and feet tied around a tree, his mouth gagged. In the next instance, he was knocked senseless and the lights went out in his brain. In the short time it took him to recover his senses, he was tied hand and foot around a tree like Lon. He tried to yell out, only to find his mouth was stuffed with a cloth. He had recovered to the point where he realized his gag was not tied in, so he started spitting the rag out until he could yell. "Look out, Preacher, it's a trap!"

"Damn!" Will cursed, having just finished securing him to the tree. He had hoped Elmo would take longer than that to recover. Lon had. Maybe he hit him harder. A minute more and he would have had the rag tied in Elmo's mouth, and maybe he would have been able to lure the other one out as well. *So much for that plan now*, he thought. He had to quickly decide what to do.

"Preacher!" Elmo yelled again. "It's a trap!"

"Open your mouth like that again, Elmo, and I'm gonna fetch you another lump on the back of your head. You and your friend here are under arrest for bank robbery and murder, so you'd do best not to rile me any more than you already have."

"Murder?" Elmo blurted. "I ain't murdered nobody!" He paused when it occurred to him. "How'd you know my name was Elmo?"

Will ignored the question. He was more concerned about the one still in the cave. He didn't have much hope for success, but he decided to give it a try. "Preacher!" He called out. "This is a U.S. deputy marshal. We've got your two partners under arrest and unharmed. If you'll come on outta that cave with your hands up, I guarantee you no one will shoot. You'll not get hurt."

Inside the cave, Preacher had been in the process of pulling on his boots when he was startled by Elmo's first yell. In a panic to collect his weapons, he was shocked again when he heard Will call out to him to surrender. *U.S. marshals,* he screamed to himself. *How many?* He looked at once toward the back of the cave where the rear door was. If they had him surrounded, he didn't hear anybody at the back. Maybe they didn't know about that way out. Will's voice broke through his thoughts again.

"Come on out, Preacher! You got no place to go. Might as well make it easy on yourself."

It struck him then, *He's bluffing, there's no posse, he's by himself.* That changed the situation completely. "Why don't you come in and get me?" Preacher yelled back.

That was not what Will wanted to hear. He must have guessed that Will was alone and called his bluff. He glanced back at his prisoners and was met with looks of scornful amusement, for they saw right away that Preacher had turned the tables on the deputy. "I reckon you're gonna have to go in that cave and get him," Elmo smirked. He looked over at Lon. "We ain't got nothin' to worry about. He can't get to Preacher without gettin' his ass shot off. I don't have no idea who this jasper is, but in a matchup, I'll bet on Preacher. He'll figure a way to get us loose." Lon, his gag still tied firmly in place, could only grunt in return.

Will realized he was stumped. It would be nothing short of suicide to try to charge into the mouth of that cave. He was sure that was what Preacher hoped he would do. It was equally foolish to think he could wait Preacher out. It was almost certain that he had provisions in the cave for the four of them, so Preacher could wait him out longer than the other way around, firewood being the only exception. He considered the rear door of the cave, but if he was detected, Preacher could either shoot him, or escape out the front to free his partners. The last option he had to consider was to take the two prisoners already in custody back and try to track Preacher down after they were locked up.

While Will was pondering his options, Preacher was making preparations to reduce them to one. For in the midst of this unlikely uncertainty, he had suddenly seen an opportunity for a financial gain worth taking a gamble on. Pinned up in this cave with him was the entire bank holdup money, more than twenty thousand dollars. With Lon and Elmo captured, it was all his, if he could escape the deputy. A gambler, he considered the odds in his favor. His success hinged upon his being able to get out the back way while the lawman was in the front. If he could do that, then the deputy would not likely leave his prisoners to go chasing after him. As quickly as he could, he hurriedly emptied Lon's and Elmo's saddlebags of their share of the bank money, while keeping a close eye on the mouth of the cave, in the event the deputy was foolish enough to rush him.

When he was ready to make his escape, he made his way up through the narrow passageway to the rear opening. As a precaution, he paused there and scanned the slope behind the cave. As he had counted on, there was no one to stop him. It was time for his final gamble, and this one was crucial. He licked his lips to try to create some moisture on them before placing two fingers to them and whistling two short bursts. Everything was now in the hands of Lady Luck, for if his horse failed this test, it might result in a footrace with the deputy, and he was carrying too much of a load to outrun him.

Still deciding what he should do, Will was startled when he heard the sharp whistle blasts. They came from up the slope, maybe near the back of the cave. If it was Preacher, why would he announce it? Maybe it was meant to draw him into the front of the cave. Then he saw the dark horse break away from the others and gallop up the slope and knew immediately what was taking place. He had no choice but to run after the roan, knowing it was in vain, but he had to try. As he ran, scrambling up the slope, he scolded himself for untying their horses, for had he not, the horse would have been unable to respond to Preacher's signal. Another mistake was not having brought Buster up from the trees where he had tied him with his packhorse while he was dealing with the capture of his two prisoners. He arrived at the back of the cave in time to get a glimpse of the blue roan disappearing into the darkness with Preacher riding bareback, saddlebag over his shoulder. In frustration, Will raised his rifle and sent one harmless shot after him. His plans were clear now, he would have to move his prisoners down off this mountain as soon as possible. There were too many ambush sites offered in these gulches and ravines. Unfortunately, there was a lot to do to get them ready to ride and he had best get at it while there were a couple more hours of darkness before sunup. He didn't like the idea of catching up the horses, saddling, and packing up whatever provisions of the outlaws he decided to borrow after it became light enough for a man with a rifle to take aim at him. It was hard to say what Preacher would do, now that he was able to choose. He might choose to try to free his partners, or simply concentrate on getting as far away as possible, thinking it just bad luck on their part.

He went into the rear opening on his way back, so he could check the inside of the cave to see what was left. By the dim light provided by the dying fire, he saw their saddles, four of them, and saddlebags with their contents strewn about. There were also the empty Bank of Sherman bags he had heard them discussing the night before. It was clear that there was no stolen money left to recover, more incentive for Preacher to desert his partners. It would depend on what kind of partner Preacher was, and Will was inclined to think he would choose to run. But he had to allow for the possibility that he wouldn't.

Back to his prisoners, he told them how things were going to be. He removed the gag from Lon's mouth, but kept them tied to the trees. "As soon as I round up all the horses and load up what food you brought with you, we'll be leavin' here. When I'm transportin' prisoners, I make it as easy as I can, dependin' on how much trouble you cause. But if you wanna be treated right, you'd best not give me any grief. You can tell me which horse is yours and which saddle goes on him. I'll throw the other two saddles on the other horses."

"Deputy," Elmo spoke up. "You're doin' a lot of talkin' for a dead man. I wouldn't be surprised if you ain't in Preacher's sights right now. The only chance you've got is to let me and Lon go and you hightail it outta here. Now, that's if you're smart enough to know that what I'm sayin' is the way things are."

"Watch your mouth, Elmo!" Lon warned. "Now he knows my name, too."

"Well, hell," Elmo replied. "What if he does? It don't make a whole lotta difference—Lon Jackson, Preacher McCoy, Elmo Black—don't make no difference. He'll take 'em to the grave with him when Preacher comes for him."

Pausing only a second to answer Elmo's warning, Will said, "If it comes down to me gettin' cornered by your partner, then let me assure you, I'll put a bullet into both of you. While I'm roundin' up the horses, think about that partner of yours. He's ridin' away with all the money, his share and your shares, too. Hard to say what that much money will make a man do." He nodded, as if agreeing with himself. "Now, I'll make you boys a little more comfortable." He untied Lon's ankles and pulled his boots off.

"What the hell?" Lon blurted, and tried to resist, but to no avail.

"I left a fellow's boots on one time when I tied him up," Will said. "While I was saddlin' up the horses, he slipped his foot outta his boot and I had to shoot him before we were done." He tied Lon's ankles again. Then he repeated the procedure with Elmo. "I'll throw your boots on one of the packhorses. You can have 'em back when we get to the jail."

"He's just tryin' to jape us," Elmo said after Will walked away. "Preacher'll be back. He ain't never let a partner down. He'll be back to get us."

"I hope you're right," Lon replied, "but I'm thinkin' about what that deputy said. That's a helluva lot of money." He was also thinking about Preacher's decision to eliminate Slick when he became an inconvenience. "I reckon we're gonna find out."

"You'll see," Elmo insisted. "You ain't rode with him as long as I have."

As the first flickers of light filtered through the branches of the trees overhead, Will prepared to move his jail train down the trail leading to the foot of the mountains. As yet, there had been no indication that Preacher was anywhere about, and the farther they traveled down the mountain, the more convinced Will became that there was no danger of getting bushwhacked. Behind him, Elmo and Lon followed on a lead rope, their hands tied behind their backs. The rest of the horses followed, two of them carrying empty saddles.

"Hey," Elmo called out. "Ain't you gonna feed us no breakfast?"

"You'll eat when I eat," Will yelled back at him. "That'll be when we stop to rest the horses, so just sit back and enjoy the ride." He figured it to be about sixty miles due east to Atoka where Jim Little Eagle had a jail of sorts, good enough to park his two prisoners for a while. And he planned to make it in one day because he had not given up on running Preacher McCoy to ground. In fact, he was more determined to catch up with him than before. He could leave the extra horses with Jim also and arrange to feed the prisoners. As he had done on other occasions, he would make a deal with the Choctaw policeman to reimburse his expenses by sharing some of the weapons, ammunition, and a couple of good saddles he had confiscated. While in Atoka, he would wire Fort Smith to bring Dan Stone up to date on the Texas outlaws.

Dan could decide whether to send a couple of deputies from Fort Smith to transport Lon and Elmo back for trial.

Will drove his train pretty hard before stopping beside a creek to rest the horses. By the time he pulled each one of his prisoners out of their saddles, one by one, and tied to a tree while he built a fire to cook some bacon, they were pretty much subdued. Elmo had quit scanning the hills and gullies they passed, searching for likely places where Preacher might be waiting. Reluctant as he was to admit it, he was beginning to believe that Preacher had, in fact, abandoned them.

"Where the hell is Preacher?" Lon demanded when Will walked to the edge of the creek to fill his coffee-pot. "On his way to Kansas to spend our money," he said, answering his own question. "The son of a bitch. There's been a hundred places where he coulda picked that deputy off with a rifle." He shot an accusing glance in Elmo's direction and added, "And don't talk to me about how faithful a partner he is."

Elmo was hard-pressed to come up with any reasonable answer. He had been so sure Preacher would make an attempt to free them, but he could not argue with Lon. It was surely beginning to look like Preacher had taken the money and run. It was doubly hard to accept, since he had held Preacher in such high regard for so long. It was as soul-wrenching as when he was a small boy and was told there was no Santa Claus. "Maybe he ain't figured out which way this feller is takin' us. There ain't no way he coulda got in front of us to set up an ambush. He might still be on the way."

"On the way to Kansas," Lon scowled. "When I get loose from this bastard, I'll damn sure find Preacher McCoy. I don't need to count on Preacher to set me free. It's a helluva long ride from here to Fort Smith. There's gonna be a time when that deputy slips up and when he does, he's a dead man." He broke off the conversation when Will approached with two plates of bacon and set them down by each man. Then he untied their hands from the trees, but left their legs tied. "This ain't much to feed a man," Lon complained.

"It'll hold you till we get to Atoka," Will said. "I'll make arrangements to feed you a little better over there. Coffee will be done directly. That'll help."

"What's your name, Deputy?" Elmo suddenly asked.

"Tanner," Will answered.

"I ain't never heard of you," Lon sneered.

"Good," Will replied, and continued with his instructions. "When you get through eatin', I'll leave your hands untied, so you can lay back on the ground if you feel like it. I know what you're thinkin'. What's to keep me from untyin' my feet from this tree? Well, I'll tell you. This Winchester 73 will do the trick, 'cause I won't be lyin' back restin'. I'll be watchin' you."

"What if I gotta take a leak?" Lon asked.

"Your hands will be free. You can unbutton your trousers and just let it fly right up against the tree trunk. But don't let me see those hands messin' with that knot holdin' your ankles together. Like I already told you, I'll treat you right as long as you behave yourself, but it's a lot less trouble for me if I shoot you."

"You've kinda got a hard bark on you, ain't you?" Lon couldn't resist asking, judging by the calm and unemotional manner of the deputy. "It's a long ride from here to Fort Smith. You might get kinda tired if you ain't plannin' to sleep between now and then."

"I expect you might be right about that," Will answered. "But you ain't goin' to Fort Smith right away. You'll be sleepin' tonight in Atoka."

Will's announcement fairly jolted Lon. He had counted on a long ride to Fort Smith and a likely opportunity to catch the deputy in a careless moment. His brain began to swirl in a panic to escape. He had no intention of being hauled into Judge Parker's court to be tried, or worse, shipped back to Texas where he would face murder charges on top of robbery. He was going to have to make his move before they made Atoka tonight. He looked up at Will and found the deputy studying him. It was almost as if they were each reading the other's mind as their eyes met. There was a silent challenge that rose between them. Will had seen it before, in the eyes of other prisoners, and cautioned himself to be wary, knowing that he was going to be tested before he reached Atoka.

When Will decided the horses were rested enough to continue, he put out his fire and went to the edge of the creek to rinse the plates and cups. Since he was about ten or twelve yards away from the two trees where his prisoners were tied, Lon decided to test Will's order not to fiddle with the rope tying their feet. He whispered to Elmo, "He ain't payin' us much attention while he's rinsin' them plates and he left that rifle he's always got in his hand propped up against a rock by the fire. I just might get this knot untied, if he keeps his back half-turned like he is right now, and I can beat him to that rifle."

Elmo didn't say anything in response, just shook his head doubtfully, as Lon raised himself to a sitting position. Very slowly, he reached around the tree and felt the hard knot holding him to it. It was not a chain-lightning response from the deputy, yet it was smooth and efficient, and unhurried, as he turned and drew the .44 from his holster. The shot that came a split second later slammed into the water oak dead center of the trunk on a level with Lon's eyes. Lon jerked backward so hard that Elmo thought he had been hit. Elmo, his eyes big as saucers, watched the solemn lawman return the weapon to its holster, showing no sign of concern, as he bent down to pick up the plates. Lon, on the other hand, was about to choke on his spit. "You coulda blowed my head off!" he blurted.

"If that tree was just a wee tad smaller, I might have, for a fact," Will said. "I ain't ever fancied myself as much of a shot with a handgun, but I figured I oughta be able to hit a tree, seein' as I was so close to it."

"Dead center," Elmo couldn't resist announcing. He was convinced the deputy was a lot better shot with a handgun than he admitted.

"I was just tryin' to scratch my foot," Lon lied.

"Best just let it itch next time," Will said. When he finished packing up the cooking utensils, he picked up his rifle before coming back to untie Lon's ankles. He stood back then, his rifle aimed at Lon. "Get on your horse," he ordered, and watched while Lon tiptoed gingerly over to the horse. Since his prisoner's hands and feet were untied, Will was especially alert for an attempt to escape. It was not long in coming. "Put your hands behind your back," he ordered. Instead of complying, Lon suddenly gave his horse a sharp kick with his heels. The horse, confused because it was tied to a lead rope to another horse, began to buck and sidestep, since it couldn't gallop. When Will tried to grab the horse's bridle, Lon saw it as his opportunity, and threw himself at him, only to be stopped in midair by the butt of Will's Winchester against his nose. Taking a step back, Will stood with the rifle aimed at Lon, who was struggling to regain his senses. "Are you done?" Will asked calmly. With blood streaming from his broken nose and busted lip, Lon could only nod weakly in response. With considerable effort, he managed to get up on all fours. Will gave him a minute or two to recover before ordering, "All right, let's try it again, we're wastin' daylight." Lon struggled to his feet and lumbered to the horse again. This time, he managed to pull himself up into the saddle and dutifully place his hands behind his back to be tied. When he was settled, Will returned to Elmo. "How 'bout you?" Will asked. "Are you fixin' to make your move?"

"No, sir," Elmo said with half a chuckle. "I druther just climb on the regular way, if it's all the same to you." When he was seated in the saddle with his hands tied behind his back, he couldn't resist japing his partner. "I swear, Lon, that was the damnest fool thing I've ever seen a man try. Does your nose hurt?"

"Go to hell," Lon snapped.

CHAPTER 6

As Will led his two prisoners along Muddy Boggy Creek, the partnership of the Cotton and Treadwell families rode into the town of Durant, over thirty miles away. Spotting the tent with the wooden façade and the sign proclaiming it to be a saloon, they headed straight for it, passing up the general store and the Texas House Hotel. "I could use a drink right now," Luther Treadwell declared.

"That goes for me, too," Liam, his eldest son, piped up.

Riding beside Liam, Cecil Cotton commented, "I reckon we could all use one." Then unable to resist teasing his brother, who was dark-complexioned with coal-black hair, he added, "All but Emmett, anyway. Don't reckon they'll serve him 'cause he looks like a damn Injun."

"You go to hell," Emmett responded, to chuckles from the others. He was a frequent recipient of his older brother's japing.

After tying the horses, the six men went inside the huge tent to be greeted by Pete Watkins. "Howdy, what's your pleasure, gents?" He made it as friendly as he could affect, seeing as how gangs this size in Indian Territory most often meant trouble for somebody. He hoped he was not that particular somebody. "You fellers passin' through on your way north?"

"Why do you wanna know that?" Jeb asked. "What makes you think we're headin' north?"

"Why, no reason," Pete replied, afraid he had said something to make him mad. "Just makin' conversation, I reckon. We see a lotta folks comin' outta Texas, headin' north. I just hadn't seen you boys around here before."

"Set up some glasses," Luther ordered. He paused while he watched Pete pour six shots of whiskey. "It's been a while since we rode through this little town and you weren't here last time we came through. You figure if we came up from Texas, we must be on the run from the law, right?" He paused to hear his answer, but when Pete began to stutter, looking for a suitable reply, Luther continued. "As a matter of fact, we're Texas lawmen and we're lookin' to meet up with Deputy Will Tanner. Has he been through here lately?"

"Matter of fact, he has," Pete answered, "two or three days ago."

"Did he say where he was headin' when he left here?" Jeb asked immediately.

Aware of the urgency in Jeb's voice, Pete paused to think before answering. He didn't believe for a moment that the gang of six men were really lawmen, and he really didn't care what their reason for being in Indian Territory was as long as it didn't include trouble for his tiny business. He hadn't been in Durant long enough to know Will Tanner, anyway, so he didn't know why he should care whether these men in his saloon right now were intent upon tracking the deputy down or not. Actually, he thought, there was another possibility. They just might like to know where Tanner was, with the notion of trying to avoid him. With that in mind, he decided there was no harm in telling them what they asked. "Well, sir," he started. "I can't say for sure where he was headin' when he rode outta here. But if I had to guess, I'd say he most likely headed up toward Tishomingo. You see, we had a little trouble here last week." He went on to relate the events that led to the murder of two men. "Tanner showed up a couple of days after the two that done the shootin' hightailed it outta here. He went after 'em. Left here on the trail to Tishomingo."

Luther turned to smile at Jeb before turning his attention back to Pete. "On the trail to catch two outlaws, is he? Well, I guess we just missed him." He cut Liam off when his son started to ask a question. "Drink up, boys, we gotta go cook up some breakfast," Luther said, not willing to discuss any plans with Pete standing there listening.

The discussion began as soon as they walked out of the saloon with Luther's chuckling comment. "Well, now how's that for luck? We were worryin' about where to run up on the son of a bitch and he was right here a couple of days ago." He winked at Jeb. "I'd say that's a sure-'nough sign that we're gonna run this coyote to ground."

"While he's trailing them two gunmen, we'll be trailin' him," Jeb said. "It won't hurt to have him thinkin' about them, but we need to catch up as quick as we can."

"When we catch up," Cecil said, "I'm thinkin' it oughta be my right to kill him."

"What the hell gave you that idea?" Emmett immediately challenged. "Billy was my brother, too. When you get right down to it, Billy would druther have me do it 'cause me and him was a lot closer. You always thought you could order him around, Mr. Big Shot."

Enjoying what promised to be an argument that might develop into a fight, Liam and Ethan Treadwell gathered close beside the two waiting to see the first blow land. In the event it developed into a fistfight, they had no doubt who would prevail. Cecil was a good two inches taller than his brother, and probably twenty pounds heavier. But Emmett would make a fight of it out of his relentless determination. Liam winked at Ethan when the Cotton brothers moved up to stand face-to-face. "You'd better step back away from me," Cecil threatened, "before I flatten that little girl nose of yours."

"I'd like to see you try," Emmett replied. "You might be older'n me, but I'll kick your ass proper." Before Cecil could reply, he was jolted by a foot in the seat of his pants when his father decided to put a stop to their childish behavior.

"You two make me ashamed I ever fathered you," Jeb sneered. "This is serious business we're about right now and if you two can't behave like grown men, I'll send you home to stay with your mama. Now, git over there and start fixin' that sowbelly. We need to be ready to ride as soon as the horses are ready." They obeyed him immediately and when they went to the fire, Jeb said to Luther, "I'm sorry, Luther. They look like grown men, but so far, they ain't growed a damn thing between their ears."

They took the time to eat some breakfast and as soon as they agreed the horses were ready to go again, they mounted up and started out toward Tishomingo, confident that the deputy's trail would not be that hard to follow.

Mary Light Walker paused when she saw the riders leading extra horses approaching her cabin on Muddy Boggy Creek. She left her bucket by the edge of the creek and hurried into the cabin to alert her husband. "Come quick. Will Tanner's coming with some men and a string of horses." Jim Little Eagle got up from the table, where he had been finishing the last of his coffee after eating supper, and hurried outside.

When the riders came a little closer, Jim could see that the two behind Will had their hands tied behind their backs. He also noticed the two empty saddles. "Hi-yo, Will," he called out when they entered the yard. "Looks like you caught those two you were chasing."

"Howdy, Jim, Mary," Will replied politely with a nod toward Jim's wife. "Turned out there was four of 'em, robbed the bank down in Sherman, Texas. I'm takin' these two back to Fort Smith, but the big one got away with the money. I'd like to park these two gentlemen in your jail while I go after him. Anybody in your jail now?" He asked the question because the log cabin Jim used for a jail was really little more than a smokehouse that had been converted to hold prisoners. And more than two or three prisoners made conditions a little crowded.

"No, nobody in there now. I just cleaned it out good yesterday. I locked a drunk Chickasaw up in there Sunday and he got sick all over the place. Better now for your two guests." He studied the two outlaws sitting grimly on their horses, especially the one with dried blood all over his mouth and chin. "You say there were four, you have to shoot one?"

"Nope. One of his friends did that job for me," Will answered. "And I appreciate it, because two of 'em was enough to handle without a jail wagon. As usual, I'd like to make arrangements to feed 'em till I can transport 'em to Fort Smith. I'd like to leave the horses here till I can come after 'em, too. Is that all right with you? We can work out your bill for the job when I get back." Jim nodded, always willing to take on these responsibilities for him because of his generosity. In fact, Jim was already admiring the bay gelding carrying one of the empty saddles. Will continued, "You still usin' that little eating place, Lottie's, in town?"

"Yeah, they'll be glad to get the business, but you might be too late to feed them tonight."

"I was afraid I might be," Will said. "I reckon I'll have to cook up something to feed 'em. We didn't really eat much of anything all day." He was actually betting on something he could usually count on, and was not surprised when Mary spoke up.

"You better let me cook something for you," she volunteered. "We already et supper, but I've got some more ham and potatoes I can fry. Won't take long. Better than what you fix, I bet." He made a weak show of not wanting to put her to that trouble, counting on her to insist, which she did. And in a short amount of time, Will and his two prisoners were fed under the watchful eye of Will and Jim Little Eagle. When they were finished eating, the two lawmen loaded the prisoners up for the short ride into Atoka.

"Son of a bitch!" Lon protested when they stopped

before the rough structure with a handmade sign that read JAIL over the door. "This ain't no jail. You might as well stick us in a hole in the ground."

"That'll come later," Will commented drily, "after your trial, I expect."

"Looks right cozy to me," Elmo said, unable to resist japing Lon. Although still finding it hard to accept Preacher McCoy's desertion of him and Lon, he was more inclined to accept whatever fate befell him. If the opportunity presented itself for escape, then he would be ready to attempt it. But he saw no good in constantly whining about the situation.

When the prisoners were locked up, Will and Jim drove the horses back to Jim's place where they unloaded the packs and saddles and stored them in the barn. Will looked over the supplies that belonged to Lon and Elmo to supplement his own and invited Jim to look them over as well. When all was done, Will fixed a bed for himself on some hay in the barn. "Tell Mary I'll be gone before breakfast. I wanna be in town to make arrangements with Lottie's Kitchen to feed my prisoners, so I might as well take breakfast there. I wanna send a wire to Dan Stone to tell him where I'm goin'. He might send somebody over here to get those two before I get back. I'll just tell him to contact you. You and I can settle up when I get back this way."

Will was the first customer at Lottie's in Atoka, which was next to a roominghouse owned by Doug Mabre and run by his wife. "Deputy Tanner, right?" Doug greeted him when he walked in.

"Mister Mabre," Will returned.

"Set yourself down and we'll have some coffee out

here before you can get settled good," Doug said. "Lottie," he called out, "bring the coffeepot."

"That sounds to my likin'," Will said. "I'll take a little breakfast and I'd like to make arrangements for you to feed a couple of prisoners locked up in the jail. Jim Little Eagle told me you've been workin' with him to feed prisoners."

"Indeed we have," Doug responded. "Be glad to work with you. You want two or three meals a day?"

"Two," Will said. "I don't want 'em to get to thinkin' they're in a hotel. Just keep a record of the number of days and when I get back I'll get you your money."

After leaving Lottie's Kitchen, satisfied that his prisoners would get decent meals, he went to the train depot and wired Dan Stone. That done, he went by the jail to check on his prisoners. Talking to them through a small barred window in the heavy wooden door, he told them that they would be fed with food from Lottie's. "I hope you catch that son of a bitch," Lon informed him, still angry over Preacher's failure to help them.

Elmo evidently realized that Preacher had made no effort to come after them and was feeling the full effects of having been deserted by one he had counted as a friend. He surprised Will when he volunteered some information that caused Will to consider it. "I doubt you'll be able to catch up with Preacher," he said. "But he used to say if he ever really struck it rich, he'd likely go to Wichita and run a whorehouse. I reckon that's outta your jurisdiction. You can't follow him up there in Kansas Territory." He paused to think about it, then said, "We've stopped at Sartain's a couple of times, up on Muskrat Creek. You ever been there?" Will said that he had. Elmo said nothing more and retired to a corner of the small room, thinking he had retaliated in some fashion for Preacher's desertion. He ignored the smug smile worn by his fellow prisoner, amused by the desertion of Preacher McCoy's faithful disciple.

Satisfied that he had taken care of everything, Will set out again to ride to the Arbuckles, this time with mixed feelings. What Elmo had told him about the possibility that Preacher might have headed for Sartain's on his way to Kansas was hard to ignore. But what if Elmo was wrong? What if Preacher took off for Texas instead? Elmo had been dead sure that Preacher would make an attempt to free him and Lon. And he had been wrong about that, so he told himself that he had to return to the cave to try to pick up Preacher's trail down the backside of that mountain. It would cost him time, but it might mean the difference in eventually tracking him down and not. With that in mind, he started out, riding south of Jim Little Eagle's place on Muddy Boggy Creek, heading straight back to the Arbuckle Mountains. With his bay packhorse heavily loaded, he was well supplied to remain on the trail for a long time before needing more.

Another long day's ride brought him back to the cave by the waterfall in time to allow him enough light to build a fire inside after unloading his horses and hobbling them. Buster would not ordinarily wander far from his master, but Will didn't want to take a chance on having to look for the bay in the morning, so he hobbled both horses. With time on his hands, he took another look through the scattered packs strewn about the floor of the cave in case he had missed something important on his first hasty search. He found nothing that would be useful to him, so after a supper of sowbelly and hardtack, washed down with strong coffee, he rolled into his blanket and went to sleep.

He was awakened the next morning by the snuffling sounds of Buster as the big buckskin sniffed around the mouth of the cave. "You're right," Will said to him. "The sun's already up and I got no business lyin' in bed. But to be honest, I had to wait for daylight to see if I can cut that jasper's trail." The buckskin showed no interest in Will's comments, so Will decided the horse was still insulted because he had hobbled him. By the time the light had filtered through the branches enough to see the ground below, Will was saddled up and ready to scout the slope behind the cave. He went directly to the spot where he had gotten his last glimpse of the fugitive galloping away in the darkness. He found the tracks he was looking for almost immediately and they pointed toward a gap between two huge boulders that formed a gateway into a thick pine forest. He rode past the boulders and entered the stand of pines to discover the tracks were gone due to the thick bed of pine straw on the floor of the forest.

He dismounted to examine the ground more closely and tried to put himself in Preacher's place when he fled. As dark as it had been, especially in the pines, he would have had to slow his horse to a walk. Consequently, there would be no obvious tracks like there would have been if the horse was at a full gallop. To add to his problem, it was still fairly dark in the pines even with the sun rising higher. He had to think like Preacher again. It was doubtful if Preacher knew the slope behind the cave very well, or at all. It was the only way left to him to escape. With that in mind, Will looked at the trees ahead and tried to guess which way would seem the most likely exit from the trees. Possibly, Preacher let his horse find its way out. That seemed like a good idea to Will, so he climbed back into the saddle and gave Buster a gentle nudge with the reins lying limp in his hands. With no guidance, the big horse walked slowly ahead, making his way through the trees until coming to a wide-open meadow. Will reined him to a halt and dismounted again to search the ground for tracks. He found what he was looking for a short distance from the point where he had exited the trees. Judging by the toe of the hoofprint, Preacher had nudged the horse to pick up the pace when he found himself in the clear. Will walked ahead until he found another track, and a little farther on until he found another. Then he looked out across the meadow in the direction the tracks indicated and picked a spot on the other side. He climbed into the saddle and rode toward that spot.

Fortunately, he was able to find Preacher's tracks and follow them down to the valley, even though the trail took a few changes in direction. He figured Preacher had to take a few detours in the darkness before coming upon the ravine that led him to the base of the slope. From that point, Preacher had ridden clear of the mountains, then turned straight north, causing Will to wonder if he had made a mistake in not heading straight to Sartain's after all. Sartain's was two full days from where he was now and he had lost a lot of time riding back here to pick up Preacher's trail. But at this point, this was all he had,

Preacher's trail leading north and Elmo's suggestion that Preacher might go to Sartain's.

He was able to follow the outlaw's tracks along the western side of the Arbuckles until he had come to an old Indian trail leading north. It appeared that Preacher had decided to follow that trail. It led him to the Washita River after a ride of thirty miles where he stopped to rest his horses. Although it seemed a logical place to stop, he saw no signs that might tell him that the outlaw had stopped there. It didn't surprise him. Traveling in the dead of night, there was no telling where Preacher might have decided to rest his horse. Will left the Washita, planning to rest his horses again when he camped beside the Canadian River that night.

As he checked his horses before starting out for the Canadian, he allowed himself to question the possibility of his tracking down Preacher McCoy. The odds were not good. He had started out trailing Preacher to the Washita, but he had not been certain he was on the same trail after that. For there were many tracks leading to the Washita, some shod and some not, so he had continued to assume that Preacher was planning to go on to Sartain's. He finally accepted the fact that he was gambling on a hunch, and if he was wrong, Preacher McCoy would vanish from Oklahoma Territory. So the only thing he could do now was to bet all his chips on that hunch. With that settled in his mind, he left the Washita, heading for the Canadian, with still a full day and a half's ride to strike the Cimarron River and the little three-house compound called Sartain's on Muskrat Creek. He tried to keep himself from fretting about the time he had lost going back to the Arbuckles, but it was hard to forget that he would have gained a day and a half on Preacher, had he not gone back. There was no thought that the lost day and a half would be a day and a half gain for someone who might be trailing him.

When he approached the Canadian River, he was surprised to discover a ferry in operation. There had not been one the last time he had ridden this way and it was a small enterprise judging by the size of the ferryboat. "Howdy, partner," a short, bald man with oxlike shoulders greeted him when he pulled Buster up to the bank. "You lookin' to take the ferry across? I was just fixin' to close her down for the night."

"Looks like maybe I got here just in time," Will said. "How much you charge to take me and my horses across?"

"Sixty cents," he said, "ten cents for you, quarter apiece for the horses." He waited for only a moment before pressing. "The river's got a lot of quicksand in spots this time of year. It'll save you a lotta trouble to let me take you across. Tell you what, since this is the last crossin' tonight, I'll take you and the horses across for fifty cents. Whaddaya say?"

"All right," Will said. He had not planned to balk at the original price.

"Lead 'em on, partner, right up to the front of the boat." When Will led his horses on, the man led his mule aboard behind them, untied the boat and picked up a cowbell and gave it a good clanging. It served to startle Will's horses, causing him some trouble to calm them down, especially the bay. "Sorry 'bout that," the ferryman said. In a few minutes, the ferry began to move slowly toward the other bank, guiding on a line stretched across the river. "My name's Cal Berry. That's my brother, Cleve, pullin' us across."

"Cowberry?" Will replied, not sure he had heard correctly.

"No, sir," he replied patiently, accustomed to having to clarify. "My name's Berry, first name of Calvin. Folks call me Cal."

"Sorry," Will apologized, "Will Tanner. You weren't here last time I rode through this way. You gettin' much ferryin' business?"

"Some," Cal replied. "Not a lotta folks know we're here yet, but I expect we'll catch on. Last week a feller tried to ford the river a couple dozen yards beyond that big oak yonder. He run into some quicksand. It was a devil of a job gettin' his wagon and horses outta there. You can still see the ruts where we pulled him back up on the bank." He paused to scratch his chin whiskers, obviously thinking about some extra money he charged for his help. "He was more'n ready to let me ferry him across then. A couple of days ago, a feller came through ridin' a big ol' black horse bareback—asked me if I had a saddle I'd like to sell. I ain't got one. Wish I'da had one though, 'cause he looked like he'da give a lot for a decent saddle. I thought about askin' him what happened to his'n, but he was a big feller, big as you, and he didn't look like he was lookin' for friendly conversation. You know what I mean?"

"I know what you mean," Will answered. This was what he had hoped for, some sign that he was, in fact, still onto Preacher's trail. "Which way did he go when he left here?"

His question caused Cal to pause before answering. He took another long look at Will. "Are you a lawman?"

"I am," Will answered.

"I knew it!" Cal exclaimed. "I told Cleve I bet that jasper was on the run from the law. He just had a look about him. What did he do, steal that horse he was ridin'? Shoulda stole the saddle, too, I reckon. Well, I'll be . . ."

"Which way did he go?" Will repeated, patiently.

"Rode straight up toward them hills in the distance yonder," Cal said, pointing toward the northwest. Will stared out across the open plains between the river and the line of low hills pointed out. It would have been the general direction he would have taken if he was thinking about striking the Cimarron where Muskrat Creek flowed into it. "Ain't that somethin'?" Cal went on, still picturing Preacher in his mind. "It ain't all that unusual to see fellers on the run from the law up here in Osage country, but he was the kinda jasper that didn't look like he'da run from anybody. Didn't have no saddle—had to carry his rifle in his hand, and a saddlebag over his shoulder. Are you one of them marshals outta Fort Smith?"

"That's right," Will answered.

Cal continued talking until the ferry was pulled up to the bank by a mule driven by Cal's brother, Cleve. It didn't seem to bother him that most of his questions were answered with one- and two-word answers. He introduced Will to his brother and immediately began telling Cleve about the rider on the blue roan with no saddle. "I figured he was on the run," Cleve immediately claimed. "Had to be—no saddle, no packhorse, no food. He gave May a dollar for some breakfast and took some cornbread with him when he left. He must notta et for a while, the way he went after that sowbelly and eggs."

Cleve's last comment sparked Cal's attention. "You never said nothin' about him givin' May a dollar."

"Musta slipped my mind," Cleve said, and immediately changed the subject. "How 'bout you, Mr. Tanner? It's gettin' on to about suppertime and my wife's a fine cook. Cal can tell you that."

"Reckon not," Will replied. "I've got a long ride to strike the Cimarron tomorrow, so I think I'll go a little farther tonight before I make camp. Thanks just the same." He climbed back in the saddle and bid them both a good evening.

"You leavin' so soon?" Elmira Tate asked when Preacher peeled off some money from a sizable roll he carried in his pocket, obviously thinking to settle his bill. "You just got here," she went on. "I figured you'd stay with us a week or two at least."

"There ain't nothin' I'd like better," Preacher said. "But I expect I'd best keep movin'. I'm figurin' on ridin' clear of Indian Territory for a while—ain't too healthy for me right now."

She was at once suspicious. "I thought you said there weren't nobody on your tail when you rode in yesterday. You weren't japin' me, were you? Is there gonna be a posse of lawmen showin' up here lookin' for you?"

"Hell, no, Elmira, I ain't ever led no lawmen to your place," Preacher was quick to insist. "I just decided it wouldn't hurt to be a little extra careful."

"Makes a body wonder," she said, still in doubt. He was in an awful hurry to be on his way. "The way you came ridin' in here with no saddle, or much of anything else, there musta been somebody chasin' after you."

"I told you I couldn't go back for my saddle or anything else when I found out them deputies had killed Elmo and them other two fellers we picked up down in Texas. I knew if I took a chance on goin' back for my possibles, they'd get on my trail for sure. I figured I'd take what little bit of money I had and head for Kansas. There wasn't anything I could do for them boys. They were already done in, or I'da sure as hell gone back to help 'em."

"You oughta hang around here for a little while," Slim Branch piped up. He had been listening with interest to the conversation between Elmira and Preacher. Already a beneficiary of Preacher's resources, having sold him a saddle, Slim was hoping he'd stay a little longer. With eyes long accustomed to observing such things, Slim couldn't help noticing that the roll of money Preacher pulled out never seemed to shrink in size. And this was even after he had peeled off forty dollars for a saddle Slim would have let him have for five, if he'd tried to bargain at all. He had a feeling Preacher had a story to tell, but he doubted it was the one he was selling. "I'm right sorry to hear about Elmo," Slim offered. "He rode with you for a long time."

"He sure did," Preacher said. "It like to broke my heart when I heard them deputies raided our camp and shot 'em all, and me not bein' able to help. I'da done anything for ol' Elmo." He looked up quickly when the door suddenly opened and Darlene Futch came in.

"Looks like I'm runnin' a little late for breakfast," Darlene announced, and headed straight for the coffeepot. After she poured herself a cup, she walked over to the table and placed a hand on Preacher's shoulder. "You feelin' any better, hon?"

"Sure," he quickly replied, seeming slightly embarrassed. "I'm right as rain. I reckon I musta got ahold of somethin' that didn't set right in my belly yesterday."

This caught Elmira's attention right away. "Well, I hope it wasn't nothin' you ate here. That beef was fresh, wasn't it, Slim?"

"Sure was," Slim answered. "It warn't nowhere close to turnin'. I just butchered it the day before."

"It wasn't nothin'," Preacher insisted, anxious to change the subject before Darlene started talking about his lack of ardor during the night just passed. He had paid her double her asking price, hoping she'd appreciate it enough to keep her mouth shut. "I'm gonna go on up to Kansas for a spell till things here quiet down. When I come back, I aim to pay you a nice long visit." He looked quickly toward the door when it opened again and Eddie, Elmira's son, walked in.

"I brought your horse up," Eddie said, "and tied him up at the rail."

"Much obliged," Preacher said.

"You'd best keep an eye on that cinch strap on that old saddle," Eddie reported. "It's lookin' frayed in a couple of places."

"Yeah, I noticed that myself," Preacher replied. "But I reckon it'll hold till I can get someplace to get a new one. I think ol' Slim skinned me on that deal, but it'll sure beat ridin' bareback." He aimed a grin at

Slim to set him at ease. He didn't plan to put up with the old single-rigged saddle very long. Being a wealthy man, he planned to buy a fine saddle, befitting one of his stature, as soon as he got the chance. But for the time being, he was ready to climb into that creaky old saddle and put some distance behind him, anxious to cross into Kansas and leave the Fort Smith deputy at the border. He still wasn't really certain that he was being followed. He didn't believe that deputy who arrested Lon and Elmo would try to follow him when he had two prisoners to contend with, but he had decided he was going to play it like he was being followed. No sense in taking chances. He reached down and picked up his coffee cup from the table, drained the last swallow, and set it back on the table. "Well, folks, I'll see you again when I'm back this way."

"Don't make it too long," Elmira said as he headed for the door. "It's always a pleasure to have you visit." She walked to the door to watch him step up on the big black horse and gave him a little wave when he touched a finger to his hat brim in farewell. *That son of a bitch is toting a lot of money he ain't talking about,* she thought. When she went back inside, she repeated the thought aloud to Darlene. "Didn't he do any talkin' about money last night?"

"He didn't do much talkin' about anything," Darlene replied. "Matter of fact, he didn't act like he was even enjoyin' bein' with me."

"I was thinkin' the same thing as you," Slim said. "I saw the size of that roll he peeled them bills off of. He had money to spare, or he wouldn'ta give me forty dollars for that old saddle."

"And right when we could use some business around here," Elmira complained. At the present time, there

were no customers seeking refuge at Sartain's, so
there were only the four of them in residence now—
herself, her son, Darlene, and Slim. Slim had originally
found her place with two partners, Pop Strawbridge
and Coy Trainer. Off and on, the three became per-
manent guests, paying their way by furnishing stolen
cattle for the cook stove. That is, until they decided to
throw in with Ben Trout and Brock Larsen to bush-
whack a fellow named Walker. None of the five ever
came back from that night until about seven months
later when Slim showed up by himself. He told a tale
about how they had been ambushed and that he was
the only one to get away. He had just rambled around,
mentally lost, with no other place to go. Elvira let him
stay, after giving him a good lecture on respecting the
rights of her guests and reminding him that Sartain's
was a haven for anybody on the run from the law. He
seemed genuinely remorseful, so she used him to
help out around the place and occasionally go with
young Eddie to hunt whenever there was news of a
cattle drive close by.

"Ol' Preacher sure seemed a mite jumpy, didn't
he?" Slim commented.

"Yeah, he did," Elmira replied. "And he was in an
awful hurry to get away from here. I'd like to have
seen what he was carryin' in those saddlebags." In
days past, she might have entertained thoughts of
finding out, in spite of the dressing down she had
given Slim about her customers' rights. But she figured it not worth the risk with someone like Preacher
McCoy, who had a killer's reputation and was generally not a man to cross. Besides that, it would be bad
for business if someone like Preacher happened to
get his throat cut at her place. "He's done led a pack

of lawmen right to us," she decided aloud, thinking again of his eagerness to depart.

"Well, if he did," Darlene said, "there ain't nobody on the run here to worry about. So let 'em come. It might be interestin' to entertain a bunch of lawmen," she added with a girlish giggle.

"That'ud be somethin', all right," Slim commented.

CHAPTER 7

The last time Will had stood on the top of this hill was a little over a year before when Oscar Moon had taken him to Muskrat Creek. Even in the fading light, he could still plainly see the three houses that made up the outlaw haven known as Sartain's. It was named for Elmer Sartain, who was a notorious stagecoach robber some years back. He built the original cabin by the creek and it soon became a hideout for other outlaws. Elmer was dead now, but the complex was run by an old flame of his, Elmira Tate. Looking at it now, it appeared that nothing much had changed that he could spot from this distance. As before, he couldn't get an idea of how many guests Elmira was entertaining because the horses were kept on the far side of the many oak trees where the cabins had been built. There was no barn. In foul weather, they huddled the horses under an overhanging ledge of the hill behind the third cabin. When he had been there before, he had come under the guise of just another outlaw on the run. They now knew he was a U.S. deputy marshal, so he was not likely to receive a welcome back. So simply riding in was not an option. He could very well be shot on sight. With that thought in mind, he stepped up into the saddle and guided Buster down the backside of the hill, planning to ride a wide circle and come up upon the compound from the north, along Muskrat Creek. He hoped by doing that, he could get a look at the horses to get an idea of how many visitors Elvira had, especially if one of them happened to be a big blue roan, as black as night.

He took his time making his circle, since he wanted to wait until it was a little darker, anyway. When he struck the creek north of the three cabins, he entered the oaks scattered along the bank just as the light began fading away. He slow-walked his horses, following the bank until he could clearly see the horses grazing behind the third house. He had no way of knowing for sure how many were owned by temporary residents, but he knew Elmira only kept one horse. When last there, he encountered three small-time cattle thieves who had been staying in one of the houses for quite some time. He counted only four horses, and no blue roan, so he couldn't be sure if Preacher McCoy had stopped here or not. The more he thought about it, the more he realized there was no way he could determine beforehand how many outlaws he might walk in on—and consequently, what his chances were of walking out alive. But with only four horses, there couldn't be more than one or two. And he needed to know if Preacher had come this way, and if he was gone, as it appeared, how long ago did he leave? He decided he'd try to account for everybody before he walked in, so he took another look at the houses.

The main house, Elvira's, was well lit up, which he expected. It was the other two that held his interest because they might tell him how many visitors were on hand. There was smoke coming from the chimney of the third house, where Darlene Futch lived, but there was no lantern light in the windows. It would appear that she was not entertaining a customer at present. Chances were Darlene was up at the main house, so there was no one in hers. There was little risk in checking for sure, so he left his horses on the creek bank and moved cautiously up to the front window. A quick look told him no one was in the house.

The windows in the house between Darlene's and Elmira's showed no light, either, so he was prone to conclude that everybody currently in residence at Sartain's was gathered in Elmira's house. Repeating the check he performed at Darlene's, he confirmed it. He decided the odds were in his favor now, so there could be no better time to pay them a call. Retrieving his horses, he led them to the front porch of Elmira's house and tied them at a corner post. A quick look through the front window told him there was no one to worry about but one. He remembered him from his last night at Sartain's and an ambush planned to take his life. Slim was what his partners had called him, and he was the only one who got away after the shoot-out on that night. Will had wondered what happened to him, but had not been interested enough to look for him. Now here he was, Slim and the two women. With his rifle in hand, he started for the door just as he heard someone behind him. "Mr. Walker?"

Will turned immediately, his rifle ready to fire,

causing the young boy to take a quick step backward. He had forgotten about Elmira's young son. "Eddie," Will said. "Didn't see you back there in the dark." He remembered then that Walker was the name he had given them when he was last here. "I was just fixin' to go inside." He stepped aside and motioned. "After you."

The three people at the table turned when the door opened and Eddie walked in. All three quickly sat upright when he was followed by Will. "Mr. Walker," Eddie announced simply, not sure what else to say. The three at the table froze.

"Evenin', folks," Will greeted them. "Sorry to disturb your supper. I was just on my way up toward Kansas, but I know you wouldn't want me passin' through without stoppin' to say howdy." Holding his rifle in a ready position, but not threatening, he nodded to Slim. "Didn't expect to see you here, Slim. Figured this would be one of the last places you'd wanna show up again."

"Now, wait a minute, Walker, you got it all wrong. I never threw one single shot at you. That was all the doin's of Larsen and Trout. They tried to kill us all. I just happened to be lucky enough to get away, else I'da been dead, too. I'm just glad to see you made it all right, too."

It occurred to Will then that they were still not aware that he was a deputy marshal. He had assumed that they knew. The reason they had all looked so stunned when he walked in was because they thought he was dead. There was no point in telling them now, he decided. He might want to call on them again. "No hard feelin's, Slim, I figured it was the work of Larsen and Trout and you and your two partners were slickered into ridin' with 'em. You and me, though, we came out of it on our feet, right?" He was well aware that Slim and the other two thought they were going to bush-whack him, trusting a partnership with the two killers.

"That's the God's honest truth," Slim exclaimed. "I'm just sorry that Coy and Pop didn't get the chance to run with me."

"Right now, I just need a little information," Will said. "I'm tryin' to catch up with Preacher McCoy. He's got some things that ain't his. I know he was here and I thought I'd catch up with him, but I see he's al-ready gone. When did he leave?"

"He left this mornin'," Elvira said, "right after breakfast."

"Did he say where he was headin'?" He knew now that Preacher was only one day ahead of him instead of two.

"No, he didn't, just said he was goin' to Kansas ter-ritory for a while." She studied his face for a moment before continuing. "I reckon you're the reason he showed up here ridin' a horse barcback, then."

"Maybe," Will answered.

"He mighta gone by Scully's tradin' post," she vol-unteered, thinking Will might be inclined to spend a little money here if she was helpful. "That old saddle Slim sold him might fall apart before he gets there."

"Much obliged," Will said. Scully's was on the Salt Fork of the Arkansas River, a distance he estimated to be fifty miles from there.

"I reckon you're gonna want some supper and a bed for the night."

"Reckon not. Some other time when I ain't in such a hurry," he replied, and turned to leave. With noth-ing more to gain, he was not inclined to waste another second there. He was gone before they could actually believe it, leaving them standing with mouths agape.

Eddie was the only one to move. He ran to the door in time to see him ride off up the creek in the moonlight. "He's gone," Eddie declared when he went back inside.

"If that don't beat all," Darlene marveled. "I reckon he don't need no food or sleep. You reckon he's really a lawman, I mean, him chasin' Preacher and all?"

"Nah," Elmira said. "I can smell a lawman a mile away. He's a son of a bitch, but not that kinda son of a bitch."

Beyond the hill where the horses were kept in bad weather, Will turned Buster's head on a course directly toward the Arkansas River. He had been operating this entire chase on information from outlaws and, so far, it had all proven to be accurate. So he decided to stay with it and head straight to Scully's. He had a full day's ride to get there, but he was not going to start out tonight. His horses needed a rest and he felt like he could use some, too. So he followed Muskrat Creek for a couple of miles until he found a spot that suited him, then went about making his camp for the night. It might not be as comfortable as a bed back at Sartain's, but he figured he had a better chance of waking up in the morning.

"We got company comin'," Deke Fanning called from the porch of the trading post on the Blue River. "Looks like a posse. I count six of 'em."

Jeremy Cannon walked out to see for himself. "Now, what the hell?" His first thought was the same as Deke's, that a deputy's posse was searching for Preacher McCoy and his gang. "Don't tell 'em a damn thing," he warned Deke. He stood there, waiting while the six riders approached his store. He offered no greeting as they stepped down and tied their horses to the rail. When he finally spoke, it was with a strong hint of sarcasm. "You fellers lost?"

Luther Treadwell frowned as he stared at Cannon for a few moments before responding. "Well, now, we might be. All of us are at one time or another. You own this store?"

"Maybe I do, and maybe I don't," Cannon answered, still convinced he was talking to a lawman.

"Like I said," Luther replied. "Maybe you're the one who's lost. You don't even know if you own this store or not. Do you always welcome strangers like this?"

Jeb Cotton stepped up beside Luther, causing Cannon to take a step back. "I sure as hell know who owns this store," Cannon declared. "And if you've come to buy supplies or somethin', I've got most of what you might need. But I ain't got no information about anybody you're lookin' for. It ain't my business to help the law do theirs." He was surprised when his comment brought a round of chuckles from the younger men standing behind the two on his front steps.

"He spotted you right off, Pa," Liam joked. "You've got the look of a marshal." This caused more laughter from the brothers.

"Yeah, Uncle Luther," Cecil said, "show him your badge."

Astonished by their reaction, Cannon exchanged glances with Deke, who shrugged in response. "You ain't lawmen?" Cannon asked. "Who are you, then?"

"My name's Luther Treadwell," he said. "This here's Jeb Cotton and these mangy-lookin' fellers behind us are our sons."

"Well, I'll be . . ." Cannon started, then paused to look at Luther again. "Treadwell and Cotton, I've heard mention of your names. From down Texas way, right?" Luther nodded. "Well, I'll be . . ." Cannon repeated, then gestured toward the door. "Well, come on in and we'll find you somethin' to drink." He stepped aside and held the door open while they filed in. "My name's Jeremy Cannon. Where you fellers headin', up in the Arbuckles?"

"Well, we didn't start out to," Jeb replied. "We've got a place up on the Cimarron, but we've got a little business to tend to up this way we're lookin' to take care of first. And I'm hopin' you can help us a little."

"If I can," Cannon said, and continued pouring a drink for each man.

"We're lookin' for a man," Luther said. "Been on his trail since Durant and we think he mighta passed this way. He's a deputy marshal outta Fort Smith."

"Will Tanner!" Cannon immediately blurted, almost joyously.

"That's right," Luther said. "Did he pass this way?"

"He sure did. He came through a few days ago, lookin' for Preacher McCoy and his gang. I didn't tell him nothin', but I'm pretty sure he went on up to the Arbuckles. Don't know if he found Preacher or not, but he ain't been back and none of Preacher's boys have been back here since then." He slapped his hand on the bar. "Ha! Ain't that somethin'? Turnaround— outlaws trackin' the deputy, instead of the other way around. Whaddaya after Tanner for?" Jeb told him about the shooting of his son Billy, done cowardly with a bullet in the back while unarmed and in custody at the time. "Well, now, that sure is a sorry piece of business, and I'm sorry for your son's death. But it don't surprise me none. That Tanner is a mean one."

"And you say you ain't seen Preacher or none of his boys since you last saw Tanner?" Luther asked. Cannon shook his head. "So it's hard to say if he found 'em or not," Luther continued. "Maybe he found 'em, but maybe they done him in, instead. I wouldn't be surprised. Preacher McCoy ain't anybody you'd wanna fool with. There's a lotta folks down in Texas lookin' for him." He turned to look at Jeb and shook his head. "I reckon the only way we're gonna find out if Tanner's still up there is to ride on up and look around."

"I gotta see him dead," Jeb replied.

"We'll have to do some lookin'," Luther said. "It's been a while since I was last in those mountains and there's a hundred places to hide. But we'll find him if he's up there," he added to reassure Jeb.

They took the time to rest their horses and eat some food. Then after buying some supplies from Cannon, they were back in the saddle again, heading for the Arbuckle Mountains, roughly twenty miles away. Recalling conversations he had overheard from other outlaws who had traded with him, Cannon had suggested they should probably enter the southern end of the mountains. He speculated that the cave Preacher McCoy and his gang had holed up in was beside a waterfall about halfway up the mountain. He apologized for the briefness of his directions, having never been there himself. His information was merely bits and pieces he had learned, but they came from quite a few outlaws who had camped there. "I think I might know where that cave is," Luther said. "I know I remember a waterfall I saw there one time."

It was still early in the evening by the time the six outlaws reached the foot of the trail that Luther felt sure was the one they sought. There was still daylight enough to follow the narrow game trail, but he and Jeb decided it was not the best of plans to start out now when darkness might overtake them halfway to the falls. The risks were two: if they ran up on Tanner, he might see them before they saw him, and there was also the possibility of getting shot at by Preacher McCoy and his men if Tanner had not found the cave. So they made their camp at the foot of the mountain and waited until morning to start up the trail.

Eager to start the next morning, they were in the saddle before breakfast and already following the winding trail up the mountain. Liam, being the more skillful in tracking, was sent on ahead by his father to scout the trail before them. "He'll let us know if we're about to run up on somethin'," Luther assured Jeb. They soon lost sight of Liam, but continued on up the path. After a lengthy climb, they came to the clearing and the pond at the base of the waterfall to find Liam standing by the mouth of the cave.

"They were here, all right," Liam announced when the others rode into the clearing. "There are plenty of tracks to see. Can't tell what happened, though. Whoever was here has done gone. There ain't nobody in the cave, but they left some stuff in there. Musta left in a hurry."

The others dismounted and searched the cave for

themselves. Jeb sent Cecil and Emmett to scout the trees outside the clearing. It was they who discovered the remains of Slick Towsen in the bottom of a gully. That was enough to convince Jeb that Tanner had found the cave and the rest of Preacher's gang must have run, with the deputy still after them. "It ain't likely they ran back down the way he came up after 'em," Jeb figured. "So they musta gone out the back somewhere." It didn't take Liam long to find the escape trail down the back side of the slope and they followed it down to the bottom where they stopped to decide what to do. "There ain't no decision to make," Jeb informed Luther. "Ain't nothin' changed. We're still goin' after that son of a bitch, even if he follows Preacher all the way to Canada. At least, me and my boys are."

Luther quickly responded. "We're all goin' after him. Like I said before, Billy was family, and we take care of family." He shrugged and said, "Besides, the direction that trail is headed is the way we wanta go, anyway, more or less in the direction of our camp on the Cimarron. So we ain't losin' nothin' if we stay on it."

Still kneeling beside the tracks of the horses, Liam remarked, "You know, these tracks ain't really that old. We might not be as far behind that jasper as we thought." That thought was enough to prompt Jeb Cotton to hustle everyone to start out at once.

"That son of a bitch!" Preacher swore when he examined the worn cinch latigo on the saddle he had given forty dollars for. When he gave it a firm tug to tighten it up, it had almost torn loose and was now held on by a small portion of the strap. Another tug and he might have broken it. He wished now that he had left the saddle on the horse when he had stopped to rest him. With half a day left to ride before reaching Scully's, he was not at all confident that he wouldn't end up on his backside in the middle of the prairie before he got there. Although he cursed Slim for his predicament, he was really angry at himself for offering him so much for the saddle. "Coulda had it for five bucks," he grumbled as he placed his boot in the stirrup and carefully pulled himself up to settle as gently as he could in the saddle. He nudged the roan with his heels and started out again, following a frequently used trail leading north.

The latigo held until within about five miles of the river when it suddenly broke. Preacher grabbed the roan's neck in an effort to remain upright when the saddle started to shift sideways. He kicked his boot out of the stirrup in time to keep the saddle from pulling him off with it while reining the horse back hard. When the horse stopped, Preacher wound up on the ground with his forty-dollar saddle. With fleeting thoughts of going back to take forty dollars' worth of satisfaction out of Slim's hide, he gathered himself together. Slim had told him that the saddle was old, so he knew what he was getting when he bought it. Still he was reluctant to take the responsibility for the poor decision. "You're damn lucky it's only about four or five miles to Scully's," he said, thinking of Slim Branch, "or I'd go back and kick your skinny ass." He gathered up his scant possessions and his saddlebags full of stolen bank money and prepared to ride bareback again, hoping he could get a saddle at Scully's. It would be a long shot because Clem Scully ran a typical trading post, selling general supplies and whiskey under the counter. He was not likely to carry saddles unless he traded for one. It was not without considerable effort that he finally got underway again; bareback, his saddlebags across his shoulders, a canvas sack in his lap, holding the overflow of cash that was too much for the saddlebags, and his rifle across his thighs. He was not in a genial mood when he arrived at Scully's.

There were two horses tied at the hitching rail in front of Scully's store. Preacher took special notice of the saddles on each horse; both appeared to be in good condition. *I'll damn sure ride out of here with a new saddle, whether Scully has one for sale or not,* he told himself. He slid off his horse and tied the blue roan next to the two horses there, picked up all his possessions, and went inside the store. He stopped at the door to look things over before walking straight to the counter. "Evenin'," Clem Scully greeted him, making no effort to disguise his curiosity when he saw the load Preacher brought in with him. "You figurin' on sellin' or buyin'?"

Preacher ignored Clem's attempt at humor. "I'll be needin' some supplies," he said. "To start, I need a saddle. I need a packhorse, too."

"Whoa," Clem interrupted. "Saddle? Packhorse? I don't sell saddles or horses. Sometimes I'll take a saddle in trade, but I don't happen to have one right now."

"I've got the money to pay you," Preacher said.

"I'm sorry," Clem replied. "I wish I could accommodate you, friend, but I ain't got horses or saddles for sale."

Preacher nodded toward the two cowhands sitting at a table at the other side of the store. They were working on a fruit jar holding corn liquor, but were watching with curiosity at the man who had walked in with all the baggage. "What about those two?"

Clem was not quite sure how to answer the question. "What about 'em? You mean, do they wanna sell their horses and saddles?" He shrugged. "I couldn't say. I reckon you could ask 'em." He was beginning to worry about the possibility of some trouble from this formidable stranger, maybe a holdup or worse. That thought prompted him to move closer to the other end of the counter where his shotgun was propped when Preacher walked over to the table.

"Which one of you fellows is gonna sell me a horse and saddle?" Preacher asked, causing both men to look at each other slack-jawed with astonishment. When there was no reply right away from either, Preacher asked, "Are you both deaf and dumb, or don't you speak English?"

"What are you talkin' about?" one of the men spoke up then.

Past patience when he came in the door, Preacher repeated, "Plain enough question, which one of you is gonna sell me a horse and saddle?"

"We ain't got no horses for sale," the other cowhand said.

"Look, friend," Preacher said. "You rode in here on a horse, didn't you? Well you've got somethin' I need more'n you do. You're lucky 'cause I'm willin' to pay you a fair price for the horse and saddle. So make up your mind which one gets the money. I ain't got all night."

"Mister, you're talkin' like a crazy man," the first cowhand said. "I can't sell you my horse and saddle. Neither can Bob, so go on back over there and leave us alone." He looked over at Scully then. "Hey, Clem, bring us over another jar of this stuff you call likker."

Preacher said nothing more, but remained for a long moment staring at the two men before returning to the counter. When Clem returned to the counter, Preacher asked, "Have you got a rig for a packhorse?"

"Yes, sir, I've got that. I just don't have any horses to sell," he repeated.

Preacher waited a moment, then said, "Well, go get it." He stood there until Clem came back from his storeroom with a pack harness and placed it on the counter.

"That'll run you eight dollars," he said. Preacher pulled a roll of money out and peeled off eight dollars. Then he called out a list of basic supplies he needed. Having seen the money, Clem jumped smartly to accommodate him.

"When you get all them supplies," Preacher instructed, "bring 'em outside. I'll be gettin' my packhorse ready. And don't forget that coffeepot." He pointed to a small pot Scully had given him a price on.

When Clem came outside with the first load of supplies, he found Preacher in the process of securing the pack harness on one of the other horses and the blue roan was already saddled. He was at a loss for words. "How much I owe you?" Preacher asked, then promptly paid him the amount he quoted. Clem thanked him but was still at a loss for words until returning to the store for the rest of Preacher's purchases. Already having his money in hand, Clem was inclined to alert the two cowhands that it might be in their best interest to see to their horses. Seeing the look of warning in Clem's face, they quickly got up and went outside to see what he was talking about.

"What tha hell . . . ?" the cowhand named Bob exclaimed when discovering his horse being stolen right before his eyes. "That's my horse, you damn fool! Whaddaya think you're doin'? You can't steal my horse!"

"If I ain't mistaken," his partner said, "that's your saddle on that black horse, too. Ain't that right?"

Struck dumb for a moment by the audacity of the somber stranger, Bob could only sputter, "You can't steal my horse!"

"I ain't stealin' your damn horse. I'm buyin' him. I gave you a chance to trade inside, but you didn't take it, so it'll be at my price, forty dollars for the horse, thirty dollars for the saddle. I think that's damn fair."

"Hell no, it ain't fair," Bob replied. "I paid fifty dollars for that saddle, even if I was of a mind to sell it, and my horse ain't for sale. Mister, you've gone loco in the head and I'm tired of foolin' with you, so get that stuff offa my horse right now." He went to Preacher's horse then and started to loosen the cinch strap.

"I'm only gonna tell you once," Preacher informed him. "Get away from my horse."

Then Bob made the mistake that Preacher counted on. His pistol was only halfway out of his holster when Preacher cut him down, then quickly turned to level his .44 at Bob's friend, who threw his hands up at once.

"Damn fool," Preacher said. "He shoulda took my offer. Now you just set yourself down on that step. Take your weapon out with your left hand and toss it back on the porch, and me and you won't have any problems." When he was packed up and ready to go, he drew the rifle from the cowhand's saddle and ejected all the cartridges before returning it to the saddle scabbard. "I wouldn't want you to get any ideas till I get outta rifle range." He climbed up into his new saddle and turned the roan away from the rail.

"What about the seventy dollars you offered for Bob's horse and saddle?" the cowhand called after him.

"He passed on the deal," Preacher called back. "I made the offer, but he decided to draw on me instead of taking the money—all the same to me—don't reckon he could spend it where he is now. You just be glad I ain't got no argument with you." Then he gave his horse his heels and loped out of the yard and back on the north-south trail to the Kansas border.

Traveling the same old Osage trail Preacher had ridden some twelve hours before him, Will spotted what appeared to be a saddle lying in the middle of his path. When close enough to confirm it, he knew that Elmira had put him on the right track, for this couldn't be anything but the old saddle Slim sold Preacher. She had been right when she doubted the saddle would make it to Scully's. "Damn near," he said aloud, "couldn't be much more'n five miles from here."

Clem Scully was standing in the door of his store when he saw the second stranger in as many days ride down the path toward his trading post. "I hope he ain't as wild as the one last night," he muttered. *At least this one has a pack horse and he's sitting in a saddle,* he thought. It had been a little difficult getting his mind back to business as usual after Preacher McCoy's call on his establishment. The young cowhand had been left with the sad task of riding back to the ranch he worked for with the body of his friend lying behind his saddle. Bob Dutton, he said his friend's name was, and they had ridden over to Scully's to celebrate Bob's twentieth birthday. Clem hoped the incident wouldn't discourage the young man from doing business with him in the future. "Hell, where else is he gonna go?" he blurted, knowing there was nothing closer than thirty miles. *Wasn't all bad, though*, he thought, *that jasper bought a hell of a lot of goods from me.* He shrugged and returned to the counter to await the stranger. "It all evens out, I reckon."

Will guided Buster toward the hitching rail and dismounted. He had seen a man he assumed was Scully watching him approach before turning to go inside. Although he had never actually been to the trading post before, he knew of its existence. The word he had been told was that Clem Scully tried to run a legitimate business, maybe selling a little moonshine, but was otherwise a man who would deal fairly with you. Will drew his rifle from the saddle sling and went inside. There was no one there except the one man standing behind the counter and a double-barrel shotgun lying on the countertop a few inches from the man's hand. "Are you Scully?" Will asked.

"Yes, sir, I am," Scully answered. "What can I do for you?"

Will walked over to face him. "You usually greet customers with a shotgun at hand?"

"After last night, I reckon so," Scully responded, then asked, "You usually carry a rifle when you walk into a man's store?"

Will smiled. "I reckon I most likely do," he said. "Tell you the truth, I never gave it a thought—it's just a habit." He laid the Winchester down on the counter beside the shotgun. "You say something happened here last night?"

"Well, I reckon," Clem started, somewhat reassured by the stranger's attitude. "Damnest thing I've ever had happen. A man rode in here on a horse with no saddle, shot a young fellow down when he wouldn't sell him his horse. Then he rode off with his horse and saddle." He refrained from mentioning the load of merchandise he had sold the man.

"That man would be Preacher McCoy, I expect, outta Texas and now raisin' hell in the Nations," Will said. "Your young cowboy last night ain't the first one he's killed in Oklahoma Territory and I'm hopin' to catch up with him before he kills many more."

"So you're a lawman?" Scully replied.

"That's right," he said. "Will Tanner, U.S. deputy marshal."

"I had a feelin'," Clem said. "You kinda looked like a lawman when you rode in."

"Sorry to hear that," Will said. "That ain't always a good thing." It brought a good-natured laugh from Scully. "What time did he leave here?" Will asked.

"It was suppertime, gettin' dark before he rode outta here, and I was mighty glad to see him go." He went over the whole episode then, telling Will about the cold, cruel way Preacher went about killing the man for his horse. "He was as calm about it as you would go about buyin' a sack of flour." When he had told him all he could remember, he asked Will if he was going to continue tracking Preacher. "You're a long way outta Fort Smith," he said. "And as far behind him as you are, he'll be over in Kansas before you catch up with him."

"You're probably right," Will admitted. "But I reckon I've come this far, I'll track him a little farther. So as soon as I let my horses rest up a little, I'll be on my way." He paused, then said, "A friend of mine, Oscar Moon, said a man could get a good meal at Scully's. Any truth in that rumor?"

"You know Oscar Moon?" Clem exclaimed. "That ol' coyote lies most of the time, but he's right about that. My wife, Louise, is a dandy cook and we'll be pleased to have you eat with us." He shook his head then, somewhat surprised that Oscar had a friend who was a lawman. "I'll be . . ." he started. "Oscar was up this way just this past week—brought me half a deer."

"It didn't have a strong beef flavor, did it?" Will joked. It brought another laugh from Scully, but he didn't say yes or no. "I'd like to buy some oats for my horses from you. They've still got a long chore ahead of 'em."

"Well, your timin' is right on the money," Clem said. "We were about to eat breakfast. It's a little later than usual today, Louise musta known you were comin'. You go ahead and water your horses and we oughta be ready to eat by the time you get done."

Clem hadn't lied, Louise Scully was a good cook and she set a generous table, even though there were no more than the three of them to partake of the food she prepared. She seemed genuinely happy to have a guest at her table. Will guessed that she led a lonely life with little opportunity to meet anyone beyond the rough breed of customers that happened upon her husband's store. She openly admitted as much and confessed to having spent most of the evening before hiding in the bedroom until she was sure Preacher had gone. He couldn't help feeling a little sorry for her and wondered what she would have done if something had happened to Clem. Those thoughts led him to thinking about Sophie Bennett, something he tried not to do too often, since it always led him to frustration. When he finished breakfast, he tried to pay for it, but they insisted that this first time was free. "You can pay next time you're up this way," Louise said. "We've enjoyed your company." She shook his hand then and said, "You be careful, that man you're after is pure evil."

"I will," he assured her, and thanked her again. He paid Clem for the oats and started out again after Preacher, feeling he had made some new friends, if nothing else came from the trip. He figured a half day's ride to the Kansas border where, legally, he should turn around. But he had never stopped at the border before on several occasions when he was this close in pursuit of a felon, so he didn't plan to stop this time, either.

He found himself still thinking about Louise Scully's plight if something happened to Clem and the parallel it offered to Sophie's life. A picture of Sophie in the apron he often saw her wear and the impish smile on her face formed in his mind as he guided Buster out of the trees along the riverbank. In the next instant, the picture vanished with the loud snap beside his ear as the bullet passed inches from his head. He didn't need to hear the report of the rifle that followed to know that he had just missed being shot in the head and his actions were immediate and automatic. Leaning forward on Buster's neck, he yanked the buckskin's reins sharply to his left to send the horse charging back into the trees. A second shot screamed through the leaves over his head, but not before he gained the protection of the large cottonwoods. Seeing a thick bank of laurel bushes topping a high spot in the river bluff, he headed for it, seeking cover not only for himself, but for his horses. He was in luck, for the bluff was high enough to shield his two horses, and the bushes would give him cover to fire from. A shallow gully running between two of the bushes provided extra protection, but only from a head-on approach.

There had not been time to think about the source of the attack as his mind was occupied with protecting his horses and grabbing his rifle. Not until he had crawled up close to the bushes in a position to return fire did he pause to wonder if Preacher had suspected he was following him and had doubled back on him. At the moment, that was the only possibility he could think of. He was not certain from what direction the shots had come, but he guessed they were probably from a long ridge about one hundred yards from the trees beside the river. There was not much cover between the ridge and the trees, and had he been thinking of something other than Sophie Bennett, he might possibly have been alert to the fact that someone could be chasing him. But that was highly unlikely, unless Preacher *had* doubled back on him. And now, although his defensive position was good, he could no longer see the ridge because the trees blocked his view of it. No doubt there was some concern in Scully's, since the shots could certainly be heard at the store. But there was little he could do for them before he found out from whom and where the attack was coming. It seemed obvious at any rate that the shooter was after him and not Scully. So there was nothing he could do now but sit tight and keep his eyes open.

"Damn it!" Jeb Cotton cursed. "I told you to wait till he rode outta them trees. Now we're gonna have to root him outta wherever he run off to."

"I wouldn'ta missed if he hadn't turned his head," Cecil complained.

"You think you're so damn good with that rifle," Emmett said. "What was you aimin' at his head for, anyway? If you'd aimed at his chest, you mighta hit him. You shoulda waited like Pa told you."

"Nobody asked you," Cecil spat back, and their father had to step between them to keep them from going after one another.

Luther held his tongue while his brother-in-law scolded his sons, then he said, "It is a damn shame Cecil didn't wait till he cleared the trees. Our business mighta been finished now and we could get on over to that cabin on the Cimarron." He tugged at his whiskers thoughtfully and said, "We don't know for sure that the feller on the horse is Will Tanner."

"Who else could it be?" Jeb responded. "He's ridin' that big buckskin Cannon told us about."

"I reckon," Luther allowed. "You never can tell. If your boy had hit him, we could go see if we could find a badge on him. Now I reckon we're gonna have to root him out to find out if he's Tanner or not." After riding like hell to catch up with the lawman, to finally spot him, only to have Cecil take a risky shot at him, was enough to try Luther's patience. If they had waited just a few minutes, they might have been able to get a little closer and guarantee a sure shot. Then they could have gone on to that cabin on the Cimarron and started getting ready to spend the winter.

"If he don't come outta there pretty soon, I'm goin' in after him," Emmett declared.

"Shut your mouth!" his father ordered. "Every time you open it, your damn ignorance spills outta your head. That's just what that damn deputy hopes we'll do. One at a time would make it real nice for him, wouldn't it?" Talking more rationally now, he turned to Luther. "I'm thinkin' we're gonna have to split up and come down on him from both sides. Whaddya think?"

"That's about all the choices we've got now," Luther answered, still a little perturbed that it was so. "And we need to do it pretty quick, else he's just liable to swim on down the river before we can cut him off."

"That's what I'm worried about, too. I wanna get him while we've got him holed up, so let's get goin' and get this business done. Me and my boys will cut over upstream near the store. You and your boys can come up from downstream. That all right with you?"

"Don't make no difference to me," Luther said. "Let's get started." He signaled to Liam and Ethan. "We'll ride down to the end of this ridge and cut over to the river from there." They nodded.

"Hey, Cecil," Liam challenged. "I'll bet you a dollar one of our shots is the one that gets him."

"You got a bet," Cecil replied, and swung his horse around to follow Emmett and his father along the ridge. They could just as well have been competing to see who was the first to shoot a deer or a rabbit. It earned him a strong reprimand from Jeb with a reminder that they were here to avenge the death of his younger brother and not playing a boy's game.

Lying in the gully at the top of the sandy bluff, Will could only wait and listen for some sound that might tell him his assailant was moving into the trees, hoping to spot him or his horses. All was quiet until he heard Scully's hound dogs barking about a hundred yards upstream near the store. His first thought was that he had attacked Scully, but he then decided differently. *Maybe he's figuring to flank me from upstream,* Will thought. *He would have been better off if he'd made his try from downstream. That way, he wouldn't have set the dogs off.* He was still thinking his stalker was Preacher McCoy. Then it struck him. *Unless there's more than one man and they're coming at me from both sides. Preacher must have gotten some help.* Right or wrong, he decided he'd better play it as if that was the case. He still had to consider that it wasn't Preacher at all. Whoever it was, he couldn't afford to get caught between them. The shallow gully he was lying in offered virtually no protection from either side.

As quickly as he could, he tried to think what his best chances were. If he tried to run for it, he would ride right into an ambush whether he rode upstream or down. And if he crossed over the river, there was nothing but open prairie on that side, making him an easy target well within rifle range for a long time. There was only one other option, and the more he thought about it, the more it seemed to be the best. There was still the risk that someone had remained in the trees in front of him to make sure he didn't do what he was about to try. It still seemed his best bet, however, so he didn't hesitate.

Moving fast, since he wasn't sure how much time he had before his assailants would be close enough to see him, he scrambled back down the bluff, grabbed Buster's reins, and led the two horses up the bluff, through the laurel and into the trees. He was banking heavily on an assumption by his attackers that he was still holed up behind the riverbank. As soon as he reached the cover of the cottonwoods, he expelled a breath in relief to have crossed the clearing without a shot being fired. Confident that his retreat from the gully had not been detected, he took his horses well back into the trees and tied them where he hoped they would be out of the way of flying lead. With his horses as safe as he could get them, he made his way back to the edge of the trees across from the gully where he had originally lay in wait.

It wasn't long before he caught his first glimpse of his assailants. Coming from upstream, they moved cautiously on foot, working their way slowly toward the gully near the top of the bank. He could see three figures, but not clearly enough to identify them. Then movement in the thick bushes downstream from the gully caught his attention, verifying his assumption that they had counted on pinning him down between them. There appeared to be three men coming up from that direction as well. *Six men,* he thought. *Who the hell are they?* He could see most of them now, well enough to identify them, but he could not remember ever having seen them before. It was fortunate that he had moved from the riverbank because the shallow gully had offered very little protection from an attack from either side. For whatever reason, they were intent upon killing him. That much was evident. It occurred to him that with his recently found wealth, Preacher could afford to hire a gang of men to kill anyone trailing him. That would depend upon Preacher being aware that he was being followed and Will couldn't really believe that to be possible. It didn't matter at the moment, for the task at hand was to keep from getting shot.

Judging by the way they carried their rifles, they appeared to be anxious to shoot. So he had escaped being the victim of a massacre when he abandoned that position. His next decision, however, would promise to be the more serious one. Should he open fire while he had sure targets? Having closed upon one another to find no target between them, they came up from their guarded stances to openly walk toward one another, evidently convinced that he had somehow fled. None of the men he saw was Preacher McCoy. He could reduce their number by two at least before they could scramble for cover. Even though they had tried to kill him, it was not an easy decision to open fire on someone without knowing who he was. There was also the possibility that they had mistaken him for someone else and weren't after him at all. *Damn it,* he thought, *pretty soon they're going to split up and start searching for me. Maybe I should run while I've still half a chance.* In the next few moments, his decision was made for him.

"Uh-oh," he grunted under his breath, for three of the men turned, climbed up the bank, and headed toward him. They had evidently concluded that there was only one direction he could have gone without their seeing him. All they had to do was look at the tracks the horses left coming up out of that gully, he thought. He was still trying to decide what to do when they pushed through the laurel bushes between the cottonwoods and the river. There was no longer a decision to be made, he had to act while he still had a small advantage. Lying flat on his belly at the base of a large tree, he took aim, pausing a moment to consider his targets. There was one older man and two young ones, all three walking crouched with their weapons at the ready. They had not picked him out as yet. He steadied his aim on the older man's chest. At this close range, he couldn't miss. On second thought, he dropped the front sight of the Winchester to the man's left leg and squeezed the trigger. Without hesitation, he rolled over to the other side of the tree, ejecting the spent shell as he did. Caught by surprise when their father dropped, the two younger men froze for an instant before frantically searching for the source of the shot. It was long enough to give Will the time to spin one of them around with a round in his shoulder. He immediately rolled back completely behind the tree and waited while a spattering of shots from the other three stalkers took chunks out of the tree trunk.

Keeping the tree squarely between himself and the rifle fire coming from the laurel bushes, Will backed away to another tree to position himself to shoot again. A hailstorm of bullets whipped the trees around him, causing him to hug the ground as flat as he could. When he could risk another peek from behind the second tree, he saw the two he had shot, with help from the third, struggling to get back under cover. He decided then to try to find out who they were, so he called out to them. "What do you want? Who are you? I could have taken kill shots, but I didn't, so why are you shootin' at me?"

Back below the bank by then, the first man Will shot yelled back, "You, you murderin' son of a bitch! Deputy Will Tanner, that's who we're after! You shot my son in the back, murdered him in cold blood."

It still had not occurred to him who the man was talking about, but at least they were talking now. "I don't know who you're talkin' about," Will yelled back. "What was your son's name?"

"Billy Cotton," the answer came back. "You shot him in the back when you had him handcuffed! My name's Jebediah Cotton, and I've come to take your life for his'n."

Billy Cotton, Will exclaimed to himself. Surprised, for he had not considered an attempt to retaliate for an act he didn't commit. "Listen to what I'm sayin', Mr. Cotton. There's no need for any more bloodshed here today because I'm not the man who shot your son. I was bringin' Billy back home when he was shot by a man named Alvin Greeley. And now, Greeley is dead, so there ain't nobody else left to blame."

"How do I know you ain't lyin' just to save your neck?" Jeb yelled back. With his leg throbbing now from the .44 slug in his thigh, he had lost much of his resolve, but he was unwilling to appear that way to the Treadwell men.

"'Cause I ain't got no reason to lie. Ask anybody who was there after the shootin'. Billy was shot in the back by a rifle seventy-five yards away, while I was riding in front of him, leadin' his horse. Now that's the straight of it. It's a damn shame I had to wing two of you just to stop you. I'm sorry for that, but I'll shoot more of you if you don't call your boys off and get the hell away from me. If you don't, from now on I'll aim to kill instead of just slowin' you down. I guarantee you you're gonna lose more of your men. So what's it gonna be?"

Luther crawled over beside Jeb. All six of them were huddled up under the bank. "You gonna make it, partner?" Luther asked.

"Yeah, the bastard shot me in the leg, got Cecil in the shoulder, but I think he ain't much worse off than I am. Whaddaya think? You think he's tellin' the straight of it about that other feller shootin' Billy? He said Greeley done it. Greeley's the name of that deputy that arrested your boys, Joe and Barney, and arrested Billy, too, just because he was havin' a drink with 'em. Ain't that right?"

"Yeah, that's right," Luther replied. "Greeley, that was his name. If this jasper's tellin' the truth, we ain't got no real reason to kill him."

"He's a damn deputy," Jeb said. "That's reason enough to shoot him, ain't it?"

"So far, we're the only ones gettin' shot," Luther reminded them. "I got a feelin' we've stirred up one helluva mean snake. Since you and Cecil ain't wounded that bad, maybe we oughta turn this rattler loose and back away before somebody else gets shot."

"He shot me and my boy!" Jeb responded angrily, lest Luther might think he was lacking in his resolve. "He's got to pay for that."

"I know how you feel, Jeb, but like he said, he didn't go for no kill shots, even though we was comin' after him. I got a feelin' this jasper is a helluva shot and he's give warnin' that he ain't gonna waste no more bullets on minor wounds."

"I ain't never run from no man," Jeb informed him.

"I know you ain't, Jeb, but this ain't exactly runnin' scared. We just made the mistake of comin' after the wrong man and it makes sense to let him be. Might be, we're lucky there ain't but two of us got hit and it'd be a smart idea to get the hell away from here while he's give us the chance. I know for sure that if we make another try to get to him, he's sure as hell gonna cut a couple more of us down, just like he said." He paused to see if his argument was making any progress in persuading Jeb. "We've done got Cecil hit. We've got to make sure no more of the boys get shot."

Jeb was halfway convinced that his brother-in-law was right about the bobcat they had aroused. Rustling cattle was their business and they had never been involved in shoot-outs in the past. But it galled him more than a little for the six of them to cut and run from one man with a rifle. "I don't know, Luther," he hesitated, his leg throbbing with the .44 slug embedded in it. Emmett and his two cousins sat up under the bank, dumbfounded, listening to their fathers discussing their plight. Jeb looked at Cecil, who was pressing his bandana against the bullet hole in his shoulder. "I reckon you're right," he said to Luther. "We need to get on over to the Cimarron where we can take care of these wounds." He shook his head, defeated. "You tell him. I can't."

"Tanner!" Luther shouted. "You win. We're gonna back outta here and let you be. All right?" Then in an effort to save face, he yelled, "But if we find out that ain't the truth what you said about Greeley shootin' Billy Cotton, this ain't over."

"Fair enough," Will's response came back, startling all of them, for it came from only a few feet directly above them. No one of them had thought to keep an eye on the bushes on the rim of the bank over them, concerned more with the business of keeping their heads down. So no one was aware that the deputy had quietly moved from the trees to stand over them, his rifle aimed point blank in their midst. Emmett was the only one to react. He started to reach for his rifle. "I wouldn't," Will calmly warned him, and shifted the Winchester to aim directly at the young man. Emmett wisely took heed of the warning. "Which one of you is Billy Cotton's father?"

"I am," Jeb answered.

"Sorry I had to wound you, but you didn't give me much choice," Will said to him. "Your son and I got along real good and I never thought he was guilty of anything—just thought I'd tell you that. And another thing, Billy's hands weren't tied behind his back. He was riding along behind me when he got hit. Now, I expect you fellows best get on your way and take care of those wounds." He kept his rifle ready to fire while they left him to get their horses. "If we meet again, at least I'll know who you are." That was his real purpose in moving to stand over them, so he would recognize them if he had occasion for contact in the future. He remained on the bank, watching until they came up from the river on their horses. He watched them disappear beyond the bend before retreating into the trees to get his horses. Luck was with him on this day, he decided, but he was not happy that he had never become aware that he was being tracked. He stepped up in the saddle and started north toward the Kansas border before turning around when it occurred to him that he might do Clem Scully a service if he went back to tell him the gunfire he heard posed no danger for him and Louise. The thought of Louise brought

Sophie Bennett to mind again and where his thoughts were when that bullet passed close to his ear. "You almost got me shot," he said aloud.

As for his encounter with the Treadwells and the Cottons, he had no interest in seeing what they were up to in the Nations. Billy Cotton had told him that they were involved in some cattle rustling in Texas, so it was fair to say they were in Oklahoma for health reasons. It was fair to assume that the Texas Rangers might be looking for them in Texas. His interest was in running Preacher McCoy to ground, and his introductions to the Treadwells and the Cottons had further delayed him in that endeavor.

After another visit with Clem and Louise Scully, during which he explained the cause of the gunfire just down the river from their store, he once again said good-bye and turned Buster north. With the Arkansas River behind him, he started out onto a seemingly empty prairie of flat, treeless land. Twenty miles or more would bring him to the boundary between Oklahoma and Kansas. There was nothing between the Arkansas and the border but endless grass. He would camp that night, hopefully by a stream or creek, under a wide starry sky, then ride another half a day to arrive at the small settlement of Wellington. It was the only thing resembling a town before another half day's ride to Wichita. And according to Elmo Black, Wichita was the town Preacher McCoy was eager to reach.

CHAPTER 8

Coming to a grove of cottonwood trees that had situated themselves in a horseshoe-shaped bend of a wide creek, he couldn't help appreciating the ideal camping spot they offered. He had planned to ride a few miles farther before resting the horses, but he decided to take advantage of the water and grass offered here. It appeared that Jeb Cotton had accepted his story about his son as the truth. There had been no sign of anyone following him, and he had been a sight more diligent about checking, so he turned Buster toward the bank of the creek and dismounted. He was still fortified by the huge breakfast Louise Scully had prepared, so he wasn't ready to fix anything to eat. But coffee was always in order on any stop of this length, so he got his little coffeepot from his packs and filled it from the creek. In a short time, he had a small fire working and his coffee bubbling away. It seemed so peaceful that he almost forgot what had drawn him all the way up to the Kansas border. The mood was quickly snatched back to the reality of his purpose there when Buster raised his head from the thick grass and whinnied an enquiry. "Damn!" he cursed, thinking he had been followed again, in spite of his diligence. Knowing he had company, whether human or animal, he didn't hesitate to pick up his rifle and roll over behind the closest cottonwood. The buckskin gelding never failed to warn him of company, but it would help a lot if the horse could learn to identify the caller.

"I hope you made enough in that pot to share a cup," a gravelly voice called out from the middle of the trees. "I've been smellin' it ever since I crossed over that ridge back yonder."

Easily recognizing the voice, for there was none other like it, Will answered, "I sure did, maybe a couple of extra cups. I'm sellin' 'em for a hundred dollars a cup."

"Damn, that's pretty steep, but danged if I don't believe a cup of coffee would be worth it right about now. How's my credit?"

"No better'n it was the last time I saw you," Will replied, laughing. He got up from behind the cottonwood to greet Oscar Moon. "Have you got a cup, or do I have to supply that, too?"

"I brung my cup," Oscar said, holding it up for Will to see as he emerged from the bushes between the trees, leading his horse. Behind the paint gelding, two horses followed on lead ropes. They were both loaded heavily with deer meat. It had been a while since he had last seen his friend, but like always, Oscar never seemed to change—same dirty buckskins, hair in two long braids, Indian-style, maybe a touch more gray in the hair and beard. "Will," he blurted, "what the hell are you doin' up here again? You've 'bout run out of your territory, ain't you?"

"Pretty much," Will said, "but I'm tryin' to catch up with a fellow named Preacher McCoy. He and three other fellows robbed the bank in Sherman, Texas, killed one of the bank's tellers, then headed up here in Indian country. I took up the trail of two of 'em in Tishomingo, where they shot two people, then I followed 'em up into the Arbuckles, where they joined up with the other two. The one called Preacher is all by his lonesome now. Two of the four are locked up in Atoka. The other one's dead. And I need to get to Preacher before he spends all the bank's money." He paused to see if his story touched off any clues from Oscar. "Don't reckon you've seen a rider pass through this section in the last day or so. He'd be easy to spot," Will said, "big man, ridin' a solid black horse and leadin' a sorrel packhorse."

Oscar scratched his beard and made a show of trying to recall. "Sorry, Will, I ain't seen nobody on this side of the river all week. You're the first soul I've seen." He read Will's casual shrug as a signal telling him he didn't really expect him to have seen Preacher. "Now," Oscar started, "whaddaya say we cook us up some of that fresh deer meat and have us a good supper."

"That sounds to my likin'," Will said with a grin. He had not planned to eat so soon, but it was hard to pass up fresh venison. "Looks like you've got a lotta meat to take care of. Whaddaya gonna do, smoke it? It ain't gonna keep long, warm as it is."

"You got that right," Oscar said. "I got the meat for Elvira and her bunch down at Sartain's and I'm gonna have to smoke cure it to keep it from turning. I'll charge her a little bit more for that. This time of year, it's most often cool enough to haul the carcasses down to her place and let her and Slim do the butcherin', but this summer don't seem to wanna call it quits."

"Too bad you have to go to the extra trouble," Will said, still inclined to jape Oscar a little. "It'd make it a whole lot easier on you if you could drive deer and antelope like cattle, wouldn't it?"

Oscar chuckled in response. "Now, it would at that, but I ain't in the habit of drivin' cattle anywhere. There's a law up here in Kansas against drivin' another feller's cattle without his sayin' it's all right. Besides, you know I wouldn't do nothin' agin' the law like rustlin' cattle, especially in your territory."

After roasting some of Oscar's venison and finishing off another pot of coffee, Will regretfully announced that he had best get moving again. His horses were rested and he didn't want to give Preacher time to increase the lead he already enjoyed. "How far are you plannin' to follow this feller up into Kansas?" Oscar asked.

"I don't know, as far as it takes, I reckon, but at least as far as Wichita. I think that might be where he's thinkin' about headin'. If I remember correctly, there's a little town I stopped at one time called Wellington between here and Wichita. You know much about that town?"

Oscar shrugged. "I've been there a time or two. Ain't much there but a post office and a store that sells dry goods in one half of it and a saloon in the other half. Feller runs the store name of Bailey and he's got a woman runnin' the saloon side of it. Her name's Emma Story. She'll pour you a drink of likker and visit with you while you're drinkin' it." He paused to smile at the image created in his head. "You can buy some supper there, too. They got an Osage woman in the kitchen that don't do too bad with the cookin'. There's a couple of other folks in town now, tryin' to make it offa tradin' with the cattle herds that push up the Chisholm Trail. A blacksmith had just set up shop last time I was there and he was talkin' about maybe tryin' to build a stable."

"I'll ride through there in case Preacher decided to light there. I reckon I'll see you when I see you," Will said in departing, as he nudged Buster forward. "Maybe we'll run into each other on my way back."

"Maybe," Oscar allowed. "Watch your back. There's a lotta folks up Wichita way that ain't got enough to do this time of year, but mischief." He had decided to stay right there until he had smoked all his venison before riding down to Sartain's.

The small gathering of buildings came into view a little before noon. He could see the modest signs of progress that Oscar had spoken of. But there were no new buildings except a barn and stable that looked to be still under construction. When he got close enough to read it, he saw the sign above the door of a board structure. It read BAILEY'S STORE & SALOON. The last time he had ridden by—the only time, actually—Bailey's store was a joining of three large tents. Will figured Bailey must have a considerable investment in his business. For starters, lumber to build his store had to be hauled in, for there were no forests to amount to anything beyond enough material to build an outhouse or two.

The town was built between two creeks, so he could rest and water his horses here. And he decided he'd take Oscar's recommendation and try out the Osage woman's cooking. In order to give the town a quick looking over before heading to Bailey's, he slow-walked his horses from one end of the short street to the other. It was just a precaution in case he happened upon a dark black horse like the blue roan Preacher rode. There were few horses of any color in the little town and most of them were tied up in front of Bailey's, so he tied up alongside them and walked inside.

A tall, thin man with dark hair and a mustache stood at the end of a long counter, filling small sacks from a barrel of flour. He turned when he heard the door open and Will walked in. "Howdy, friend," he greeted Will as he looked him over. "Don't believe I've seen you in here before."

"Never been in before," Will replied as he glanced over toward the other side of the building where the saloon was located. The only division between the two businesses was provided by a couple of steps up to the saloon floor, which was a couple of feet above the store. There were two men seated at a table, drinking, and one man standing at the bar. He noticed that the man sacking flour seemed to be frequently taking nervous glances toward the saloon, as if worried about something.

"Well, welcome to Bailey's Store. My name's Jack Bailey. What brings you to Wellington? You ridin' with a herd?" He asked the question in hopes there might be a large cattle herd approaching town, although he knew it was late in the season to be expecting one.

"Nope," Will replied. "I'm just on my way to Wichita. Thought I'd stop in. A friend of mine told me I could buy a good meal here if I hit town at the right time of day. Any truth to that?"

"Yes, sir, there sure is," Bailey answered. "And you've hit town at the right time. You go on over to the saloon and the lady there, Emma, will fix you right up. You picked a good day to try out the cookin'. Lily cooked up one of her specialties, Cowboy Stew." This was the first time Will had heard anyone referring to Cowboy Stew other than Gus Johnson at the Morning Glory back in Fort Smith, bragging about Mammy's beef stew. So he braced himself for the punch line that Gus never failed to deliver—that the stew was so good because Mammy only used fresh cowboys. But it didn't come. Evidently, Bailey wasn't as clever as Gus, or maybe whatever seemed to be making him nervous in the saloon had taken his appetite for humor. "You go get yourself something to eat," Bailey said. "Then if there's something I can help you with in the store, I'd be glad to do it."

"I'll do that," Will assured him, then paused. "You ain't by any chance seen a big man ridin' a black horse come through town a day or two ago, have you?"

Bailey hesitated before answering, wondering now what manner of man he might be talking to. Preacher McCoy had stopped in the saloon long enough to have a couple of drinks before buying some supplies in the store. Bailey wished then that he had more customers like the big man riding the dark horse. He was free with his money, never bickering or bargaining. The man he was talking to in his store today, holding a rifle as if it was a part of him, looked capable of handling himself in a shoot-out or a fistfight. He was reluctant to answer, fearing that he might be causing trouble for Preacher.

Will sensed Bailey's reluctance, so he opened his

vest to reveal the badge he wore on his shirt. "I'm a
U.S. deputy marshal," he said. "The man I'm lookin'
for robbed a bank in Texas where one man was killed,
and he's responsible for the deaths of three other
men that we know about in Oklahoma Territory."

"Well, I'll be go to hell," Bailey responded. "He
sure as hell fooled everybody here." He shook his
head in disbelief. "He was here, all right and, like I
said, nice a feller as you're likely to run into. I swear."
Then he showed a little excitement when another
thought occurred to him. "Might be a good thing
you dropped in today, deputy. See that feller standin'
at the bar? He goes by the name Bill Pike—rode in
here two nights ago and he's been hangin' out at the
bar ever since. He's already run a couple of my regular customers away and I ain't got so many I can afford
to lose any."

"What's he doin' to make 'em leave?" Will asked.

"One thing and then another," Bailey said. "It's like
he's lookin' to draw down on somebody. He must be
fast with that .44 he's wearin'. I was hopin' he'd move
on to Delano, that little town across the river from
Wichita. I expect he wouldn't be actin' so big up
there."

This was not news that Will wanted to hear. His intention was to stop here long enough to rest his
horses and get something to eat. He hadn't planned
to tell Bailey that he was a deputy marshal, since he
had no real authority in Kansas. But it had appeared
that Bailey had been reluctant to admit having seen
Preacher before Will told him he was a lawman. "Well,
I'll tell you the truth, Mr. Bailey. So far, this Bill Pike
ain't committed any crime from what you tell me,

other than bein' a blowhard. Have you asked him to leave and he refused to go?"

"Well, no," Bailey replied. "Tell you the truth, I wasn't sure I wanted to."

"Like I said, I'm on an important job right now and I need to catch Preacher McCoy before he disappears somewhere I can't find him. You say this Pike fellow's been here a couple of days?" Bailey nodded. "Was he here when Preacher was?"

"Yeah, but he didn't start botherin' everybody till after Preacher left."

"Sounds like he had sense enough not to poke a coiled rattlesnake. But I do plan to get something to eat while I'm here, so I'll go on over and do that and we'll keep an eye on Pike. I wouldn't be surprised if he isn't about ready to move on, since it sounds like he ain't havin' much luck buildin' a reputation here."

"Maybe you could show him your badge and tell him to move on outta town," Bailey suggested.

"It ain't against the law to be born a son of a bitch," Will said. "As long as he ain't caused no real trouble, there ain't much I can do legally." He could see the disappointment in Bailey's face, but he figured the man worrying him would probably move on pretty soon. "I'll go on over and try out the cookin'," he said, and started toward the other side of the room.

Just then remembering Will's earlier question, Bailey asked, "Who's the feller that told you you could get a good meal here?"

"Oscar Moon," Will called back over his shoulder.

"You know Oscar?" Bailey replied at once. "I expect it's been a month or more since he rode through here." Will merely shook his head, once again thinking that Oscar must know everybody in Kansas as well as Oklahoma.

The woman named Emma was trying to stay busy by washing glasses and cleaning her counter, obvious to Will's eye that she was doing so in an effort to disengage from conversation with Bill Pike. It was apparent that Pike was not discouraged as he followed her from one end of the bar to the other. Seeing Will coming up from the general store, she gave him her full attention. "Howdy, friend, what'll it be, whiskey?"

"No, ma'am," Will replied. "It's a little early for that. I was thinkin' I might try some of that Cowboy Stew that Mr. Bailey was braggin' on." He was not oblivious to the outright scrutiny of Bill Pike as he walked up to the bar.

"Why, sure," Emma responded cheerfully. "I'll have Lily fix up a plate for you. Set yourself down at one of the tables and she'll bring it right out. You want coffee, I reckon." He nodded and she went immediately to the kitchen to give the Osage cook his order.

As she had suggested, Will sat down at a table close to the bar, avoiding eye contact with the glowering man leaning on the bar. He laid his rifle across the arms of the chair beside him, already knowing he was going to be forced to confront him. He was typical of troublemakers that most saloons had to deal with. It didn't take long. Pike favored him with an undisguised sneer for only a few moments before beginning. "Cowboy Stew," he said. "Are you a cowboy?"

"Nope," Will answered. "I used to be, but I ain't now."

"Is that a fact? Well, maybe it ain't fittin' for you to eat Cowboy Stew. It's like you're pretending to be somebody you ain't." When Will responded with no more than a shrug, Pike continued to press him.

"You know, you interrupted a conversation me and the woman was havin', without so much as a 'pardon me.' That kinda riled me a little."

"Well, I didn't have any notion to rile you, so pardon me," Will calmly replied. "Does that satisfy you?" They were interrupted briefly when Lily came from the kitchen with Will's supper. She was followed by Emma carrying a cup of coffee. Lily favored him with a shy smile, then returned to the kitchen, but Emma stood by the table for a few moments, waiting to see his reaction to the food.

"No, it don't satisfy me," Pike muttered, barely over a whisper, then raised his voice to a warning. "It don't satisfy me a-tall. I don't think I like your smart-mouthin' me. The only thing that's gonna satisfy me is for you to get up from there and get your ass outta my sight. You can just leave that plate of food on the table and get out before I get mad. Do I make myself clear?" He walked over, shoved Emma aside, and stood over the table, his hand resting on his gun belt close to the handle of his .44.

Will could not help a small sigh. He did not want to deal with a saloon loudmouth at this point, but it was obvious that he was not to have a choice in the matter. He could certainly see why Jack Bailey wanted the belligerent man to depart. Very patiently, he looked up to meet Pike's surly gaze. "Yep, you make yourself very clear, so maybe I'd best do as you say. But first I'll take a little taste of the stew, just to see what I'll be missin'. That'd be all right, wouldn't it?" The question only served to frustrate Pike, causing him to move right up against the side of the table. With his hand resting on the handle of his pistol, he hovered over

Will in an obvious intent to intimidate him. Moving deliberately then, Will took his fork and stabbed a chunk of beef, put it in his mouth, and chewed it thoroughly before swallowing. He looked up at Pike and with a little shake of his head, he said, "I don't know, that's mighty good stew. I think I'm gonna have to stay right here and finish it. So I'm gonna need to have you back off a little bit and give me some room to eat."

"Why, you dumb jackass . . ." Pike started. Flustered, he made a move to draw his .44, only to cry out in pain when he was stabbed in the back of his hand with Will's fork before he had time to draw the weapon. Yowling like a wounded calf, he stepped back from the table and shook his hand violently in an effort to dislodge the fork, but it had been driven in too solidly to fall. He had to yank it out with his other hand. It only took a few brief seconds, but that was all the time Will needed to come up out of his chair, grabbing his rifle as he did, and slam the butt of it squarely against the bridge of Pike's nose. Pike dropped like a stone. Stunned by the vicious blow to his head, he lay still for a few seconds until he regained his senses. Still too groggy to get up, he uttered a low moan and slowly rotated his head back and forth. He made no effort to resist when Will pulled his pistol from his holster and emptied the cartridges out on the floor. Then, as if all at once, he realized what had happened and he opened his eyes to discover the muzzle of a Winchester rifle only inches from his face.

With his other hand, Will reached inside his vest and pulled his badge from his shirt. "You know what this is?" Will demanded. "It's a U.S. deputy marshal's badge and I could lock you up for threatening an

officer of the law. And I would, if I didn't have business
to take care of that's a helluva lot more important
than wastin' time with you. So I'm gonna let you go,
but I want you to clear out of this town and don't
come back. If you wanna give me trouble, I'll just
shoot you down. I don't have time to haul you back to
a jail cell somewhere." He backed away from him
then, but held the rifle on him. "So what's it gonna
be?" Will asked.

Pike, in no position to object with the eye of the
Winchester staring at him, rolled over to get to his
hands and knees. He paused there for a few moments
before trying to get to his feet as blood dripped from
his crushed nose. Still groggy, he tried to wipe some
of the blood off his face with the back of his hand, but
only succeeded in smearing it with the blood coming
from the puncture wounds on his hand. On his feet
now, though still not steady, he took the hat that Emma
handed him, having picked it up from the floor. Only
then did he look Will in the eye defiantly.

"I know what you're thinkin'," Will said, "and I'm
tellin' you to forget it. You lost a little blood and a
little pride, but you're still alive and that's out of the
kindness of my heart. So count yourself lucky, get on
your horse, and clear outta here." He handed him his
empty .44.

"I can't wait to leave this sorry town," Pike mumbled, glaring at Bailey, who had come to the steps that
divided the two businesses. "Things woulda been a
helluva lot different in a fair fight." This he directed
at Will.

Will quickly brought his rifle up as if ready to shoot.
"Are you threatenin' a peace officer?"

"I'm goin', I'm goin!" Pike blurted. He started

toward the door on unsteady feet with Will following right behind him to keep an eye on him until he climbed on his horse and rode out the end of the street. To be sure, Will remained on the saloon porch until Pike disappeared into the flat prairie of grass.

"Maybe it's the last you'll see of him," Will said to Emma and Bailey when they came outside to join him. When Pike was clearly out of sight, they went back inside. Will went directly to the table where his supper was waiting and sat down. "I'm gonna need another fork," he said to Emma.

She threw her head back and laughed delightedly. "I'll get you another one right away." She turned toward the kitchen and was back with a clean fork in a few seconds. "Deputy, if you ain't something. I swear. What's your name?"

He hesitated a moment to decide, studying the smiling face. She was a large, sturdy woman, and he figured her to be in her late thirties or early forties with streaks of gray already appearing in her hair. He decided there was no reason he couldn't tell her the truth. "My name's Will Tanner," he said. "And I'll let you in on a little secret. I wasn't lyin' when I said I was a deputy marshal, but I ride outta Fort Smith, Arkansas. I was out of my jurisdiction as soon as I crossed the Kansas border."

"Well, I declare . . ." Bailey reacted, having overheard the conversation. "What are you doin' so far from your territory?"

"Like I said when I first came in," Will answered, "I'm on Preacher McCoy's trail." He went on to give them a little more background on the outlaw out of Texas. When he had finished his supper, he prepared to leave, and Emma wondered what they would do if

Bill Pike returned seeking revenge. "I reckon he could," Will said. "But I doubt he'll show up here again. A bully like him most times won't wanna come back to a place where he got his bluff called. If he's gonna think about revenge, I'll be the one who has to worry." It was not much to reassure them, but there wasn't anything else he could do for them. As was his custom, he told Emma to tell Lily that he thought she was the best cook in the territory. Then he said, "So long," climbed back in the saddle, and headed for Wichita. Although sounding unconcerned when he talked to Bailey and Emma, he did not discount the possibility of an ambush if he followed the common wagon road leading to Wichita. So he abandoned the road and set his own course across the prairie.

A ride of thirty miles brought him to the confluence of the Arkansas River and the Little Arkansas River and the town of Wichita. It was commonly called Cowtown because of the many herds of cattle driven up from Texas on the Chisholm Trail to be shipped east on the railroad. Starting out as a trading post created by Jesse Chisholm, it grew to be a thriving cattle town with the arrival of the Atchison, Topeka, and Santa Fe Railroad. Will could well imagine why Preacher McCoy was anxious to reach the bustling cattle town, but he expected to find him in the little town of Delano across the river. Delano was more suited to the outlaw's taste, with its saloons and houses of prostitution and the total absence of law. Will was familiar with Delano, especially a corrupt establishment called the Rattlesnake Saloon where he had come close to cashing in his chips one night. That was another occasion when he had followed an outlaw over the line to Kansas. With that thought in mind, he decided he'd best go to the telegraph office and let Dan Stone know where he was. He had just as soon not, but it had been quite a few days now since he had telegraphed Dan to tell him about the two prisoners he had left in Jim Little Eagle's jail in Atoka. *First thing in the morning,* he thought. At the present time, he was more interested in taking care of his horses, and after that, treating himself to a fine supper at the Parker House Hotel. *This time of night, Dan's probably gone home and it might upset his supper to get a telegram delivered at his house, telling him that his problem deputy had crossed the line again.*

He slow-walked Buster and his packhorse down the main street of the town. There were more than a few people on the street, in spite of the fact that it was suppertime and it was late in the season for Cowtown. The last herd had surely been delivered before now. That thought reminded him that the last time he was in Wichita it was the same time of year. *Hope I have better luck finding Preacher than I did with Brock Larsen,* he thought, and continued on up the street until he came to a stable.

"How much to stable my horses for the night with a portion of grain for each?" Will asked the owner.

Walter Hodge glanced over Will's shoulder at the two horses, then answered, "Fifty cents apiece."

"How much if I sleep in there with 'em?"

"Another fifty cents."

"Why as much as my horses? I don't want any oats."

Hodge took a hard look at him then. "You were in

here before. It was a while back, though, a year maybe, right?" Will nodded. "I thought somethin' about you looked familiar." He smiled and extended his hand. "Walter Hodge," he said. "I won't charge you to sleep in the stall."

"Will Tanner," he returned. "I 'preciate it."

"If I remember correctly, you didn't come up with a herd," Hodge said. "What brings you to Wichita? You just passin' through?"

"Matter of fact, I'm hopin' to catch up with a fellow. Maybe you mighta seen him—big fellow, rides a solid black horse—goes by the name of Preacher McCoy."

Hodge shook his head. "Don't think I've seen him in town," he said. "But the town stays pretty busy now, even this time of year. So I coulda missed him. I know he didn't bring his horse here. I'm sure of that."

After relieving his horses of their saddle and packs, Will walked up the street toward the Parker House at the opposite end of town. On the way, he came to the Chisholm Saloon, which was the first saloon he had checked when he hit town the last time he was here looking for Brock Larsen. He decided to check it again, even though he was still thinking that he would more likely find Preacher across the river in Delano. He paused at the door and looked the room over. As he expected, there was no sign of Preacher McCoy, so he walked over to the bar to ask the bartender if he had seen him. He remembered the bartender, but not his name. Barney Smith remembered him, however. "Been a good while since you came in," he said. "What's your pleasure?"

"I'll have a shot of rye whiskey if you've got some," Will replied. "If you ain't, I'll take whatever you're sellin'. I'm fixin' to go get some supper and a shot of whiskey might help my appetite."

"I've got rye," the bartender said, and reached behind him to pull a bottle off a shelf. Making idle conversation while he poured, he asked, "What brings you to Wichita?"

"Supposed to meet a fellow here," Will said. "Preacher McCoy, has he been in here?"

"I remember you now," Barney said. "Last time you were in here, you were lookin' for some fellow. Did you ever find him?" Will nodded and the bartender continued. "Don't recall anybody named Preacher McCoy. 'Course a lot of men come in and I don't usually ask them their names, so he mighta been in." Will shrugged, then tossed the drink of rye back. He was thinking if Preacher had been in the saloon recently, the bartender would have remembered him. Preacher was the kind of man who stood out anywhere he went. He paid Barney for his drink and promptly left for the Parker House where he got the same result when he asked there about Preacher. If his hunch was wrong, and Preacher was in Wichita, and not Delano, Will felt he would very likely have dined at the Parker House. It was the best place in town for a man of means to have supper, and based on his trail so far, Preacher favored the finer things that money can buy, courtesy of the Bank of Sherman, Texas. As in the Chisholm Saloon, however, no one remembered having seen Preacher McCoy. It was the same story everywhere else in town when he asked around after eating his supper.

He allowed himself to enjoy his supper without the feeling of urgency he had felt in the days leading up to this and that was due to the belief that he had reached Preacher's destination. He was convinced that he would find his man across the river in Delano, hopefully tomorrow. He felt now that he should have trusted Elmo Black when he said Preacher would head for Wichita. He could have saved a lot of time had he ridden straight to the town, instead of trying to catch up by trailing him. But at the time he wasn't really sure Elmo felt he had been betrayed by his partner. When he had finished eating, he took a walk around town to see if anybody remembered seeing Preacher. Then he returned to the stable, planning to wire Dan Stone in the morning.

CHAPTER 9

"Wichita!" Dan Stone almost screamed. "What the hell is he doing in Wichita?" He read the telegram again to make sure he had not misread it. "Damn it! He's crossed over into Kansas again," he complained to no one in particular since he was alone in his office. That didn't keep him from swearing at the innocent piece of paper a boy from the telegraph office had just delivered moments before. He had received Will's wire from Atoka informing him of the two prisoners he had left in the jail there, but Dan had no one available to send over there to pick them up. He wired back to Atoka, telling Will that, but evidently Will didn't wait around for a reply. Even so, Stone expected to see Will show up any day with the two prisoners. Unwilling to waste another minute to remind his deputy that his jurisdiction ended at the Kansas border, Dan slipped into his jacket and went out the door, locking it behind him. He headed straight to the telegraph office.

* * *

Will had barely finished his cup of coffee at the Chisholm Saloon when he looked up to see the boy from the telegraph office looking around the room to find him. He raised his hand to signal him. "If I need to reply, I'll be over directly," he told the boy and gave him a nickel for his trouble.

YOUR AUTHORITY LIES IN THE WESTERN DISTRICT OF ARKANSAS STOP
RETURN AT ONCE TO ATOKA TO TRANSPORT TWO PRISONERS TO FORT SMITH STOP KANSAS AUTHORITIES HAVE BEEN NOTIFIED TO TAKE RESPONSIBILITY FOR TRACKING FUGITIVE STOP
DO NOT DELAY RETURN STOP REPLY THIS WIRE AT ONCE STOP THIS IS AN ORDER STOP

"Damn," Will muttered when he read Stone's telegram. He expected his boss to be upset to learn where he was, but he hadn't counted on Stone's being adamant about his returning to Oklahoma. *Hell, I'm only a little way over the line,* he thought. *I reckon I'd best reply.* The tone of Dan's wire suggested that he was not to be disobeyed, but he felt he was so close to running Preacher to ground that he couldn't abandon the hunt at this point. He paused to chew a generous bite of pork chop while he considered his options. *Order or not,* he decided, *I ain't leaving till I check over there in Delano.* Satisfied then, he turned his attention back to his breakfast.

When he had finished eating, he went directly to the telegraph office and sent the following wire:

WILL COMPLY STOP SLIGHT DELAY STOP
HORSES NEED SHOES STOP

Then he promptly left the telegraph office in case
Dan might respond to his wire right away. He wasn't
sure of the exact distance, but he guessed that he was
over three hundred miles from Fort Smith, so Dan
couldn't be sure how long it would take him to return,
especially since he had to go to Atoka first to pick up
his two prisoners. And then there was the problem of
transporting three prisoners from there to Fort Smith.
That might be difficult without a jail wagon and the
help of a posse man. With all that in mind, he determined to proceed to cross the river to Delano and try
to find Preacher McCoy. He felt pretty confident that
Stone's attitude would change if he came back with
the notorious bank robber.

"What the hell are you doin' back here again?" Roy
Bates exclaimed when he saw Will walk into the
Rattlesnake Saloon. "You ain't got no business here.
This ain't Oklahoma."

"Howdy, Roy," Will returned sarcastically. "Glad to
see you again, too." He would have expected nothing
different in the form of a greeting from the owner of
the saloon. The last time he had been there, a shooting had resulted that cost Roy two of his customers.
"I was thinkin' I might need a place to stay for a spell
and I know you've got rooms to rent upstairs. So I
thought I'd like to have a look at 'em to see if they'll
suit me. Let's go see." He started toward the stairs
without waiting for a response from Roy.

"Hey, wait a minute!" Roy yelled, and started after him. "You can't just do what you want to in my saloon."

"I just wanna take a look at your rooms. I'll try not to disturb any of your guests, unless one of 'em's named Preacher McCoy."

"Who?" Roy responded, and Will repeated the name. "I don't know nobody by that name," Roy claimed. "And I can tell you for sure there ain't nobody named Preacher McCoy in one of my rooms. Matter of fact, ain't nobody upstairs right now. All my rooms are empty."

Already on the bottom step by then, Will stopped and said, "Well then, there ain't no harm in just lookin' at the rooms, is there?"

Roy paused a moment to think. "No, go ahead and look for yourself, then get your ass outta my saloon, or I'll call the sheriff to come throw you out."

Will started up the steps again. "I swear, Roy, I'm beginnin' to get the feelin' I ain't welcome around here."

"You ain't."

Will was already of the opinion that he was wasting time, since Roy didn't put up more of an effort to stop him from looking around. Evidently, Preacher wasn't using one of his rooms, but he thought he should check just to be sure, so he continued up the steps. As Roy had said, there was no evidence that any of the four rooms were being rented at that time, they were all empty with no apparent belongings. When he came out of the last room at the end of the hall, Roy stood in the hallway waiting. "Well, Mr. Deputy Marshal, are you satisfied? And if you were tellin' the truth when you said you might be interested in takin' one of 'em to let, I'm sorry, but I ain't got no vacancies."

"Tell you the truth," Will replied, "I druther sleep in the stable with my horse. Maybe I'll get a chance to visit with you again before I leave town, though."

"Maybe the sheriff might be interested to know there's an Oklahoma lawman hasslin' the folks here in town," Roy threatened.

"Might at that," Will said. "Only problem is there ain't no sheriff in Delano and the sheriff in Wichita doesn't give a damn." Roy followed him to the front door and stood there to watch him until Will untied Buster's reins and walked down the street, leading the buckskin and his packhorse behind him.

One by one, he checked every saloon and whorehouse in town. He checked with the blacksmith and the stables, where Seth Thacker met him with much the same welcome as he had received from Roy Bates. Then he checked the legitimate businesses where he hoped to encounter a few honest merchants. At the end of the day, he had no evidence that anyone had seen Preacher McCoy, or had even heard of him. The blank expressions he witnessed led him to believe that they weren't lying. With no place else to look, he had to admit that his gut feelings had led him astray. As difficult as it was to do, he was forced to say he was wrong, that he had come all this way on a meaningless hunt, and Preacher had proven both him and Elmo Black wrong. Preacher was evidently smarter than they had credited him, or maybe Elmo had not lost faith in Preacher after all and had sent him off on a wild goose chase. Faced with the fact that he didn't know where to look for Preacher now, Will had no option but to do as his boss had ordered and get back to Atoka to transport Elmo and Lon to Fort Smith. It was going to be a difficult thing to do. After tracking Preacher all the way across Oklahoma and into Kansas, it was not in Will's nature to give up and return to Fort Smith. And he felt so close, he thought he had cornered the notorious outlaw. Reluctantly, he resigned himself to the return trip, empty-handed and likely facing a dressing-down by Dan Stone for riding seventy miles out of his jurisdiction.

Asking Buster and the bay for a little extra, he rode hard for almost five days to reach the town of Atoka late one Sunday afternoon. With both horses and man in need of rest, he rode directly to Jim Little Eagle's cabin on Muddy Boggy Creek, short on rations and out of coffee for the last day's ride. He was counting on Jim's wife, Mary Light Walker, to insist upon cooking him supper, and he was not disappointed. "You're looking wrung out," Jim said. "You have a rough trip?"

"You could say that, I reckon," Will answered. "I'm down to nothin' as far as supplies and I'm comin' back with no prisoner. Dan Stone wired me to come transport Elmo Black and Lon Jackson to Fort Smith. I was surprised he didn't send somebody over to do that since I was tryin' to follow Preacher McCoy across the whole territory. Those two must be about half-crazy after spending so many days in that little jail of yours."

"I think those two crazy when you put them in there, but they don't complain," Jim Little Eagle said. "I think they getting fat on Lottie Mabre's cooking and they in no hurry to get to Fort Smith, anyway."

"In that case, I reckon they can spend one more night there," Will said. "I'll have to go to see Tom Brant at the general store in the mornin' and buy enough supplies to get the three of us to Fort Smith. That is, if I've got any money left after paying Doug Mabre what I owe Lottie's for their meals." He figured to be broke, or damn near it, by the time he got back to Fort Smith. He would be reimbursed for the money he had to pay Mabre, and he was due mileage for transporting the prisoners all the way from the Arbuckle Mountains. That was money he would have lost if Stone had sent another deputy to transport his two prisoners, so at least he would recover that. Maybe if Stone wasn't too sore at him for chasing Preacher so far, he might allow something for the trip back from Kansas, even though chances were not too good. He wasn't bringing a prisoner back from there. The thought of that made him want to curse. He had been counting on that before Preacher gave him the slip.

After camping for the night close by Jim's cabin on the creek, Will enjoyed breakfast with Jim and Mary before he and Jim rode into Atoka. As payment for taking care of the horses and overseeing the prisoners, he left Jim the bay he had been admiring, saddle and all. His bill at Lottie's Kitchen wasn't as much as he had figured, so he had money enough to make sure he didn't starve his prisoners before they reached Fort Smith.

"Damn, look who's back," Elmo said when he saw the two lawmen leading the horses up before the jail. He left his position beside the one tiny window to face the door when Jim opened it and Will walked in behind him. "To tell you the truth, I never figured to see you again, Deputy. You must notta caught up with

Preacher. That mighta been the luckiest thing that coulda happened to you."

"Maybe so," Will replied. "He ran off somewhere up in Kansas, so the Kansas authorities have that job now."

"Did you look for him in Wichita?" Elmo asked.

"Yep. He never showed up there, or Delano either."

Elmo looked genuinely surprised to hear that. Lon, silent and sullen to that point, and still not recovered from having his nose flattened, expressed his opinion. "The son of a bitch got away with all that money and to hell with us. I wish you'da caught him." He got up from the cot he had been sitting on. "I reckon we're gettin' ready to leave our plush accommodations in this damn smokehouse now."

"Reckon so," Will replied. "I figured you'd enjoy a little ride."

"I wish to hell Preacher was here to enjoy it with us," Lon grumbled when Jim unlocked the cell door and motioned for them to come out one at a time so Will could tie their wrists together. As before, when he brought them down from the cave in the Arbuckles, he helped them up into the saddle, their hands behind their backs, with the reins tied to a lead rope. This time, however, Will decided to tie their feet together under the horse's belly as well. He was well aware of Lon's determination to escape at the slightest opportunity, knowing the potential for that would increase with each mile closer to Fort Smith.

With his prisoners secured, Will said so long to Jim Little Eagle and started out on a trail leading past the Jack Fork Mountains and between the San Bois Mountains and the Winding Stair Mountains. It was a trail he had traveled many times, so he was confident he could make Fort Smith late on the third day with ample time to rest the horses. After riding about twenty-five miles, they came to a small creek where there were plenty of trees for his purposes, so he called for a stop to rest the horses. Then, one at a time, he helped his prisoners dismount, tying each one to a separate tree and promising himself that he was going to start using a posse man whenever he had to transport more than one man in the future. But for now, he had to continue securing each man completely before attending the other. It made for a lot of grumbling on the part of his prisoners, but he was in no position to give them any freedom at all. The job was made quite a bit more troublesome without the convenience of handcuffs. He had come to this hunt straight from his ranch in Texas, and he had no manacles with him, so he had to make sure his knots were tied properly.

Allowing his prisoners nothing more than water during this stop, he reminded them that they had been fed a good breakfast from Lottie's and he would feed them again when they stopped for the night. Back in the saddle, they rode until near the feet of the San Bois Mountains. Ordinarily, he would plan to camp overnight with his old friend Perley Gates in the San Bois Mountains, but due to the urgency he felt to deliver Lon and Elmo, he decided not to delay any more than necessary. *Besides,* he thought, *I don't have an extra sack of coffee and Perley always expects me to bring him some.* The thought of his friend brought a smile to his face. *Hell,* he thought, changing his mind, *I ain't seen Perley in a hell of a long time. If he's out of coffee, I'll just let these two buzzards go without.* Perley would be glad to see him and Will had a feeling the feisty little old man wouldn't be around for many more years. The more he thought about it, the more he felt like he should check on him. It wouldn't delay his arrival in Fort Smith enough to matter.

He pushed the horses an extra five miles before coming to the gap in a long line of hills that marked the mouth of a long narrow passage that ended at a small meadow and Perley's cabin. Buster seemed to know where he was going because the big buckskin turned toward the gap without any direction from Will. He followed the long winding trail through the hills until reaching the meadow. Certain that Perley would know he had company, he halted his prison train at the edge of the meadow, expecting Perley to be watching with a rifle trained on his visitors. "Perley!" Will called out several times, but there was no response. He looked at the cabin, built back up against the base of the mountain, realizing then that there was no smoke coming from the chimney. He shifted his gaze toward the tiny corral and saw no horse there.

It appeared that Perley was off somewhere hunting. Will nudged Buster and rode on up to the cabin, only then realizing that the cabin was deserted. "What the hell is this place?" Lon blurted. Will didn't bother to answer. He was interested more in the whereabouts of his old friend, but he couldn't do much looking around until he made sure his prisoners were taken care of. Once Elmo and Lon were secured to their own private trees, however, he went inside the cabin, hoping he wouldn't find evidence that Perley had come to some tragedy. Inside, he waited for a little while to let his eyes adjust to the darkness. When he could see better, it was obvious that the cabin was deserted and had been for some time. It occurred to him that he could let his prisoners sleep in the cabin that night, but he rejected the idea immediately. It was better to keep them tied up outside where they could be kept farther apart. The stale air in the little shack was not appealing to his nostrils, anyway. He turned to leave when his eye caught sight of a piece of cardboard propped against the fireplace. He picked it up when he noticed some writing on it. But it was too dark to make it out in the cabin, so he took it outside to look at it in the fading light of evening. *Whoever finds this place is welcome to it. This is a good warm cabin. I bilt it and it has served me good. I won't be back. Perley Gates.*

"Well, I'll be . . ." Will exclaimed softly. "Perley finally did what he's been threatenin' to do for as long as I've known him. I reckon he's off somewhere in the high mountains he's always claimed he was gonna see some day." He was distracted then by a complaint from the trees beside the cabin.

"Ain't you gonna feed us nothin'?" Elmo wailed.

Will brought his thoughts quickly back to the business at hand. "Just hold your horses," he said. Then after silently wishing Perley luck he went about the chore of making camp. He built a fire to boil coffee and fry bacon slices to go with the hardtack he had bought in Tom Brant's store. When it was ready, he freed their hands and guarded them while they ate.

"It's a helluva job havin' to watch two men, ain't it, Deputy?" Lon taunted. "Makes it a lot harder when you got both of us untied at the same time, don't it? We might decide to just take off in opposite directions. What would you do then?"

"The marshal service gives us a standard procedure in that case," Will declared. "I shoot the one who runs the fastest, then tell the closer one to halt. If he doesn't, I shoot him, too. As long as I bring in both bodies, I get credit for the arrest and save court costs in the process."

"Ha!" Elmo grunted. "Damned if I don't believe he's tellin' the truth."

He let them finish eating and answer nature's call while he watched them with his rifle ready. Then he put them down for the night, each one between two trees, with hands tied to one tree and feet to the other. He kept enough slack in the rope to give them some movement in their arms and legs, but not enough to bring their hands down to their ankles. Only then did he eat, telling them that he would not sleep, but would stand guard over them all night while they slept.

"You tellin' me you ain't gonna sleep till we get to Fort Smith?" Lon scoffed.

"That's right," Will replied. "I can go without sleep for three and a half days and we'll be in Fort Smith in less time than that." It was not the absolute truth, although he had gone many a night without sleep, but not two or more nights in succession. He planned to catch a short nap when he was sure they were sleeping.

When morning came, he woke with the first rays of the sun after a nap of almost an hour in the wee hours of the night. When his two prisoners showed signs of waking, he had a fire going and his coffeepot working away. Ordinarily, he would have gotten everybody in the saddle and on the trail, stopping to eat and drink coffee when the horses needed rest. But he thought a cup of hot coffee might help their spirits, considering the rough conditions of their trip to the gallows. It might also help to keep his senses alert since he was short on sleep.

"I swear," Elmo commented to Lon. "I believe the son of a bitch wasn't japin' us. I believe he did stay awake all night."

"I hope to hell he did," Lon replied, "'cause I don't believe he can stay awake two nights in a row and I still don't have no intention of gettin' dragged into that jail in Fort Smith."

"You thinkin' 'bout makin' another try like you did when you got your nose busted?" Elmo asked, unable to resist japin' him about it. "You're still talkin' kinda funny with your nose flattened out like that."

"I'm glad you're enjoyin' this ride to Fort Smith so much. When I do get my chance, I just might leave you here with him," Lon threatened.

Elmo got serious then. "I ain't wantin' to go to jail anymore'n you do, but I can't help you if you make another damn fool try like you did before. This jasper is too damn good to get took that easy. If we get a chance to jump him, we'll both have to take him. We'll just see how lucky we get between here and there."

"I'll make my own luck," Lon insisted as he glanced over at the small fire where Will was busy filling two cups with coffee. When Will brought the coffee over and untied Lon's hands, he asked, "How many more nights you figure before we make it to Fort Smith?"

"One more night is what I'm goin' for," Will answered. "Then you'll have a nice comfortable cot to sleep on. Sorry it's gonna be a lot of hard ridin' to make it there by day after tomorrow, but I reckon you're as anxious to get there as I am."

"Day after tomorrow, huh?" Lon repeated, and glanced at Elmo to make sure he was listening.

It was not difficult to imagine why Lon was interested in the planned time of arrival. It only served to make Will more cautious in his handling of his prisoners. From the first, Lon Jackson was the one Will knew he had to watch. But he figured Elmo might be just as dangerous, in spite of his nonthreatening guise. He might be the one to attack when he least expected it.

Things went well enough through the long day of travel, but when Will led his prisoners down to a clump of trees in a wide curve of the Poteau River, he was aware of a definite change in their demeanor. This was the last night on the trail. By the afternoon of the next day, they would reach Fort Smith and jail. If there was any time to strike, it would surely be now, so Will tried to be as careful as he could be and not give them any opportunity. He halfway wished he had not taken pity on them and tied their hands in front of them instead of behind, as he had before. But it was mighty uncomfortable to sit in the saddle all day with your hands tied behind your back, so he relented.

"Damn," Lon was the first to complain. "You're gettin' harder on us every day." He was still sitting in the saddle while Will helped Elmo dismount and secured him to a tree. "Wouldn't hurt you none to at least untie my feet, so I can get 'em outta these stirrups. I got a terrible cramp in my ankle." When Will ignored him, Elmo spoke up.

"What you bellyachin' about, Lon? You oughta be used to settin' in that saddle, as long as we've been settin' in 'em the past two days. You oughta look at it like I do, least ol' Tanner didn't make us walk all the way from Atoka. I'm kinda lookin' forward to gettin' to that jail with a cot to sleep on and a little walkin' around room. Least, that's what I heard about the jail at Fort Smith, ain't no individual cells, just two big rooms. Ain't that right, Tanner?"

"That's right, Elmo," Will answered. "Just like stayin' in a fancy hotel."

"Just like ol' Gaylord Pressley," Elmo crowed, "only we won't have all the women and whiskey that money can buy."

"Who the hell's Gaylord Pressley?" Lon asked.

Elmo laughed. "Preacher!" he exclaimed. "Ain't you ever heard Preacher joshin' 'bout callin' himself Gaylord Pressley when he struck it rich? He just made it up, thought it sounded like a real highfalutin son of a bitch." He laughed again when he thought about his present situation. "Yessir, I reckon ol' Gaylord has set himself up with the rich folks and bigwigs, and he can thank me and you for helpin' him get all his money."

"I ain't never heard him call himself that," Lon said, failing to find the humor in it that Elmo had.

"I reckon that musta been back before you joined up with me and Preacher," Elmo said. He glanced up at Will, wondering what had suddenly caught the deputy's attention.

Dismissed as nonsense by Lon, Elmo's rambling had indeed struck a chord in Will's brain, causing him to consider a bizarre possibility. Should he have been searching Wichita for some stranger calling himself Gaylord Pressley, maybe in the Parker House instead of the low-class saloons of Delano? He had the money to pull it off. It was probably a ridiculous notion, but it reopened the void left in Will's mind for having to end his unsuccessful mission to find Preacher McCoy.

Now the possibility that Preacher had been in Wichita all the while he had searched in all the wrong places was a thought that he could not easily let go of. Quickly fetching his thoughts back to what he was doing, he finished tying Elmo and turned to take care of the scowling Lon Jackson. He was anxious more than ever now to deliver the two outlaws to jail, his mind awhirl with the possibility of going after Preacher again. Right away, he feared it might be impossible to persuade Dan Stone to let him go back to Wichita. Stone had already shown a reluctance to having his deputies work with Kansas deputies. The need to finish the job he came so close to completing was too strong to resist. For his own satisfaction, he had to go back to Kansas, if he had to take a leave of absence to do it unofficially.

He untied the rope under the horse's belly that had held Lon's feet in the stirrups in case he really did have a cramp in his ankle. He stood back to give him room to dismount. "All right, grab the saddle horn and get down," Will said, while holding his rifle on him, but Lon still sat, unmoving, his face screwed up as if in pain. "Get off the horse," Will commanded.

"I swear, I'm tryin'," Lon replied. "It's my damn leg. The cramp's moved up into my whole leg and I can't get it to move."

Not ready to buy that story, Will gave him a few seconds longer, then took a step closer, intending to jerk Lon's foot out of the stirrup. An interested spectator, Elmo watched to see what Lon was going to attempt, for, like Will, he didn't believe Lon had a cramp. But in case Lon had a plan, he was ready to offer his help. "Yeah, he gets them cramps every time we take a long ride," he said.

"Is that so?" Will responded, then jerked Lon's boot from the stirrup. Lon let out a long sigh of relief and slowly stood up on one leg in the stirrup. He then made a dramatic show of lifting his leg ever so carefully in an effort to swing it over to dismount. Instead of stepping down, however, he suddenly leaped from the saddle to land on Will's shoulders, sending both of them to the ground. With his wrists tied together, Lon fought to throw his arms over Will's head to clamp down on his neck from behind while wrapping his legs around Will's waist to ride him like a pony. Unable to shake him off after a couple of attempts, Will charged like a bull at the nearest tree, turning his body enough to give Lon the full force of the collision. It was enough to make Lon grunt with each blow as he was repeatedly thrown against the bark of the trunk. Finally, Will was able to grab Lon's wrists and force them back up over his head. Then, using Lon's arms for leverage, he forced him down until Lon had to give way with his legs and drop to the ground. Unwilling to give up, he got on his feet again and charged at Will, who was ready for him this time. With his feet set wide apart to brace himself, Will aimed his first punch to land squarely on Lon's already battered nose. Capable of throwing a right-hand punch with considerable force, Will stopped the desperate outlaw's charge with one blow. The excruciating pain of the broken bones as they were smashed anew was enough to stun Lon and he dropped flat on his back. Will stood over him for a few moments to make sure he was through, then he grabbed his ankles and dragged him over to a tree.

After Lon was tied securely, Will picked up his hat, which he had lost during the scuffle. Placing it squarely on his head again, he turned his attention to Elmo, who had been feverishly working to unearth a sizable rock that was halfway embedded in the ground near his feet. Will looked at the rock, then back at Elmo again. "A rock?" he asked. "Was that your part of the plan? If Lon rode me over by this tree, you were supposed to hit me in the head with that rock? How were you supposed to pick up the rock, tied to the tree like that?"

Elmo grinned sheepishly. "I hadn't figured that out yet." He shrugged. "Hell, you never can tell, I mighta worked somethin' out."

Will shook his head, amazed. "Well, I reckon if the rodeo is over, I might as well build a fire and fix us something to eat." He started toward the horses to unsaddle them, but stopped, turned around to take another look at Elmo. Then he went to his packhorse to get his hatchet. Returning to the tree, he used the hand ax to loosen the dirt around the rock. When he had uncovered enough dirt to loosen it, he picked the rock up and carried it to the river and threw it in.

In a short time, Will had coffee working and sowbelly frying in the pan. When it was ready, he took their supper to each of them, although it was a little while longer before Lon felt well enough to eat. Elmo, on the other hand, had his usual appetite, as well as feeling he was unable to resist japing with Lon. "I swear, Lon," he said when his partner showed signs of life, "I don't never get tired of watchin' you tryin' to escape." He received a dark scowl in response as he watched Lon taking cautious sips of hot coffee. "If you ain't gonna eat that bacon, I'll take it," Elmo said. He was rewarded with another scowl as Lon picked up a piece of the sowbelly and forced himself to chew it.

* * *

They arrived in Fort Smith late the following afternoon. Finally resigned to the improbability of escape, the two outlaws made no further attempt, so the ride was uneventful. Will walked the horses straight through town to the courthouse where he turned his prisoners over to Sid Randolph at the district jail. "What happened to this one?" Sid asked when he saw the shape Lon's face was in. "He looks like he got kicked by a mule."

"He's just a slow learner," Will said, as he untied the rope binding Lon's hands. "But you gotta give him credit for tryin'." He looked at Elmo, who seemed to be studying him intensely. When their eyes met, Elmo spoke.

"Well, Deputy Will Tanner," he said, "looks like our little journey is over. I gotta say you treated us fairly, but I can't say it was a pleasure knowin' you."

"I'd say the same goes for me," Will replied. "You and Lon behave yourselves and they'll treat you fair in here." He turned to leave, but Elmo caused him to pause with another comment.

"You're goin' back after Preacher." It was not a question.

"Maybe," Will said. "Maybe not."

"Take my advice, you'd best be careful."

"Always am," Will replied. He was almost convinced that Elmo was sincere in his advice to be cautious. He went out the door then, with only a wave of his hand to acknowledge Elmo's parting comment.

"I'll see you in hell," Elmo promised.

Will led the horses down to the stable to leave them in Vern Tuttle's care. "They've worked hard, Vern.

Let's give 'em all a portion of oats." He placed what was left on his packhorse in the small storeroom he rented in the stable and piled the extra saddles in a corner of one of the stalls. He purposely took his time putting everything away because he knew he should report at once to Dan Stone. There was something he wanted to do before he saw Stone, however, and if he killed enough time, maybe Dan would leave the office for the day and Will would have to wait till morning to report.

CHAPTER 10

Leaving the stable, Will walked directly to the telegraph office where he found an operator on duty. The operator recognized him as one of the deputies, so he automatically charged the call to the marshal's office. Will didn't bother to tell him otherwise. "I wanna send a wire to Gaylord Pressley. He's at the Parker House Hotel in Wichita, Kansas."

"Right," the operator said. "Whaddaya wanna say? You can write it down on that pad there."

Will had to pause for a moment to think how to word the telegram. He really had no message to send, he just wanted to know if someone took delivery of the telegram. "I don't need to write it down. Just say, 'everything all right here,' that oughta do it." The operator shrugged indifferently and sent the message. "I'll check back with you later to see if there's a reply," he said, then thought, "if there ain't no reply, they'll still let me know if it was delivered, won't they?"

"Yep, we'll know if somebody accepted the telegram, but I might not get the confirmation right away, maybe not till tomorrow."

"Well, like I said, I'll check with you later tonight. If you don't have it, I'll check first thing in the mornin'." He walked back to the courthouse then, hoping Dan Stone was already gone, so he could tell him tomorrow that he had reported in, but just missed him. He happened to meet Deputy Ed Pine coming down the stairs from the second floor of the courthouse where Stone's office was. Always a friend to Will, he stopped to visit. "Just gettin' back in town?" Ed asked. Will said that was the case, so Ed said, "If you're lookin' for Dan, you just missed him. He's already gone home." That was the news Will wanted to hear because now Ed could tell Stone that he had tried to report. Will had a lot riding on nothing more than a hunch and if that telegram was accepted by somebody claiming to be Gaylord Pressley, Stone might be willing to hear him out. "Come on over to the Smith House with me and I'll buy you a drink," Ed offered. "I just got back from deliverin' a couple of subpoenas. That's about all Dan lets me do ever since that time I got shot up so bad."

Knowing Ed was paid just fifty cents for each subpoena he served, plus six cents a mile to deliver it, and nothing for the return trip, Will thought it best to decline the invitation. "'Preciate the invitation, Ed, but I'm gonna miss my supper if I don't get on down to the boardin' house. Ruth doesn't know I made it back to town yet, so she won't be savin' anything for me if I'm late. And I've got to check by the telegraph office on my way home. Maybe we'll have a drink tomorrow sometime, if you ain't ridin' out somewhere in the mornin'."

"We'll see you tomorrow then," Ed Pine said. "I'll be around the office most of the day, I expect." They parted company then with Will heading toward the telegraph office, and Ed to the Smith House where he kept a room. Will didn't want to drink there, anyway, since that had also been Alvin Greeley's hangout.

After checking for a confirmation at the telegraph office, and finding that there had been no reply so far, Will told the operator he would check again in the morning. He headed for home then because he really did want to get there before the women threw the food out.

"Well, hello stranger," Sophie Bennett greeted the tall man with his saddlebags slung on his shoulder and carrying a Winchester rifle. "If you're looking for a room for the night, you'd best try the hotel. We don't have any vacant rooms here."

"I'll sleep on the porch if I have to, as long as I'm not too late for supper," Will said, making a concerted effort to be as casual as she, even as his emotions were churning inside his head. The declarations of his feelings for her that he had rehearsed during long hours in the saddle seemed woefully immature upon facing her now.

Sophie laughed. "Where in the world have you been? Mama was about ready to rent your room out."

"Just about everywhere, I reckon. What are you doin' out here on the porch? It's gettin' kinda chilly without your coat, ain't it?" *Say it*, he thought. *You were determined to do it. Say it now while you have her alone.*

"Mama sent me out here to watch for strays and doggoned if you didn't show up just when I thought I'd never find one." She laughed again, then said, "It got so hot in the kitchen over that stove that I decided

I needed to get a breath of cold air. I'd better go in and tell Mama there's gonna be another one at the table." She paused to give him a long look. "You look like you need to clean up before supper. You've got time if you don't take too long."

He immediately reached up to feel the whiskers on his chin. "I guess I do need a little polishin'. I ain't had much time to think about that." Her comments suddenly made him feel embarrassed and all the thoughts he had had about the possibility of approaching her to confess his feelings for her now seemed foolhardy, maybe even to the point of terrifying him.

She studied his face for a moment longer before asking, "Are you going to be in town for a while now?"

He didn't want to say that he hoped not, since he had it in mind to return to track Preacher down. "I can't say for sure how long I'll be here right now. It depends on what my boss says in the mornin', I reckon."

"Well, come on in and clean up a little," she said. "It won't be long before supper." She held the door for him and as he passed by her, he was aware of a hint of baked bread mixed with her natural gentle fragrance. He was immediately struck with a fear of what he must smell like, causing him to glance quickly at her face. She only smiled in return, leaving him to wallow in doubt, his resolve to declare his love for her rapidly losing strength. "Hurry up," she prodded him. As he walked down the hall past the kitchen, Sophie's mother glanced up to see him and called out a welcome home. He acknowledged her greeting with one of his own and continued walking.

When Sophie swung in the kitchen door, Ruth studied her face intently for a few moments before commenting, "Well, it's nice to see that Will came home safely. There's always a chance that a deputy marshal won't, so I'm glad he made it back this time." Accustomed to her mother's suggestive comments when it came to Will, Sophie responded with nothing more than a sweet smile. She always frustrated her mother with that typical response, for Ruth wanted to discuss her obvious interest in Will Tanner and she wanted to convince her that the chances were high that one day he wouldn't return home. Although her mother's thinly veiled warnings became tiresome to Sophie, she knew that she was acting purely out of concern for her daughter.

As was the usual case, Will was afforded a warm welcome home from the other boarders at the supper table with the usual questions about where he had been. Will answered with his typical conservative use of words, to the disappointment of Ron Sample, who always seemed to press him for gory details of the confrontations. "When are you goin' out again?" Ron asked.

"Maybe in a day or two, I ain't sure," Will answered, and glanced at Sophie to see her reaction and noticed that Ruth was watching her, too. Neither made any comment.

After supper, when the kitchen was cleaned up, Sophie made it a point to find him in the parlor when he was alone. Determined to finally express his feelings while he had the chance, Will swallowed hard and started. "Sophie, I'm considering this trip in the morning as maybe my last one as a deputy. It depends on what my prospects are for settling down with someone." It was obvious who he meant by that someone.

"You know I care for you, Will," she said. "I just don't know if you really can give up your life as a lawman. And as much as I care for you, I don't want to sit alone on lonely nights wondering if you're all right, or if you're lying wounded somewhere, or worse."

"I can give it up," he was quick to assure her. She had said she cared for him, but was it enough to marry him? He was afraid to assume as much. "Shorty and the boys have done real well with the J-Bar-J, better than I expected. When I get back there, we'll make it even bigger. I know we can, and I'll be ready to have a family. But I've got to go this one last time. I'm the best chance to put this outlaw where he belongs. Then I'm comin' home."

"I'll hold you to that promise," she said, then turned around and returned to the kitchen, leaving him to stare after her, still uncertain if he was standing on firm ground or not, and still having failed to express his love for her.

Right after breakfast Will was on his way to the telegraph office. Finding a different operator at the desk, he identified himself and what he was looking for. The operator checked a log in front of him and told Will what he had hoped to hear. "That message was delivered last night to the party in the Parker House in Wichita."

"Does that mean the party's name was Gaylord Pressley?" Will asked.

The operator shrugged. "I don't know," he said. "It means that somebody accepted the message that was sent to Gaylord Pressley. That's all I can tell you." He saw Will's concern and added, "At least it didn't come back as undeliverable."

"That's right," Will said. "Thanks." To him that was as good as verifying Preacher was there in Wichita. He felt certain that Elmo had unwittingly given him the information that would lead him to Preacher's capture. Now the job ahead of him was to convince Dan Stone to let him go back to find him and that might prove to be more difficult at this point.

"Well, there you are," Dan greeted him when he looked up from his desk to see Will walk in. "Kinda thought I'd see you first thing this morning. Ed Pine said you got in last night."

"Yeah, I did. I saw Ed when I tried to catch you last night. I'da been here earlier this mornin', but I had to check by the telegraph office first."

"I got word that you brought in two of those four that robbed the bank in Texas. That left one of them dead and the other one in Kansas somewhere, right?"

"The other one, Preacher McCoy, is still in Wichita," Will was quick to inform him. "He was the leader of the gang, and he's using another name, Gaylord Pressley."

"Gaylord Pressley?" Stone responded. "How do you know that? What kinda prissy name is that, anyway?"

"One he's used before, according to what one of the men I brought in told me," Will answered. He went on then to tell Stone why he knew Preacher was still in Wichita, about the telegram he sent, and reminded Stone that Preacher was still in possession of most of the total twenty thousand dollars stolen from the bank. When Stone shook his head, still unconvinced, Will repeated, "Somebody accepted the telegram addressed to Gaylord Pressley. It ain't hardly a common name."

"Sounds to me like you're still working this case, even though I ordered you to leave it to the folks in Kansas." Stone could already see where this was leading and he wasn't inclined to go along with it. "Damn it, Will, it doesn't make sense to send you all the way back out there. It's hard for me to justify it when the man is in the state of Kansas. It's now their problem and they've got capable men to handle it."

"Kansas wouldn't have the problem if I'd stopped Preacher McCoy in Indian Territory," Will insisted. "And it's my fault I didn't. I was just before arrestin' him, but I didn't get a gag tied in quick enough." When Stone asked what he meant, Will told him about the setup with the cave having a front and rear door. He told about luring the outlaws out one by one until Elmo yelled a warning before Will could tie his gag in securely. "There wasn't any way I could get Preacher then," he explained. "If I try to rush him, I'll get shot for sure. If I go in the front, he goes out the back and if I go in the back, he goes out the front and unties the other two to boot."

"I see what you mean," Stone said. "I couldn't picture that from that brief telegram you sent from Atoka." He took a little time to think about the situation. He could certainly appreciate the frustration Will felt to have been so close to arresting all three, only to have the biggest fish slip through his fingers. Still reluctant to give him permission to go into Kansas, now that he had already alerted the Kansas authorities, he continued to stall.

"I'll get him," Will stated, matter-of-factly, without emotion.

"Damn it, you'd better!" Stone blurted, finally giving in to Will's persistence. "But I'll tell you this, if you don't get him, you'll be taking a little trip there and back without any pay whatsoever."

Will nodded. "Fair enough, I'll be leavin' in the mornin'." It wasn't for the money he stood to earn. He was sure Stone knew that, too. He also knew that Stone would love to find a way to justify the expense incurred from a trip that long because the marshal was paid twenty-five percent of every deputy's earnings.

He started out the door, but was stopped by a word from Stone. "Will . . . Be careful, damn it."

"Yes, sir, I will."

His first stop after leaving Stone's office was at the stable to check on his horses and inventory what supplies he had left. After the extensive trip he had just completed, he had to go to the bank to withdraw some money from the little bit he had put aside. It would be some time before he realized any of the expense money he was due and his supplies were down to the point where he couldn't wait to restock. When all his preparations were completed, it was later in the afternoon, but still a couple of hours before suppertime at Bennett House. His stomach was sending him signals reminding him that he had not eaten since breakfast, so he considered stopping in at the Morning Glory Saloon on his way home. He decided against it, however, telling himself that he might be tempted to have a couple of drinks and maybe that wouldn't be good on an empty stomach. Had he been willing to be honest with himself, he would have admitted that his talk with Sophie the night before was weighing heavily on his mind. *I care for you, Will,* she had said, but she was clearly concerned about committing herself to a man always in danger. Then he had talked about the ranch in Texas he was half owner of and thoughts he had had of returning to it if there was a possibility that she might consent to go with him. She seemed not to fully believe he could leave the marshal service. And now he was going to leave again right away and would be gone for a long time. In his heart, he knew that it was not fair to any woman to ask her to live the life of a deputy's wife. So he would have to make a decision. When he thought about telling Dan Stone that he was going to quit, he realized that it would be a difficult thing for him to say.

The problem was still swirling around in his mind when he reached the boardinghouse. For the first time, he was not anxious to see Sophie, so he went up the back stairs to his room. He was not anxious to tell her he was leaving the next morning. He busied himself laying out the extra shirt and underwear he would take with him. In a short while, she appeared at his open door. "Didn't hear you come in," she said. "Looks like you're packing up to leave right away."

"Yeah, I guess it does at that."

"Leaving in the morning?" she asked.

"Yep, most likely before breakfast."

"Be gone long?"

"I reckon so," he stammered. "Dan Stone is sendin' me back to Wichita to finish up the job I started. Gotta bring this one outlaw to justice, gotta finish the job I started."

"I suppose you're the only deputy Dan Stone could send to Wichita to arrest this man," she replied. "It seems to me that if this outlaw is in Kansas, the Kansas marshal would take charge of his arrest."

"That's right," he replied. "That's the way things usually work. But in this particular case, it would be better for me to go after him. I'm the only one who knows what this outlaw looks like and where to go to look for him right now. And since it's my work that's brought it to this last point, it makes sense for me to see it through." He couldn't confess that he had to go because he didn't like to leave the job unfinished.

She listened patiently and when he finished to stand there looking helpless, she remained silent for a long moment while she considered his words. While he stood there looking as if in a daze, she strode up to him, threw her arms around his neck, and reached up to kiss him. It was not a friendly peck on the cheek. She stood on her tiptoes and pulled his head down to receive a warm, passionate kiss. When she finally released him, she stood back a couple of steps to gaze at him for a moment before speaking again. "When you come back—if you come back—I'll be your wife, if that's what you want, but only if we're planning to go to Texas right away. Understood?"

"Yes, ma'am," he replied, still in a state of shock and totally at a loss as to how he should react to her aggressive embrace. "But I might be gone a good while—at least as long as I was gone this time." He was trying desperately to think of what he should do at this moment, a moment he had only dreamed of before. *Should I tell her I love her?* he wondered, but thought surely she must already know that.

"I don't want to think of the possibility of you getting

shot or something like that. If you don't come back, I'd rather think it's because you decided you didn't want to marry me."

"I'll be back," he stammered. "I wanna marry you, but I have to finish this thing."

"Good, that's settled. Supper's almost ready. Don't be late." She turned then and left his room and a completely flustered, but happy deputy marshal.

With about six or more days of riding between Fort Smith and Wichita, Will left before breakfast the following day. Sophie made him drink a cup of coffee and gave him a couple of biscuits to carry. They had just come out of the oven and he thought he could still feel the warmth of them inside his jacket as he rode down along the ferry slips by the river. His intention was to generally follow the Arkansas River most of the way. His first stop to rest the horses and to eat something himself would be Sallisaw Creek. That would be one of a dozen stops during the long days of hard riding before he reached Wichita.

At the end of the first day, he rode his weary horses into Muskokee, thinking it common courtesy to check in with the Creek policeman when stopping in his town. He slow-walked Buster along the street in the fading light of evening, past the stone Council House that the Creek Indians had built to serve as the capitol for the Creek Nation. As he anticipated, Sam Black Crow was not there, so he continued on to Sam's cabin, which was a short distance from the little town. The cabin was built beside a strong creek with plenty of grass for his horses. He had camped there several times before, about fifty or sixty yards from the cabin, far enough away so that Sam's dogs didn't aggravate his horses. Buster and the bay did not escape some harassment from the two hounds entirely, however, when he rode up to the cabin to announce his presence.

"Will Tanner!" Clara, Sam's wife exclaimed when she looked out the cabin door to see what had set the dogs to barking.

"Howdy, Clara," Will greeted her. "Sorry to raise such a racket, but I thought if you didn't mind, I'd make camp up the creek a ways." He remained in the saddle and tried to steady Buster. The big buckskin was shifting back and forth, trying to keep the hounds away from his hooves.

Sam Black Crow came storming out of the cabin then and threw a stick of firewood at the closest dog, yelling some words at the top of his voice that Will assumed were Creek swear words. It served to cause the dogs to cower a safe distance away. "Howdy, Will," Sam said. "What brings you up this way tonight?"

"Sam," Will acknowledged. "Just passin' through on my way up toward Kansas. Thought I'd camp in that little spot I camped at last time I was here." He eased back on the reins when Buster steadied down a little. "Why don't those dogs bother your horse like that?"

Sam chuckled. "They used to, till my paint kicked one of 'em up against the side of the barn. They decided they could live in peace then, just like the white man and the Creek."

"You take care of your horses," Clara said. "I fix you something to eat."

"Thanks just the same, Clara," Will replied. "I expect you and Sam have already had your supper. I don't wanna put you to the trouble of fixin' more. I'll build me a little fire and make some coffee. I've got plenty of bacon and I've still got one of the biscuits Sophie Bennett gave me this mornin'.'"

Clara was not to be denied. "No such thing. We got plenty coffee left, corn cakes, too. I fix."

"No use to argue with her," Sam said. "Come on, I'll help you with your horses."

Not at all surprised by Clara's reception, Will stepped down and opened a pack on the dun pack-horse and pulled out a sack of flour and a sack of coffee beans, and handed them to her. He had antic-ipated their usual hospitality and added them to his supplies. Visibly pleased to receive the staples, she gave him a warm smile along with her thanks. He and Sam led the horses up the creek then.

When they returned to the cabin, they found Clara frying up new corn cakes to go with some beans left over from their supper. She offered to fry some bacon as well, but Will insisted the beans, corn cakes, and coffee would be more than enough to satisfy him. When Sam decided he could eat a couple of the corn cakes, she gave him a playful frown. "You eat enough already. You get so fat, I have to help you on your horse." She poured a couple more of the cakes in her big iron skillet, anyway.

As usual, the conversation consisted mostly of what was going on in Sam's district. And according to him, there had been no real disturbances during the past several weeks. An occasional fight, most often gener-ated as a result of some illegal whiskey, was about all Sam had been called upon to handle. The evening passed quickly and soon Will announced it was time for him to retire for the night. He thanked them both for their hospitality and declined Clara's invitation to have breakfast with them, claiming a need to be in the saddle early. "I've got a long ride ahead of me and I'm kinda anxious to get where I'm goin'," he said. "I probably woulda rode a little farther today, but I haven't been in your town for quite a while. So I thought I'd like to stop by and see how you're doin'." He said good night and retired for the evening. The next morning he was saddled up and on his way with the first rays of the sun.

CHAPTER 11

Preacher McCoy tied his horses at the rail in front of a two-story frame building, then took a few minutes to look down the street toward the main part of the little town where the saloons and retail stores were huddled. "El Dorado," he mumbled critically, then turned and gave the weathered building before him a good looking over. It was in bad need of repair, with some broken windows, and the paint on the sign proclaiming it THE PRAIRIE PALACE was faded to the point where it would soon be illegible. Were it not for the rocking chairs on the wide front porch, all empty now because of the chilly weather, a person would doubt that the place was open for business. The thought caused him to chuckle to himself because patrons would come here to buy the product no matter the condition of the structure housing it. And when he completed what he planned to do, there would be a higher number of customers, and a higher class to boot. *Yes, sir,* he thought, *this is just what I'm looking for.* He stepped up on the porch and went in the door to find himself in a large parlor.

A full-figured woman of taller than average height walked in from a hallway door to greet him, having heard the tiny bell attached to the front door. Preacher could well imagine that she had been a right comely woman when she was younger, for she wasn't bad looking now. "Well, howdy, friend. Welcome to the Prairie Palace." She took note of the solid build of the stranger, his shoulders almost as wide as the doorway, and his obviously tailored clothes. This was no ordinary cowpoke looking for companionship. "What brings you to our door this afternoon?"

"I think I'm the man you've been waitin' to see," Preacher replied. "Are you the owner?"

"I'm the manager," she said, "Dolly Plover. Luke Barton owns the place, but I reckon I run it. What can I do for you? You lookin' for some special lady companion for the night?"

"Nope, I expect I'd need to talk to Mr. Barton, and from the looks of the place, I think he'll wanna talk to me."

"I expect you'll have to talk to me," Dolly replied. "Like I said, I run this establishment and Luke ain't here right now, anyway. So whatever you're sellin', you'll have to try to sell it to me." She was rapidly coming to the conclusion that he was some kind of slicked-up drummer, hoping to sell something she didn't need or want. Patience was not her strong suit by any measure and she was already becoming impatient to return to her sofa to finish her nap before the house got busy.

"Lady," Preacher started. "Dolly, was it?" She nodded. "Well, Dolly, I ain't sellin', I'm buyin'. I'm lookin' for a place like this, only I'm thinkin' this one needs a helluva lot of fixin' up. But I've got the money to do it. I can build my own place, but it'll save me a little to buy into this business as a partner with Luke, say a sixty-forty deal, with me being the sixty percent. So I need to talk some business with Luke. Where is he?"

She hesitated before answering, reluctant to tell him that Luke was where he always was this time of day, upstairs in his room, sleeping off his afternoon drunk. "He ain't here right now," she finally said. "He'll most likely be back in an hour or so."

"Well, where is he?" Preacher repeated. "I'll go talk to him." He waited, and while she still hesitated, he asked, "I wouldn't be far wrong if I guessed ol' Luke was drunk, or asleep, or both, would I?" She didn't answer, but the expression on her face told him he was right. "Let me put it to you this way, Dolly. I picked this town to build a high-class gentleman's club, with high-class women to entertain the cattle buyers. From the looks of this dump, Luke ain't got the money to fix this place up. So he's got a simple decision, take me as a partner, or have me across the street as his competition. And I guarantee you he ain't gonna like that. So go wake his ass up. I wanna get the work started before hard winter sets in."

"Where does that leave me, if you build your high-class whorehouse?"

"In a classier position," he said with a smile. "You're still gonna be my manager."

"I'll go get him, Mr. . . . ." She paused, realizing he had never introduced himself.

"Pressley," he said, "Gaylord Pressley."

She said nothing at first, her reaction a simple raising of one eyebrow. Then she repeated it. "Mr. Gaylord Pressley . . . I'll go get Luke."

* * *

Luke Barton was as astonished as Dolly had been by the unabashed frankness with which the total stranger told him that he was going to build the Prairie Palace into a classy establishment. One, that in a short time, will pull those owners and buyers over from Wichita to El Dorado. Still only half-awake from a typical afternoon of drinking, Luke was not in a receptive mood. "What the hell gave you the idea my place, or any part of it, was for sale? You come in here with your fancy getup and your big talk about all the money you've got. That's all it is, just talk."

Preacher didn't bother to respond to Luke's comments. He was already satisfied that he had sized him up pretty accurately. Eager to see the rest of the building, he walked into the hallway, leaving Luke and Dolly no choice but to follow. Passing several doors, he went straight to the kitchen where a short, gray-haired woman was busy working over the stove. Across the hall from the kitchen, he saw a second parlor presently occupied by three tired and slovenly looking women in various stages of undress. More interested in them than he was the cook, he walked into the parlor. The women were drinking coffee, one of them eating a biscuit, evidently preparing for the coming evening. Preacher gave them no more than a glance, in contrast to the bored stares he received in return. When he turned back to face the two following him, he commented, "Might wanna keep the young one eatin' the biscuit, maybe use her as a maid. We're gonna need one."

Left slack-jawed in disbelief to this point, Luke was

pressed to protest. "I done told you this place ain't for sale. This is my business and it's doin' damn good without no fancy-dressin' dude to run it."

"Is that a fact?" Preacher responded. "Then where is the dinin' room? Over in Wichita at the Parker House a cattle buyer from Chicago gets a fine dinner and a decent room for him and his lady for the night. He sure as hell couldn't get that here, could he? You got a washroom?" When Dolly suppressed a chuckle, he continued. "I didn't think so. What you've got here, Luke, is a cheap, run-down whorehouse and I'm givin' you a chance to pull yourself up to be a legitimate businessman."

"He might be makin' a lotta sense," Dolly interrupted, "if he can really raise the money to do all he's talkin' about."

Starting to get interested after Dolly's comment, Luke hesitated before asking, "How do I know you can raise the money you're talkin' about?"

"I don't have to raise any money," Preacher replied. "I'm talkin' about cash money, ready to get started. And if I go into this place, I'll already have a building, so I might get most of the fixin' up done by the time a hard winter hits."

Luke finally began to see the potential offered him with this rich dude paying all the cost. He hesitated only a moment more before attempting to sweeten his part of the deal. "Dolly said you were talkin' about a sixty-forty split." When Preacher nodded, Luke went on. "Well, that ain't gonna happen. The best you'll do is a fifty-fifty split and I'd have to approve everything you do to the place."

"You're a better businessman than I thought," Preacher said. "All right, then, fifty-fifty, but I'll have all the say about how I spend my money fixin' up the place."

His quick acceptance surprised both Luke and Dolly, so much so that Luke decided to press for more. "All right," he echoed. "Now let's talk about how much you're gonna give me for a piece of my building."

Preacher responded with a wry smile of amusement. "Not a nickel," he said. "I'm payin' for all the fixin' up and you ain't investin' a damn penny."

"It was worth a try, partner," Luke said, and extended his hand, a wide grin across his unshaven face. They shook on it.

"Now, I need a room to stay in," Preacher said. "Have you got one that's halfway clean?"

"You can take the room next to mine, behind the kitchen," Dolly said. "Ain't nobody been in that room for six months." She still found it hard to believe Preacher settled for a fifty-fifty split with Luke. She knew that she wouldn't have. She held the same opinion of Luke that Preacher had had from the start, and she could imagine that Luke would more likely get in the way of turning the Prairie Palace into the fancy bordello that this strange new partner talked about. Had she known more about the man calling himself Gaylord Pressley, she would have figured that he accepted the deal for the simple reason he wasn't planning to have Luke around for much longer.

"You show him the room," Luke said to Dolly. "I gotta get some coffee and see if I can get rid of this damn headache."

Dolly waited for Preacher to get his saddlebags and rifle off his horse, then she led him through the kitchen to the back hallway. "This is my room," she said as they passed the first door. When they got to the next door, she handed him a key. "These are the only rooms in the house with locks on the doors. The girls live upstairs."

"What about Luke?" Preacher asked. "Is that his room?" He motioned toward the next room on the hallway."

"No, he likes to stay upstairs where the girls sleep. He uses the last room at the end of the hall by the back stairs."

"Does he get drunk like that every day?" Preacher asked.

She grinned. "Unless it rains, then he gets twice as drunk."

"Looks to me like he ain't much use around here," Preacher said. "Looks like you're runnin' the place all by yourself." He shook his head as if in concern. "Man does a lot of drinkin' like that is liable to find out it'll do him in."

"Try to tell him that," Dolly said. "Might as well talk to that door over there."

"Well, if he's gonna be my partner, I'll expect him to pull his weight around here. I aim to make this the place to come to spend your money."

His comment brought a smile to her face. She was just beginning to imagine how it would be to be part of a fancy place like he described. There was one worry, however, and she felt she had to know. "From what you said a while ago, sounds like you're thinkin' about gettin' rid of some of the girls."

"Hell, yeah," he quickly replied. "Them girls you're talkin' about are more like old ladies. We've got to get some younger stock in here to entertain the customers we're goin' after. You get a rich cattle buyer from Chicago to stay here, he ain't gonna want a woman that looks like his grandma."

"Reckon that means me, too," she said.

"Hell, no," he replied, just as quickly as before. "You're still the manager. I told you that right off. I think me and you are gonna make this business go. I'll work on ol' Luke and maybe we'll get some help outta him." He formed a wide grin for her. "Now, let's see about gettin' some supper. Have we got a decent cook?"

"We sure do. Rena can cook with the best of them," Dolly assured him.

"Good," Preacher said. "You tell her to cook up somethin' while I take my horses down to the stable and we'll celebrate our new partnership."

Paul Perry was duly impressed by Preacher when he came into his stable, just as Dolly Plover had been. The big, broad-shouldered stranger was dressed like the moneyed gentry that usually came through El Dorado in the summer on their way to the cattle markets in Wichita. But there was also a cruel, rugged look about the man that suggested he might have known the harder way of life as well. "Evenin'," Paul greeted him. "You lookin' to stable your horses for the night?"

"Nope," Preacher replied. "I'm lookin' to get your best rate to stable my horses from now on. If you give me a fair rate, I won't have to build a barn and corral myself."

Not expecting such a response, Paul said, "I figured you were passin' through town on your way to Wichita. I'll sure give you a fair rate." Before he did, however, he had to satisfy his curiosity. "What brings you to El Dorado?"

"I just bought the Prairie Palace," Preacher replied. "I'm plannin' to fix it up to where it'll bring more folks to town."

"You don't say . . ." Perry uttered in surprise. "Well, welcome to El Dorado." He extended his hand and said, "I'm Paul Perry and I'll take good care of your horses for you."

"Gaylord Pressley," Preacher replied, shaking Paul's hand.

"Well, I'll be . . ." Paul went on. "So ol' Luke sold out to you. I didn't think he'd ever let go of that place. It was doin' just enough business to keep him in whiskey. What's he gonna do now?"

"He'll still be here. He'll stay on at the Prairie Palace, kinda like my partner."

"Well, he oughta be happy about that," Paul reckoned, then asked, "Is Dolly stayin' on?" Preacher assured him that she was.

When he had concluded his arrangement with Perry, Preacher left the stable and returned to the Prairie Palace. Supper was ready when he got there, and as Dolly had declared, Rena cooked a good meal for them. Preacher did his best to keep the talk at the table friendly and positive with much speculation on the saloon's promise in the future. Luke merely dawdled with his supper and soon became glassy-eyed, since his coffee cup held rye whiskey instead of coffee. The first to get up from the table, Luke announced he was going to the outhouse and then going up to his room.

"Good idea," Preacher said. "When I finish my supper, I'll grab a bottle of that whiskey you've been drinkin' and I'll come up and have a drink with you. We've got a lot to celebrate after what we agreed on today." He looked at Dolly, laughed, and shook his head when Luke made no response, even seeming not to have heard him. As he stumbled toward the back door, Preacher chuckled and said to Dolly, "I don't think he heard a word I said. I'll go up later and have that drink with him. It'll kinda make our deal official."

"Bet you didn't think anything big was gonna happen today when you got up this mornin'," Dolly commented to Rena Peters after Preacher left the kitchen and went to his room.

"I surely didn't think nothin' like this was ever gonna happen," Rena replied. "He just blew in here like a big ol' dust storm." She paused to think about it. "How much money you reckon he's really got? He's doin' some awful big talk."

"Acts like he's got all the money in the world, don't he?" Dolly responded. "I hope to hell it ain't all talk. I'd like to see this place fixed up like he's talkin' about." She laughed then. "I don't think poor Luke knows what he's in for. He ain't gonna have any say on what Mr. Pressley does with his business."

"Gaylord," Rena said with a giggle, reminding Dolly of his first name, "Gaylord Pressley, ain't that a fancy name?" They both giggled. "Luke didn't hang around long at the table, did he? I think he still ain't figured out what happened to him today."

"I reckon Gaylord is gonna try to straighten Luke out," Dolly said. "He had me get him a bottle of rye whiskey, the kind Luke likes, and he gave me the money for it, said he promised Luke he'd go upstairs and have a drink with him. And, honey, you shoulda seen the roll of money he pulled outta his pocket to pay me. It'd choke a horse."

After the women had finished cleaning the kitchen and Dolly had gone to the front parlor to receive any customers that might happen to call, Preacher picked up the bottle of whiskey and went up the stairs to the small room at the end of the hall. Turning the knob, he pushed the door slowly open until he could see the unconscious man lying on the bed. He went on inside and walked over to stand beside the bed. *Sleeping like a baby*, he thought. "We'll have that drink to celebrate our partnership," he muttered as he pulled the cork out of the bottle and took a healthy swig from it. Then he placed the bottle down on the dresser beside the bed, pulled the pillow out from under Luke's head, and hesitated to see if he would waken. When he did no more than grunt a few incoherent sounds, Preacher clamped the pillow down firmly over Luke's face, making sure his mouth and nose were covered. There was no reaction from Luke at first. In a few seconds, he began to move slightly in an attempt to get air. A few seconds more and he started to struggle, but to no avail. Then he suddenly became conscious enough to realize he could not breathe and he fought frantically for breath. Helpless to fight against the powerful hands that clamped down even tighter, he began to kick and twist, again to no avail. After a few more minutes, he finally relaxed in death. To be certain, Preacher continued smothering him for several minutes longer before releasing him.

He grabbed Luke by the hair and raised his head while he placed the pillow under it. Then he splashed a little from the bottle around the empty glass on the floor beside the bed. After taking another drink himself, he walked to the window, raised it, and poured out almost all of the remaining whiskey. That done, he placed the bottle beside the glass on the floor, threw his head back, and laughed loudly. Pleased with his results, he gave Luke one last look. *Been nice doing business with you, Luke,* he thought, and walked to the door. He began talking as he opened the door, in a voice loud enough to be sure he would be overheard. "Yeah, Luke, I believe we're gonna do a lot of business together. Glad we worked it all out. You go easy on that bottle, though. I think we both mighta hit that whiskey pretty hard. See you in the mornin'." He smiled to himself when he passed the room next to Luke's and noticed the door slightly ajar, enough for someone inside to hear. Satisfied with himself now, he went back downstairs to his room.

"Good mornin'," Rena greeted him when he walked into the kitchen. "You're an early riser. Coffee's ready and breakfast is on the way." She poured a cup of coffee for him and placed it on the table when he sat down. "You sleep all right in that old bed?"

"Like a baby," Preacher answered, "couldn'ta had a better night." He made a point to look over his shoulder toward the door. "Has Luke been down yet?"

"Not yet," Dolly answered him as she walked in. "It's a little early for him. He'll come stumblin' in after a while." She poured herself a cup and sat down at the table opposite Preacher. "I didn't expect to see you this early."

He gave her a wide grin. "Why not? There's a lot to be done. I've gotta get to know the other folks in town, make sure they understand things are gonna be different around here. I'll wait for Luke to get up, so he can go with me."

Dolly and Rena exchanged amused glances before Dolly remarked, "Luke don't usually show up downstairs till just before noon. And if you and him did much drinkin' last night, we might not see him till afternoon."

"He's gonna have to get started a little earlier than that," Preacher said, just as the young prostitute he had seen eating the biscuit when he first arrived came into the kitchen. He stopped her on her way to the stove and the coffeepot. "Wait a minute, there, darlin'," he said. "What's your name?"

"Angel," the frightened girl replied, afraid that she might have already done something to anger him.

"Angel, huh?" Preacher responded. "Well, Angel, why don't you run upstairs to Luke's room and tell him I need him down here right now? We've got to get started on some of the things we talked about last night."

Angel hesitated, unsure. "Luke don't like for nobody to bother him in the mornin'." She looked at Dolly for confirmation, but Dolly just smiled and nodded toward the door.

"It'll be all right this mornin'," Preacher said to her. "You tell him I sent you up there to get him outta bed. We got things to do, ain't we, Dolly?" He gave Dolly a wink. "Pour me another cup of that coffee." Dolly got up to get his coffee while Angel headed for the stairs.

He had barely sipped his fresh coffee when they heard Angel's scream from upstairs. "What the hell . . ." Dolly blurted, and paused to listen. When Angel continued to yell, she scrambled out of her chair and headed for the stairs with Preacher and Rena right behind her.

By the time they reached the second floor, both of the older prostitutes were in the hall with Angel and she was standing in front of Luke's door, frantically pointing into the room. "What is it, girl?" Preacher asked, pushing his way past the women.

"It's Luke!" Angel exclaimed. "He's dead!"

"Whaddaya mean, he's dead," Preacher replied, playing his part. "Dead drunk, maybe, did you try to wake him up?"

"Yes, sir, I tapped him on the shoulder two or three times and he didn't move a muscle." She suffered an involuntary little shudder when she added, "The look on his face, it's like he saw the devil or something."

"It does look like it," Dolly said, standing at Preacher's shoulder.

"Maybe he did," Preacher said. Then he reached down, grabbed Luke by the shoulder, and shook him violently. "He's dead, all right, he's already got stiff, musta died in his sleep."

"Musta died in his sleep right next door to me while I was sleepin'," Angel said, and shuddered again with the thought. "He was all right last night. I heard him and you talkin' when you left his room."

"Yeah, he didn't give no sign that anything was botherin' him," Preacher said. "I reckon whiskey finally got him." He pointed to the almost empty bottle beside the bed. "He sure as hell hit that bottle hard after I left. He ain't the first man that whiskey has done in." He turned to Dolly. "Who's the man in town to take care of the buryin'? I expect we'd best get ahold of him right quick before ol' Luke starts to get too ripe." He glanced at the gathered faces and saw no sign of grief in any of them. It didn't surprise him.

"That would be Tom Hawkins," Dolly answered. "He's the barber and undertaker and the closest thing we've got to a doctor." She turned to Angel. "Why don't you run down the street and fetch him, honey?"

Already over the shock of trying to wake a dead man, Angel responded with a pained expression. "Can I have my coffee first? I was just startin' to get it when Gaylord sent me up here."

Before Dolly could answer, Preacher said, "Yeah, drink your coffee, ol' Luke ain't goin' nowhere." He looked at Rena then. "Matter of fact, we might as well go ahead and eat some breakfast."

"My biscuits!" Rena almost screamed as she turned and ran from the room, having forgotten they were still in the oven.

There was plenty of time before Tom Hawkins showed up to pick up Luke Barton's body, so the inhabitants of the Prairie Palace enjoyed a hearty breakfast, even if the biscuits were baked a little too brown. "It's a funny thing, ain't it? I mean how things worked out," Preacher remarked. "I reckon it was mighty lucky I came along right when I did to keep this place goin'. I don't know what you folks woulda done, if I hadn't come along."

Everybody nodded in agreement, although the two older women had not yet been told that they were soon to be sent packing. And Dolly thought to herself,

I know what we would have done, the Prairie Palace would be mine and good enough to take care of my needs without any fancy improvements. It was a thought that she had entertained more than once before on prior occasions when Luke had drunk so much that he didn't come out of his room for most of the day. She had no choice now, but to hope Gaylord's arrival would indeed bring the prosperity he promised.

When Tom Hawkins pulled his buckboard up in front of the house, Preacher introduced himself and went upstairs with him to help carry the corpse down. "I can stick him in the ground with a wooden cross for twenty dollars," Hawkins said. "For seventy-five, I can give you a small marble headstone with 'Rest in Peace' engraved on it."

"Well, then," Preacher replied. "We'll take the seventy-five-dollar funeral. I didn't have time to get to know the feller, but he was my partner the short time I've been here, so that's the least I can do for him." He pulled a roll of bills from his pocket, peeled off seventy-five, and handed them to Hawkins. His intention was to impress the barber, and from the reaction on Tom's face, he was satisfied that he had. Before he was through, Preacher planned to own El Dorado and everybody in it. He smiled to himself when he thought about the twist of fate that brought him to El Dorado, loaded with enough money to build the business he had always wanted. He owed a special thanks to U.S. Deputy Marshal Will Tanner for luring Elmo and Lon out of that cave up in the Arbuckle Mountains. Tanner was the name of the deputy looking around Wichita for Preacher McCoy. The desk clerk at the Parker House told him that and Preacher had a notion he was the same lawman who'd tricked Elmo and Lon out of the cave. *The son of a bitch must have trailed me all the way from Oklahoma,* he thought. But Preacher had lain low until he'd heard that Tanner didn't find the man he'd hunted and was no longer in town. Only then did Gaylord Pressley reappear around town after being confined to his hotel room with a slight case of consumption.

He frowned as the business of the telegram came to mind. It came to him from Fort Smith, Arkansas. What that was about, he couldn't figure out. Why would the marshal service send him a telegram, addressed to Gaylord Pressley? The message didn't make sense and it didn't ask for a reply. Where'd they get the name, anyway? *Unless,* he thought, *Elmo Black told them.* That was the only way, he decided. At any rate, it had caused him to decide to move on out of Wichita and find another town to suit his purposes. Twenty thousand dollars was a lot bigger in El Dorado than it was in Wichita. He had made a smart move.

CHAPTER 12

It was early evening when Will stepped down from the saddle and tied Buster and the bay to the hitching rail in front of the Parker House. Although tired after covering over fifty miles from his last camp near the Kansas-Oklahoma border, he came straight to the hotel. Before going to the desk, he decided to take a look in the hotel dining room on the chance he might find Preacher eating an early supper. The dining room was almost half-full already, but there was no Preacher McCoy, so he went to the desk.

"Good evening," the desk clerk greeted him. "Can I help you?" Although his greeting was polite, his raised eyebrow signaled his disapproval of the rifle in Will's right hand.

"I hope so," Will answered. "I'm supposed to meet Gaylord Pressley here in Wichita. He said he was stayin' at the Parker House."

"Mr. Pressley was here, but he checked out last week." The clerk seemed relieved to tell him so, thinking that possibly the hotel might have missed some trouble. He remembered Will, he recalled that he had come in before, looking for another man. He didn't recall that man's name now, but it wasn't Mr. Pressley. He couldn't imagine that a man like Gaylord Pressley could have any legitimate business with a trail-hardened drifter like this individual appeared to be. He was pleased to think that Mr. Pressley had been fortunate to have avoided him.

Damn! Will thought. He had missed him. Disappointed, but at least he knew there was a man walking around who called himself Gaylord Pressley. And he felt it would be an unlikely coincidence that it was anyone other than Preacher McCoy. "Did he say where he was goin' when he checked out?"

"No, he didn't say," the clerk answered curtly. "He just said he enjoyed his stay at the Parker House." He couldn't resist adding, "He didn't say he had an appointment to meet someone here."

"He wouldn't," Will replied. "Well, thanks for your help." He turned and walked out the door, convinced that the clerk had been honest with him in spite of his cold attitude. Another thought struck him that had not occurred to him before, but thinking of it now, he realized he should have thought about it at the time. When he was in Wichita before, he had checked the stable to see if Preacher's dark black horse had been stabled there. Walter Hodge had no recollection of the horse Will had described. It occurred to him now that the hotel had a small stable of its own for their carriage and horses and he had not thought to look there for Preacher's blue roan. Preacher didn't tell the desk clerk where he was heading, but he might have told someone in the stable. Taking Buster's reins, he led his horses around behind the hotel to a small barn and stable about twenty yards from the main building.

He dropped Buster's reins in front of the barn and walked inside. Seeing no one there, he started to continue on to the stables when he heard someone call out above him, "You lookin' for me?" Then a young man appeared at the top of the ladder to the hayloft.

"I reckon so," Will replied. "Maybe you can help me out a little." He waited while the young man climbed down. "I'm lookin' for a man I'm supposed to do some work for. I was supposed to meet him here at the hotel, but I got hung up and didn't get here till too late. I was hopin' maybe you had talked to him before he left."

"Most likely the fellow you're lookin' for kept his horse down at Hodge's stable. The hotel charges a lot more than Hodge. Don't nobody but a few rich folks keep their horses here."

"This fellow could afford it and mighta thought it was worth it to have his horse real handy. He was a big fellow, most likely had two horses and you mighta remembered the one he rode, a big black horse."

The young man smiled at once. "You must be talkin' about Mr. Pressley. He had his horses in here, gave me a couple of dollars to make sure they got some oats."

"That's the man I'm lookin' for," Will said. "Gaylord Pressley, did he say where he was headin' when he left here?" The young man shrugged and shook his head. "Maybe you saw which direction he took outta town." Once again, a shrug and a head shake was all he received in reply. "Well, 'preciate it."

Back on the street, he pondered his next step, while reprimanding himself for not having thought about checking the hotel stable when he was there two weeks before. It would have saved him a hell of a lot of time and travel back and forth to Fort Smith if he had known that Preacher's horse was there. Surely he couldn't have remained holed up much longer before Will would have found some trace of the man. *There ain't nothing I can do about that now*, he thought, *just have to start over*. He considered Delano across the river, but decided Preacher wasn't likely to go there. From what he had learned recently, Preacher had no interest in falling back into the outlaw crowd that hung out in Delano. He had money and he wanted to be part of the high-class crowd that made up the upper crust of the town. Will remembered Elmo's comments about Preacher's ambitions, so he decided Delano was a waste of time. But where to look? To start, he decided to take his horses back to Walter Hodge's stable. They were tired and hungry and he wasn't going to ride anywhere that night. After they were taken care of, he planned to call on every store and shop in the little town on the chance Preacher might have talked to someone before he left.

One of the first places he decided to visit was Baine's Store, a general merchandise establishment, thinking if Preacher was leaving for another town, he may have needed supplies. How much he bought might indicate whether he planned a short trip or a long one. He needed a new bandana, anyway. His had become almost ragged, so he decided he might as well get one here. Inside, a short, bald man, wearing a soiled apron, welcomed him from behind a long counter. "Howdy, stranger. What can we do for you today?"

"Well, I'm just havin' a little walk around town,"

Will said. "Never really took a good look at the town before. I was supposed to meet a fellow here, but I got here too late. Looks like you've got a nice little business here."

"Yeah, I'm doing all right, so far," Jim Baine replied. "Who's the fellow you were supposed to meet?"

"Gaylord Pressley."

"Mr. Pressley," Baine responded. "He was in here a couple of days ago, but I think he's left town."

"He mighta mentioned where he was headed," Will said hopefully.

"No, he didn't," Baine said. "He didn't even say he was leaving town when he was in here, but I wondered why he was buying things he bought since he was staying in the hotel. And he didn't buy much of that."

Will guessed that meant he was planning a trip, but not a long one. His first thought had been Dodge City, but Dodge was a hundred and fifty miles west of Wichita. Preacher must have been thinking about somewhere closer. There weren't very many towns of any size within a day's ride of Wichita, so Baine's information was of little help. "'Preciate your help," Will said. "I need a new bandana, long as I'm here."

"I've got a big selection of bandanas," Baine said. "Come right over to this end of the counter and take your pick." At that moment, another customer came in, so Will told Baine to go ahead and take care of him while he looked the bandanas over to decide which one he wanted.

"Howdy, Frank," Baine greeted the customer. "You come to pick up that load of supplies?"

"No," Frank replied. "If it's all the same to you, I'll

bring my wagon by in the mornin' and load up then. Did you have everything on that list I left you?"

"Sure did, and I checked it twice to make sure I didn't miss anything. That was a sizable order, I appreciate it. Looks like you're got a big job to do. If it's a new business, I hope it ain't another general merchandise store."

His comment brought a chuckle from Frank. "Ain't no need to worry, it ain't even in this town. I gotta haul all my tools and stuff thirty miles from here to El Dorado. Feller that owns the Prairie Palace is wantin' to fix the place up, damn near rebuild it, accordin' to what he told me."

"The Prairie Palace," Baine repeated. "Ain't that the name of that old whorehouse?"

"Sure is," Frank said, chuckling again. "And if my ol' lady knew it, she might not let me go over there to do the job." They both enjoyed a good laugh at that and the customer looking through the box of bandanas was more than a little interested.

Will walked over to the end of the counter where they were talking. "Couldn't help overhearin' you talkin' about the job you've got in El Dorado," he said. "What's the fellow's name that owns that place?"

"The feller that used to own it was Luke Barton, but he just died and this other feller just bought it. He's plannin' on fixin' it up real fancy, but he couldn't find no real carpenters over there. So he came to see me about doin' the job—told me not to advertise it, 'cause he wants a surprise openin'. He told me he's lookin' to pull some of the Parker House's business over to him. I bet he didn't tell the folks at the Parker House what he was up to while he was stayin' there last week."

"Gaylord Pressley," Baine guessed aloud.

Gaylord Pressley, Will repeated silently, and couldn't help wondering how the previous owner happened to die.

"That's right," Frank said. "That's the gent, all right."

"I'll take this red one," Will said, his mind racing now, in spite of the calm demeanor he displayed.

"What?" Baine responded, not understanding.

"Bandana," Will said. "I'll take the red one."

Outside, after paying Baine for his new bandana, Will untied his old one and dropped it in a barrel filled with trash. There was an urge to start out for El Dorado immediately, but his horses had already been worked hard that day, and according to Frank, the town was thirty miles away. He could afford to be patient now, since Preacher was no longer on the run. He thought about what Elmo Black had told him about Preacher and he certainly knew him as well as he thought. Preacher was planning to build the fanciest house of prostitution in Kansas. Elmo also warned him that Preacher was a dangerous man to confront, so Will decided it best to heed that part of Elmo's ramblings as well.

With nothing more to prepare for, he decided to treat himself to a good supper at the Parker House before retiring to the stable to sleep with his horses. He would check his weapons to make sure both rifle and handgun were in good operating condition tonight and plan to make an early start in the morning.

The more Dolly Plover listened to Gaylord Pressley talk about the plans he had for the Prairie Palace, the closer she came to changing her mind about the sudden turn of ownership of the place. Maybe, in the long run, she might be better off with Gaylord running things. For one thing, he obviously had the money to get things done, and he believed in spending it. He took her with him when he went back to Wichita a couple of days ago and gave her money to buy a couple of nice dresses while he talked to a carpenter about doing the work on the Palace. On the way back he told her that he was duly impressed by her and it was his plan for the two of them to run the business together. By the time they returned to El Dorado, she believed he meant every word he said and was convinced that it had been her lucky day when he arrived at the door. So convinced was she, that when he suggested it, she accompanied him to his room that night to keep him warm.

It had not occurred to Dolly that this tall, broad-shouldered stallion might have developed a passion for something other than building the Palace into something glorious. During the night they spent together, he talked of long-term plans that included her beside him every step of the way. She couldn't help feeling that he might be thinking about marriage even though things had not gone that far at this point. She had questioned him about his decision to come to El Dorado, instead of Wichita, a town that was thriving, with so much more to offer than this little settlement. Reluctantly, he had confided in her that he left Wichita to escape a murderous outlaw who had stalked him for weeks, seeking to rob him. "I wouldn't try to avoid him if he would stand up to me, face-to-face, but he's a back-shooter and a coward. I figured he'd have a harder time sneaking up on me in a smaller place like El Dorado." She was shocked to think he had suffered such a threat and her heart went out to him. Reading the compassion in her face, he assured her then, "Don't worry your pretty head about it. If the time comes, I'll be ready to settle his hash for him, once and all."

Her life had changed the day he walked in the door and she had to smile when she remembered what he had said to her on that day. "I think I'm the man you've been waitin' to see." She shook her head in wonder. *At my age*, she thought, *I never figured it could happen to me again.*

One member of the Palace staff was not yet won over by the bigger-than-life persona presented by Gaylord Pressley. And when Rena happened to walk down the hallway in time to almost bump into Dolly coming out of Gaylord's room, she became immediately concerned for her friend. If Dolly felt like giving her boss a ride just for the hell of it, that was her business. It had been a few years since Dolly had participated in boy-girl games, maybe she was on a lark to see what she'd been missing. On the other hand, if Dolly was really developing deep feelings for this stranger at their door, she might be setting herself up for a hell of a letdown. *After all*, she thought, *Lola and Violet don't know they're going to be kicked out just as soon as Gaylord can replace them with younger women.* As for herself, Rena was confident that she and Angel need not fear for their jobs, that is, if Angel fully accepted the fact that she was being kept as a maid and nothing beyond that. The poor girl was young enough, but the Good Lord had not smiled favorably upon her when it came to looks. *Thank goodness I'm a hell of a good cook*, she thought. Her mind came back to Dolly again. *I may have to talk to that gal.*

"I thought you were gonna run me over when you came outta that room a while ago," Rena said to Dolly when she came into the kitchen to get her morning coffee.

"I had to pee," Dolly explained with a giggle. "I'm sorry. I didn't see you till it was almost too late."

"I thought you were running because you went in the wrong room and you wanted to get outta there before he woke up and saw you," Rena said.

Fully aware that Rena's remark was pure sarcasm, Dolly snickered again. "If that's what you thought, then we'll go along with that." She filled another cup with coffee. "But he wants a cup of coffee and said I'd best be quick about it." She picked up the cup, gave Rena a wink, and hurried out the door.

Oh my, Rena thought, *it looks like she's heading for trouble all right*. It was especially disturbing to her because Dolly was normally not inclined to believe everything she heard come out of a man's mouth. She certainly was not that way with Luke, but Luke was no more than a harmless, no-account drunk. Rena had her doubts about this Gaylord Pressley person. Ambitious, that went without saying, but she had a feeling that he wouldn't stop at anything to get what he wanted. In fact, her first thought when Angel found Luke dead was to question whether Gaylord might have had something to do with it. She discarded the notion only after Angel said she heard them talking when Gaylord left Luke's room and went to bed. She still had a slight feeling of distrust for the man, however. She would just have to reserve her judgment until she knew him better and hope he proved her wrong. She needed the job.

In a short time, Dolly returned to the kitchen while Gaylord went to the outhouse. She was carrying the two empty coffee cups. Angel had appeared in the kitchen by then and was busy helping Rena prepare breakfast. "Lola said she ain't feelin' too good this mornin'," Angel said to Dolly, "said she'd fix herself somethin' later on when she's feelin' better. I think it might be her time of the month."

"Well, don't say nothing about it to Gaylord," Rena quickly responded, thinking Lola might be thrown out right away if he heard about it.

"Don't say nothin' to Gaylord about what?" Preacher asked, having overheard her remark just before entering the kitchen.

Having to think fast, Rena hesitated only a few seconds before answering. "I was planning to cook you a fresh steak for your breakfast this morning, but the fellow that brings us most of our beef didn't get here yesterday. Now I reckon you'll have to settle for bacon."

"Steak would be more to my likin'," Preacher said. "But ain't nothin' wrong with bacon if there's potatoes and biscuits to go with it."

"There's plenty of that," Rena assured him.

"Who's the feller you get the beef from?" Gaylord asked.

"Man by the name of Oscar Moon," Dolly answered for Rena. "He showed up here one day leadin' a stray cow he said he'd found out on the prairie and wanted to know if we'd like to buy it. The price was right, so we bought it. Turns out Oscar's one of the luckiest men you'll ever meet. He seems to find stray cows on a regular basis."

Preacher laughed, he was well acquainted with men like Oscar Moon. "Next time he shows up, I'll have to talk to him about messin' up my breakfast this mornin'. We need to celebrate an occasion, anyway. Feller by the name of Frank Welch oughta show up here today or tomorrow to start work on the new Prairie Palace." He glanced over at Dolly and gave her a wide smile. She returned it with a little girlish touch. Witnessing what looked to her like flirtatious smiles, Rena experienced the sour taste of disgust. She was going to have to give her a mother-daughter talk, in spite of the fact that she was only a half dozen years older than Dolly.

"'Mornin','" Will called out to the man driving the wagon when he overtook him less than a mile out of Wichita.

"'Mornin','" Frank returned. "You're the feller I talked to in Baine's Store last night. You headin' to El Dorado?"

"Yep, I've got a little piece of business over there. I ain't ever been there before. Does this trail lead all the way to El Dorado?"

"Sure does," Frank replied. "The road's pretty well traveled, just stay on it and it'll take you to the Walnut River. Then the road runs right up beside the river and you'll strike El Dorado in just a few miles. I'd invite you to ride along with me, but I'd slow you down too much."

"I expect so," Will came back. "Thanks just the

same." He nudged Buster into an easy pace and loped off ahead of the wagon.

"Maybe I'll see you over there," Frank called out after him. Will responded with a wave of his hand.

He figured he couldn't be more than ten miles from El Dorado when he tried to decide whether to ride on into town without stopping to rest his horses. Although he usually made it a rule to rest the horses after twenty or twenty-five miles, he would not hesitate to push Buster and the bay farther if there was a need. There was no particular strain on them, traveling over this mostly flat terrain, so they could make the entire thirty miles to El Dorado without his asking too much of them. Knowing with certainty that Preacher McCoy was only thirty miles away, he was anxious to get there as soon as possible. Still, when another five miles brought him to the first good creek he had seen all morning, he had second thoughts about resting the horses. He had to remind himself that Preacher was no longer on the run, he'd be there no matter when he got to town. And it would be better not to arrive with horses tired and thirsty, in case there was a need to call upon them again right away. "What the hell," he muttered, "I ain't had no breakfast. I could use a cup of coffee."

While the horses drank at the edge of the creek, he kindled a fire large enough to heat some water for coffee. Then he sat down to watch the pot while he tried to frame a mental picture of this saloon-whorehouse he had never seen before. It might not be as simple as walking in the front door to find Preacher waiting for him. Preacher might be in another part of the building, away from areas where customers gathered. It would not be so difficult if he could go in pretending to be a passing stranger. But Preacher might recognize him, even though he had, at best, gotten no more than a hazy glimpse of him from inside that cave in the Arbuckles. Will had not found him the first time he searched for him in Wichita, trying to find Preacher McCoy, but had Preacher gotten a look at him? He must have figured Will would be back looking for Gaylord Pressley this time in Wichita. Most likely the telegram Will sent spooked him, causing him to decide to leave town. These were the thoughts occupying Will's mind as he watched the horses munching on the grass near the creek bank. Maybe, he thought, his best option would be to wait until dark to call on the Prairie Palace.

When he felt the horses were fresh and ready to go again, he took his time to get underway. Frank had told him that the little town lay on the west bank of the Walnut River, so he decided to leave the wagon road and follow the creek to its conjunction with the river. He figured he would strike the river about five miles south of the town. And from that point, he planned to enter the town from the south, hopefully unnoticed.

After a short ride, the tiny gathering of buildings came into view through the oak trees that lined the banks of the river. He continued on until within a hundred yards of the settlement, stopping then where he still had the cover of the trees. As it was early in the afternoon, he had time to study the town, if he waited until dark. Seeing the drab, two-story building sitting a little distance apart from the others, he figured that it was most likely the Prairie Palace. It was the only two-story building in town. There was a sign out front, but from that distance, he couldn't read what it said. With the simple layout of the town, it would be almost impossible to ride in without being noticed right away, so he decided to wait.

CHAPTER 13

With the setting of the sun on the far horizon, the usual sprinkling of patrons began to show up to drink and talk to Lola and Violet, which sometimes led to one or two with enough money left to go upstairs with one of the women. On this night, however, Violet would be their only choice, since as Angel had reported, Lola wasn't feeling well. Occasionally, someone would want to buy something to eat, so Rena always prepared a big pot of stew, or soup, to handle that request. Leon Williams, who had a small farm on the eastern side of the river, came in every day about sundown to tend bar. His farm was really little more than a garden. He had no family, so he often slept in one of the rooms upstairs, instead of returning to his cabin across the river. Luke Barton had paid Leon a minimum amount of money to tend bar, but Leon also was allowed occasional visits with Lola or Violet, and he had free access to Rena's cooking. Dolly felt sorry for the poor man's plight and she dreaded to tell him he was scheduled to be fired along with the two women. *I guess it just has to be*, she thought, *if Gaylord plans to make this the classiest house in the state. Maybe we'll find another job that Leon can do.* That thought prompted her to glance toward the door to the hallway. Gaylord and Frank Welch had been in the back office talking about the work to be done on the building for more than an hour. She wondered when they would come out.

From about one hundred yards away, his horses tied in the trees, Will decided it time to get on with the job he came to do. Earlier, he had watched Frank Welch when he drove his wagon into town and pulled up before the Palace. It occurred to him that thirty miles was a long haul for a horse pulling a wagon. He had halfway expected Frank to show up first thing in the morning and he would have preferred it that way. *Just as long as he doesn't get in the way*, he thought as he stepped up into the saddle. He pulled Buster's head around and headed him toward the Palace. The big buckskin padded slowly toward the building where Frank's wagon was still tied out front.

He took a long look down the nearly empty street after he dismounted. The little town seemed to have already gone to bed for the night. Satisfied that there should be nothing outside the Palace to interfere with what he had to do, he stepped inside the door. With his rifle in his right hand, he quickly scanned the room, searching for one he knew he would recognize as Preacher McCoy. Unlike a typical saloon, the room was more akin to a big parlor, but with a long bar across one end of it. There was no one in the room who would fit Preacher's description. He glanced toward the bar where Rena was talking to Leon, after having brought him a plate of stew. He shifted his gaze to the other end of the bar where Dolly was standing, watching the room. Her gaze promptly shifted toward him when he paused in the doorway before entering.

Certain now that he was going to have to search the building for Preacher, he walked across the parlor toward a door at the back wall, it apparently being the only door to the rest of the house. He was in the middle of the room when that door suddenly opened and Frank Welch walked out, immediately followed by Preacher. Outlaw and lawman reacted immediately, with Will a split second faster. His rifle up and cocked in an instant, Will leveled the Winchester at Preacher, who was caught without a weapon. His reaction was to grab Frank by the arm and pull the startled carpenter in front of himself, using him as a shield. "Don't do anything stupid, Preacher," Will warned moments before he was slammed in the back by a blast from the shotgun held by a terrified Dolly Plover. The impact dropped him to the floor immediately.

"Shoot him again!" Preacher blurted. "Shoot him again! He ain't dead!" He looked around him frantically searching for a weapon when Dolly seemed to be too deeply in shock to respond. When she continued to stand there, stunned by what she had just done, he shoved Frank aside and grabbed a handgun from a wide-eyed customer who had been visiting with Violet. By the time he had turned around again, he was to be confronted by Will's Winchester rifle in the hands of Rena Peters and it was aimed directly at him.

"Throw that gun down, or so help me, I'll cut you down where you stand," Rena commanded. "This man's dying. There ain't any use to shoot him again.

I ain't ever killed anybody, but by God, I'll kill you if you don't drop that gun and get your sorry ass out of here. And I mean out of this house and don't ever come back." Whether she meant everybody, or just him, the few customers there wasted no time in exiting the parlor, with the exception of Frank Welch, who was still standing petrified by the hallway door.

Preacher hesitated for a brief second, thinking to test the woman's bluster, but the cold look in her eye told him it would likely cost him his life. "All right, you crazy bitch," he said, satisfied that Will was dying. "I'll gladly leave this damn dump behind. It was a bad idea in the first place." He was already thinking that the word would spread quickly and there would soon be another deputy, or a posse, showing up to look for him.

Unable to believe all that had happened in the span of two minutes, Dolly recovered enough to scream, "Rena! What are you doin'? He came to kill Gaylord!"

"Shut up, Dolly," Rena snapped. "You just shot a U.S. deputy marshal—maybe killed him, I don't know yet." When Will went down, she had run to him, not to help him, but to get the rifle in case he was not dead, to prevent him from returning fire. When he struggled to turn over on his side, she saw the deputy's badge under his vest. In that instant, she knew that every suspicion she had held about Gaylord Pressley was justified. Now she looked at Dolly for help, but realized right away that Dolly had gone into shock again, so she turned to the bartender. "Leon, help me drag him over behind the counter." When they had done so, she said, "Get that shotgun from Dolly and we'll stay behind the counter till we find out what Gaylord is planning to do." In a very short time she found out, for he suddenly came through the door, carrying his rifle and his saddlebags over his shoulder.

Seeing Rena and Leon behind the bar, their weapons pointed straight at him, he paused for only a moment before asking, "Where is he?"

"He's lying on the floor, dead," Rena answered. "I hope you're satisfied."

Preacher smiled, pleased. "Good, that's where he oughta be." He smiled at Dolly, who was still trying to understand what had just happened. "Thanks, Dolly, you done the world a favor when you shot that son of a bitch." Finished then, he lingered only a moment longer to say, "You're lucky I don't care enough to break your neck before I go." He directed this at Rena. "I shoulda done for you like I done for Luke, but I'm just glad I didn't waste my money on this place. So we'll call it square. Next time I see any of you, it'll be in hell." With that, he walked out the door, heading for the stable to get his horses, unwilling to waste any more time, in case there was a posse following Will Tanner.

"Leon, look out the door. Is he gone?" Rena asked. Moving quickly now, she tried to take a closer look at the wounded deputy, who was struggling to get up on his hands and knees. "You just take it easy, young fellow," she said when Leon said Preacher had gone. "We're gonna take care of you." She turned to Angel, who seemed to be the only one of the other women to show a sense of helping. "We need to get him on a bed while somebody goes for Tom Hawkins." Leon volunteered and was out the door immediately. "Give us a hand!" Rena snapped at Dolly, who was still lost in the chaos caused by what she had done. Acting as if in a nightmare, she finally moved to help them carry

Will. "We'll take him to my room," Rena directed. "It's the closest to the kitchen." With some effort, the three women carried the wounded man into Rena's room. The job was made more difficult by Will's struggles to help himself as he gradually became aware of what had happened. The impact of the shotgun blast at such close range had knocked the wind out of him and now that he could breathe again, his natural tendency was to fight. Finally when Rena yelled at him to be still, he realized that they were trying to help him.

"He's gonna get blood all over that quilt," Angel said. "We'd best get something to spread over that."

"You're right," Rena said. "That's my good quilt. There's an old one I was saving to cut up for patches in that dresser in the corner." They lowered Will to the floor while Rena got the old quilt and spread it on the bed. Then they transferred him from the floor to the bed. "I'm glad that's over," Rena announced. "He's heavier than he looks."

Before long, Leon returned with Tom Hawkins, who came in apologizing. "You know, I ain't no doctor, I'm better at buryin' 'em, but I have tended some gunshot wounds. I'll do what I can." With help from Rena, he rolled Will over on his side. "Shotgun," he announced. "Sure made a mess of his back." He glanced at Rena. "I reckon we'd better clean him up as best we can, then maybe we can see where to start on the wounds."

Tom spent the better part of two hours digging shot out of Will's back, most of it concentrated between his shoulder blades. Since it had been at such close range, the pattern had not had time to expand. There was a good number of shot that had driven too deeply in the muscles of his back to make it practical for Tom to try to dig them out. "I'd do more damage than good," he explained when he'd extracted all that he safely could. "He needs to see a doctor," he stated when he had finished.

"Well, we ain't got a doctor," Rena said. "So I reckon he's just gonna have to make it without one." At Tom's suggestion, she took an old sheet from the same drawer the quilt had come from and ripped it into bandages. Then after applying some lard lightly over the many wounds to keep the cloth from sticking to them, she wrapped the bandages around him.

During the entire procedure, the patient did not make a sound, causing those administering to his surgery to wonder if their efforts were in vain. It was not until Rena asked him if he wanted to remain on his stomach, or switch to his side, that he spoke. "I reckon I'd do better on my side," he answered, his voice calm and steady, surprising those attending him. "Is Preacher still here somewhere?"

Misunderstanding, Tom answered, "No, I'm sorry, we ain't got no preacher in town yet. We're hopin' to build a church one day soon."

Will winced with the pain caused by his efforts to talk. "No, Preacher," he grunted, "Preacher McCoy, Gaylord. Is he still here?" He felt around him on the bed, searching for his rifle.

A step ahead of the others from the start, Rena responded, "Preacher McCoy, is that his real name? No, he's gone and I doubt he'll be back. What I wanna know is who the hell are you? Are you really a deputy marshal, or did you take that badge off a dead man?"

"Will Tanner," he said, still finding it painful to talk. "I'm a deputy outta Fort Smith. Preacher robbed a bank in Texas and I've been chasing him all the way through Indian Territory." He paused to catch his breath before continuing. "And he killed a couple of men."

"Three," Angel interjected, recalling Preacher's parting comment about Luke.

"I've gotta get on my feet," Will said, thinking he had to be prepared for Preacher's return. "I've gotta see to my horses." He dropped his leg over the side of the bed and tried to stand up, but found that he couldn't do it.

"Mister," Tom said to him, "you ain't in no shape to get outta that bed. You've lost about a gallon of blood. You're gonna have to build your blood back up, and that's gonna take a little while." *If you don't die from blood poisoning,* he thought to himself.

They were distracted by a comment from the hallway, where Violet and Lola had stood watching through the open door. "Martin Weed came back lookin' for his pistol," Violet announced. "He found it where Gaylord dropped it in the parlor. He said Gaylord got his horses and hightailed it outta town." Hearing her, Will lay back and relaxed his body, knowing he had no chance of stopping Preacher McCoy until he recovered. He was still in a fog regarding what had happened and who had shot him when he was so close to making an arrest.

"We'd best let you get a little rest now," Rena said. "I'm gonna go to the bar and fix you up a little drink to help you relax. You might just as well stop worrying and let those wounds heal up. Gaylord . . . or Preacher, is it? Anyway, he's left town and there's nothing you can do about him till you get better. Leon will take care of your horses for you. He can take 'em down to the stable and leave 'em with Paul." She turned around and ordered, "All right, everybody out, he needs some sleep." She waited until they all moved toward the door before turning back to Will. "I'll be right back with a little shot of whiskey for you."

After she had taken care of Will, Rena left him to rest and went back to her kitchen where she found her next patient waiting for her. "What the hell have I done?" Dolly wailed when Rena walked in. "Gaylord told me that he came to El Dorado because there was an outlaw who had been trying to murder him and steal his money, and I thought that's who that man in there was. What if he dies?"

In the three years that Rena had known Dolly, this was the first time that the usually iron-willed, self-sufficient woman had ever broken down emotionally. "If he dies, then that's just the way things were supposed to be. Maybe he won't die. No matter, you did what you thought was right. Hell, it's my fault, too. I shoulda given you a strong dose of my doubts about that son of a bitch." She paused to give Dolly a smile. "I do wish you'da missed, though. I'd liked to have seen that lying bastard get arrested and hauled off to prison just for what he did to you."

"You mean make me into the world's biggest fool?" Dolly asked, hanging her head in shame. "I believed every lie he told me. It's gonna take me a long time to get over this."

"No such a thing," Rena was quick to reply. "You just gave a stranger a double load of buckshot. It ain't like it was anything serious."

Dolly laughed in spite of herself. "How can you joke about what I did?"

"Listen, honey, I got a feeling about this fellow, just like I had a feeling about our Mr. Gaylord Pressley, or

Preacher McCoy, or whatever his name is. Only the feeling I got with this deputy is a good one. He's tough. I think he'll heal up faster than you think and thank you for giving him a chance to rest for a while."

"What if he wants to arrest me for shooting him?"

"Well, then, we'll shoot him again."

Rena's feelings proved to be accurate in regard to Will Tanner. The morning after he was bushwhacked by Dolly, he was able to sit up in bed and drink the coffee Rena brought him, even though he could not get out of the bed for a couple more days. When he could move a little better, Rena transferred him to Preacher's room, so she could return to hers. During that time, and the days that followed, he was treated royally by the women of the Palace and Dolly bought him a new shirt to replace the one ruined by the buckshot. He was healing fairly rapidly although it would take some time before he became unaware of the pieces of shot lodged deep in the muscles in his back. While he could not deny the frustration of having walked into an ambush, even though it was not a planned one, he understood the reason it had happened. He blamed himself for being careless when he walked into the Palace. There was one other who was disappointed in the confrontation that revealed the outlaw, Preacher McCoy. Frank Welch headed back to Wichita the morning after, minus the big job he thought he had, but at least he had his life—and three hundred dollars Preacher had given him to buy some materials. The three hundred was worth making the trip for, he decided, and he could use the supplies he had loaded in his wagon in Wichita.

In a short time, Will came to know the people at the Prairie Palace as decent folks who had simply been victims of Preacher McCoy's charade as a moneyed gentleman. Dolly, of course, was the most remorseful for having been taken in so completely that she was inspired to protect the vicious outlaw. And she, even more than Rena, was there to fulfill his every request. As far as Will himself, he was healing rapidly physically, but knowing he had come so close to arresting Preacher, only to lose him again, created a frustration bigger than he had ever experienced before. He had no idea where to start looking for him, and it served no purpose for him to stay on in Kansas without a lead of some kind. With no other choice, he concentrated on getting well enough to ride, with the intention of going back to Fort Smith to report to Dan Stone that he had failed to deliver Preacher McCoy once again. It was a ride he didn't look forward to.

"You must be feeling fit as a fiddle," Rena commented when Will walked into the kitchen to get his morning coffee. He was wearing his cartridge belt and holster. "You thinking about going somewhere?"

"I'm thinkin' it's time I got on a horse again," he replied. "I feel ready to ride. Most of those smaller wounds have healed. I expect my back's healin' over those deep wounds and maybe before too much longer they'll quit achin'."

"Ain't nobody knows better'n you," Rena said. "But if I was you, I'd be darn sure I was well enough before I started out anywhere. You've still got a lot of lead in your back and you go bouncing around on a horse, you're liable to start that bleeding again."

"And you need more iron in your blood," Dolly said, having heard Rena's comment as she walked in carrying a large cut of fresh meat. She placed the meat on the table next to the stove. "So you're not going anywhere till you eat a good portion of this. We finally got some fresh butchered beef and that's what you need to build your blood back up."

"Dolly's right," Rena said. "We waited long enough for him to show up with some beef. Is he about finished butchering that cow?"

"Already finished," another voice from the hall boomed out, one that had a familiar twang Will thought he recognized. In a moment, he walked in. "Will Tanner! What the hell are you doin' here?"

"Oscar Moon!" Will blurted at almost the same time. They were both speechless for a moment.

"I'll be damned . . ." Moon sputtered. "Dolly said she was wantin' to cook up some of this beef for a wounded man, but she didn't say it was you."

Will had to laugh. "I've been laid up in the bed so long, I reckon I don't pay attention to what's goin' on around here. Dolly said she was expectin' a fellow to bring her some beef, but she never called your name. I heard her go out in the yard when you showed up." He chuckled again. "If I'd known that was you out there, I'da got my rifle and shot you, 'cause I know that cow was stolen."

Moon pretended he was insulted by the remark. "That poor cow wandered off from the herd. It had a lame foot and I was just lucky enough to save it from gettin' et by some wolves."

Rena and Dolly watched the exchange between the two men, amazed that they knew each other. It was Dolly who spoke first in Moon's defense. "Oscar's

right, Will, I'm sure he didn't steal that cow and he is
lucky that he finds a stray like that from time to time."
Her plea caused both men to laugh all the more.

"Don't worry," Will told her. "We'll be able to tell
for sure after you cook some of it up. Stolen beef has
a strong flavor that other beef don't have."

"Now I know you two are just japing me," Dolly said,
realizing then that they were friends.

"That's a fact," Moon said. "And it looks like things
didn't go the way you wanted 'em to after you left me
down on that creek below the Kansas line. How bad
are you hurt? It don't look like it slowed you down
none, settin' up here at the table, drinkin' coffee.
Dolly said you got shot in the back with a shotgun."

"She did?" Will responded, trying to shoot a playful
smirk in her direction. "Did she tell you who shot me?"

"No, she didn't. Was it that feller you were trailin',
that McCoy feller?"

"Nope," Will said, smiling when he saw Dolly
scrunching her face up, embarrassed. "It was some
gunslinger called Shotgun Plover that got the jump
on me," he said, unable to resist teasing Dolly. He
went on then to tell Moon about tracking Preacher to
Wichita and from there to this brothel-saloon here
in El Dorado. When he reached the part where he
got shot, Moon looked at Dolly as if unable to believe
she did it. "When you shake it all out," Will said when
he had finished, "Preacher got away again and I've
been holed up here tryin' to get well enough to ride."

"I'll swear . . ." Moon started, then only shook his
head. "Whaddaya gonna do?" he finally asked.

"I don't know," Will said. "I didn't ride all the way
up here from Fort Smith just to ride all the way back
by myself. But I don't know where to start lookin'. I

don't even know if he took off north, south, east, or west. When he rode outta the stable, I was flat on my belly, lookin' at the parlor floor."

"Reckon he went back to Wichita?" Moon asked.

"I don't think he'd go back there, 'cause that's where we picked up his trail before and found out what name he was usin'. No, I think he'll light out for someplace where he can start all over and nobody knows him. So I figure that rules out Texas, where the Rangers are lookin' for him, and Oklahoma, where I'm lookin' for him. If I just knew what direction he started in, maybe I'd have half a chance to pick up his trail. So I reckon I'll go talk to the fellow that owns the stable. What's his name, again?" He aimed his question at Dolly.

"Paul Perry," Dolly answered.

"Right," Will continued. "I'll go talk to him. Maybe he saw which way he rode outta town."

Will left Moon and Rena to finish the preparations to dry the major portion of the cow he had delivered, while he walked down the street to the stable. He found Paul Perry mucking out one of the stalls. "Howdy," Perry greeted him. "I reckon you're the owner of that buckskin and the bay. I figured you'd show up pretty soon." He propped his pitchfork against the side of the stall and walked out to meet him. "Looks like you're recoverin' pretty well after Dolly shot you." He shook his head slowly. "That was a helluva thing about that feller, Pressley. He had us all fooled—thought he was gonna put El Dorado on the map."

"He's fooled a lotta folks everywhere he's been, I reckon," Will said. "Maybe you can help me a little. Is he still ridin' that black horse?" Perry said that he was and that he had a sorrel he was using as a packhorse. Knowing there wasn't much in the packs, that left a possibility that Preacher might seek out a place to buy the supplies he would need, if he was planning to travel far. "What's the closest place where he could buy supplies?"

"Right here," Paul said. "I expect he could get anything he needs at the general store." Then he thought about what he had just said. "I reckon he was in too big a hurry to get outta town to do that." He paused to recollect. "I reckon the closest place would be back at Wichita, thirty miles, and he rode out that way when he left here." That was going to be Will's next question. Preacher appeared to be heading back to Wichita, but Will still didn't think Preacher would return to that town and expressed that opinion. Perry thought a moment longer, then suggested, "He coulda gone to a little tradin' post about three miles north of Wichita on the Arkansas River. Feller by the name of Calvin Green owns it."

Well, that's something, Will thought, immediately discarding any notions of returning to Fort Smith without Preacher. *It's a long shot, but it's somewhere to start.* If Preacher was concerned about being followed, he would change directions as soon as he was out of sight of the town and he would try to disguise his trail after that. But Will believed Preacher was not in fear of that. According to Rena and Dolly, Preacher believed that Will was dead. "I 'preciate your help, Mr. Perry. I reckon I'll get my horses in the mornin' and I'll settle up with you then." He knew Rena would strongly insist that he was not recovered enough to leave, but he felt he couldn't wait any longer. And if push had come to shove, he figured he could have started today, so he would surely be ready tomorrow.

Back at the Palace, he found Dolly and Moon, with help from Angel, laying out the cuts of meat to be smoked. When he told them he planned to leave in the morning, Moon was quick to volunteer to ride along with him. "Suit yourself," Will said to him. "Are you sure you can tear yourself away from your busy schedule?"

Moon grinned in response. "I'll check my calendar, but I don't think I've got any important appointments in the next few days. I'll go along with you for a couple of drinks of corn likker. Whaddaya say? Ain't nobody better'n me at trackin' . . . Couple of shots of corn likker," he repeated, "that's my price."

"All right," Will said. He figured he might need his help with the trackin' before he caught up with Preacher again.

"Where are we headin'?" Moon asked. Will told him about the trading post Perry mentioned and Moon nodded. "Calvin Green's store, I know him. He's an honest man." Will wondered again if there was anyone in the whole of western Kansas and Oklahoma who knew more people than Oscar Moon, or the territory itself. He was glad he wanted to ride with him.

As he had expected, Rena thought it a bad idea to start out on what could be a long trek at this stage of his recovery. She made one attempt to reason with him to allow at least two more days before leaving. But she quit trying when she was met with the same stone face encountered by Sophie Bennett when she had complained about his leaving town again so soon after having been away so long. "Well, if you find out you need a place to heal up after all, you can always come back here. I think we owe you that. Ain't that right, Dolly?"

"Sure is," Dolly was quick to reply. "We owe you that, at least I do."

"'Preciate it," Will said, "but I think I'm ready to go." He looked at Moon. "Sunup tomorrow, right?"

Moon shrugged. "How 'bout in the mornin' after breakfast? You don't get many chances to eat like you do at Rena Peters's table."

"I reckon you're right," Will conceded, "tomorrow after breakfast then."

Rena nodded her approval. "At least, I can get a little more of that good beef in your system."

CHAPTER 14

The good-byes the next morning were brief with an invitation to Will to make sure to stop in to see them, if he was ever back that way. One final time, Dolly asked and received Will's forgiveness for shooting him in the back. Then Will and Moon went down the street to the stable to get Will's horses.

There was little information to be gotten from Paul Perry regarding Preacher's destination when he had left town on the night of his escape. Perry pointed in the direction he remembered Preacher had ridden from his stable. Even though it was dark by that time, he felt sure Preacher had headed to the left of the single oak tree standing on a knoll about fifty yards behind the stable. Will settled his bill with Perry, then he and Moon rode to the tree pointed out to look for tracks, knowing they would be pretty old by now. They figured it highly unlikely there would be tracks left by anyone else on the same spot, so they might at least determine the direction Preacher started out in. "Looks like Paul was right," Moon said after a brief look around the tree. "He rode out this way." They followed what tracks they could find and all of them were consistently in the same direction, leading Moon to speculate, "Looks to me like he sure as hell headed back toward Wichita. Maybe we can track him enough to see if he changes his direction."

"I reckon so," Will agreed, still thinking that Preacher would avoid the town. "I'm thinkin' about that place you talked about outside of town. I think Preacher might need supplies if he's plannin' to put a lotta distance between him and Wichita. If he knows about that store north of town, that might be where he'd go to get what he needs. So far, it looks that way because he's headin' straight west and if he stays on this line, it's hard to say exactly where he'd most likely strike the Arkansas River. That's about thirty miles from here, but he might strike it somewhere within a few miles north of Wichita."

"I can't disagree," Moon said. "You're thinkin' don't waste time tryin' to follow his trail, just ride on to Green's Store?"

"That's what I'm thinkin'," Will replied, thinking that would be the logical thing to do.

"Well, I'll be damned . . . Oscar Moon," Calvin Green blurted when he saw the two men tying their horses at the hitching rail in front of his store. He walked out to greet them. "Howdy, Moon, ain't seen you in I don't know when. Who's this you got with you?" he asked as he looked over the rangy younger man riding the buckskin horse.

"Calvin," Moon returned the greeting. "This here's U.S. Deputy Marshal Will Tanner," he announced.

"Deputy marshal?" Green questioned. "Are you

under arrest?" He was not joking. As Green was well aware of Moon's tendency to walk a line between what was lawful and what was not, it seemed a natural assumption.

"Hell, no," Moon quickly responded, pretending to be offended. "Me and Will's friends. I'm helpin' him track down an outlaw and we figure he mighta stopped here a while back."

Green stepped forward and offered Will his hand. "Welcome to my store . . . Deputy. Tanner, was it?"

"That's right," Will said. "I'm hopin' you can help us out a little. I'm lookin' for a big fellow ridin' a black horse and leadin' a sorrel packhorse. I'm thinkin' he mighta needed some supplies."

"Yes, sir, he was here, all right, bought a right smart load for that packhorse, and didn't fuss about the price of anything," Green said, and gave a little appreciative shake of his head as he recalled the order. "Now, are you sayin' that fellow was an outlaw?"

"That's a fact," Will answered. "His name's Preacher McCoy. He's wanted for murder and robbin' a bank in Sherman, Texas, and anything you can tell us about him, where he's goin', or anything else, I'd appreciate it."

"Dang," Green responded, stroking his chin as he tried to recall. "There ain't much I can tell you about him. He showed up one day, bought a load of supplies, and left, said he had a long ride ahead of him. That was all. He didn't seem to be in a talkative mood."

Will was not surprised. He hadn't expected to get much information from the store owner, but at least he was glad to know his impulse to ride straight to

Green's Store had been a time-saver. "Which way was he headin' when he left here?"

"He crossed the river, headin' west," Green replied.

"I reckon we'll be headin' that way, too, as soon as we rest the horses," Will said.

"You got any of that corn likker you used to sell?" Moon asked Green. He cut his eyes over at Will. "That ride over here this mornin' musta riled up my rheumatiz. It's painin' me some. A couple of shots of that whiskey always eases it a little, so I reckon I'll have that drink you promised me now."

"I never thought about how hard a ride like that can be on a man your age," Will japed. "Maybe I'd best leave you here in Wichita while I ride on alone. How 'bout it, Mr. Green, have you got any of that corn whiskey?"

"I sure do," Green said.

"Well, give us a couple of drinks before we go take care of our horses and I need a sack of oats. Buster's most likely gonna need some before we're done," Will said.

"I'll have to sell you a jar of whiskey," Green said. "I ain't got a saloon inside. I don't sell it by the drink."

Will did not miss the smile on Moon's face. "I got a feelin' you knew that," he said to him. He paid Green for the whiskey and the oats and added a sack of coffee beans to the order, since there would have to be enough for two now that he had a partner.

After leaving Green, they crossed the river before resting the horses. Will wanted to scout the other side for evidence of Preacher's tracks and he figured he could do that while the horses were watered. Moon was quick to open the jar Will had bought and sample its contents. After a couple of snorts, he offered it to

Will. After Will declined, he put it away and started gathering wood for a fire to roast some of the ample quantity of smoked beef he had supplied. When the fire had caught up enough to let him put on larger pieces of wood, he added some, then went over to the bank where Will had found hoofprints. "I can't say for sure," Will said. "These tracks have been here for a while, but I'd bet they're Preacher's. It looks to me like two horses came outta the river right here and they're in about the right spot to be on a line to Green's Store."

Moon agreed and turned to line up the direction the tracks started in when they left the river. "If he keeps up in that direction, he'll be headin' back toward Oklahoma."

"I didn't think he'd go back there," Will said. "Maybe they ain't Preacher's tracks." They had to be, however, they were the only tracks they found on that side of the river. "Who else could it be? We'll just follow those tracks and see where they go." With that settled, they went back by the fire and ate some of their smoked beef, and washed it down with some strong coffee. When the horses were rested, they climbed back into the saddle and started out after Preacher again.

They had not ridden far when they realized the trail continued to turn toward the south as if Preacher had just planned to ride around Wichita. Late afternoon found them about twenty miles from Green's Store when they struck what appeared to be a well-used wagon road, running east and west. The tracks they had followed disappeared on the other side of the road. "He's headin' to Dodge City," Moon suddenly realized. "This here's the road to Dodge!" Since there

were no tracks across the road to dispute it, Will had
to agree that Preacher had turned onto the road. To be
sure, they rode on opposite sides of the road for about
five miles in case Preacher turned off again. "He's goin'
to Dodge City," Moon declared for certain. "Hell, that's
about a hundred and fifty miles from here."

"Looks that way," Will agreed. "You sure you wanna
keep goin'?"

"Hell, I ain't got nothin' else to do," Moon replied.

"All right," Will said. "So I reckon we'd best find a
place to camp before we wear the horses out. That
little creek up ahead looks like it might do." When
they reached the creek, they turned the horses upstream and rode along the bank until they found a
spot that pleased them.

Starting before breakfast the next morning, they
set their horses at an easy, but steady pace, no longer
concerning themselves with trying to follow Preacher's
tracks. The road had been traveled enough to make it
hard to determine one horse's tracks from another.
They were going with what seemed to be the most
likely gamble. Preacher probably figured he could
blend in with the lawless crowd in Dodge City, so it
made sense that he might go there. They didn't stop
to rest the horses and cook their breakfast until reaching the South Fork of the Ninnescah River. On the
hope he might be lucky, Will scouted the area they
stopped in to see if he could find any signs that
Preacher had stopped there, too. But there were no
tracks except those left by some deer. In the saddle
again, they went back on the road, which followed the
river for approximately thirty miles before it veered
slightly away from it. By then, the horses were showing

signs of fatigue again, so when they came to a small creek, they decided to make camp there. Moon figured they were still a day and a half from Dodge City.

Once the horses were taken care of and a healthy campfire was blazing, they cooked their supper and relaxed while they ate. Moon complained about his rheumatiz again and sought some corn medicine to soothe it. Feeling a stinging stiffness in his back from the shotgun wounds he was still recovering from, Will took a couple of drinks from the jar when Moon offered it. "I reckon I could have telegraphed Dan Stone before we left Wichita," he thought aloud. "He's already put out with me for not lettin' him know what I'm up to."

"I reckon you can wire him when we get to Dodge City," Moon said.

"Yeah, I reckon," Will said, but his mind was already working on things unrelated to the job at hand. He had already been gone from Fort Smith a long time and he was thinking about Sophie's last words before he left. *If you don't come back, I'll know why.* She had said it in the form of an ultimatum and he interpreted it to mean just that. If he changed his mind about wanting to marry her, don't come back. Remembering her kiss, he knew there was no question. He would be back, no matter what. "What?" he said, just then realizing that Moon was talking to him.

"Damn, I thought you'd gone to sleep with your eyes open," Moon said. "I asked you if you wanted another snort of this whiskey."

"No, thanks," Will replied. "I think I'll take a look around while there's still a little light left, ease my back from sittin' in the saddle all day." He got up and began to scout their campsite as he had done when they had stopped before. And, as before, there was no evidence of anyone else having stopped there. For no reason, other than trying to free his mind of thoughts of Sophie, he walked back to the wagon road. Crossing the creek, he walked on for a few yards before coming to what he figured to be a game trail, leaving the road to the south. He turned about, preparing to return to the camp, since the light was now rapidly fading, but something caught his eye. He paused, then decided to satisfy his curiosity with a closer look. Two steps onto the game trail, he discovered the faint mark on the ground that had attracted his attention was, in fact, a clear imprint of a horse's hoof. He considered the possibility that this might be an old Indian trail, as he pushed through the bushes on either side of the trail to come to a low spot where water no doubt seeped from the creek. In the soft dirt there, he found more tracks, clearly from shod horses, and not Indian ponies. "Moon!" he yelled, knowing that as soon as the sun dropped below the horizon, it would be totally dark. "Bring a light!"

Moon sat up straight, looking all around him, startled by Will's call. His first reaction was to grab his rifle until he heard Will say to bring a light. He knew what he meant then, so he took a stick of wood that was flaming brightly from the fire. "Where the hell are you?" he called back and Will told him where he was. In a couple of minutes, he saw him standing at the head of the game trail. "What'd you find?" Moon asked, blowing on his torch to keep it from dying out.

"Take a look," Will said, "tracks, shod horses."

"Damned if they ain't," Moon exclaimed. He knelt down to take a closer look, having only moments before the flame on the limb he had chosen for a torch died out, leaving only a streamer of smoke behind. "Might be the tracks we've been followin'— hard to say. We can take a better look in the mornin' when we got some light. Could be that feller we're followin' mighta camped here, too, and just rode down this trail to find him a good spot."

Those were the same thoughts going through Will's mind. "If they are Preacher's tracks, and they keep followin' this trail, then he's sure as hell not goin' to Dodge City. This trail is headin' straight south."

"Don't make much sense, does it?" Moon replied. "I'da thought he was headin' for Dodge. If he keeps on in this direction, he'll wind up back in Injun Territory."

"Well, I reckon we'll see what's what in the mornin'," Will said. "We can't see much standin' out here in the dark." They returned to the campfire and the coffeepot.

After finishing the coffee, both men lay propped up on one elbow, each in deep thought, with no more than an occasional word of conversation between them. After a while, it was Will who spoke first. "I'm beginnin' to wonder if we ain't off on a wild goose chase, and find out when we get there, we've been followin' some cowhand ridin' the grub line, lookin' for work."

"Might be," Moon said. He had been doing some heavy thinking, figuring out about exactly where they were between Wichita and Dodge City. Unlike Will, he had traveled this part of the country more times than he could remember and feeling sure he knew where they were now, he expressed his conclusion. "That trail is an old Injun trail that heads straight south into

Injun Territory. I have an idea those tracks belong to Preacher and I know where he's headin'." His statement captured Will's attention, causing him to sit up to listen. "If I'm right, that feller is headin' to a cabin about twenty miles below the Kansas line, settin' in a pocket of oak trees on the Cimarron River. It ain't far from a hilly place that's full of caves and tunnels with colored rocks on the inside. Some outlaws from Texas built it a few years back and there's somebody there from time to time. I never stopped by when there was somebody there, but the last time I was over that way it was empty. I don't think any lawmen on either side of the line know about that place." He paused to ask, "Did you know about it?" Will shook his head. "Like I said," he went on. "Too many people has found out about Sartain's—this'un's still a good place to go, if you're hidin' out."

Up at sunup the next morning, they saddled the horses and loaded their packhorses, waiting for the sun to get up high enough to afford a little light. When it was enough, they returned to examine the tracks Will had found the night before. It was not difficult to determine the tracks were left by more than one horse, with two being the best estimate. After there were no indications that the rider had been looking for a place to camp, but continued following the narrow trail straight south, Will and Moon paused to talk it over. "I think it's your man," Moon stated. "It makes sense to me now. He wants to hide out to give the law a chance to get tired of lookin' for him. Then he can go wherever he wants. If I was in his shoes, and I knew you were comin' after me, that's what I'd do."

"Accordin' to what Rena told me," Will replied, "Preacher thinks I'm dead."

"Yeah, but the Kansas marshals and the Oklahoma marshals ain't dead, so he's worried about them now."

"You're probably right," Will said, but he had to think it over for a few minutes before he could decide for sure. It made sense, but the night before, it made sense that Preacher would head for Dodge City. It was a gamble either way, but Oscar seemed convinced they were on Preacher's trail. "All right," he decided, "let's follow this trail to the Cimarron and see what we find in that cabin." He figured that at least these tracks were something to bet on, whereas going to Dodge City would just be wagering on a hunch, since there were too many tracks to identify any one particular horse. The tracks were old, but it had been some time since Preacher had fled, so his tracks would be about as old as these. And in some parts of the trail they disappeared altogether, but always reappeared farther along, leading them straight south. According to Moon, the distance to the Cimarron was about the same as it would have been to Dodge City, one long day, or one and a half, if they didn't want to push the horses too much. They agreed that it was about fifty miles to the Oklahoma line, so Will decided it would be better to ride that distance on this day. That would leave them no more than twenty miles to the Cimarron, if Moon remembered correctly. Will preferred to reach the cabin early in the day to get a chance to look the situation over.

"You're the boss," Moon responded. "That'll put the Medicine Lodge River at the halfway point between here and the line."

As Moon had predicted, they arrived at the Medicine

Lodge River after what Will estimated to be close to twenty-five miles. They rested the horses there, then crossed the shallow river to find there were no longer any tracks to follow. Some time was spent searching for Preacher's point of exit from the water, but to no avail. "Looks like he finally decided it'd be a good idea to hide his trail," Moon commented. "And he done a pretty good job of it." They talked it over for only a few seconds, but Will decided they were so close they might as well continue on to the cabin. Moon agreed, convinced it was no coincidence Preacher had ridden almost straight to the cabin. So they pushed on south until striking the Salt Fork of the Arkansas at a point Moon knew to be only a few miles north of the boundary between Kansas and Oklahoma. "I ain't dead sure exactly where the line is," he said. "Ain't nobody put up a sign, or built a fence." He chuckled in appreciation of his remark.

Will made no response to Moon's attempt to be humorous, his immediate attention having been captured by the remains of a campfire hidden behind a hedge of laurel bushes. "Take a look at this," he called to Moon. "Somebody went to a lot of trouble to hide their camp."

Moon came over to inspect it with him. After a brief search, he discovered tracks leading to the ashes. "There's tracks here," he said. "But they're headin' north. Must not be our man. Wait a minute," he bellowed then. "I found some more tracks and they're headin' south."

"Comin' and goin'," Will remarked. "Most likely not our man, since we lost his tracks back at the Medicine Lodge River. How far you figure it is from here to that cabin?"

"Half a day's ride," Moon answered.

"Well, let's get started then."

The country they rode through for the last half day of their journey was rugged and harsh, with many small ridges and draws. And as they approached the Cimarron River, Moon pulled up to get his bearings. After a few moments, he pointed to his left. "That way," he said, and led out along the bank of the river.

It was close to midday when Moon reined his horse to a stop, raised his hand, and signaled to Will to come up beside him. "You see that place up ahead, where the river takes a turn?" He pointed to a sharp bend with a thick stand of trees on both banks. "About fifty yards around that bend is where that cabin sets. And the best way to get a look at what's what there is for us to swing out around those trees till we ride past the cabin and tie our horses in the trees. Then to get a close look, we'd best go on foot to see if there's anybody there." Will didn't question it, just nodded and motioned for Moon to lead out.

As Moon had suggested, they rode a wide circle around the river bend, keeping the screen of oak trees between them and the river. By the time they turned to enter the oaks, they found themselves about one hundred and fifty yards below the cabin, which they could see through the trees when the breeze moved the branches aside. They tied the horses where they were not likely to be seen, then worked their way in closer to the cabin until they were close enough to see it. Will understood then why it was so hard to see from any distance. Built of logs with a sod roof, the back of it was jammed right up against the almost vertical slope of a rugged draw and sat on a low rock ledge. The front of the cabin required three steps up to the porch to make the floor level. A stone chimney rose at the back of the cabin and there was a stone fire pit outside for use when the weather permitted. There was no sign of anyone outside, but there was smoke coming from the chimney.

Will felt a tap on his shoulder and turned to see Moon pointing to the far side of the cabin. Looking in that direction, he saw what had caught Moon's eye. A horse came from the trees behind the cabin and walked down to the edge of the river. In a few minutes, another horse appeared and was soon followed by several others. This was not good news, for it meant that Preacher, if he was here, was not alone. Suddenly, Will grew tense when a dark black horse followed the others to the water. *There could only be one horse like that.* "Lookee yonder!" Moon whispered, and pointed. "Right there! Is that that blue roan you been chasin'?"

"Looks like it to me," Will said. There was little doubt in his mind. Now it was a question of who else was in the cabin, so he thought it only fair to discuss his intentions with Moon. While they watched, a few more horses came down to the water's edge. "I count ten horses," he said. "You see any more?" Moon said that was the same number he came up with. "I need to see how many there are in that cabin," Will said. "I know Preacher was leadin' one packhorse, so that still leaves eight horses and could mean eight riders, or one or two riders with a string of horses. And I can't do much about arrestin' Preacher till I find out how many I've got to deal with. The way I figure it is I can't do anything until I wait 'em out a little while and get a chance to see just what I'm up against. And that might take a while."

"Looks to me like two, maybe three saddles stacked on that little porch," Moon said. "It must be pretty crowded inside that cabin. Might be more saddles inside, though."

"Might be," Will said.

"You figure to just set on 'em awhile then, right?" Moon asked, repeating what Will had just said.

"Reckon so," Will replied. "And I reckon you've done your part in this party. You led me to ol' Preacher, so now you might wanna back on outta here before any shootin' gets started."

"Well, if that ain't a helluva note," Moon replied at once. "You think I'd take off and leave you to take on however many outlaws there are in that cabin?"

"I'm just sayin' it ain't your responsibility to fight 'em and I didn't bring you along to get yourself shot tryin' to help me. I ain't gonna take any chances if there's too many for me to handle. I might just have to wait till I can catch Preacher by himself sometime." He was certain that he saw a genuine hurt in Moon's eyes. "You saved my bacon once already in that saloon in Delano," he went on. "I don't wanna put you in the way of a bunch of gun-slingin' outlaws."

"Is that a fact?" Moon came back, obviously perturbed. "I reckon I'd best be the judge of whether I oughta help you flush this gang of polecats or not. This gray hair growin' outta my head oughta tell you I ain't that easy to kill and I didn't come with you all this way just to take a long ride. Tell you the truth, you need somebody to help you. You're the only deputy I ever heard of that works by hisself. That's the reason it was just luck that I came along and kept you from gettin' shot in the Rattlesnake Saloon. And, hell, that's the reason you're achin' now with a load of buckshot in your back. You need a posse man to ride with you and I reckon I'm him on this trip."

"Damn!" Will exclaimed, fairly well astonished by the wizened little man. "That was one helluva speech. I believe I really got you riled up." He shook his head and chuckled. "I guess we'll go partners on this one."

"Damn right," Moon grunted.

"All right, then," Will said. "I expect the only thing to do right now is to lay low here and watch the cabin. It won't be much longer before they're gonna start thinkin' about cookin' some supper. Somebody's gotta come outta that cabin sometime, if it's just to take a leak. I'd like it a lot better if somebody would come out and build a fire in that fire pit in the yard, there. Then maybe all of 'em would come out and we'd know how many we've gotta deal with."

"Are you thinkin' about arrestin' all of 'em?" Moon couldn't help asking.

"Hell, no," Will answered. "I'm here to get one man, Preacher McCoy. The two of us can't handle more than two, three at the most."

"I'm glad to hear you say that," Moon remarked.

"Besides," Will continued, "I don't know who these other men are, or if they're even wanted anywhere. I'm lookin' for a way to get to Preacher and hopin' the rest of 'em don't wanna help him out."

As Will had figured, it wasn't long before someone came outside to build a fire in the stone-encircled fire pit, causing him to blink several times to be sure he was seeing accurately. It was one of the brothers, Treadwell or Cotton, he didn't know which, but he remembered him as the one who started to react when he surprised them under the riverbank. "Well, I'll be . . ." he murmured. A few minutes later, Jebediah Cotton limped outside, his wounded leg evidently slow in healing.

Aware of Will's surprised reaction, Moon asked, "You know them fellers?"

"Yeah, I know 'em," Will answered. "Two families in the cattle-rustlin' business down in Texas. I had a little run-in with 'em on the Arkansas River a short while back and had to shoot two of 'em before we came to an understandin'." He went on to explain exactly what had taken place and the terms under which they agreed to back down.

"So there's six of them, seven countin' Preacher?" Moon replied. "You reckon they'll throw in with him?"

"I don't know. They might decide they want another chance to shoot me. If they find out how much money Preacher is carryin', they might throw in with him. It's hard to figure what they'll do." The discussion continued as they sat watching the outlaws from the cover of the trees. "There he is!" Will suddenly whispered, when the tall, broad-shouldered man came out to join the others.

"Preacher McCoy?" Moon asked. When Will nodded, while keeping his eyes on Preacher, Moon whispered, "He's a big'un, ain't he?"

Unwilling to simply thin out their numbers by laying down a barrage of rifle fire while the seven were easy targets and unaware of their peril, Will was still of the opinion that his responsibility was the arrest of one person. In spite of the fact that they had trailed him before with the intention of killing him, their real crime was cattle rustling and didn't justify cold-blooded execution. He could forgive them for coming after him to avenge Billy Cotton's murder. In their position, he would have done the same. There was still the possibility that the six cattle rustlers might throw in with Preacher, so the problem was how to catch Preacher alone. "What we need is an Indian attack," he muttered as he watched Preacher help himself to more of the beef haunch roasting over the fire.

CHAPTER 15

"I'd like to get a look at what he's carryin' in those saddlebags," Luther Treadwell said to Jebediah Cotton when Preacher came out of the cabin. "He don't never get very far away from 'em."

"You noticed that, too," Cotton replied. "I'm thinkin' that tale he told us about losin' all that bank money was somethin' he just made up. And he don't never take that .44 off. I swear he even sleeps with it in his hand. It's a wonder he ain't shot one of us in our sleep on accident."

Preacher had showed up at the cabin on the Cimarron, surprising them as well as himself, for both parties expected to find the cabin empty. Crowded though it was, they welcomed him to claim a few feet of cabin space for himself when he explained that he was on the run from Deputy Will Tanner. "Tanner!" Jeb Cotton had exclaimed at the time. "He's the reason I'm limpin' and my boy Cecil's shoulder is still stiff." Preacher had sympathized with him and told him that he had lost his three partners to Tanner, so that gave them a bond against the ruthless deputy.

As for Preacher, he didn't trust Luther or Jeb, or the four boys, but he made a lot of talk about how outlaws always stood together against the law. "That's why I'll stand with you folks if he comes after you again," he had said.

"I reckon you got a pretty fair payday at that bank," Luther had remarked.

"Not as good as you might think," was the answer he received from Preacher. "There wasn't but about four thousand dollars in that vault," Preacher lied. "And there was four of us, so it wasn't all that worthwhile. I've already spent most of my share and I've run all the way from Texas clear up to Wichita before I lit here. When Tanner jumped us, we had to leave that bank money behind. Maybe I can go back and look for it one of these days after they give up lookin' for me. I need to find somethin' else I can do, maybe cattle rustlin', like you boys."

And now, while the brother-in-law team of rustlers watched the poor-mouthing bank robber sitting on the porch steps, helping himself to the roasting beef they had provided, they were wondering if there was a word of truth in anything he said. "If he's as poor as he claims," Luther finally decided, "it's because he's buried that money somewhere. Maybe if we just play along with his game for a while, he'll lead us to it." Their conversation was interrupted then, when Preacher got up from the step and walked over to join them.

"I surely do appreciate you boys sharin' your meat with me," he said. "I've got enough bacon and flour to carry us for a while that I'll gladly share with you. I'll take a little ride tomorrow to see if I can't find somethin' to shoot. There oughta be some deer around this river somewhere."

"We're glad to share with you," Luther said. "A little venison would be right tasty at that." *And I'll have Liam on your tail to see where you go to hunt that deer*, he thought.

"I'm pretty lucky when I'm huntin'," Preacher boasted. "The boys that used to ride with me would always start raggin' me to go huntin' when they got sick of bacon. I'd ask 'em to come along with me, but they said I was always luckier when I hunted by myself."

"Well, maybe you'd best go by yourself tomorrow then," Jeb said. To himself, he thought, *You lying son of a bitch.*

"Yeah, I'll do that," Preacher said, "tomorrow after breakfast. So I think I'm about ready to turn in for the night." He rinsed his plate in the river, then went inside the cabin.

"He's fixin' to take off tomorrow," Luther said to Jeb after Preacher was gone. "Sure as hell, he's gonna go dig up that money and he ain't comin' back here. I'll put Liam on his tail. There ain't no tellin' how much money he's got buried somewhere."

Luther and Jeb weren't far behind Preacher, leaving their young sons to sit around the fire until one after another got sleepy enough to call it a night. Liam and Cecil took it upon themselves to check on the horses before joining the others. Satisfied that the horses were bunched close by the riverbank and would probably not wander far from there, the two cousins retired for the night.

* * *

Sometime after midnight, a three-quarter moon rose high over the peaceful Cimarron River to peek through a scattering of low clouds. The only sounds of the night came from the crickets and frogs at the river and the chorus of snoring inside the cabin. The fire in the fireplace had burned away all but a bed of glowing embers as the snoring competition deepened to a steady hum. Suddenly all were awakened by the sound of a piercing scream. Startled and confused in the empty space between sleep and consciousness, they all bolted upright when the cry went out again, this time from more than one voice. "Injuns!" Jeb sang out. "They're after the horses!" There was no doubt now, the screams that had awakened them were Indian war cries to stampede the horses.

In an instant, all seven bodies were in motion, snatching up weapons, pulling on boots, bumping into one another in the cramped space of the cabin as they all tried to go out the door at the same time. There was no need to give any orders. Every man there knew he could not afford to lose his horse. Outside, they looked all around them, expecting arrows or gunshots to be flying, but there were none. "They ain't attackin'!" Luther exclaimed. "They're just after the horses!"

"They're runnin' 'em up the river!" Cecil yelled. Still the war cry continued and they saw most of the horses galloping away along the riverbank with only a few straying away from the bunch. "Go after 'em!" It was an unnecessary command. Without their horses, they were as good as lost.

Frantic, like the others, Preacher ran after the galloping herd until he suddenly caught a glimpse of a dark horse higher up the bank when the moon peeked through the clouds again. It was the blue roan, he was sure of it, and it was moving at a slow trot toward the ring of oak trees. There were no thoughts about the other horses, he saw the chance to save his, so he ran after it, thinking the Indians were driving the main herd and not concerned with the strays. Running up the bank as fast as he could, he almost stumbled as he strained to run faster. With a glimpse of the horse's rump as it trotted into a dark opening between two trees, he could see that he was beginning to catch up. Encouraged, he pushed himself even harder, plunging into the dark shadows between the trees. "Whoa, Samson, whoa," he called the horse's name brief moments before he was knocked to the ground by the butt of a Winchester rifle.

Dazed and confused while his head seemed to ring like a bell, he was helpless to defend himself or prevent his assailant from rapidly tying his hands behind his back. He tried to force himself to recover his senses, certain that he had been captured by Indians until he heard the clear, sober voice command him. "You can have it either way, quiet with no trouble, or fight it and get a .44 slug in your skull. It doesn't make any difference to me."

Still confused and his head aching as if it had been cracked open like a gourd, Preacher rolled over on his side, unable to get to his knees. "Who the hell are you?" he slurred.

"Deputy Will Tanner," was the response. "And I'm takin' you back to Fort Smith. There's a lotta folks there anxious to make your acquaintance."

"Tanner!" Preacher gasped, unable to hide the distress of being caught by the deputy he thought was dead. The last, and only, time he had seen Will Tanner, the deputy was lying facedown on a barroom floor, obviously dying. Slowly, Preacher's brain began to function again and he was aware of the shouts of the men in the distance as they chased their horses, in contrast to the silence there among the trees.

When it appeared that Preacher might be able to, Will commanded him to get on his feet. Desperate now, Preacher responded, "Hell, I can't get up with my hands behind my back like this. You're gonna have to help me."

Will considered that for a moment. Preacher was a big man. It was going to take an effort to get him up. And if he was recovered more than he let on, he might be thinking about trying something, hands behind his back, or not. "All right," Will decided. "I'll give you a hand." He drew his pistol from his holster before propping his rifle up against a tree trunk. "Get on your knees," he ordered. Preacher started to protest, claiming that he couldn't. "Let's get one thing straight," Will said. "I'd just as soon put a bullet in your brain if you're gonna cause me trouble. So you tell me if it's worth dyin' right where you lie." He aimed the .44 at Preacher's head.

"All right! All right!" Preacher responded. "I'll get on my knees, but you're gonna have to give me a hand if you want me on my feet."

"I said I would," Will replied. He stepped back to give Preacher room to struggle to his knees. When he had done so, Will stepped back close enough to take hold of his arm, at the same time jamming his pistol hard up against his ribs. "This Colt has got a hair trigger, in case you're thinkin' about showin' me some tricks," he warned. Preacher's only reply was a grunt when the barrel of the pistol struck his ribs. With an assist from Will, Preacher was promptly on his feet. With one end of a long rope he had coiled, Will made a loop, put it over Preacher's head, and drew it up tight around his neck. Then he picked up the rifle Preacher had been carrying, as well as his own, and started walking toward the blue roan standing patiently several yards away. Preacher had no choice but to stumble along after him.

When they approached the horse, Preacher blurted, "What the hell . . . ?" He realized only at that moment that his horse was saddled. Will cranked the cartridges out of Preacher's rifle until it was empty, then put it in the saddle sling. Preacher knew then that the saddle had to have been taken from the porch while they were all sleeping inside. Silently cursing the unlucky circumstances that caused his horse to stray off from the others, he was then further infuriated to discover the long rope tied to his horse's reins. It wasn't happenstance at all, Tanner had led the roan away from the others, tricking him into following. Although his head was still throbbing, he could think well enough to realize the deputy did all this because he didn't want to chance having to fight everybody in the cabin. He wasn't confident that they would be inclined to fight for him or not, but it was the only hope he had at the moment, so he started to yell out, "Luther! It's the law! Come help me!" He started to yell again until Will gave the rope around his neck a strong yank, choking off a second attempt.

"I thought I made myself clear," Will stated. "You mighta just signed your death warrant, 'cause if they come to find us, you're a dead man. I don't have the patience to put up with any trouble from you. You've already caused me more trouble than your sorry hide is worth. You're under arrest. If you behave yourself, you'll go to trial. If you don't, it's easier for me to deliver your body and it costs me a helluva lot less. So it's up to you how you wanna arrive in Fort Smith."

"All right," Preacher grumbled, thoroughly convinced the deputy meant what he said. "I ain't gonna cause no more trouble."

"Step up in that stirrup," Will directed. "I'll help you up." It took no small effort to boost a man Preacher's size up into the saddle when his hands were tied behind him, but Will managed. When his prisoner was seated, Will said, "I'm gonna let you ride while I lead your horse, but I think I oughta tell you how I'm gonna do it. You can see I'm leadin' your horse by the reins in this hand. But I'm still holdin' the rope around your neck in the other hand." He held it up so Preacher could see it. "So if you take a notion to give the horse a kick, he might take off but it's most likely gonna break your neck if he does."

Preacher sat, sullen, fully understanding, as Will started walking through the grove of trees in the opposite direction from that the horses had taken in stampede. Helpless to prevent his capture, the frustrated outlaw bit his lip in anguish over thoughts of close to nineteen thousand dollars disappearing. His only hope was to get an opportunity to escape somehow. At least he was confident that, if he failed to escape from this cursed lawman, no one else would benefit from that money. He had been smart enough to scout the cabin before riding in and it was a good thing that he did, for he had not expected it to be occupied. As soon as he had seen how many men were there, he promptly backtracked until deciding the best place to hide all but a few hundred dollars of the stolen money. He was satisfied that he had decided on a place that would be easy for him to find again, but not obvious to the occasional passerby. But for now, there was nothing to do but wait for an opportunity to overcome his captor.

Out of the oaks and up a dry stream bed, Will walked close to a mile in the darkness before coming to a scraggly clump of trees where Buster and the two packhorses were tied. "You just sit right there," he said to Preacher while he tied the roan to a tree. "We oughta be on our way pretty soon." In a short time, they heard a horse approaching and Will grabbed his rifle in readiness.

Seconds later, Moon rode up the dry stream. "I see he took the bait," he crowed as he rode up beside them. "I drove them horses off toward the west before I let 'em scatter. It'll take a while before them boys find all their horses." He moved a little closer then to take a good look at Preacher, who scowled at him in return. "Damned if you didn't lead us on a long ride," he chided. "I believe if I was Will, I'd just shoot you instead of haulin' you all the way to Fort Smith."

"Ain't nobody asked you what you'd do, old man," Preacher snapped back, regaining some of his usual bluster.

Moon chuckled in response. "How 'bout all that bank money?" He directed this question toward Will. "I don't reckon he was totin' that with him, was he?"

"Nope," Will replied. "I reckon the Treadwells and the Cottons will split that money up. I was hopin' to recover the bank's money, but I'm not anxious to fight six of 'em for it. I've got the man I was sent to capture. So that's just the Bank of Sherman's loss." He hesitated before adding, "And Preacher McCoy's."

His last remark caused Preacher to snarl. "Them saddle tramps ain't gettin' that money. I got better sense than to put it where they could get their hands on it. Don't nobody know where that money is but me." Hoping to strike a deal at this point, he made a proposition. "How likely is it for you boys to get a chance to see almost twenty thousand dollars in one pile? It'd take a helluva long time to save up that much cash money on a deputy marshal's pay, wouldn't it? If you were smart, you'd have a chance to set yourselves up in high style with that much money. And all you'd have to do to get it would be to turn me loose. Whaddaya say, Deputy?"

"It might make it easier on you, if you tell us where that money is hidden," Will replied. "If the bank recovered the biggest part of what you stole, the judge might go easier on you."

Preacher reacted as if astonished. "You mean if I take you to that money, you'd just hand it over to the judge? I can't abide a man with an honest streak that wide. You'd take it, all right."

"I doubt he would," Oscar said. "Now, me, I'd take it in a half a second," he joked. "But then I'd have Will on my tail."

"I reckon we won't sit around here talkin' about it," Will said. "We're got some ground to cover. What I just said might still help you with the judge. When we get to Fort Smith, you can tell him where you hid it and we'll let him send somebody back to get it."

"The hell I will," Preacher spat defiantly. "That money can rot before I'll turn it over to the judge."

"Suit yourself," Will said. "Let's go." He gave Buster a nudge with his heel and started off at an easy lope. An interested party to the discussion that had just ended, Oscar shook his head thoughtfully, amazed that Will gave all that money no more consideration than that. He wheeled his horse and loped after him.

They rode for most of the rest of the night, following the Cimarron River southeast until the horses had to be rested, then they stopped to get a little sleep before starting out again in the morning. Will was anticipating a solid week of riding to reach Fort Smith, as always, strapping himself with the responsibility of transporting a prisoner without benefit of a jail wagon. Like others before him, Preacher was a dangerous man to transport, but Will had his set routines that took as few risks as possible. Moon rode with him for almost ninety miles before deciding Will could take his prisoner in without his help. Will had assured him that he could. Watching the way Will handled his prisoner for a couple of days, Moon was satisfied that his friend knew what he was doing, so he told Will of his plans to head back to his camp. He had moved his camp to a new spot, this time on the Canadian River. "With winter right on our heels, I've got a lot of work to do on my new camp," he said. "And I need to do a heap of huntin' to make sure I don't run outta meat. I ain't got no reason to wanna go to Fort Smith, but I'll stay with you, if you need me to help you get this jasper to jail."

Will assured him that he had done this many times before without help and had not figured that Moon was going all the way to Fort Smith with him. "I appreciate your help once again. It's gettin' to be a regular habit. Before long, you're liable to start runnin' when you see me comin'." So the next morning, Moon struck out straight west to strike the Canadian, while Will continued to lead his prisoner southeast along the Cimarron.

As he had done with Elmo Black and Lon Jackson, Will pushed the horses for a full day every day. Sullen for most of the time when Moon was still with them, Preacher became more talkative as each day rolled by. Will was aware that it was intended to cause him to become careless, so in effect it encouraged him to be more wary. He knew that Preacher would make an attempt to escape and the closer they got to Fort Smith, the more desperate that attempt would likely be. At the end of the seventh day after leaving the cabin on the Cimarron River, Will was forced to stop when within fifteen miles of the Arkansas River crossing into Fort Smith. Both men and horses were weary from the extra-long day of travel as Will ordered a stop beside a small creek.

He couldn't help noticing the look of severe fatigue in the face of his prisoner when he marched him over to a small tree and handcuffed his hands around it. Accustomed to the ritual after a long week, Preacher offered no resistance to being shackled to the tree while Will took care of the horses, then built a fire. Will could pretty well guess how Preacher was feeling; with no opportunity to escape, he had apparently finally accepted his fate. The only resistance he demonstrated now was his refusal to say where he had hidden the stolen money. And that was not a huge concern to Will because he really didn't care if the bank recovered it or not. In the midst of filling the coffeepot, he was suddenly struck with the realization that he was weary of the quality of life afforded him in his chosen profession. He turned to glance over his shoulder at the sullen figure handcuffed to a tree and told himself he was tired of spending virtually all of his life with men of Preacher's character. He shook his head, trying to rid it of such thoughts, for the image that usually followed them in his mind was one of Sophie, and the thinly veiled ultimatum she had given him. *Fifteen miles from home,* he told himself, *it's time to make good on the promise I gave her.* His mind made up, he turned his attention back to the chore of cooking some food for his prisoner and himself.

It was a good thing there were only fifteen miles to travel in the morning, he thought, for he was cooking up the last of the bacon for their supper. Sowbelly and coffee was all they had to eat for the last half of the week. "This oughta make eatin' at the jail seem like the Parker House," he joked when he walked over and placed Preacher's supper on the ground.

"I wouldn't be surprised," Preacher murmured, and held his hands up to be freed. Will unlocked the handcuffs, quickly stepped back and drew his .44 as Preacher shook the manacles off and moved away from the tree to eat his supper. He took a bite of the bacon and chewed it thoroughly before chasing it down with a swallow of strong coffee. "We're damn near Fort Smith, ain't we?"

"Be there in the mornin'," Will said, "and you can sleep on a cot tomorrow night, instead of huggin' a tree."

"Don't reckon you've changed your mind about gettin' rich," Preacher said.

"Reckon not. Might be you can make a deal with

Judge Parker to go a little easier on you, if you tell him where the bank's money is hid."

"Maybe so," Preacher allowed, and shook his head doubtfully. He finished his coffee and placed the cup on his empty plate. "I need to get rid of that coffee now, all right?" Will nodded and backed away a few steps while holding his .44 on Preacher. Then he stood, guarding him while he relieved himself. "I 'preciate it," Preacher said when he'd finished, then he walked back to the tree. "You know, it's been a real pleasure travelin' with you, Tanner, but I'm damn tired and I'll be glad to get to that jailhouse in the mornin'." He chuckled. "I never thought I'd ever hear myself say I was gonna be glad to get to jail. I don't know, though. You've got me used to sleepin' settin' up with my arms around a tree. I might have to talk 'em into lettin' me sleep on the floor with my hands tied around the bed."

Will smiled in acknowledgment of Preacher's attempt at humor and followed him back to the tree where the manacles were left on the ground. Preacher sat down behind the tree and thrust his wrists out on either side of it to be handcuffed. Still holding the Colt handgun in one hand, Will picked up the manacles in the other.

Preacher watched passively while Will locked one of the cuffs on his left hand. When Will shifted the Colt to his other hand, Preacher suddenly seized the hand, trapping the pistol in it. Caught by surprise, even though he expected a desperate attempt by the outlaw, Will fought to keep Preacher from wrenching the weapon out of his hand.

In a fight to save his life now, Preacher tried to pull Will over on his side to pin him to the ground. Equally desperate, Will fought to keep the larger man off of him and struggled to his feet. Both men were on their feet now, each with one hand free and the other locked in a desperate grip with his opponent's, the Colt .44 trapped between them.

After the initial struggle to control the pistol, and finding themselves stalemated, the two combatants started to slowly move in a deadly circle, looking for an opportunity to gain advantage. Only one had a weapon free now and that was the heavy iron manacle locked on Preacher's wrist, the unlocked bracelet dangling on a short chain. Preacher grinned at Will as he moved his hand from left to right, causing the iron bracelet to swing back and forth. Will knew whatever else happened, if he released his grip on Preacher's hand, he would lose the gun and his life with it.

Suddenly Preacher struck, swinging the manacle like a mace, landing a blow on Will's shoulder when Will ducked sideways to avoid it.

"How'd that feel?" Preacher taunted. "I'm gonna beat you into the ground with it, Mr. Deputy Marshal."

They continued moving around in a circle as Preacher struck again and again, trying to land his iron mace where it would be a deciding blow. But Will managed to absorb the beating he was taking on his arm and shoulder until, finally, both men began to tire from the desperate strain. Along with it, Preacher became more and more frustrated. Being larger and heavier than the persistent lawman, he expected the battle to be over once he succeeded in fighting him hand to hand. And the longer Will was able to withstand the punishment he was receiving from the rain of blows from the manacle, the more frustrated Preacher became. Breathing hard, he realized how tired he was and decided to overpower Will in one desperate charge. So he roared like a lion and took a giant step in before Will understood his intention to bowl him over backward. Will responded with a knee thrust between the big man's legs.

The blow shocked Preacher to the extent that he involuntarily released his grip on the hand that trapped the pistol between them. Doubled over with the sudden pain, he tried to retaliate with a wild swing with the handcuff. The blind swing caught Will on his forehead, knocking him to the ground. Almost senseless, he lay helpless, unable to think. Still doubled over, Preacher realized that Will was totally vulnerable and he forced himself to finish him. Trying to clear his head, the injured deputy sensed he was about to die, but he couldn't make himself resist. About to lose consciousness, he only remembered feeling the Colt in his hand and pulling the trigger, unaware of where it was aimed.

Slowly, his senses returned to him, although he wasn't quite sure if he was alive or dead. The only sensations that registered were a feeling of being smothered and pain like a bolt of lightning splitting his head. A few moments more and he realized what caused the feeling and he struggled to roll Preacher's heavy body off him. He sat up beside the body, still holding the Colt in his hand, and stared at the startled face of the big outlaw, frozen in an expression of surprise, a bullet hole in the center of his forehead. Aware now of the pain in his own forehead, he reached up and wiped away some of the blood that had run down in his eyes from the cut. He looked again at the neat dark hole in Preacher's forehead, scarcely able to believe he had shot him. For the only memory he had of those final moments was that of sliding helplessly into unconsciousness. It seemed impossible to him—someone or something had to have had a hand in it because the pistol must have aimed itself. He surely had no memory of aiming it. *Ain't for me to question*, he thought, *just be thankful for it.*

He struggled to his feet, becoming more aware of the many blows he had absorbed on his arms and shoulders. He remembered Preacher's boast that he was going to beat him into the ground with his manacles. "He damn near did," he muttered.

Standing over the body, he couldn't help berating himself for being careless, in spite of anticipating a desperate attempt from the boastful outlaw. To make matters worse, he was now faced with the loss of pay for the mileage traveled, for Preacher was not delivered alive for trial. On top of that, he would have the responsibility of paying for Preacher's burial.

He turned to face east, as if looking toward his destination. "And only fifteen miles to Fort Smith," he lamented aloud. Looking back at the huge body, he commented, "You cost me a lot of money with that fool move."

CHAPTER 16

"Damn, Will, what the hell happened to you?" Ed Kittridge exclaimed upon seeing the deputy pull up in front of his shop, his shirt splotched with blood-stains and his new bandana tied around his forehead. "You look like you got into it with a grizzly."

"That pretty much describes it," Will answered, and dismounted while Kittridge took a quick look at the body riding across the saddle of the coal-black roan gelding. "I woulda buried him myself, but I didn't feel like diggin' the grave. Besides, I don't know if Dan Stone wants to see the body or not, but I'd like for him to verify my claim that this is the outlaw called Preacher McCoy. I'll check with him before you bury him—like always, nothin' fancy. I have to pay for it myself."

"What happened to your forehead? Looks like it's been bleedin' a lot," Kittridge said.

"Yeah, it has," Will said. He reached up and pulled the bandana up so Kittridge could see. "The damn thing don't wanna heal up."

"That's a nasty-lookin' cut, all right. You might

better have Doc Peters take a look at it—probably
need a few stitches. When did it happen?" He asked
because the blood was dry except for a few rivulets
seeping from his forehead.

"Last night," Will answered. "I reckon I didn't do
much of a job of cleanin' it up. Come on, I'll help you
carry him in. He's a heavy bastard. I wished I'd had
some help loadin' him on that horse this mornin'."

After leaving the undertaker, Will took the horses
to the stable where Vern Tuttle met him with the same
questions he had just answered with Kittridge. Like
Ed, Vern advised him to see Doc Peters to take care of
the gash on his forehead. Will said that he would and
he intended to, but he thought he'd best report in to
Dan Stone before he did anything else. As usually happened, Vern was interested in what Will planned to do
with the blue roan. He was obvious in his appraisal of
the dark horse. "I'll talk to you about it later," Will
said. It was a fine horse and one he might consider
keeping to add to the small herd he was accumulating
over in Ward's Corner. He was also thinking about the
cost of this second trip to Wichita. He might have to
strike a deal with Vern to pay for it.

"Good Lord in heaven!" Dan Stone blurted when
Will walked in, "I swear, for a while there, I wasn't sure
you'd make it back this time. Looks like you had a
little trouble arresting Preacher McCoy."

"Yes, sir, I did," Will answered matter-of-factly.

"You take him to the jail?"

"No, I was plannin' to, but I took him to Ed Kittridge

instead." Stone didn't answer, instead he struck a patient pose that conveyed a need for an explanation. Will continued. "I almost made it," he said, "got within fifteen miles of here before he made his move to escape. I shot him, but I don't remember doin' it."

"Whaddaya mean, you don't remember shooting him?" Stone responded, obviously in need of more explanation.

"Well, I reckon when he was beatin' the hell outta me with my hand irons, he got in one good lick that knocked me silly and I don't remember anything after that till I came to with him lyin' on top of me." He went over the details leading up to the actual fight as best he could remember, right up to the final moment before getting struck on the forehead.

"And you think you shot him while you were unconscious?" Stone asked, finding the story difficult to believe.

"Unless he decided to commit suicide and shot himself," Will replied, having no explanation for the incident ending the way it had. Stone still looked as if he doubted his young deputy's account of the killing.

"You're sure the corpse lying over there at Ed Kittridge's place is the man calling himself Preacher McCoy and Gaylord Pressley?" Stone asked. Will said there was no doubt in his mind about the identity, but he had instructed Ed not to put Preacher in the ground until Stone okayed it. Stone nodded, then asked, "What about all that money he was supposed to be carrying? Were you able to recover any of it?"

"'Fraid not," Will replied. "He said he hid it and he didn't say where, so I reckon that money's gone forever." He went on to explain the circumstances under which Preacher was captured and the reason there was no opportunity to search for the bank's money. "He claimed those six outlaws he was sharin' the cabin with didn't know where he hid the money. He was the only one who knew where it was and he wasn't tellin' anybody. I figure he mighta been thinkin' to buy himself a lighter sentence from the judge if he told him where they could recover it."

"Damn," Stone muttered, thinking about it. "That's a helluva lot of money to disappear. I wonder how much of it was left."

"Well, Elmo Black claimed Preacher got away with all of the twenty thousand, his share and Lon Jackson's share, too, when he escaped from the cave up in the Arbuckles. And Preacher said he still had almost all of it left when I captured him, so I reckon the bank is the loser on this deal."

"I expect so," Stone said. "We'll notify the Texas Rangers that McCoy is dead and no money recovered. They held up on coming after Black and Jackson until they got word that we had arrested McCoy, so they could transport all three of them at the same time." He got up from his desk and extended his hand. "Glad to have you back. I think you'd best stop by Doc Peters's office now and have that cut taken care of. Then you can rest up a little. You look like you need it. I'll send for you if I need anything else today or tomorrow."

Will took his leave, carrying a feeling that Stone might harbor some suspicions that he might know the whereabouts of that twenty thousand dollars. *Ain't nothing I can do about it,* he thought as he headed up the street to the doctor's office. His mind was working on more important things now and he was anxious to get finished with the doctor, so he could go home to Bennett House. There was a lot he wanted to talk about with Sophie.

Dr. Peters opened his office door to Will's knock and said nothing for a moment while he stared at the bandana around Will's head. "What did that?" he finally asked.

"Handcuffs," Will answered.

"Well, at least you came to see me before I sat down to eat my supper this time. Come on in and let's take a look at it." He stood aside, holding the door for him. When Will passed by, Doc asked, "What's that on your back?" He saw a wide pattern of small dried bloodstains on the back of Will's shirt.

"Shotgun," Will replied. "You might better take a look. A barber up in El Dorado, Kansas, picked most of the shot outta my back, but he said I oughta have a doctor look at it."

"Take your shirt off," Doc said. When Will removed it, Doc shook his head, astonished when he saw the pattern of shot. "Well, I've seen worse, but there's a little work to be done on some of those wounds to keep you from dying of gangrene. Let's take care of that cut on your forehead first." While he worked away, stitching up Will's forehead, he was unable to keep from lecturing his patient on his foolish choice of occupations. "I used to try to talk some sense into Fletcher Pride and it looks like you're heading down the same road. Let me tell you, young man, you can't be shot at but so many times before you finally get hit with one I can't fix." Will sat, silently patient until Doc finished his treatments and said, "That's about all we can do. Let's take a look at your back now." He spent less than an hour removing a few more of the shotgun shots that the skin had already grown over. "That barber did a pretty good job from what I can see. He was right in not trying to go after those deep ones— better off just leavin' 'em. You ain't the first deputy carrying a load of lead around. I reckon that'll do it for this time. I'll try to patch you up next time, too. Just don't come in at suppertime."

Over three hundred miles northwest of Fort Smith, a stocky little gray-haired man wearing dirty buckskins and riding a paint horse approached the banks of the Salt Fork of the Arkansas River. Oscar Moon was in the process of scratching an itch that had played on his mind ever since he had parted company with Will Tanner a week before. After Will had left with his prisoner, Oscar started thinking about an incident on the Salt Fork that had continued to goad his curiosity until he had to do something about it. When he and Will had crossed the river at this point, they had found it strange that someone had taken such pains to hide their campfire. They made nothing of it at first, since the tracks were heading north, instead of south. Even after they found more tracks that led in the opposite direction, they dismissed it, figuring the rider had forgotten something, or simply changed his mind about where he was going. They hadn't even speculated that the tracks might have been left by Preacher McCoy. They had lost Preacher's tracks back at the Medicine Lodge River and had decided to ride straight to the cabin on the Cimarron. It would have been too much of a coincidence to have stumbled on Preacher's tracks at that point on the Salt Fork. But now, Oscar could no longer resist taking another look around that small clearing in the bushes by the river.

Retracing the trail they had taken to the Cimarron, Oscar found the point where they had crossed the river. Guiding his horse up through the ring of bushes close to the bank, he found the ashes of the campfire again, and dismounted. Then he began a careful inspection around the base of each bush, looking closely for any signs that might indicate someone had dug in the soil around them. He proceeded to repeat the process all around the tiny clearing. After completing the circle, he felt positive that the soil had not been disturbed. Disappointed, he sat down and looked around him. There was no place to hide anything, no rocks, no logs, nothing. *So much for hunches,* he thought, concluding that he had ridden all the way back there for nothing. *Unless,* he thought, *he hid it somewhere else around here.* With that in mind, he pushed through the ring of bushes again and took a sweeping look around the riverbank. There were hundreds of possibilities for a hiding place, he decided. He could spend the rest of his life digging holes, moving logs, climbing trees, and would still have to be lucky to strike it rich. He had ridden a long way to humor his idea of instant riches, so he had to continue his search. He wore away the afternoon in a fruitless search for the hidden money before deciding it useless. Since it was getting late and he had not eaten since breakfast, he decided to build a fire and cook some supper.

"You warn't meant to be a rich man, anyway, Oscar Moon," he finally announced to the world in general. "Although I'da liked to have give it a try." And then it struck him, as he went about the business of gathering wood for his fire, the one place he had never thought

to look. Excited again, he grabbed his shovel, pushed
back through the bushes, and scattered the ashes of
the fire with his boot before starting to dig. Laboring
in earnest, he stayed hard at it as he went deeper and
deeper, knowing if the money was there, it would have
to have a solid layer of dirt over it to protect it from
the fire. At last, when over two feet down, the blade of
his shovel struck a heavy canvas bag and he blurted,
"Hot damn!" He was tempted to dance a little jig, but
there was still work to do. The hole had been dug
straight down, much deeper than it was wide. Preacher
had evidently dug the hole this way so as not to leave
a large circle of dirt under the fire to cause suspicion.
But the labor now was joyous.

When at last he was able to draw the long sack out
of the hole, he sat back to regain his breath and patted
the canvas bag affectionately for a few moments before
untying the laces at the top. He was almost afraid to
open it, fearing it might not be the money at all. After
a brief pause, he slowly pulled the bag open and
peered in, stunned for a second by what he saw. Then
a grin formed slowly on his weathered face. He had
never seen that much money in his whole life. Impul-
sively, he hurriedly looked around him, in case someone was watching, but there was no one, no witnesses,
no one to know what became of the money stolen
from the Bank of Sherman, Texas. He paused again
for just a few moments to think about Will Tanner. A
slight tinge of guilt caused him to wonder if he should
share his find with Will, since it was through Will that
he had been led to this place. After all, he and Will
were partners in the capture of Preacher McCoy.
"Nah," he decided. "Will would feel duty-bound to
turn it over to Judge Parker. Best I just keep it and

keep my mouth shut." He tied his treasure on his horse behind the saddle in case he had to leave suddenly, still afraid someone might be watching him. After a hasty supper, he started out for his camp that night, reluctant to camp there. As he rode up from the river, he thought about moving a step up in life and feeling as confident as Gaylord Pressley had. *Maybe I might think me up a fancy name like that*, he thought as a wide smile parted his whiskers.

She didn't say a word upon first seeing him as he approached the porch, his saddlebags on his shoulder, his rifle in hand, but this time with a large bandage around his forehead. She propped her broom beside the front door and stood watching him intently, her hands on her hips. Finally, when he reached the steps, she shook her head slowly, released a long sigh, and murmured, "Oh, Will . . ." But she did not move forward to greet him. Instead, she continued to stare at him as if confronting an unruly child. "What in the world happened to you?" Before he could answer, she cut him off. "Never mind, I don't really want to know. Come on inside and get ready for supper." She picked up her broom again and gave the porch a few quick swishes in the direction of the steps, then followed him in the door. Inside, she took hold of his arm to stop him while she took a closer look at the bandage on his forehead, concerned by the spots of blood seeping through. "How bad is it?" she asked.

"Not too bad," he answered, a little disappointed by her reception. He had hoped for something more joyful upon seeing him safely home. "Doc Peters put nine stitches in it."

"I don't wanna know who knocked you in the head, but I hope it knocked some sense into you," she said. "What's this on the back of your shirt?" she asked, just then noticing. When he explained the reason for the small spots of dried blood, she bit her lip in frustration. "Does Dan Stone plan to send you out somewhere right away as usual?"

"Don't know," Will answered bluntly. "I've been thinkin' I might take another ride down to Texas."

Already frustrated by his attitude, she scolded him. "You were just down there a couple of weeks ago. Why do you have to go back again so soon?"

He tried to keep a straight face, but he couldn't hide the beginnings of a shy smile. Feeling like he had been caught stealing chicken eggs, he confessed. "'Cause you ain't ever seen the J-Bar-J and I need to know if you'd be happy livin' there."

"Is that so?" she answered, taken completely by surprise, since the Will Tanner she had come to know would have trouble proposing such a thing. "What kinda girl do you think I am?" she responded, pretending to be shocked. "I won't go riding off to Texas with a man I'm not married to."

"I reckon that's what I was kinda hopin'," he said.

"Are you asking me to . . . ?" she started, then stopped. "That's the worst proposal I've ever heard. Are you asking me to marry you?"

"I reckon so."

"Well then, ask me proper."

"Will you marry me?"

"Of course."

She turned as if heading for the dining room, then stopped abruptly, spun around, and jumped up in his arms. Taken by surprise, he managed to catch her in one arm, but he dropped his rifle and saddlebags in the process. They landed with a clatter on the floor, but he didn't care. The feel of her in his arms was enough to make him know he never wanted to release her. She kissed him hard, as if firmly sealing the contract. Still locked in his arms, she said, "Now comes the hard part." When he gave her a questioning look, she continued, "Going in to tell Mama."

TURN THE PAGE FOR AN EXCITING PREVIEW!

*National bestselling authors William W. Johnstone
and J. A. Johnstone spin a breakneck tale about a
heroic chuckwagon cook who knows just what to do
when cowboys get hungry—for revenge . . .*

THE CHUCKWAGON TRAIL

Framed for murder, Dewey "Mac" McKenzie is
running for his life. Though Mac's never even made
a pot of coffee, he talks his way onto a cattle drive
heading west—as a chuckwagon cook. Turns out he
has a natural talent for turning salt pork and dried
beans into culinary gold. He's as good with a pot
and pan as he is with a gun—which comes in handy
on a dangerous trail drive beset with rustlers, hostile
Indians, ornery weather, and deadly stampedes.
Mac can hold his own with any cowboy twice his age.
At least until the real showdown begins . . .

Mac's trail boss, Deke Northrup, is one mean spit
in the eye. Before long, he's made enemies of all
his men. When Mac learns that Northrup is
planning to double-cross the herd's owner,
Mac stands up to the trail boss and his henchman.
He might be outgunned and outnumbered, but
Mac's ready to serve up some blazing frontier
justice—with a healthy helping of vengeance . . .

THE CHUCKWAGON TRAIL
by WILLIAM W. JOHNSTONE
with J. A. JOHNSTONE

On sale now, wherever Pinnacle Books are sold.

LIVE FREE. READ HARD.

CHAPTER 1

Dewey Mackenzie shivered as he pressed against the wet stone wall and blinked moisture from his eyes. Whether it came from the chilly rain that had fallen in New Orleans earlier this evening or from his own fear-fueled sweat—or both—he didn't know. He supposed it didn't matter.

Right now, he just wanted to avoid the two men standing guard across the street. Both were twice his size, and one had the battered look of a boxer. Even in the dim light cast by the gas lamp far down Royal Street, Mac saw the flattened nose, the cauliflower ears, and the way the man continually ducked and dodged imaginary punches.

At some time in the past, those punches hadn't been imaginary, and there had been a lot of them.

A medium-sized young man with longish dark hair and what had been described by more than one young woman as a roguish smile, Mac rubbed his hands against the sides of his fancy dress trousers and settled his Sunday go-to-meeting coat around his shoulders.

Carrying a gun on an errand like this was out of the question, but he missed the comforting feel of his Smith & Wesson Model 3 resting on his hip. He closed his eyes, licked his lips, and then sidled back along the wall until he reached the cross street. Like a cat, he slid around the corner to safety and heaved a huge sigh.

Getting in to see Evangeline Holdstock was always a chore, but after her pa had threatened him with death—or worse—if he caught him nosing around their mansion again, Mac had come to the only possible conclusion. He had been seeing Evangeline on the sly for more than two months, reveling in the stolen moments they shared. Even, if he cared to admit it to himself, enjoying the risks he was running.

He was little more than a drifter in the eyes of Micah Holdstock, owner of the second biggest bank in New Orleans. Holdstock measured his wealth in millions. The best the twenty-one-year-old could come up with was a bright, shiny silver cartwheel and a sweat-stained wad of Union greenbacks, but he had earned the money honestly at a restaurant in the French Quarter.

Mac held his hands in front of him and balled them into fists. He had worked as a farmhand and a half dozen jobs on riverboats before he washed ashore in the Crescent City three months earlier. Every bit of that work was honest, even if it didn't pay as well as sitting behind a bank desk and denying people loans.

He tried to erase such thoughts from his mind. Holdstock's bank served a purpose, and the man made his money honestly, too. It just wasn't the way

Mac earned his. It wasn't the way anyone else he'd ever known in his young life had earned their money, either.

If he wanted to carry out his mission tonight, he had to concentrate on that. He had gotten himself cleaned up for a simple reason.

Looking his best was a necessity when he asked Evie to marry him.

"Mrs. Dewey Mackenzie," he said softly. He liked the sound of that. "My wife. Mrs. Evangeline Mackenzie."

A quick peek around the corner down Royal Street dampened his spirits a mite. The two guards still stood in front of the door leading into the Holdstock house. Shifting his eyes from the street to the second story revealed a better way to get in without being caught and given a thrashing.

More than likely, Evie's pa had told those bruisers they could toss him into the river if they caught him snooping around. This time of year, the Mississippi River roiled with undertow and mysterious currents known only to the best of the riverboat pilots. It wasn't safe to swim anywhere near the port.

"Besides," he said softly to himself, "I don't want to muddy up my fancy duds." He smoothed wrinkles out of his coat, then boldly walked across the street without so much as a glance in the guards' direction.

He stopped and looked up when he was hidden by the wall. A black iron decoration drooped down from the railing around the second-story veranda just enough for him to grab. He stepped back a couple paces, got a running start, and made a grand leap. His fingers closed on the ornate wrought iron. With a powerful heave, he pulled himself up and got a leg over the railing.

Moving carefully to keep from tearing his trousers or getting his coat dirty, he dropped to the balcony floor and looked down to see if he had drawn any unwanted attention. Mac caught his breath when the guard who must have been a boxer came around the corner, scratched his head, and looked down the street. Moving quickly, Mac leaned back out of sight before the man looked up.

Senses acute with fear, he heard the guard shuffle away, heading back toward the door where his partner waited. Mac sank into a chair and used a handkerchief to wipe sweat from his forehead.

If this had been a couple of months later, he would have been drenched in sweat and for a good reason. Summer in New Orleans wore a man down with stifling heat and oppressive humidity, but now, late April, the sweat came from a different cause.

"Buck up," he whispered to himself. "Her pa can't stop you. You're going to marry the most wonderful girl in all New Orleans, and tonight's the night you ask for her hand."

Mac knew he had things backward, but considering how Mr. Holdstock acted, he wanted to be sure Evie loved him as much as he did her. Best to find out if she would marry him, *then* ask her pa for her hand in marriage. If Evie agreed, then to hell with whatever her pa thought.

He took a deep breath, reflecting on what she would be giving up. She claimed not to like the social whirl of a young debutante, but he had to wonder if some part of her didn't enjoy the endless attention, the fancy clothing, the rush of a cotillion followed by a soirée and whatever else they called a good old hoedown in New Orleans society.

A quick look over the railing convinced him the guard had returned to his post. Stepping carefully, knowing from prior experience where every creaky board was, he made his way along the balcony to a closed window. The curtains had been pulled. He pressed his hand against the window pane, then peered into Evie's bedroom. Squinting, he tried to make out if she stood in the shadows. The coal-oil lamp had been extinguished, but if she was expecting him, she wouldn't advertise her presence.

He tried the door handle. Locked. Using his knife blade, he slipped it between the French doors and lifted slowly. When he felt resistance, he applied a bit more pressure. The latch opened to him, as it had so many times before. Evie liked to playact that he was a burglar come to rob her of her jewels, then ravish her.

The thought of that made him blush because he enjoyed it as much as she did. More than once, he had sneaked into her room and gone through the elaborate ritual of demanding her jewels, then forcing her to disrobe slowly to prove she had not hidden anything on her body. Both of them got too excited to ever carry on with the charade for more than a few minutes. He went to the bed now and pressed down on it with his fingers, remembering the times they had made love here.

Mac swung around and sat, wondering how long he should wait before he went hunting for her.

For all he knew, her ma and pa were out for the night. Their social life mingled with Holdstock's banking business and caused them to attend parties and meetings throughout the week to maintain their standing in the community. Mac got antsy after less than a minute and went to the bedroom door. Carefully opening it, he looked down the hallway. Evie's room was at the back of the house, while her parents had the room at the front, at the far end of the hallway lined with fancy paintings and marble sculptures. The Persian rug muffled his footfalls as he made his way to the head of the stairs.

The broad fan of steps swept down to the foyer. He ducked back when he heard Holdstock speaking with someone at the door. From the guest's accent, he was French. That meant little in a town filled with Frenchmen and Acadians. French Creole was almost as widely spoken as English or Spanish.

"I am glad we could meet, Monsieur Leclerc. Come into the study. I have a fine cigar from Cuba that you will find delightful."

"*Bon*, good, Mr. Holdstock. And brandy?"

"Only the finest French brandy."

The two laughed and disappeared from sight. Mac cursed his bad luck. It would have been better if Holdstock were out of the house rather than entertaining— or conducting business, judging by the formality the two showed one another. Some high-powered deal was being struck not fifty feet away. That deal would undoubtedly make the banker rich. Or richer than he already was.

But Mac didn't care about that. His riches were wrapped in crinoline and lace, with flowing blond hair and eyes as green as jade. He stepped back and wondered where she might be.

Then he heard her soft voice below as she greeted Monsieur Leclerc and exchanged a few mumbled pleasantries. The sound of her slippers moving against the foyer floor set his heart racing. He hastily retreated to her bedroom and closed the door behind him. From past times here, he knew the exact spot to stand.

Beside her wardrobe, hidden in shadow when she lit the oil lamp, he could cherish her for a few seconds before she realized she was not alone. Mac pressed into the niche just as the door opened. He closed his eyes and took a deep whiff. Jasmine perfume made his nostrils flare. This was her favorite perfume, but he told her often she did not need it, not with him. Just being around her intoxicated his senses more than enough.

He opened his eyes and squinted as he stared directly into the burning wick of Evie's bedside lamp. She bent over slightly, hands on the bed, her bustle wiggling delightfully.

"I have never seen any woman so lovely," he said. "If I live to be a thousand, I never will forget this moment, this sight, this beautiful—"

She straightened and spun. Her eyes went wide. His heart almost skipped a beat when he realized it wasn't surprise that caused her face to contort. It was fear.

"What's wrong, my dear?" He went to her, but she pushed him back.

"Go, Mac. Get out of here now. Please. Don't slow down. He knows we've been seeing each other."

"I don't care. I love you. Do you love me?"

"Yes, yes," she said, flustered. She brushed back a wayward strand of lustrous, honey blond hair and looked up at him. True fear twisted her face. "I love you with all my heart and soul, Mac. That's why you have to leave."

"Then let's go together. Let's elope. We can find a justice of the peace. We don't have to get married in the St. Louis Basilica."

"Mac, you don't understand. I—"

"I can't give you a fancy house or fine clothing or jewelry like this." He touched the pearl necklace around her slender throat, then moved to caress her cheek. "Not now. Someday I will. Together we can—"

"You have to go before he catches you!"

"I'll go down and beard the old lion in his den. We'll have it out, man to man. I won't let him chase me off from the love of my life." He moved her around so he could go to the door.

Before he could get there, the door slammed open, reverberating as it smashed into the wall. Silhouetted against the light from downstairs, Micah Holdstock filled the frame.

"I should have known you would come, especially on a night like this!"

Mac began, "Mr. Holdstock, I—"

"Papa, please, you can't do this. Don't hurt him." Evie tried to interpose herself between the men, but Mac wouldn't have it. No woman he loved sacrificed herself for him, especially with her father.

"Evie and I love each other, sir. We're getting married!"

Micah Holdstock let out a roar like a charging bull. The attack took Mac by surprise. Strong arms encircled his body and lifted him off his feet. He tried to get his arms free but couldn't with them pinned at his sides. Still roaring, Holdstock went directly for the French doors and smashed through them. Shards of glass sprayed in the air and tumbled to the balcony as he used Mac as a battering ram.

The collision robbed Mac of breath. He went limp in the man's death grip. This saved him from being driven against the iron railing and having his back broken. He dropped to his knees as Holdstock crashed into the wrought-iron railing and fought to keep from tumbling into the street below.

"Papa," he heard Evie pleading, trying to stop the attack.

Mac got to shaky feet to face her pa.

"This is no way for future in-laws to act," he gasped out. "My intentions are honorable."

"She's betrothed. As of this very evening!" Again Holdstock charged.

Mac saw the expression of resignation on Evie's face an instant before her father's hard fist caught him on the side of the head and sent him reeling. He grabbed the iron railing and went over, dangled a moment, then fell heavily to the cobblestone street and sprawled onto his back. He stared up to see Evie sobbing bitterly as her father grabbed her by the arm and pulled her out of sight.

"You can't do this. I won't let you!" He got to his feet in time to see the two guards round the corner. From the way they were hurrying, he knew what they had been ordered to do.

Shameful though it might be, he turned and ran.

The guards' bulk meant they were slower on their feet than Mac was. Three blocks later, he finally evaded them by ducking into a saloon in Pirate's Alley. He leaned against the wall for a moment, catching his breath. The smoke in the dive formed a fog so thick it wasn't possible to see more than a few feet. He coughed, then went to the bar and collapsed against it. "I say this to damned near ever'body what comes into this place," the barkeep said, "but in your case I mean it. You look like you could use a drink."

CHAPTER 2

The bartender poured a shot of whiskey.

Mac knocked it back, and it almost knocked him down. He wasn't much of a drinker, but this had to be the most potent popskull he had ever encountered. He choked, swallowed, then said, "Another."

"The first was on the house. The next one you pay for."

"I just had a run-in with my lady friend's pa." He sucked in a breath and endured the pain in his ribs. Micah Holdstock had a grip like a bear. The powerful liquor went a ways toward easing the pain. He fumbled out a greenback for another drink. He needed all the deadening he could pour down his gullet.

The bartender picked up the bill, examined it, and tucked it away. "Don't usually take Yankee bills, but seeing as how you're in pain, I will this time." He splashed more whiskey into Mac's empty glass.

Mac started to protest at not getting change. As the second shot hit his gut and set his head spinning, he forgot about it. What difference did it make anyway? He had to find a way to sneak Evie out of the house and get her to a judge for a proper marrying.

"Do tell."

Mac blinked and frowned. He hadn't realized he had been talking out loud, but obviously the bartender knew what he'd been thinking. He ran a shaky finger around the rim of his empty shot glass and captured the last amber drop. He licked it off his fingertip. The astringent burn on his tongue warned him that another drink might make him pass out.

"I'll find a way," he said, with more assurance than he felt. He needed both hands on the bar to support himself.

As he considered a third drink, he noticed how the sound in the saloon went away. All he heard was the pounding of his pulse in his ears. Thinking the drink had turned him deaf, he started to shout out for another, then saw the frightened expression on the barkeep's face. Looking over his shoulder, he saw the reason.

The two guards who had been stationed outside Micah Holdstock's front door now stood just inside the saloon, arms crossed over their chests. Those arms bulged with muscles. The men fixed steely gazes on him. Out of habit—or maybe desperation—Mac patted his right hip but found no revolver hanging there. He had dressed up for the occasion of asking Evie to marry him. There hadn't been any call for him to go armed.

He knew now that was a big mistake. He turned and had to brace himself against the bar with both elbows. He blinked hard, as much from the smoke as the tarantula juice he had swilled. Hoping he saw double and only one guard faced him, he quickly realized how wrong that was. There were two of them, and they had blood in their eyes.

"You gonna stand there all night or you gonna come for me?" He tried to hold back the taunt but failed. The liquor had loosened his tongue and done away with his common sense. Somewhere deep down in his brain, he knew he was inviting them to kill him, but he couldn't stop himself. "Well? Come on!" He balanced precariously, one foot in front of the other, fists balled and raised.

The one who looked like a boxer stirred, but the other held him back.

"Waiting for the bell to ring? Come on. Let's mix it up." He took a couple of tentative punches at thin air.

"Mister, that's Hiram Higgins," the bartender said, reaching across the bar to tug at his sleeve. "He lost to Gypsy Jem Mace over in Kennerville."

"So that just means he can lose to me just east of Jackson Square."

"Mister, Gypsy Jem whupped Tom Allen the next day for the heavyweight championship."

"So? You said this man Higgins lost."

"He lost after eighteen rounds. Ain't nobody stayed with the Gypsy longer 'n that. The man's a killer with those fists."

Mac wasn't drunk enough to tangle with Holdstock's guard, not after hearing that. But the boxer stepped away deferentially when a nattily dressed man stepped into the saloon. The newcomer carefully pulled off gloves and clutched them in his right hand. He took off a tall top hat and disdainfully tossed it to the boxer. Walking slowly, the man advanced on Mac.

"You are the one? *You*?" He stopped two paces away

from Mac, slapping the gloves he held in his right hand across his left palm.

"I'm your worst nightmare, mister." Still emboldened by the booze, Mac flipped the frilled front of the man's bleached white shirt. A diamond stud popped free. The man made no effort to retrieve it from the sawdust on the floor. He stared hard at Mac.

"You are drunk. But of course you are. Do you know who I am?"

"Not a clue. Some rich snake in the grass from the cut of your clothes." Mac tried to flip his finger against the man's prominent nose this time. A small turn of the man's head prevented him from delivering the insulting gesture.

"I am Pierre Leclerc, the son of Antoine Leclerc."

"I've heard the name. Somewhere." Mac tried to work out why the name was familiar. His head buzzed with a million bees inside it, and he was definitely seeing double now. Two of the annoying men filled his field of vision. He tried to decide which one to punch.

"He owns the largest shipping company in New Orleans. It is one of the largest in North America."

"So? You're rich. What of it?"

"You will leave Miss Evangeline Holdstock alone. You will never try to see her again. She wants nothing to do with you."

"Why's that, Mister Fancy Pants?"

"Because she and I are to be married. This very night my father arranged for her hand in marriage to unite her father's bank and our shipping company."

"Your pa's gonna marry her?"

"You fool!" Leclerc exploded. "You imbecile. *I* am to marry Miss Holdstock. You have given me the last insult that will ever cross your lips." He reared back and slapped Mac with the gloves. A gunshot would have been quieter as cloth struck flesh.

Mac stumbled and caught himself against the bar. He rubbed his burning cheek.

"Why you—"

"You may choose your weapons. At the Dueling Oaks, tomorrow at sunrise. Be there promptly or show the world—and Miss Holdstock—the true depth of your cowardice." Leclerc slapped his gloves across his left palm for emphasis, spun and walked from the saloon. The two guards followed him.

"What happened?" Mac said into the hollow silence that hung in the air when Leclerc was gone. He was stunned into sobriety.

"You're going to duel for this hussy's favor at sunrise," the bartender said.

"With guns?"

"You'd be wise to choose pistols. Leclerc is a champion fencer. He can cut a man to ribbons with a saber and walk away untouched."

"Heard tell he's a crack shot, too," piped up someone across the saloon.

"Eight men he's kilt in duels," another man said. "The fella's a fightin' machine—a killin' machine. I don't envy you, boy. Not at all."

Mac found himself pushed away from the bar by men rooting around in the sawdust looking for the diamond stud that had popped off Leclerc's shirt. He watched numbly, wondering if he ought to join the hunt. That tiny gemstone could pay for passage up the river.

Then he worked through what that meant. Evie would call him a coward for the rest of his life. And running would show how little her love meant to him. He loved her with all his heart and soul.

If it meant he laid down his life for her, so be it. He would be north of town at the Dueling Oaks at dawn.

After another drink.

Or two.

Connect with

Us

Visit us online at
KensingtonBooks.com
to read more from your favorite authors, see books
by series, view reading group guides, and more.

Join us on social media

for sneak peeks, chances to win books and prize packs,
and to share your thoughts with other readers.

facebook.com/kensingtonpublishing
twitter.com/kensingtonbooks

Tell us what you think!

To share your thoughts, submit a review,
or sign up for our eNewsletters, please visit:
KensingtonBooks.com/TellUs.